# Praise for Girls' Weekend:

"By page three, I was hooked. If I could have, I would have read it in one sitting."
– *When I Grow Up*

"The book made me think (and highlight many passages). It's a fun read, but also goes deeper, too. Really enjoyed it."
– *We Imagine She Must Lead a Rather Dull Life*

"Mom lit at its finest!"
– *Mommy's New Groove*

"Very real and completely engrossing."
– *Emma b Books*

"Had I known I'd still be sitting in my favorite chair at 2am, racing to the finish, I probably would have put on my pajamas before I started. (Sometime before lunch...) Yeppers, it was that good. It was compelling, touching, and a bit soul-searching. Oh, and it was fun, too."
– *Momma on the Rocks*

"A beautiful book that has fabulous characters, lots of wine, and will have you wanting more."
– *Whispering Stories*

"A very entertaining, intriguing story of female friendships, and determining who we are and what we want from life."
– *Book Babble*

# Girls' Weekend

## Cara Sue Achterberg

THE
ST RY
PLANT

Studio Digital CT, LLC
P.O. Box 4331
Stamford, CT 06907

Copyright © 2016 by Cara Sue Achterberg
Cover design by Barbara Aronica-Buck

Story Plant Trade Paperback ISBN: 978-1-61188-228-5
Story Plant Mass Market Paperback ISBN:
978-1-61188-289-6
Fiction Studio Books E-book ISBN: 978-1-943486-88-5

Visit our website at www.TheStoryPlant.com

First Story Plant Trade Paperback Printing: May 2016
First Story Plant Mass Market Paperback Printing: September 2020

Printed in the United States of America
0 9 8 7 6 5 4 3 2 1

For Nicholas, thank you for believing I could do this. (I promise I'll always come home from my girls' weekends.)

# Dani

Predictably, ten minutes before the alarm was due to sound, Joe reached his arm around Dani's side and began inching his hand towards her breast. Dani was definitely not in the mood; she'd been awake for the past twenty minutes running through her to-do list for the day. But she hadn't been in the mood for the last few days, and she'd have to weigh the stress of a grumpy husband against the cost of delaying the start of her morning. When they'd married amid all that passion, she had not predicted it would come to this.

Dani rolled over and looked at Joe. His eyes were still closed, but he was definitely awake. His dark hair was speckled with gray at the temples and the front of it stuck up in a vague Mohawk shape. She never *really* looked at him anymore. He was just there, like the living room set that had been in her life for over a decade, generally in the same place doing the same thing day after day.

When she first met him nearly twenty years ago, she would wake up next to him amazed to find him there (and almost always in the mood). Joe had been a real man with a job and a future, not one of the college boys she'd dated who thought the future was the keg party next weekend. He was interesting, intelligent, even funny. She'd been crazy about him. Somewhere along the line, that magic had faded, leaving just an impression, like the rings left by her water glass on his mother's antique end table. She needed to remember to sand that spot before the in-laws visited at Easter.

Ten minutes later, the alarm sounded, her now-satisfied husband bounded out of bed and jumped in the shower while she was still fishing for her panties at the bottom of the bed. Fine, she thought, this would give her the opportunity to make good on yesterday's plan to start working out again. She was tired of looking like the mommy. No more sweatpants. No more makeup-less, baseball hat-wearing, just-get-out-the-door days.

Stumbling around in the dark bedroom, she cursed silently as her bare feet landed on the Lego bricks Joey Jr. had left scattered across the carpet. She had repeatedly asked him to pick them up yesterday, but when she crawled into bed at eleven, they'd still lain everywhere like little land mines.

Sweating on the elliptical machine in the basement, Dani could hear Joe above her brewing his coffee, talking to the dog, preparing to make his escape. She could also hear her knee click with every revolution of the machine. How did she ever get so old? She didn't feel like a grown up, especially after the fight she'd had yesterday with Jordan. At twelve, Jordan knew precisely where the hairy edge lay that would make her nuts. She would push right up to that brink and then she'd watch Dani self-destruct in frustration. After Dani had yelled all the things she'd sworn she would never say to her own kids, Jordan would shrug, roll her eyes, and exhale loudly, as if Dani were the child. Her stomach knotted up thinking of their argument yesterday. It had spiraled from a small dispute about Jordan forgetting to unload the dishwasher before school to a screaming match about respect and kindness and treating adults the way they should be treated. Joe had laughed when she'd told him about it last night. Some days she felt completely inadequate as a parent, but it infuriated her when Joe made light of her daily battles. They were supposed to be partners in this war.

Enough of the torture machine, she looked around for a spot to do sit-ups. The dimly lit basement was crowded with boxes of clothes for Goodwill, toys in permanent time-out and Christmas decorations stacked next to the green and red plastic tubs Dani had bought at Walmart back when she'd vowed to organize her life or at least her basement.

She cleared a space on the kids' play mats and sank to the filthy floor. She'd meant to come down here last night and run the vacuum. Somewhere around the twentieth abdominal crunch she noticed the mouse poop on the floor next to her. Damn cats. They were absolutely useless. As if to reiterate her point, Jolly rubbed against her side mewing for breakfast. The fat orange tabby gave her a demeaning look. She heard the door close upstairs as Joe left for work. So much for *30 Days to a Beach Body*.

In the shower, Dani tried to piece together her day: make the dentist appointments; change the sheets; call the furnace guy to come for the yearly cleaning; finish the phone calls for the PTA fundraiser; sew the patches on Jordan's Girl Scout uniform; mail the packages for her grandmother's birthday; and try not to forget Joey's Gymboree class again. And she had to get at least four hours of real work in or she wouldn't get a paycheck this week. Dani transcribed medical records. It was mindless work she could do at home, hence the sweatpants.

With a loud bang, the bathroom door flew open and hit the side of the tub. Dani felt the rush of cold air as Joey bounded in, "Mommy! You're in the shower?" he asked.

"Yep," she said with a sigh.

"I need to watch *Thomas*," Joey said.

"No videos today."

"I need to watch *Thomas*."

Joey's obsession with Thomas the Tank Engine was wearing on her. Never mind the eerie faces on the grumpy trains and the mind-numbing voice of the narrator, the stories themselves made no sense and she found herself humming the annoying intro music at inappropriate times, like while signing her credit card slip at the gas station as a line of teenagers waited nervously behind her to buy cigarettes, or while the ob-gyn was washing up and putting on gloves to begin her exam.

"Maybe later, we'll see. Go get dressed."

Joey ignored her suggestion and turned on the sink faucet, causing the water pressure in the shower to plummet. He ran his fingers beneath the steady stream and began chanting, "*Thomas, Thomas, Thomas . . .*"

"Mom, did you wash my red sweater?" Jordan yelled, entering the bathroom just as Dani shut off the water.

Dani peered around the shower curtain at her children. "Look, I don't want to start my day screaming. Please, please, please, can the two of you leave me alone for just ten minutes?"

"I HAVE to have my red sweater. It's spirit day. Everybody else will be wearing red and I don't own anything else red," explained Jordan, not budging from the sink.

"I NEED TO WATCH *THOMAS*!" Joey yelled with as much melodramatic angst as a four-year-old could muster.

"Out."

"But Mom," Jordan began.

"OUT!" yelled Dani.

Jordan took Joey by the hand and reassured him, "C'mon, I'll put your show on."

---

Later, with Joey comatose in front of the DVD of his favorite anamorphic metal friends, Dani finally sat down with her coffee and the week's work. It was impossible to escape the insistent blare of Joey's show in their tiny old house and Dani struggled to focus on the doctor's scribbly notes. There was talk of going to all laptops for notes and that might spell the end of this cushy, if boring job. What would she do then? She'd never finished college, dropping out when she met and married Joe. Not much call for a half-finished art major with plenty of typing experience.

The phone rang. Dani stared at the receiver. She shouldn't answer; she was finally getting some work done. She sighed. It might be the school.

"Hello?"

"Hello, yourself."

"I suck as a mother."

Charlotte laughed. "DVDs won't kill him."

"Twenty a day might make him brain dead, though."

It was good to hear Charlotte's voice, somebody who didn't demand anything but friendship and the occasional home-baked cookies. Having only one child and working out of her home, Charlotte was also more available for impromptu coffee dates or a quick consultation when Dani couldn't make up her mind about any number of issues— what to wear, what to cook for dinner, what to say to her mother-in-law when she called with her latest invitation.

Just last week she'd called Charlotte in a panic because she couldn't find Joey. She'd sent him to get ready for his Gymboree class and went to put another load of laundry in the dryer. When she'd looked for him he was gone. After five minutes of yelling and threats hadn't produced him, she'd panicked. Charlotte had talked her down from her mental ledge and hadn't even laughed when Dani spotted Joey hiding in the car, dressed and ready for the Gymboree class they were now too late to attend.

"What do you think about a girls' weekend?" asked Charlotte.

"I think you're crazy."

"No, I mean it. We should go away for a weekend. We could invite Meg, too."

"I can't afford it. Besides, where would we go?"

"Sweet Beach! It's only ninety minutes away—far enough that we're really away, but not so far away that we'll waste the weekend getting there. There are tons of vacation houses for rent there. It's the off season; I'll find something reasonable. I can spot you if necessary."

"I have no time. Who would take care of the kids?"

"Hello? You do have a husband. Remember him?"

Dani laughed. Why couldn't she go away? Joe traveled for work on occasion and thought nothing of leaving her with the kids. Last month he'd had that conference in Orlando and she'd been stuck home with sick kids and a foot of snow. Time alone with them might be good for him.

"Meg will never go."

"Going away for the weekend might be the best thing for Meg."

"Maybe, but she doesn't go anywhere anymore."

"Which is precisely why she should come."

"I don't know, Charlotte. It might be too soon."

"Too soon? It's been almost two years! Look, I'm not trying to be mean. I just think it's time she moves on or at least does something for herself for a change."

"I'll ask her."

"Does that mean you'll go?"

"Sure. I'll go."

"I'll call the realtor today!"

"Let me find out Joe's schedule first. I do need to get away from here. My kids are making me into such an awful person."

"That's their job. I'll work on the place, you work on a weekend."

"You're serious about this? What does Brett think?"

"He doesn't know yet, but Will is leaving for Spain in a few weeks, so he won't care too much about my whereabouts." Will was Charlotte's

Girls' Weekend

thirteen-year-old son who was the most balanced
and mature thirteen-year-old Dani had ever met.
Joey followed him around like a shadow and Will
spent hours with him playing Legos, army men,
even watching the wretched *Thomas* DVDs. She
could only hope Joey would turn out like Will, but
doubted there was much chance of that. Will had
two parents devoted to his every moment.

Dani rarely admitted they hadn't planned on a
second child. Joey's birth had added a stress to her
life that she only acknowledged after several glasses
of wine. His birth had meant she couldn't go back to
school, couldn't get a real job, and four years later,
couldn't lose the baby weight. He was a fun kid, but
there was no end to his energy and lately, Dani gave
into his demands for DVDs just to pacify him. Lucky
for them all, Joey thrived on neglect.

"I'll talk to Joe and figure out a weekend that
would work. God, it would be great to get away. I
don't know if I would come back."

"I've got to get back to work, got a client breathing down my neck. Hang in there, babe, and don't
let them get to you. Let me know what Meg says."

## Charlotte

Charlotte sifted through the carpet samples. She
chose a smoky chocolate color and turned to the
paint chips. She wondered about the young entre-
preneur whose office she was designing. He was
handsome and loaded. His name had just turned
up on the list of most eligible bachelors being auc-
tioned off for a local charity fundraiser. She'd have
to be sure to get a ticket. Maybe she'd take Dani
instead of Brett.

Charlotte and Brett had been married for sev-
enteen years. When they started out, she never

imagined they would be where they are now. They
had a beautiful house, two successful businesses,
and an amazing child who was proof positive that
parenting was as much luck as know-how. How
Will had turned out to be such a nice kid despite
her neurotic tendencies was still a mystery to Charlotte. Brett was a great dad. He spent hours with
Will, not because he had to but because he actually
enjoyed being with him. On summer nights, they
would throw a Frisbee or a football until darkness
chased them indoors. They spent hours in Brett's
woodshop designing, building, fixing, but mostly
talking. Charlotte would hear the low murmur of
their voices until late in the night.

She envied Brett's easy rapport with Will. She
loved her son so much it hurt sometimes, but she
was startled by how uncomfortable she could be with
him. Many times she would watch him and feel awed
by the sheer wonder of him. Somehow all the best
genes in both of them pooled together to produce
Will. He had Brett's easy confidence and Charlotte's
charm, Brett's calm happiness and Charlotte's sense
of adventure. By some means, he had missed getting
Charlotte's insecurities or Brett's lack of initiative.

Will would be leaving this spring for three
months in Spain through an exchange program at
his school. St. Tim's was a private Catholic school
with a bigger emphasis on private than Catholic.
The exchange would be reversed in the fall, when
the child from the Spanish host family would come
and stay with them. Lucky for Charlotte, this visiting child would speak English. Although she'd had
three years of Spanish in high school and two in
college, she couldn't say much other than "*Como se
llama usted*?" And just how many times could she
ask the poor child his name?

Charlotte wondered if things might be different
without Will at home. Somehow they'd become that
couple she never wanted to be. Recently they'd gone
out to dinner and Charlotte had laid a ground rule,
"No talking about Will, okay?"

"Why not?" Brett had asked.

"Because he's all we ever talk about."

"That's not true," Brett insisted, but the conversation had been forced the rest of the evening and they'd finally skipped dessert and gone home where Brett had joined Will for *SportsCenter* and Charlotte had taken a glass of wine and a book to bed.

When they were first married, they'd gone to gallery openings, exotic restaurants, and museums. They'd taken impromptu trips to warm places to indulge their mutual love of snorkeling. They'd gone to movies and stayed up talking in trendy coffee bars until the owners kicked them out. They'd played darts for drinks, and had sex wherever the urge took them— the kitchen, the hallway, the balcony.

But all that changed when they became parents. Charlotte thought back to the day she told Brett she was pregnant. He cried and she'd been stunned by his tears. He doted on her during pregnancy and she'd loved the attention. He had treated her like a queen.

It was a difficult pregnancy, most of it spent in hospitals or on bed rest. When Will was born healthy, they'd cried tears of joy, but they both knew they would not go through it again. He would be enough. After that, their world revolved around their beautiful boy.

She wasn't sure when it happened, but something had changed. It was as if Brett had lost interest in their relationship. She began attending the black-tie fundraisers, gallery openings, and trendy restaurants alone. "You go without me," he would say. "I'm just not in the mood." Or he would claim he had work to do. On occasion he would join her, but insist they bring Will along.

When Charlotte protested and said Will would be better off at home, he asked, "Why would we leave him? We love Will." It was as if Charlotte was suggesting they abandon him in a shanty town.

Charlotte knew college was still five years away for Will, but suddenly it seemed just around the corner. Will going to Spain was a foretaste. What would be left of their world without Will? She couldn't remember the last time Brett even told her he loved her except to echo her own sentiments.

Charlotte tried to focus on her work. Besides the office design, she also had a new house to decorate. The construction was supposed to finish this week and it was time to begin the interior so the client could move in by Easter. Charlotte was a very successful interior designer because she could see possibilities other people never imagined. She took the time to get to know her clients and to design a home that fit their personalities and their needs. She had more work than she needed, but lately found herself taking jobs based on the client. She gravitated towards jobs working for men who were attractive, connected, and interesting. She knew her flirting was growing dangerous, but Brett was such a cold fish anymore, what was the harm? She didn't intend to take it anywhere.

Maybe with Will out of the house, she and Brett could rekindle whatever still existed beneath their busy schedules and Will-focused lifestyle. Maybe she should be going away with Brett instead of the girls. He was leaving for a conference the day after Will, but when she'd hinted that she might like to attend, he said, "You'd be bored out of your skull. And anyway, the schedule is crammed with seminars and meetings. I won't have any free time."

Charlotte knew she could have insisted, but she was hurt he didn't seem to want her there, so she let it drop. Yes, it would be good to spend some real time with Dani and Meg. Girlfriend time. That's what she needed.

❧

# Meg

That afternoon, Meg sat on the bleachers with Dani in the sweaty air of the indoor pool. Their girls took swimming lessons together every Thursday at the local Y. She glanced at Joey, strapped into his stroller sound asleep with a soggy cookie still clutched in his hand. She missed having a little guy. Logan would have been five now.

She shook her head and squeezed Timmy's shoulder. He sat beside her, eyes glued to an iPod. Timmy was seven and needed her less and less. She knew she babied him. She did too much for all her kids: Michael was thirteen and she still packed his lunch and laid out his clothes. He didn't seem to mind. Sarah was nine and Lizzie was eleven and they both fought her for the independence she wasn't ready to give. It was ridiculous to think she could control every detail of their lives, as if she had any power. No matter how careful she was or how closely she watched them, there was nothing she could really do to protect them. There was nothing she could have done to save Logan and she'd been standing right there. She knew that logically. The doctors and so many well-meaning friends had said it again and again, but still she couldn't help herself.

Logan's death had been so sudden. He'd never had an allergic reaction to anything before. Meg and Peter had taken the kids to a May Day party at the club where Peter played golf. No one even saw Logan eat the cashew from the bowl of mixed nuts at the bar. He'd climbed up on one of the stools and was spinning the stool to amuse himself. When he toppled from the stool, it looked like he'd just gotten dizzy and lost his balance. But then he hadn't moved. It was like watching a horror movie in slow motion. Logan turned blue. The bartender hopped over the bar and started CPR, to no avail. It wasn't his heart that stopped, it was his airway that had closed. By the time the paramedics arrived, it was too late.

Since his death, Meg had struggled to find her footing. She propelled herself forward even when she thought she couldn't take one more step—toting the kids everywhere, volunteering at school, getting them to Girl Scouts and swim lessons. They even took the kids to Disney World last year. But beneath her makeup, she knew the circles under her eyes contrasted with her pale, pasty skin. She'd never been thin, but she'd gained so much weight she'd begun wearing some of her maternity clothes. She just couldn't get herself to the gym. Peter suggested she might want to take up tennis. It was his not-so-subtle hint that her weight bothered him.

Meg could hear Dani chatting away about some teacher that was giving Jordan a hard time. She watched Michael, where he sat on a different set of bleachers diligently working on his homework. At thirteen he was deep in the throes of the "uglies," as Charlotte had called them when they'd commiserated about their thirteen-year-old boys. Pimples dotted his face, his greasy hair was rarely combed, and he was as awkward as a baby giraffe. He always looked like he'd rather be somewhere else. "I can't think with all the heat and noise," he said, gathering up his books and taking them out into the hall.

"Charlotte called me this morning with this wild idea," Meg heard Dani say.

"Does she want to do your living room over in purple zebra stripes?" asked Meg, never taking her eyes off of Sarah, who was a weak but determined swimmer.

"She wants us to go away for a girls' weekend in Sweet Beach next month. Just the three of us. You, me, and her. What do you think?"

Meg turned to look at Dani. She frowned. "I don't think it's possible."

"Why not? It'd be great. We all need to get away."

Meg shook her head and turned back to watch Sarah. "You'd really go away and leave your kids?"

"Sure, Joe can handle two days. The kids will survive. Peter can handle it, too."

"Peter can *so* not handle it," said Meg.

"Peter manages lots of people and millions of dollars at work, surely he can handle four kids for two days. Besides, I'm sure you'd leave him with twelve pages of instructions and every meal pre-packaged in ziplocked baggies."

Meg cheered as Sarah jumped off the swimmers block and swam out to the instructor, who handed her a kickboard and sent her on her way up the lane. She sat back down and turned to Dani, "I wouldn't leave all the food in baggies."

"I was kidding."

"What did Joe say when you told him?"

"I haven't asked him yet. I'm sure he'll grumble and try to make me feel guilty, but he'll do it."

"I'll think about it," said Meg, reaching over to take the soggy cookie from Joey's fingers and absently putting it in her mouth.

"Really?" asked Dani.

"I didn't say I was going, I just said I was thinking about it."

"Charlotte says she'll find a place in Sweet Beach; we just need to pick a weekend. So look at your calendar."

"I haven't said I'm going."

"Oh, Meg, you have to go. It will be great—just think, we can sleep as late as we want and not have to share our bed with anybody with cold feet or wet jammies."

"I'll think about it. It's not that easy for me to just up and leave."

"It's only a weekend. They can handle it."

Class ended and the girls came running towards them and Meg shrieked, "WALK!"

## Dani

When Joe got home at 7:30, Jordan was playing on the computer and Joey was lining up his Hot Wheels cars on the sofa to race off the edge. Dani had just finished cleaning up the kitchen and was sitting down at the counter with a cup of tea. Joe entered quietly. He set his briefcase down next to the door and said, "Sorry."

"We had spaghetti; there's a plate for you in the microwave."

Later, when the kids were in bed, Dani found Joe sitting on the couch clicking through the channels. She picked up the Hot Wheels scattered around his feet and throughout the room. Joe watched her, but made no move to help. When she finished, he said, "There's nothing on."

He continued to click through the channels. Dani stretched out on the sofa and put her head in his lap. He absently ran his fingers through her hair and paused at a soccer game on a Spanish station.

"I want to go away with Charlotte and Meg for a weekend."

"Why?" asked Joe.

"I don't know. Just to get away."

"All of us?"

"No, no kids or spouses. Just girls."

"What would I do?" Joe asked, turning off the TV. Dani sat up.

"You'd take care of the kids. Do whatever we would normally be doing. I'm sure Joey will have a soccer game and Jordan will probably have a Girl Scout function. You could have your folks over for dinner, so you wouldn't have to cook. You could rent a movie."

"You don't have to plan it all out for me. I can handle it, I guess. When do I get to go away? Or better yet, when do you and I get to go away without the kids?"

"You go away for work all the time."

"That's different."

"It is, but still you don't have to make your bed or cook or clean up or deal with kids."

"There are other stresses on my trips."

"I realize that. Look, this isn't about you. This is about me needing a weekend away." Dani could feel unexpected tears at the edge of her eyes. She blinked them away and put her head on Joe's shoulder. He sighed and laced his fingers through hers.

"Honey, it's fine. We'll be fine. You go have fun with the girls."

She'd expected Joe to resist, and when he didn't she felt her unexplainable tears wash down her face. Maybe she needed this weekend away more than she knew. She didn't understand the unhappiness that remained just under the surface of her life lately. Where did the dissatisfaction come from? Was something missing? Or was she doing something wrong? She wished she could talk to Joe about it. But she couldn't begin to explain it to herself, so what would she say to him? Besides, for the most part, her life was perfect; how could she be unhappy? Joe wiped a tear from her cheek.

"You seem pretty stressed out."

"I am, but I don't know why. Nothing's any more crazy than usual. I don't know why I'm crying; maybe I'm just tired."

"A weekend away will do you good, then. I can only imagine what kind of trouble Charlotte will find for you."

"She's good at that."

"Remember the last time you and I went away?" he asked, smiling.

"I'm reminded of it every day when I negotiate *Thomas* videos and Oreos."

Joe pulled her closer and kissed the side of her head.

The year before Joey was born, her parents had given her and Joe a weekend away together without Jordan for Christmas. Later that winter, they'd snuck away to a little cabin by a lake. It snowed ferociously, but the snow shoes the owner left for them had remained hanging on the wall. She and Joe spent the weekend rediscovering why they'd gotten married in the first place. They never left the comfort of the little cabin, except to bring in more wood for the huge fireplace. They couldn't even bring themselves to leave the cabin to try some of the fabulous restaurants their hosts had recommended. The food they brought along—cheese, fruit, bread, too many bottles of wine—had been enough. They'd been afraid to break the spell. She'd been a little careless with her diaphragm, letting her passion get the best of her. The weekend was magical, but what were the odds?

And so the next Christmas there had been Joey.

"This will be a different kind of weekend away," said Dani, leaning up to meet Joe's kiss.

## Meg

Meg couldn't stop thinking about Charlotte's idea. A weekend away? She'd barely been able to let the kids go to school without her since Logan's death. It wasn't that she imagined she could keep them safe. She only wanted to be near them, just in case.

When she couldn't find an excuse to be at their school volunteering, she busied herself at home— cleaning, cooking, preparing. As long as she was moving, she didn't have time to think about how much she missed her baby boy. She didn't have to crave his skin, his laugh. She didn't have to imagine his last moments: what he thought, how he hurt, or how she could do nothing to help him. It had been almost two years since Logan's death and it still felt fresh. She still had to remind herself that he was gone every morning when she woke up.

The rest of the family seemed to have recovered. Peter threw himself into his work and his golf game. He was rarely home, and when he was he never talked about Logan. The other day when Timmy was playing with the toy cars they'd given Logan for his third birthday, she commented on how much Logan had loved those cars. Timmy said, "These are my cars, Mommy." The girls hardly mentioned him anymore. She worried they were forgetting him. Not Meg. Logan's death followed her everywhere she went; it felt like an invisible cloak that only she could see. Wasn't there a cloak like that in *Harry Potter*? Jordan would know. No, the cloak wasn't invisible, it made *you* invisible. That might be nice.

She'd done her best to push the pain aside, to keep it hidden from even herself. When images of Logan's still body lying on the floor at the club filled her mind, she would turn up the music on her iPod and begin making lists. She made lists for shopping, cleaning, and vacations. She listed ideas for Christmas presents, teacher gifts, and birthday parties. Anything to keep her mind busy. When there was nothing to list, she worked on crossword puzzles. Painstakingly researching clues, consulting crossword dictionaries online, even e-mailing strangers when all else failed. She'd contacted the president of the Shirley Temple fan club to find out which Beatles album had a picture of Temple on it. She was working her way through every puzzle in the book Peter had bought her—*1001 Beyond Challenging Crossword Puzzles.*

The idea of leaving for a weekend to do nothing terrified Meg. Peter would veto the idea anyway. She was sure of that. She wouldn't have to make excuses, he was her built-in excuse. He was the reason she'd quit the book club. "*Peter has a standing conference call that night and it's just gotten too hard to find a sitter.*" He was the reason she'd stepped down from evening PTA commitments. "*Peter's work has gotten so busy—I can never be certain which nights he'll be home.*" She even used him on the kids. "*No, Lizzie, sorry, your father doesn't think ski club is a good idea this year. Sorry, Sarah, no sleepover at Michaela's; Daddy's going to be home tonight and he wants us to have a nice meal together and watch a movie."* Peter didn't know and probably wouldn't care that Meg used him this way, but it wasn't as if Meg was making it up. Peter was absent more than he was present in their family. It hadn't always been that way. Meg knew she should confront him on it, but she wasn't any different, was she? She was present, but only going through the motions, getting through her days.

Meg put aside the crossword puzzle she was working on. It was from last Sunday's paper. She felt an irrational pressure to finish each day's puzzle. She'd been busier than usual and was three days behind on her puzzles. What was the 1979 hit whose title is sung with a stutter? That was way too easy for a Sunday puzzle. She hummed "My Sharona" to herself as she helped Timmy and Sarah get ready for bed.

When she returned to the crossword puzzle, Peter was sitting at the counter helping Lizzie with her homework. Meg was as surprised as she was glad to see it. He normally came home late and was often too tired to be of any help with the kids.

"Okay, Dad. I got it. I don't have to do anything after page 192."

"But this is the best part. That way, when your teacher goes over this stuff tomorrow, you'll be ahead of the game."

"I don't want to be ahead of the game. I just want to have my homework done," explained Lizzie as she closed her book.

"It's time to get ready for bed anyway," interrupted Meg. "You only have fifteen minutes, sweetie. Why don't you get your pajamas on and brush your teeth and I'll be up to tuck you in."

Lizzie gathered her books and headed upstairs. Meg heard her drop the pile on the bottom step as she went up.

"I wish she was more excited about math. I worry she's not living up to her potential. She's smart, why doesn't she use it?" Peter seemed genuinely puzzled.

"She's eleven. Give her time. Not every kid has that academic drive, especially in elementary school. They already do so much more than we ever did at that age. When I was in fifth grade, I didn't have half the homework she does."

"Maybe that's the problem. They give these kids so much work it just drills the enthusiasm right out of them. It becomes a chore to get through. Maybe we should rethink our choice of schools."

Meg put aside her crossword puzzle and began assembling lunches for the next day.

"So, have you given any more thought to seeing that counselor I mentioned?" asked Peter.

He'd been trying to get her to see a shrink ever since Christmas. She suspected it had more to do with her lack of interest in having sex than in his concern for her happiness. Well, maybe that wasn't fair, but he seemed to equate sex with happiness. If she didn't want to have sex, there must be something seriously wrong with her. He sat at the counter watching her.

"I'm not sure I need that," she said.

"Look, you've got to do something. You can't keep going like this."

"Like what?"

"Like, I don't know, like a zombie. It's like you're here, but you're not here."

Meg didn't say anything. She filled five bags with cookies and began filling five more with pretzels. She never used to make Peter's lunch. But the first night she made lunches and included one for Logan's preschool lunch bunch, she'd started crying and Peter had said, "Hey, can I have it? I've always wished you made my lunch, too. They always look so good." She'd kept making it ever since, even though she knew he went out to lunch with clients most days.

"What would you think about me going away for a day or two with Charlotte and Dani for a sort of girls' weekend?"

"I would think, who's going to take care of the kids?"

"Well, it would only be for a day or two. I think you could handle it."

"Why now? I'm swamped with work. Couldn't you wait 'til this summer when school is out and my parents will be back from Florida? Besides, I'm not sure you're ready for that yet."

"You're the one who said I have to snap out of it." She glared at him, one hand in the pretzel bag as her other shook open a plastic baggie. Peter didn't meet her eyes. Instead, he checked his phone, unwilling to respond to her shrill tone. She sighed.

"Anyway," she continued, "The timing's not up to me. They're going next month with or without me. Is it so ridiculous to ask you to take care of your own children for two days?" Meg stormed out and went upstairs to tuck in Lizzie. She didn't know why she was so angry. She didn't want to go on the stupid weekend anyway. Or did she? She'd wanted Peter to say no, and now that he had, for some strange reason, it made her angry.

Lizzie was already asleep when she looked in. She closed the door softly, then scooped up the discarded clothing and wet towels lying in the hallway. Stopping to turn off the bathroom lights, she caught her reflection in the mirror. She looked horrible. When had those lines appeared on her forehead? Lately, she felt a hundred years old, and now she was beginning to look it. She scanned her bright blond hair for signs of gray. She could find none. Leaning in close, her breath fogging the glass, she examined the dark circles under her eyes, the pale, dull skin. Did it matter what she looked like anymore? She ran her fingers through her reckless curls and repositioned her headband. She looked like a housewife. That was all. An *old* housewife.

She splashed water on her tired face before heading to Michael's room. Peter was lying on Michael's bed, tossing a football up and down while Michael worked at his desk. She heard Peter asking him about signing up for baseball. Knowing she didn't want any part of that conversation, she tip-toed downstairs to finish making the lunches.

When Dani first suggested the weekend, Meg had dismissed the idea as out of the question. Even if she wanted to go, it would be too complicated, and not worth the effort to convince Peter and prepare the kids. Now she felt differently. Peter's annoyance with the idea made her angry. He could take care of his own children for two days and two nights. He was a powerful, well-educated attor-ney; he handled million-dollar lawsuits and hostile divorce cases. Dani was right; he could certainly handle this house for two days. She would make lists of all that needed to be done and which kids had to be where. She would plan the meals and have everything they needed.

Peter entered the kitchen quietly and Meg watched him as he made a cup of coffee. He was so careful and meticulous. She had always appreci-ated that about him. He liked order.

"Who hosted the winter Olympics after Van-couver?" she asked. Meg knew the answer; it was a common clue, but she knew Peter liked to have the answer.

"Sochi!"

"Thanks," she said. He was a good man. He just didn't handle surprises well, and the idea of the girls' weekend had definitely surprised him.

"Look, instead of a girls' weekend, maybe you could all go out for a nice lunch at some place fancy, like La Fontana? I'd even spring for it," he offered.

Meg looked at him, an odd fury building inside her. Had he always dismissed her ideas so readily? Peter smiled at her and took a sip of his coffee. She watched him take his coffee to his study and close the door. Robotically, she assembled sandwiches for the lunches, laying out five sets of bread. Peter always got what he wanted. It's how he'd gotten as far as he had at work, and probably why she'd married him. She finished four peanut butter and jelly sandwiches, and started to make Peter's ham sandwich. She stared at the bread slices, mayonnaise knife poised. Why did he always get his way? When had she asked for anything like this before? She set down the knife, closed the jar, returned the ham to the fridge, put the knife in the dishwasher and closed the empty sandwich, wrapping it neatly in tin foil. She placed his lunch next to his car keys and turned off the kitchen light.

Saturday afternoon, Meg curled up on the sofa in her bedroom with a crossword puzzle. A movie blared on the TV downstairs. Her three younger children were alternately watching the movie and fighting with each other over the seating arrangement. Michael was in his room working on his latest invention with the door closed. She hadn't seen much of him all day. It was nearly three. Where was Peter? How was it that Saturday morning's golf game always continued into the afternoon?

She couldn't stop thinking about the girls' weekend. Of course, Charlotte would suggest it. Charlotte, whose life was so simple and uncomplicated she could just up and leave for a weekend and happily wave to her perfect little family who'd wish her a good time. It wouldn't be so easy for her. She would have to convince Peter. She could only imagine what he was thinking. First among his concerns would be the loss of his Saturday morning golf game. Maybe she could hire a sitter to cover Saturday morning.

Her thoughts were interrupted by her son's quiet presence. Michael could do that—just appear as if from thin air. He waited for her to notice him. It was sad he had to do that so much lately. She was always busy refereeing the girls' fights, and dealing with Timmy's tantrums, she took for granted Michael would look after himself.

"Hey sweetie."

"Hey," he replied, toying with the paper in his hands. "You doing the crossword? Ask me one."

"Okay, who was the last Pope Pius?"

"I wouldn't know that. We never go to church anymore."

"Pope Pius the twelfth. Do you need something?"

"Can you take me to the hardware store? I need some stuff."

"What kind of stuff?"

"Some stuff for my experiment. Wires and switches and maybe some tape."

"How about when your dad gets home you can tell him about your experiment, and the two of you can stop at the store on the way to pick up pizza for dinner?" Peter needed to spend more time with Michael. Maybe he would get involved with Michael's project. Peter was not very mechanically inclined; he was more comfortable with words. Science seemed to intimidate him, but he was proud of Michael's aptitude for it. Meg's eyes glazed over when Michael tried to explain his theories and experiments, but he could be counted on for the science clues.

"Will he be home soon?"

"I think so. Why don't you make a list of what you'll need?"

"Let me know when Dad gets here."

Michael's disappointment was evident in the slump of his shoulders as he walked away.

"Hey! Here's one you could help me with—Galileo's birthplace?" she called after him.

"Duh. Pisa." Meg was rewarded with a shy smile. She hoped Peter would be receptive to the idea of helping Michael with his experiment. She was about to call his cell phone when she heard the familiar squeal of the garage door opening. She heard him place his clubs against the wall and come up the stairs into the house. She knew he'd sneak upstairs as quietly as possible, avoiding the kids until he had showered and changed and was ready to deal with them.

But Timmy spotted him as he slipped through the kitchen.

"DADDY!" he yelled.

Meg smiled. She could hear a brief wrestling match ensue downstairs. When Peter finally entered the room, he looked sheepish. He made for the bathroom, saying, "We got stuck behind a bunch of old geezers. They wouldn't let us play through, so it took all day. Sorry sweetie. I'll be right out."

She wanted to be angry, but she wasn't so much mad as resigned. He needed his golf. He worked hard and needed the break, but they all missed him. The weekends were their only chance to be together.

Peter finally emerged from the bathroom in only a towel. Meg put down her crossword. She had no idea which president signed the Sherman Antitrust Act. Peter was still a handsome man and, for a moment, Meg felt a stirring she hadn't felt in months. After Logan died, she'd clung to Peter. She was hungry for him every night, as if somehow he would fill the void that threatened to swallow her up. And then the casseroles stopped coming and the friends stopped calling, and everyone assumed she would pick up the remnants of her life and carry on. Only she couldn't. So she put all her energies into her children, shutting out everything else, even Peter. She pretended everything was fine in the hopes that it would be.

She watched him comb his hair in the mirror and considered locking the bedroom door. Instead, she took a deep breath and began the speech she'd prepared. "I realize it could be an inconvenience for you if I went away for the weekend, but I think I deserve it. I work just as hard as you do and I need a break. You play golf every Saturday, and if I added up the hours, I'm sure it equals at least a weekend away. I want to go away with my friends. Not just that, I need to go away."

Meg could see Peter already dismissing her as he sifted through his dresser drawer looking for underwear, not making eye contact. Her anger returned and she plowed on, "It'll only be two days, and maybe . . . maybe it'll help. It's not that much to ask. Michael will help."

When he didn't reply, Meg wondered if he was even listening.

"Well?"

"Well, what?" asked Peter as he emerged from his cavernous closet stuffed with expensive suits, shirts, and ties for every occasion. Even his T-shirts were on hangers.

"Peter, did you listen to anything I said?"

"Honey, we talked about this. I said it wasn't going to work. Maybe instead of a nice lunch, I could spring for dinner for you and the girls at the club. We could even make it an occasion and invite the husbands. I don't think a weekend away is going to help you. I think it might be better if you talked to Dr. Ayers, like I suggested."

Meg struggled to find the words to voice her anger. She stood up, automatically smoothing the bedspread and replacing the pillow. Peter, thinking it was settled, went back to the closet in search of his shoes.

Meg started to leave, but then turned, and in a quiet voice said, "No." She stood in the doorway, waiting to hear if Peter had registered her reply.

"Did you say something, honey?" he called from the closet.

-◠-

Thursday found Meg and Dani sitting by the pool again. Dani kept a firm hold on the back of Joey's overalls as they watched the girls in the pool. Michael sat beside them with his nose in a book, and Timmy played on Meg's cellphone. Periodically, Joey pleaded, "Look at my trucks, Michael," offering him his tanker truck as he held tight to his cement mixer. When he didn't respond, Joey began driving the tanker up and down the page Michael was reading.

"Joey, I'm in the middle of something. Let me finish, and then I'll race the trucks with you in the hall."

"Okay, you have the tanker, I have the mixer." Joey turned to run for the door, but Dani scooped him up on her lap and gave him a candy cane she'd found in her purse, left there since Christmas.

"So, I think I can do this weekend thing," Meg said quietly, not wanting Michael to hear her. Burrowed in his book, he didn't appear to be listening.

"You're kidding! That's great! Charlotte's rented this awesome house just a few blocks from the beach. We can each have our own bedroom and bath. Can you imagine? A bathroom all to yourself? What did Peter say?"

"That it wouldn't work for him."

Dani raised her eyebrows in question, and Meg shrugged.

"I've never been away more than two nights from my kids, and you know what happened the last time I did that. Not that I don't love Joey. I am *so* looking forward to this. You really think Peter will come around?"

"I don't care. I'm doing this, and to hell with what doesn't work for him. Maybe it'll be good for them to have a weekend without me."

"Yeah, they'll figure out that dishes don't do themselves and clothes don't make it to the hamper without assistance."

"Not in one weekend they won't. I'll return to a sink full of dishes and a house that is completely trashed."

Joey finished his candy cane and climbed off Dani's lap. He tapped Michael on the knee. Michael closed his book and took Joey out to the hall to race the trucks.

"Probably, but it'll be worth it," said Dani.

That night, Meg lay in bed waiting for Peter. It was already past eleven, but she wasn't even tired. She was keyed up and hoped her plan would work. That afternoon she'd bought a new lace teddy with a built-in push-up bra. She hadn't realized how much weight she'd gained and was embarrassed at the store to ask for a larger size.

It wasn't a very original plan, but it was a classic. First she'd have sex with Peter, and then she'd tell him she was going away for the girls' weekend. In the end, she couldn't think of any other way to make Peter receptive to her idea. They hadn't had sex in months, and even then it'd been a quick affair, Meg giving in so she could get some sleep.

After all the kids were asleep, she lay on the bed, rearranging her ample cleavage, which spilled out of the bra each time she changed positions in her attempt to look seductive. Finally, she couldn't wait any longer. She found the sheer robe Peter had bought her for Christmas and tore the tags off. Wrapping it loosely around herself, she went downstairs to find him.

Peter was still in his office, working at the computer. When Meg entered, he didn't look up.

"I know, I know, it's late; I'll be right up."

Meg leaned against a bookcase, feeling overly self-conscious, waiting for him to see her. Finally, he glanced up, shocked. He took off his glasses and leaned back in his chair, smiling as he ran his eyes up and down her. Without even pausing to save his work, he led her to the leather couch in the corner by the window.

He laid her down gently, but she could tell he was more than thrilled by the sight of her. She'd thought this part would be difficult, but his reaction had been so raw. His desire instant. She could still make him quiver. When he held her, instead of going through the motions as she had been doing this past year, she found herself desperately aware of how much she wanted him, too. She missed this connection; she did still love him. Peter couldn't hold out long and it was over too soon. He brushed the hair back that had fallen in her eyes and kissed her cheek.

"You okay?" he asked afterwards, rolling to his side and pulling her to him.

Meg nodded. She lay against his chest, feeling the quick thump of his heart.

"Peter?"

"Yes?"

Meg softly touched his cheek and he closed his eyes. She touched his thick eyelashes and nuzzled his neck. "I need to tell you something."

He didn't respond. Meg ran her hands through his hair.

"I'm going away for a weekend in April with the girls. I've already arranged a babysitter so you won't miss golf."

When he didn't say anything, Meg began to cry. She didn't know what else she could do to convince him. Peter sat up and pulled her into his arms.

"You really want this, don't you?"

She nodded, wiping at her tears.

"It won't be easy for me, but I'll figure it out; I guess I'll have to. Please stop crying. You're making me feel like such a jerk."

He smiled and kissed her forehead.

"Did you think I wouldn't let you go?"

Meg nodded.

"Honey, all you had to do was tell me how important it was to you. I want you to be happy."

Meg hugged him, wanting to believe everything he said.

# FRIDAY, APRIL 12

## Dani

Charlotte arrived to pick up Dani at one that afternoon. Meg would drive herself down later. She insisted she needed to stay with the kids until Peter got home, and of course he was late.

Dani took three trips back into the house to tell Joe something else, and to kiss Joey again, before she finally climbed in beside Charlotte and slammed the door.

Charlotte was on her headset debating carpet weights with a client. She raised her eyebrows at Dani silently asking if she was ready to go. Dani grinned and nodded.

She listened to Charlotte's side of a conversation that seemed much longer than necessary. The only people Charlotte ever indulged were clients. Dani felt as if she'd just jumped in a getaway car after robbing a bank. She smiled to herself, but said nothing, afraid to break the spell. Finally, she couldn't stand it any longer and put on a CD.

"Oh, this takes me back. Indigo Girls, right?" said Charlotte when she was finally off the phone.

"It brings back my college days, when I was a single woman full of angst."

"I forgot you went to college. What were you like? Wild and crazy? Serious student?" Charlotte asked.

"Oh, not much different. I was studying art, though, so you know I was a little odd."

"Outrageous clothes? Moody? Dark? Heavy drinker? What?"

Dani laughed. "Some of all that, but I was always broke, so there wasn't much drinking."

"So, does the music bring back good memories or bad?"

"Both, probably. Lost loves, old dreams. All the things I was going to do and the woman I was going to be."

"I don't think any of us turn out like we plan to."

"Yeah, well, I guess you can't spend too much time mourning the roads not taken. Joe happened along and he seemed like a good idea, and before I knew it we had Jordan and life was just buzzing by. When I put on this CD, it takes me back. But no regrets, right?"

"Hmmm. We'll have to dig deeper into this over a bottle of wine. Speaking of which, I'm going to stop before we get any further and pick up a few bottles. What else do we need?"

"I've got enough groceries for a month, but I probably didn't bring enough chocolate."

---

A little more than an hour later, they pulled into a gravel drive leading to a beautiful old house tucked between two much larger modern homes. The house had worn gray siding with baby blue shutters. Huge, wide trees sheltered it like protective arms. The front porch wrapped around one side of the house and ivy crawled over its railings. A hand-painted sign crookedly declared, *Paradise Found*. A widow's walk on the roof was barely visible above the tree tops. It was a cottage right out of a storybook.

"How did you find this place?" asked Dani, awestruck.

Charlotte laughed. "You just have to know what you're looking for." She grabbed several bags of groceries and started up the steps.

Inside it was just as amazing. The furniture was unique and tasteful. Nothing matched, but it still worked. The walls were painted a peach color, creating a beautiful warm light in the late afternoon sun. Dani stood in the elegant, sparse living room and studied the books filling the shelves. She loved the place. She felt like she had come home.

Charlotte called from the kitchen, "Isn't this place darling? It's better than it sounded on paper. I thought quaint would mean tiny, and cozy would mean dark. But it really is quaint and cozy. Let's check out the upstairs."

Upstairs were two small bedrooms, each with its own bathroom. On the third floor was a converted attic bedroom with a tiny bathroom and steps leading up to the widow's walk on the roof. The room was painted a soft robin's egg blue and furnished almost completely in white. Four sky lights brought the sunset in.

"Who sleeps here?" asked Charlotte as she followed Dani up the steps to the widow's walk. As they stepped out on the narrow porch, Charlotte grabbed for the railing. Dani walked to the end. It was only about eight feet across and maybe three feet wide, but from their perch they could see the ocean. Dani stood against the rail and breathed in deeply. The smell of the ocean always calmed her. The waves were beautiful, although this early in the spring they looked pretty rough. There wasn't a soul on the beach. Dani turned to ask Charlotte what she thought of the view, but she was gone.

Dani found her downstairs inspecting the two smaller bedrooms.

"I think I'll take the lavender room. It's really me, don't you think?" she called from one of the rooms. Dani walked in to admire the room. Lavender walls and a soft gray carpet. The collection of throw pillows on the bed rivaled the mound on Charlotte's own.

"Charlotte, you should have the loft. It's the best room. This was all your idea and you made the arrangements. It's only fair; I know Meg will think so, too."

"I don't like being up so high and that widow's walk freaks me out. It seems so unstable up there, balancing on the top of the house. Besides, I love this room. It's me, completely. You take the loft."

"I'll wait to debate it with Meg. Seems presumptuous of me to take the best room."

"Put your stuff up there, I'll tell her I assigned rooms. Anyway, she won't care."

"You're sure?"

Charlotte nodded as she opened drawers and inspected the closet.

"Let's walk to the beach before it gets dark."

---

"How about we order Chinese tonight," suggested Dani when they returned to the house. "I want to eat out of a box and throw away my utensils. No dishes for me tonight."

"Whoa—don't get crazy on me, now," teased Charlotte. She selected a bottle of wine and opened it, filling two glasses to the brim.

"To us," she offered as she raised her glass.

"To no husbands, no children, and no whining," said Dani.

---

Later, Charlotte and Dani waited on the porch for Meg. She should have been there hours ago and wasn't answering her cell phone. Dani worried she'd never find the house in the dark.

"Maybe she changed her mind," said Charlotte.

"I don't think so. I get the feeling she had to move heaven and earth to make this happen."

"I bet Peter's pissed off."

"I can just see him. He might actually have to do some dishes and miss his precious golf game," said Dani.

Charlotte laughed. "He sure is Mr. Perfect. I wonder if he always was. Didn't Meg meet him in high school?"

"I bet he was hot back then. Can you imagine being together so long?"

"No," said Charlotte before taking a long drink of her wine. Then she smiled mischievously. "Do you suppose she's never slept with anyone else?"

Dani smacked her. "Charlotte!"

"I mean, seriously, can you imagine?"

"I think it's kind of nice."

"That's not the word I'd use," said Charlotte. "Think of all you'd miss out on!"

Dani laughed. "Some of us more than others!"

"Ouch! But I have no regrets! How many men have you slept with?" asked Charlotte.

"I don't know."

"Yes, you do. Everyone does. Unless it's so many you can't keep track?" Charlotte poured more wine in Dani's glass.

"Let me think." She took a sip of wine and started counting on her fingers.

"Five. But really four and a half," said Dani.

"How is that possible?"

Dani shrugged. "I was drunk and I didn't mean to sleep with the one guy. So I don't count it because it didn't mean anything."

"Oh my God! I did not expect that from you Danielle Harper!"

"Oh c'mon! I was young! It may be hard to believe but I wasn't always such a model of good behavior!"

"I'd say not!"

An owl hooted in the trees and they both jumped.

"It's nice here," said Dani. "I'm so glad we did this."

They sat in companionable silence for a few minutes, then Charlotte asked, "Do you ever think about what your life would be like if you'd married one of those other guys you slept with?"

"I don't know. Not really. They were just kids. I think one of the reasons I married Joe is he seemed like a grown up."

"Are you glad you chose him?"

"Of course," said Dani, climbing in the hammock that swung gently in the corner of the porch. "Now this is nice."

"Room for me?" asked Charlotte, climbing in. Dani shrieked as the hammock tipped, but after the initial dip, it leveled back off again.

"Here," said Charlotte, handing her a napkin to wipe the wine that had spilled on her jeans. The hammock shifted slowly in the slight breeze.

"Why all these questions about the men not chosen? Aren't you glad you married Brett?"

Charlotte ran her finger around the rim of her glass. "Not lately."

"Really? I thought you two were happy."

"We are. I mean, I guess Brett is, but I wouldn't know since we never talk."

"How is that possible? Especially now with Will away?"

Charlotte shrugged. "I don't know. I always feel like I'm the only one doing the talking. He's usually willing to go along with my plans, but he never initiates anything—not dates, not conversations, lately, not even sex."

Charlotte was quiet. Dani knew it wasn't easy for her to admit this. She thought of Charlotte as the friend who had it made—great husband, perfect son, and a successful business. Plus, she was always upbeat. To most of the world, Charlotte appeared to have life on a string. Dani knew it wasn't as perfect as all that, but she hadn't realized there was a problem.

"I wonder sometimes if he wishes he weren't married to me."

"Charlotte! That can't be true. Brett loves you," insisted Dani.

"I think that may be apparent to everyone but me." She shook her head and took a drink of her wine. "I suggested maybe we should have dinner last night, before I left today, and he didn't even show up. He called later and said he'd forgotten."

"Wow," said Dani. "That sucks."

Charlotte nodded. "Here's what sucks even more. We haven't had sex in probably six months."

"How is that possible? Don't you sleep in the same bed?"

"He usually goes to bed before me. And when I suggest a little action, he always has an excuse. After a while, the rejection starts to feel personal. Our relationship feels more platonic these days anyway."

"Still, he's a guy. That doesn't make any sense. Joe would do it every night if I agreed. The man is insatiable. I always feel like the party pooper. Any chance Brett's having an affair?"

"I've thought of that, but I don't think he would. Not because of me, but because of Will. He'd never want to do anything to disrupt our family. And beyond that, it wouldn't be in his character. He always does the right thing. Brett's a great dad. He's a fun guy." She took the last sip of her wine. "Maybe he's tired of me."

"I can't imagine anyone getting tired of you, Charlotte. You're the most exciting person I know."

"I am, aren't I?"

"And modest, too. That's what I love in a friend."

Charlotte jumped up quickly, causing the hammock to tip and dump Dani on the floor.

"Hey! What's that for?"

"You needed a little excitement. Besides, I'm out of wine."

When Charlotte returned with a fresh bottle of wine, Dani was sitting on the steps, picking dead leaves off the ivy curling around the railing. Charlotte handed her a glass of wine and a fortune cookie.

"Thanks. Where's yours?"

"I already ate it."

"What was your fortune?"

"*In the end all things will be known*," said Charlotte in a deep, serious tone.

"Huh," said Dani, pulling her fortune from the cookie. She squinted in the porch light. "*There are no mistakes, just lessons to be learned.*"

"Profound," said Charlotte, clinking her glass with Dani's.

"Look at all those stars," said Dani looking up at the dark sky. "It seems like there are more here than at home."

"They're there, we just can't see them because of all the light pollution," said Charlotte. "It's getting late, I hope Meg's really coming."

"She'll be here."

"I was surprised she agreed to this. I haven't seen her without the kids since Logan's death."

"Maybe she's afraid to leave them alone."

"Yeah, or maybe she's afraid to be alone."

---

Meg's car pulled in at ten thirty. Her puffy eyes and exhausted look said it all.

"Peter didn't get home until eight, and then Timmy had a fit because I was leaving."

"But you're here now," said Charlotte.

"Thank God. I need a drink and a big comfy bed, in that order."

"I know just the place," Dani assured her.

They fed Meg leftover Chinese food and red wine.

"I almost didn't come," said Meg. She took a big swallow of wine. "Everybody was mad and the house was a mess and I was so stressed by it all. Peter was laying it on, complaining that he didn't feel well and was exhausted. I almost turned around several times. I still can't believe I'm here." She shook her head and wiped away fresh tears. "Thank you for making me do this."

"I'm just glad you didn't turn around," said Dani, putting her arm around Meg.

"You know, once I was finally on the road, I thought—what if I keep going?"

"You mean, not come here, just run away?"

"I would never really do that, but sometimes I just feel like trying a new life. That probably sounds crazy."

"Not really," said Dani.

"Sometimes I wish Brett would have an affair so I'd have an excuse to start over."

"Charlotte! You don't mean that!" said Dani. Turning to Meg, she said, "We've already had two bottles of wine."

"How do you know I don't mean it?" challenged Charlotte. "Wouldn't it be great to create a new life?"

"That's easy for you to say," said Meg. "You only have one kid and he's practically grown up."

"I think Will was born grown up," said Dani.

"I don't think that makes a difference. I'm almost forty-three years old. For all intents and purposes, my life is at least halfway over. I just wonder sometimes, if this is all there is. If this is all the happiness I get."

"My mother always told me that happiness is relative," said Dani. "Course she didn't have the happiest life married to my dad."

"I'm not saying I'm going to do anything crazy. But think about it. Are you happy with your life at this point?"

Meg was quiet and Dani didn't say anything. The question was too loaded. The silence quickly grew deafening.

Dani got up. "And that's a wrap. I'm going to bed. I want to get up and go for a run on the beach in the morning."

"Not me. This weekend is all about indulgence and decadence. No exercise. No healthy food," said Charlotte.

"I'm exhausted. I just want to sleep until noon," said Meg.

"Okay, ladies. This weekend is whatever you want it to be." Charlotte raised her glass and waited for the others to raise theirs.

"To a weekend of absolute self-indulgence. Do what makes you happy!"

---

After she brushed her teeth, Dani pulled on an extra sweatshirt and climbed the stairs to the widow's walk. It was a clear night and the temperature had dropped to the forties. Dani wished her mittens weren't three floors down.

On the roof, in the darkness, the air smelled sweeter. She lifted her arms and stretched, breathing deeply. She needed this airing out. She'd been feeling sluggish and foggy lately, as though she were weighed down by some invisible force. She was easily annoyed by stupid stuff and never seemed to have energy for the things she used to enjoy, like working in her garden or playing cards with Jordan. Mostly, she felt like she was simply going through the motions.

She knew from the psychology course she took in college and the women's magazines she read, that these were symptoms of depression. She should see the doctor, probably. But that would cost money. Besides, she didn't want to be on some drug that artificially pumped up her happiness because, really, what did she have to be depressed about? There was nothing wrong with her life. In fact, it was nearly perfect. She had two wonderful children and a reliable, loving husband. Sure, money was tight, but there had never been a time in her life when it was not.

No, she had no excuse. She had it good. All she had to do was look at Meg to realize that. She couldn't imagine losing Joey. It was a wonder Meg could put one foot in front of the other. If anyone had a right to a few pills to get through the day, it would be Meg.

Nothing terrible had happened in Dani's life. The days bled together with mind-numbing monotony: meals, laundry, kids, errands—life. The most exciting thing that had happened of late was Joey getting kicked out of the YMCA's childcare for eating paste and stealing Legos. She had no reason to be sad, but a melancholy colored her days. She'd find herself motionless, not even sure what she'd been doing. Sometimes a heaviness came over her and she'd sit down, only to pop up moments later when a child or the phone or the dryer buzzer startled her out of her funk. She'd thought being an adult would be more exciting.

When Jordan started school, the plan had been for her to get a real job or maybe even go back to school herself. They hadn't expected Joey.

Joey was not an easy child. From the moment he could crawl, he was never content to play with baby toys, but sought his own excitement in the form of his father's tools, his sister's belongings, and his mother's reactions. But Dani was certain Joey was not responsible for her unhappiness. On the contrary, he was the one person who could make her smile. If it weren't for him, Dani might have slunk off back to bed after Jordan got on the bus in the mornings.

No, the kids weren't the cause of her restlessness. Maybe this weekend away would help her refocus her energies, and send her home with renewed excitement for her life.

The sky was clear and the stars burned brighter here. She stared out at the dark ocean, listening to the tide's endless give and take.

"Why aren't I happy?" she whispered.

Dani considered herself a spiritual person. Even though she didn't attend any church on a regular basis, she felt as if there was a hand on her life and in the world, but she wasn't sure whose it was. Growing up, her parents' church had left her feeling confused. Much of what had been preached on Sundays wasn't a part of life on Mondays.

She felt like her life was spinning by too fast, like Charlotte said, and what did she have to show for it? Oh sure, she knew raising kids was important, but sometimes that felt like a crapshoot. The lady at the Y sure made Dani feel like she wasn't doing such a bang-up job with Joey. The quiet of the stars and chill in the breeze left her feeling deserted. Did it have to be this hard? Why couldn't she have faith like Meg, who was so sure of her religion and her purpose and what was right and wrong. Why couldn't it be clear for her, too? Why couldn't she just accept things and be content instead of always feeling this disconnect with her world? She could hear Meg now, telling her to "Let go and let God." Meg's favorite advice sounded like nails on a chalkboard to Dani. She could let the ball go if she really thought God would pick it up. And how far had that gotten Meg, anyway?

She listened to the ocean only a few blocks away. The beach town was deserted. In just a few months, the area would be bustling with tourists and day trippers. Dani sometimes brought her kids to the beach for the day. She and Meg usually made the trek a few times each summer, but she'd never been here in the off-season. It was a different place. It seemed to be resting, catching its breath and waiting. The quiet creating a huge void only the crazy, crowded days of summer could fill. Dani liked it much better this time of year.

# SATURDAY, APRIL 13

## Meg

**M**eg pulled on khaki pants and a lavender sweater set, completely inappropriate for a wild girls' weekend getaway. She wished she had Charlotte's fashion sense. Fishing around in the outside pocket of her suitcase for the tissues she'd stuffed in at the last minute, she found three packs of flavored condoms. She smiled to herself as she studied them, wondering if they were still effective. She sure hadn't been concerned about their effectiveness back when she and Peter bought them on a rare weekend away several years ago. They could never have too many children. Maybe what she needed now was another baby, but at forty that was crazy. And it wasn't like another baby could replace Logan.

She sank down on her bed. The thought still stole her breath away every time. Logan was gone. His sweet little dimpled hands were underground in that cemetery, covered by manicured grass and plastic flowers. How could that be? She shook her head. She wasn't going to spend this weekend crying. Dropping the condoms on the bed, she closed her suitcase and went downstairs in search of caffeine.

She found Charlotte in the dining room sipping coffee and reading one of three newspapers sprawled out across the enormous table. She poured herself a cup and moved aside a few papers to sit down.

"Guess you needed to catch up on the news?"

"I just couldn't resist, I had to buy them all. I like to read the *Post*, and Brett will only subscribe to the *Times*, and then I just saw the *Herald* and I didn't know what you all read. There's nothing better than a cup of coffee and a good newspaper."

"Except a cup of coffee, a good newspaper, and some breakfast. Any food in there?" Meg nodded towards the kitchen.

"Dani brought a ton of food, but I'm not sure what's for breakfast."

Meg pulled out the crossword puzzle from the *Herald*. She'd just get her puzzle out of the way and then it wouldn't hang over her all day. She sighed, it was a tough one. Saturdays' usually were.

"Do you do those puzzles every day?" asked Charlotte.

Meg nodded. "It's my therapy."

"I tried one once; it was impossible."

"There are tricks to it and clues inside the clues."

"Way over my head."

"You could do them if you wanted to. Anyway, it keeps my mind busy."

"You are the busiest person I know; maybe instead of crosswords you should do yoga. Maybe your mind needs a break."

"Maybe," said Meg as she tried to think of a classic 1986 sports movie that started with *h*. Peter was always helpful with the sports clues. *Hoosiers.* That fit.

"Is Dani already out running?" asked Meg.

On cue, they heard Dani hurrying down the stairs from the third floor.

"Nope. Guess she wasn't serious about that run this morning," teased Charlotte in a loud voice.

Dani appeared in the doorway dressed in her running gear.

"Yes, I was! I just wasn't serious about the crack of dawn timing. Back in thirty!"

Meg and Charlotte watched her go.

"She's a better woman than I," said Charlotte. She turned to Meg, "So, Peter was a jerk about you leaving last night?"

"Pretty much."

"Well, I hope the kids are total brats for him all weekend."

"You mean for the babysitter. He's playing golf all day today. I'm sure tomorrow he'll take them to church for the hour's quiet and then let them watch videos all day. And then he'll act like he had it so bad."

Charlotte put her hand on Meg's arm. "I'm so glad you came. I just wish Peter wasn't being such a prick about it."

"Me, too," said Meg. "But let's not talk about pricks." Meg blushed and Charlotte laughed.

"I don't think I've ever heard you use that word!"

"So what's the plan today? Will we just sit around this gorgeous house stuffing our faces, or are we going somewhere?" asked Meg.

"I thought we could walk down to the board-walk after breakfast. Some of the shops and restaurants down there are open year-round."

"Sounds good. I'm hungry, you trust me to come up with breakfast?"

"Of course," said Charlotte.

Meg felt her emotions find firmer footing as she began cooking. She was going to enjoy this weekend, and Peter was not going to ruin it for her with his infantile behavior. He could handle it. She shouldn't have bad-mouthed him to her friends. It wasn't fair to him. Besides, she couldn't blame him for feeling overwhelmed. Ever since Logan's death, he'd been distant, seemingly uninterested in what was happening at home. Or maybe she had pushed him out, who knew. She'd taken over every decision in their daily life from play dates to meals to vacations to home improvements. She told him where they were going, what they were doing, and when it had to be done. Had it always been that way? She could hardly remember their life *before*. Surely, he was more involved. Did he defer to her now on everything because he hoped it would make her happy? That it might make everything normal again?

There would never again be *normal*. Couldn't he see that? Or, like always, did she have to tell him? Sometimes she wondered how Peter could make so many decisions, big decisions, on a daily basis as a trial lawyer, yet be incapable of deciding something as simple as what clothes to put on their seven-year-old. He couldn't even decide what to have for lunch on Sundays. After church, they would all troop upstairs to change out of their church clothes. He would come downstairs first while she made sure the kids hung up their clothes. When she made it to the kitchen he would be sitting at the table picking through the morning paper for articles he'd missed. Even now she could see his untroubled face as he'd ask, "So what's for lunch?" The man was incapable of even deciding what to have for lunch!

Meg knew she'd created the monster. Isn't that what she wanted? A man who couldn't live without her? A family that revolved around her? Isn't that what she always pictured? She would be the perfect wife, the perfect mother, and they'd have the perfect life.

And they had. Or at least she thought they had. Now it was gone. Replaced by an absent father and a mother who spent every moment keeping their lives running perfectly so no one could possibly be sad—least of all her. She shook her head and turned back to the pancakes. "Be here, not there," she whispered.

When Dani returned from her run, she seemed rejuvenated. While she showered, Meg set the table, folding Charlotte's abandoned papers neatly in a pile in the corner. She was just filling juice glasses when Dani reappeared.

"Meg, you are a goddess!" she exclaimed.

"Really, I'm happy to do this for you all. I wouldn't be here if you hadn't planned it and brought the groceries to boot. Think of it as a thank you."

---

### Dani

After they feasted on pecan pancakes with sautéed bananas, Dani convinced Meg to leave the breakfast dishes and her crossword for later so they could start their day's adventures. They set off for the boardwalk, walking the two blocks to the beach and following it south to town.

"It's weird being here in the off season," said Charlotte. "I've never seen it so quiet. Will loves the beach. Brett does, too."

"My kids love it but I wish there wasn't so much sand," moaned Meg. "I spend months getting it out of everything after we get back."

Dani laughed. "The sand is the point! I love the sand!" said Dani. "I'd live here if I could."

"I wonder if we'll still find a weekend to come down when Will returns or if we'll skip it this year. Brett's planning a family vacation to a dude ranch in July to experience what he calls *Americana*." Charlotte rolled her eyes. "But maybe when our Spanish guest arrives in August we can bring her to Sweet Beach. That would be a classic American experience."

When they reached the boardwalk, Charlotte plopped down on a bench that looked out over the water. "Wait, I need to catch my breath."

"I've got to get the sand out of my shoes," said Meg, joining her and removing her tidy white sneakers.

Dani sat down on the boardwalk steps and waited.

"It's amazing to have a day with nothing to do," commented Meg.

"I'm sure we'll find something," said Charlotte.

Dani said nothing, soaking in the sun and the quiet of the sleepy beach. It was a welcome treat after the long winter. She'd be happy to spend the entire weekend right there on that step, but she was sure Charlotte was itching to go to all the expensive boutiques in town. Dani didn't have any spare cash to spend. The weekend was a splurge she couldn't really afford, but worth every penny she didn't have.

She watched as a tow-headed little girl in a pink dress arrived, stumbling across the sand, chasing after the gulls. The child's parents sat on a dune not far from her. The father fished around in his bag and pulled out a camera.

Dani remembered when her own daughter was that young. She and Joe recorded her every move. They had scrapbooks filled with pictures of Jordan playing in the tub, chasing bubbles in the yard, dumping the Tupperware all over the kitchen floor. Dani couldn't stand the idea of leaving her in daycare. She'd planned to continue at her job as the office manager for a group of architects, but found it impossible. Thank God for Charlotte. As usual, she'd saved the day.

Dani had met Charlotte just a few months before Jordan was born. Charlotte had been redecorating the offices where Dani worked, and as the office manager, it was Dani who'd worked with her. Considering it was an office full of architects, they'd had surprisingly little interest in the appearance of their offices. While they considered carpet samples and furniture upholstery, Charlotte had shared her advice about pregnancy and childbirth. She'd had a rough go of it with her own son. The two women bonded immediately when Dani confessed that she only planned to have one child. Charlotte said she and Brett had made the same decision.

When Jordan was born, Charlotte had showed up with an enormous box of diapers, a bouquet of irises, and a plate of Godiva chocolates. When Dani decided not to go back to the office, it was Charlotte who suggested she try medical transcription. She'd even called one of the medical practices she'd worked with and made a connection for Dani. It paid well and didn't require child care, pantyhose, or makeup.

"Let's see what we can find on the boardwalk," said Charlotte, pulling on her strappy sandals.

"I'm game," said Meg.

They wandered along the boards, glancing in the mostly closed storefronts. Most of the beach concessions selling tacky T-shirts, big straw hats, and hermit crabs had yet to open for the season.

While Charlotte and Meg browsed in one of the boutiques with prices way beyond her budget, Dani found a bench outside to people watch. The boardwalk was a very different place in early spring. Kids on skateboards enjoyed the freedom to ride on the boards, knowing in a month or two their presence would be outlawed, crowded out by the summer people. A cluster of old men sat together at a picnic table, throwing scraps to the seagulls that screamed and dived and fought with each other.

Young couples walked hand in hand, probably enjoying a quiet weekend of hotel sex at off-season rates. Dani laughed at herself, she sounded like Charlotte. Lately, Charlotte had a way of turning every conversation back to sex. After hearing about the state of her marriage, Dani wasn't surprised at her frustration. But she seemed more than frustrated, maybe volatile was the word. Charlotte was always outrageous, but she was acting odd, as if she was on the verge of something. Was she planning on leaving Brett? It was surprising that Charlotte had let things get to this point. If she knew her friend, change was coming. She hoped Brett was ready.

Charlotte emerged with a bulging bag and Meg was wearing a gorgeous new silk scarf that went beautifully with her lavender sweater. They continued along the boardwalk.

Dani stopped in front of the purple door of an art gallery she'd seen last summer. She'd been dragging Joey off the beach for a time-out and couldn't stop in, but she'd wanted to. The sign on the door said it was open.

"Hey, let's check out this place," she suggested.

Meg groaned. "I'm gonna go find some salt water taffy for the kids. How about I meet you back at the Pelican for lunch in thirty minutes?"

"You sure?" asked Charlotte.

"I'm not the art person—that's for you girls."

Dani and Charlotte entered the gallery. The bright white walls were covered with large, almost gaudy prints, but also more traditional art. Dani was impressed with the display. Free-standing glass shelves in the center of the small space held colorful sculptures made of a variety of mediums. The gallery seemed eclectic, not leaning toward any particular style. Dani stopped in front of a Wyeth-like painting of horses in the snow. The horses stood close together, backs to the wind and heads bowed in the cold, their tails whipping around them.

"I think I could use something like this," said Charlotte. "I'm doing an old-money lawyer's office and he's always talking about foxhunting."

Dani moved on to the next print. It was another horse, nothing special, a dull brown color, but somehow the artist had brought him to life. He stood on the crest of the hill at sunset; his ears pricked forward and his eyes focused on something far away.

She was startled by a deep voice. "What do you think?"

Dani turned to see a handsome man dressed in jeans and a ragged green sweater. On his feet were worn leather sandals. He looked to be in his late twenties. His curly dark hair almost hid the earring in his left ear. He waited for Dani to reply.

"They're very real. It's as if they might move any moment."

"The artist lives on a farm a few hours from here. He brings me paintings several times a year. Are you looking for anything in particular?"

Dani smiled at the question. Was she looking for anything in particular? That was certainly the question. "Actually, we're just browsing. It's a beautiful gallery."

"I'm glad you think so; I've invested a lot of time in it."

"Are you the owner?" asked Charlotte.

"Yes. I own the space, but I don't own the art. I display the work and artists earn a percentage. I have an eye for talent, but no talent myself, sadly." He smiled at Dani. "Are you an artist?"

"She is!" exclaimed Charlotte barging in on their conversation.

Dani shook her head. "I wanted to be. I used to make stuff a long time ago." She used to paint *on* things. It wasn't real art. She'd find old picture frames, furniture, dishes, pretty much anything, and clean them up and paint them with doodles, flowers, patterns, sayings, anything to give them new life. Then she'd give them away as presents. She even sold a few at a high school art fair. She started when she was in middle school and had continued until she went to college to study art. Somewhere along the line, she'd become convinced that she could be an artist. Everyone had made such a fuss over the things she created as a kid, so when it was time to go to college, she chose art.

She knew now that what she made was actually crafts, not art. A professor her freshman year had made that clear when she'd shown him her portfolio filled with photos of the things she'd painted. Even now she remembered that hot, embarrassed feeling when he'd flipped through the book and pronounced it, "Immature. Really something anyone could do."

She'd pushed the hobby aside at that point and got serious about her painting. A year later, the same professor had said, "Maybe you should consider giving ceramics a try." The ceramics professor grew quickly frustrated with Dani's "lack of vision" as she called it. Thankfully, Joe came along not long after that and rescued her.

She'd brought a few of her old pieces with her when she moved into the apartment. Joe had loved them. He'd wanted her to make more "art," and she couldn't bring herself to tell him that they weren't really art.

Now the only "art" she made was posters for the PTA. Meg recruited her for every function, saying she was the *artist*. She told Meg that neat handwriting and doodles did not qualify as art, but Meg would insist, saying, "And you studied art in college!" as if that automatically made her an artist.

"Do you have any samples of your work?"

Dani laughed. "I haven't made anything in years."

"Well, if you start again, let me know." He handed her his card.

*JEREMY JENKINS*
*Art collector and dealer*
**Sweet Beach Art Gallery**

She tucked the card in her jeans.

He gave them both a tour of the gallery, showing off his favorites and a few controversial pieces he kept near the back. Dani was impressed by Jeremy's knowledge. He was easy to talk to and seemed interested in her opinions on each piece, listening intently, asking questions, and sharing his own opinion. Dani was flattered by his attention. She hadn't talked so much about art in years.

When they'd seen everything in the gallery, Jeremy pulled down the two prints Charlotte was interested in and took them to the back workroom to package for shipping. The room was filled with boxes, tools, cleaning equipment, and tarps. There was a radio playing heavy metal rock music that seemed incongruent with everything else about Jeremy and his gallery.

"Oh, you have to see these. They just came in," he said, opening a box filled with tiny carved figures made of soapstone. Some were white, some pink; all smooth and cool to the touch. The carvings were intricate and tiny. Dani examined a tiny carved dancer. She wore toe shoes and her skirt flowed around her as if picked up by a breeze. The detail was remarkable. You could even see the pins holding the bun in her hair. How had the artist made this without the fragile stone cracking beneath his hands? She thought of Jordan and the dance lessons she'd taken last year. There wasn't money for lessons this year, and Jordan had been gracious and said she was getting too old for ballet anyway. She already knew how to dance she said. Dani handed the dancer back to Jeremy. Maybe she would enroll Jordan next year.

She glanced at her watch. It was one already. "We need to go meet Meg," she said to Charlotte.

They thanked Jeremy and promised to come back in the summer. Charlotte asked him to keep her in mind when he got more "horse stuff" as she put it.

Walking to the Pelican, Charlotte asked, "How come you never finished your art degree?"

Dani sighed. "Lots of reasons, but mostly Joe and then Jordan. Plus, my parents didn't see the point in paying for it once I married Joe. He'd always wanted me to go back, but there was never time or money."

"What do you think your life would have been like if you'd become an artist?" asked Charlotte, with a gleam in her eye. "Maybe you'd be living at the beach with a man half your age who wears sandals year round and has pierced ears."

"Or maybe I'd be waiting tables at the Pelican and living out of a box!"

They'd reached the Pelican and it was nearly deserted.

"Meg must have lost track of time. Let's get a table and have a drink," suggested Charlotte.

When Meg arrived, Dani and Charlotte were both on their second glass of wine. They were sharing a plate of bruschetta and comparing notes on what their husbands might be up to in their absence.

"No talking about husbands or children or what they are doing without us," declared Meg. "I want to enjoy my lunch. Guilt is not good for my digestion. So how was the gallery?"

"It was fabulous," said Dani.

"But not as fabulous as the handsome young owner who gave us a personal tour and couldn't get enough of Dani!"

"Not true!" protested Dani. "He just wanted to talk art."

"Okay, that's what you're going with?" laughed Charlotte, taking a sip of her wine and winking at Meg.

"Just how cute was he?" Meg asked with a raised eyebrow.

"He's almost young enough to be my son! But he was quite adorable in a granola, crunchy sort of way. Sandals, earring, messy hair, you know. But he knew his stuff and he gave me his card!"

"What was his name?" asked Meg.

"Jeremy."

"Oh, that's such an artsy name. Let's go back and see him after lunch!" suggested Meg.

Dani shook her head. "Did you find taffy for your kids?"

"I decided they would only fight over the taffy, so I looked for something else. The younger three were easy, but Michael's so hard to shop for. I finally found a quirky little book store and got him a copy of *Gullet*, the latest in the pulp fiction series he's reading."

After lunch, the journey back to the cottage was slow going. It had grown warm, and the deep sand and wine at lunch slowed their pace. Once there,

Meg disappeared to call home and take a nap. Charlotte selected a book from the packed shelves in the sun room and curled up in one of the comfy chairs. Dani decided to run a bath.

Soaking in the tub, Dani pictured Jeremy's face. Maybe he was just very good at his job, but he'd made Dani feel special. He obviously loved art and knew a lot, but he'd acted interested in her opinions and the work she'd done, even though none of it had amounted to anything. She remembered a time when she would have swooned over a guy like Jeremy. The art school had been crawling with them. Interesting, philosophical boys who could stay up all night drinking cheap wine or herbal tea, talking about art, politics, imagery, commercialism, and the deeper truths hidden beneath the surface of contemporary life. They were destined to careers at Starbucks, sacrificing for their art.

So why had she abandoned her ideal when she met Joe? Because he took her seriously? Because he could talk about more than art? No, she'd fallen for him because he was a real man. He was so confident and funny. He had a real job, a future, and beyond all that—he was handsome. Artists were all well and good when you were young, but you couldn't build a life with them. She remembered her parents' relief when she'd brought Joe home. He wore socks. What more could they ask for?

She wondered if Jeremy had a girlfriend. She was probably an equally artsy, hippie-happy person—someone like Dani had been.

She let herself day dream about him while soaking in a hot bubble bath far, far away from the distractions of her children and husband. A guy like that—so sensitive and attentive, not to mention gorgeous—could have any girl he wanted. Maybe the hot water and bath oils were going to her head. She tried to focus on Joe. Even if her passion for him had cooled lately, she knew it was still there, buried beneath their harried lives. She would find it again, wouldn't she? She just wished her body still reacted to Joe like it did to Jeremy today. Was that something exclusive to youth or novelty? She'd had too much wine to give it serious consideration and instead gave in to her own pleasure beneath the warm water, remembering Jeremy's young body. No harm done. She'd probably never see him again.

◆

## Charlotte

Charlotte tried another book. There was an eclectic selection on the shelves of the cottage, but she couldn't seem to still her mind and read. Instead, she decided to go for a drive. She left a note on the table, lowered the top on her Saab, and wrapped her long red hair in a scarf. She felt better already, a drive was just what she needed.

She drove south along the coastal road out of Sweet Beach. Most of the area was protected seashore and there weren't many cars on the road. In the summer, this road would be jammed with people on their way from sleepy Sweet Beach down to Oceanside with its bars and outlet malls and resorts. Before she knew it, she was entering Oceanside. She parked on the street outside a new restaurant she'd seen a review about in the paper that morning. The Rum Runner boasted a celebrated chef from somewhere down south and live music nightly. She remembered there was even a dance floor.

The restaurant was quiet, very few tables full. She took a seat at the bar and watched a man setting up equipment for the evening's performance. Still feeling the effects of the wine from lunch, she ordered cranberry juice and 7up.

Charlotte wondered if Brett was expecting her to call. She hadn't left a number or even a goodbye note. He'd already gone to work when she got out of bed yesterday morning. It seemed hopeless and, honestly, she wasn't sure she could do much more. Relationships were a two way street. There was a time when Brett had been the romantic and she was the busy one. She smiled thinking of the time he surprised her with a picnic on the floor of the office where she'd stayed late working, or when he'd planned a one-day getaway to Atlantic City with champagne waiting in the hotel room. Those first years of marriage had been magical. But then Will arrived and they were deliriously happy, but everything was different. Brett was different. He thrived as a father. He was still a good husband, but the extra effort he used to make stopped. Maybe she was spoiled, expecting him to romance her after all these years.

Without Will around, they'd had nothing to say to each other. Ever since he'd gone, Brett didn't feel the need to be home at any particular hour. Charlotte couldn't fathom what he was doing at the office until nine. If Brett was any other man, she'd worry he was examining one of the hygienists. But Brett was nothing if not faithful. He liked his life simple. He was probably spending his evenings e-mailing Will or surfing the Internet, planning their Americana experience. Or maybe he was reading dental journals. Brett was zealous in his efforts to stay on top of his game. Ever since returning from the conference in California, he seemed to be spending more time studying. He never even asked Charlotte what she'd done while he was away for four days.

He took no more notice of her than the wallpaper, despite the efforts she'd made lately to get his attention. She'd gotten a haircut, a pedicure, several manicures, a massage, a facial, and a bikini wax. She'd spent nearly three thousand dollars shopping online, buying clothes she would never have the opportunity to wear. So much had piled up, she'd brought only new things with her on this trip. She'd even splurged on perfume that sold for six hundred dollars an ounce. It made her feel expensive. Brett hadn't said a word. She wasn't sure if he didn't notice or didn't care. And she wasn't going to beg. If he wasn't interested, maybe she'd find someone who was.

Besides, the purchases were presents she deserved. Brett hadn't given her anything in years. At Christmas, they always agreed on a joint gift. This year it had been a pool table for the new game room he and Will had built in the basement. Her birthday was typically marked by a dinner out, although she wondered if that would even happen this year since Will would be in Spain.

The man setting up the equipment finished his work. He sat down at the bar, and the bartender brought him a beer. They kidded each other like old friends. She heard his Irish accent and looked over. When he laughed, his green eyes twinkled like Santa's. She watched as he downed a quick beer while scanning his phone. He had thick, sandy bed-tousled hair and the build of a man who used his body more than his mind. She couldn't help admiring him. When he caught her staring, he winked, which made her blush.

After he left, Charlotte picked up one of the handbills scattered around the bar. Martin O'Keefe would be playing Irish folk music tonight.

Paying her tab, she smiled at the gray-haired bartender and left him a big tip.

When Charlotte got back to the house, it was quiet. She didn't know where the others were. She searched in her purse for the cigarettes she'd bought while she was out and took them out on the deck.

A few minutes later, she was startled by a knock on the window behind her. Meg waved a bottle of wine and an opener. Charlotte gave her a thumbs up. Meg joined her on the deck a moment later with two glasses of wine and coasters. Only Meg would think to bring coasters.

"I didn't know you were here. Were you sleeping?" asked Charlotte.

"Actually, I was awake. I finally have an afternoon available to nap and it figures I can't. My mind won't stop spinning."

"Anything good?"

She shook her head. "No. Just how angry I am with Peter."

"Did you call home?"

"I did," Meg hesitated, before continuing, "The sitter answered and said Peter had called to see if she could stay until after dinner. He told her to order a pizza and use money from the cookie jar on the counter."

"Where was he?"

"He didn't say. He just told her that he was going to be a little later than planned, and if he wasn't back by eight, to go ahead and put Timmy to bed. I'm so angry! What is his problem?"

"I don't know. Maybe he doesn't know how to handle things without you. Has he ever had to before?"

"I never leave him with the kids. I mean, I used to when I had PTA meetings or whatever, but he's hardly home before bedtime since . . ." Meg didn't finish her sentence. Instead, she gulped her wine.

"This is good for him. The kids are probably fine with the sitter and I'm sure Peter will pay her well. He's got to come home sooner or later," reasoned Charlotte, watching her friend drain her wineglass.

"I need a cigarette."

"Really?"

"No, but I'm so mad, I feel like doing something rebellious, something dangerous."

"Wow, this is a new side of you. I think I like it."

Charlotte tossed her the pack. Meg struggled to light the cigarette, fumbling with the matches in the wind. Her hands were trembling and a tear slid down her cheek. Charlotte leaned over and took the cigarette. She used her own to light it and handed it back.

Meg took a long puff and began coughing. Looking at the cigarette hostilely, she laid back on a chaise lounge.

"Smoking is such a filthy habit," she said.

### Dani

Dani sat on one of the rickety wooden folding chairs on the widow's walk and dialed home. She could smell the cigarette smoke and knew Charlotte was on the porch. She reached Jordan on the first ring.

"'Lo?"

"Hey, Jordan, it's Mommy. How's it going?"

"I'm waiting for Carly to call. I can't talk now."

"Honey, I just need a minute. Carly will call back, I'm sure."

"But this is important!" complained Jordan.

"When did you talk to her last?"

"An hour ago, but that doesn't matter! This is about something else! If I had a cell phone, I would use that, but I don't, so I can't!" cried Jordan. She had been lobbying for her own phone for months.

"You don't need a phone; you're too young," replied Dani.

"That is so not fair," whined Jordan.

"So, what have *you* been doing today?"

"Played on the computer mostly. Talked to Carly. Watched a video."

"You mean you spent the entire day inside? It was a beautiful day!"

"So?"

Jordan was only twelve, but she already seemed like a teen.

"Can I talk to Daddy?"

"He's outside working in his shop."

"How about Joey?"

"He's watching a video. He wouldn't take a nap and Daddy yelled at him."

"Can you tell your dad that I called?"

"Uh-huh."

"Don't forget, okay? I love you."

"Uh-huh, bye."

"Bye, sweetie."

Dani pressed the end button before she realized her daughter had not answered her I love you with her own. She and Jordan used to be so close. These days she could feel Jordan pulling away and was never sure how tight to hold onto her.

---

"What did Joe have to say?" asked Meg when Dani joined them on the porch.

"He was outside, so I talked to Jordan. Sounds like he's doing the typical man thing, putting on videos, saying yes to everything, and then exploding when they don't do what he asks. But it sounds like they're doing okay." Dani realized she was relieved to not have to talk to Joe. She wasn't sure what to say. He'd been so good about her going away this weekend and she felt somewhat guilty. She didn't want to tell him she was having a great time. She couldn't tell him about Jeremy. She couldn't tell him that for the first time in months, quite possibly years, she felt like she could breathe.

"Who was that model who was married to David Bowie?" asked Meg, pencil poised.

"Iman. Listen, you guys, how about we try this new restaurant in Oceanside tonight. They have live Irish folk music," said Charlotte.

"I love Irish music. You do know I can jig, right?" said Meg, setting down her puzzle and taking a long swig of her second glass of wine.

"You just jump around and kick your feet!" laughed Dani, "I've seen you!"

"That's authentic Irish dancing, I'll have you know. I learned it on our honeymoon when Peter and I went to Ireland."

"I don't know, Charlotte. Are you sure this place is ready for Meg, the supposed Irish dancer?" Dani asked.

"We'll sit on her as much as possible, or better yet, we can take pictures and use them to blackmail her later."

"Just you wait," said Meg, going inside to change her shoes.

---

"How'd you know about this place?" asked Dani when they pulled in the parking lot.

"I just did," said Charlotte, helping Meg climb out of the backseat of the car. Meg looked great in her slinky red dress.

She stood up, tugging at her bra straps and pulling her hemline back down. "I had this dress made for the New Year's bash at Peter's firm two years ago. It's a little tight now. I guess I've gained some weight."

"It still looks good," said Charlotte. "It's tight in all the right places!"

"I don't know," said Meg, hesitating and reaching for her wrap.

"Meg, you look great," said Dani. She wished she'd brought something as nice, not that she owned anything half as nice. She wore a simple black T-shirt dress and low heels.

"Peter loves this dress," said Meg.

"Yeah, I bet he does," said Charlotte with a laugh. Charlotte was wearing a skintight leather skirt and a see-through shirt with a black cami beneath it. Next to them, Dani felt more than a little dowdy.

The restaurant was crowded and Charlotte led them to the far end of the bar. They ordered several appetizers and chose beers from the huge selection on tap.

"Charlotte, you're shameless," accused Dani, watching her flirt with the young bartender who didn't look old enough to shave.

"Don't be silly. It's just fun to see if they will still flirt with me."

"For the record," said Dani, "Yes, he will, but he also knows the old ladies tip well."

Charlotte gave her the finger and probably would have said more, but the recorded music ended and the musicians appeared on stage. The guitarist began to play. He was talented and the crowd acknowledged it with their yells and clapping. Soon, a long-haired keyboardist joined in, generating sounds not typically expected of a keyboard. He was his own percussion, woodwind, and brass section. He grinned behind John Lennon shades and nodded to the singer. The tempo picked up, and then Martin O'Keefe began singing in a sweet tenor.

## Charlotte

Charlotte was captivated. Martin O'Keefe might look young, but the lines around his eyes showed him to be closer to her age, maybe even older. Still, he was a beautiful man. He caught her eye, recognizing her from earlier and winking. She smiled and turned back to her friends.

Dani shook her head. Charlotte shrugged and gulped her beer. Dani knew her too well. Meg seemed to be scanning the crowd, as if she would know someone here, but she smiled and lifted her beer when Dani asked if she was okay. There was no point in trying to converse with the loud music. They watched the set, clapping along when appropriate and sipping their beers. Meg's cheeks were getting rosy; Charlotte knew it was only a matter of time before she would be dancing.

The set ended and the canned music came back on.

Dani remarked, "Now that is one good-looking Irishman, but somehow I'm certain you knew that, Charlotte."

"And he's talented, too," added Meg.

"I had a premonition," said Charlotte.

"That's what you're going with?" teased Dani.

"It's amazing what the keyboardist can do. He's like a one man orchestra over there. I'm just about ready to dance," announced Meg in a giddy tone.

"Oh no, here we go," warned Dani.

"And you, Dani, are going to be my partner."

"No way, you aren't dragging me out there to make a fool of myself. You'll have to go solo on this one."

"Well, it'll have to be a solo show then, girls. Buy me another beer, I need to fortify myself and get on my happy feet."

When the musicians came back out for the next set, Charlotte couldn't take her eyes off Martin O'Keefe. "He's everything and a pack of gum," she said to Dani.

"I believe he knows that," laughed Dani.

When Martin O'Keefe smiled, Charlotte thought she saw the flash of a dimple. The freckles covering his nose gave him a boyish charm, and he wasn't wearing a wedding band. Charlotte glanced around; she wasn't the only woman watching him. A cute man with a guitar and an accent, wasn't that what every woman wanted?

When the music started, it was a fast tune. The crowd immediately started clapping. Meg was off her seat in a flash. Out she went to the dance floor, breaking up the small crowd that was gathered there waiting for a table. She began to dance. She held her torso straight just like the dancers in the videos Charlotte had seen, but her breasts were bouncing up and down to the rhythm. Her dress wasn't exactly made for Irish dancing; it was riding up her thighs. The crowd moved back to give her more room and Charlotte saw the guitarist eye her and smile. Definitely a dimple.

Dani laughed as she watched Meg, who motioned for them to come dance. Dani took another swig of her beer and said, "What the hell," bounding out to join Meg.

A moment later, Charlotte was on the floor, too. They all did their best imitation of Irish dancing and laughed till it hurt.

At the break between songs, Martin acknowledged the "Irish lasses" on the dance floor and invited others to join them. When no one did, he said something to the other musician and laid down his guitar. He hopped down off the stage and began to dance. Everyone stepped back to let him have the floor. He was amazing, kicking and turning and hopping and doing a real Riverdance. He motioned to Meg to join him and the two of them jigged side by side. Then he turned to Charlotte and took her hands, pulling her out to dance, too. She let him guide her around the floor, trying to keep her feet moving to the beat. They both laughed when she tripped over her own feet and he caught her and turned it into a mock dip. When he returned her to her feet, he winked and released her, hopping back on the stage. He picked up his acoustic guitar and launched into a slow, sad ballad.

Back at the bar, Dani gushed, "Meg, you can really dance!"

"I told you I could. You kept up pretty well, and Charlotte, I think that Irishman has his eye on you! His Irish eyes are smiling!" Meg nearly fell off her stool laughing at her own joke.

"I don't remember when I've laughed so hard or had such a good time," said Dani.

Meg looked at her and said, "Me too, it's been too long. I think this weekend needs to be a yearly event." She raised her glass in a toast.

"Forget yearly, I think it should be monthly," said Dani.

"Weekly," Charlotte agreed, finally tearing her eyes away from Martin to join them.

"Just so long as we do it again." Meg raised her glass and they all clinked together.

The bartender interrupted their celebration to tell them a table of men had sent a pitcher for them. Did they have a preference?

"Men or beer?" joked Charlotte.

Dani pointed to a tap and thanked the bartender.

"Does this mean we have to talk to them?" asked Meg, looking around trying to figure out which table.

When the bartender brought the pitcher, Meg asked, "Who sent it?"

He shrugged. "They liked the dancing."

"Wow, I don't remember the last time a strange man bought me a beer," Meg said happily. "I'm not sure I want to go home."

The music started again, and Meg dragged them back out on the floor.

They closed the place down. Driving back to the cottage, Charlotte pulled into a 7-Eleven for Ben & Jerry's and coffee, then decided to stop at the pier. She parked the Saab at the edge of the parking lot, where they could see the ocean, and pulled the top down. They ate their ice cream watching the moonlight dance on the surf. The stars created a shimmering canopy over the unseasonably warm night.

"So, Charlotte, what's with the Irishman?" asked Dani.

"He was some kind of hot, wasn't he?" she asked, lighting a cigarette.

"Put that nasty thing out," said Meg, grabbing it and flinging it out of the car.

"Excuse me? I think someone's had a little too much to drink!" said Charlotte, pulling out another cigarette.

Meg started giggling. "What?" asked Charlotte, but Meg was laughing hard now, smacking the dashboard and snorting. Her hysteria was contagious and soon they were all in tears from laughing so hard.

When she could finally get her breath, Meg said, "This is the first time I've been out, had too much to drink, danced like a fool, and didn't have to have sex afterwards." She started giggling again.

"Meghan Elizabeth, you surely are drunk," said Charlotte. "I don't think I've ever heard you say the word sex so many times in a weekend."

"What?" Meg laughed, leaning into Charlotte, "Sex, sex, sex!"

Charlotte shoved her away.

"Peter's usually embarrassed when I get drunk or dance too much. So I always feel like I owe him something by the time we get home. Sex is the easiest way to make him happy."

"Definitely too much information," said Dani.

"Oh come on, doesn't drinking and dancing make you want to go home and have sex anyway?" asked Charlotte.

"Drinking and doing almost anything makes me want to have sex," laughed Dani.

"Actually, whenever I go out, it's to some hoity-toity function for Peter's work. He makes me stay sober so I won't start dancing and carrying on and embarrass him."

"You have got to be kidding!" said Charlotte.

"No, that's why I never get to dance anymore."

"You should dance every day Meg," said Dani, reaching over the seat to take Meg's hand.

"I know," said Meg.

"God, it's so good to be here!" exclaimed Charlotte suddenly, honking her horn. "I so needed this. I feel like a different person."

"Why haven't we done this before?" asked Dani.

"A million reasons," said Meg. "But at least we're here now."

"I wish we didn't have to go back," said Charlotte.

"Me, too," said Dani.

"Me, three," said Meg with a loud hiccup that set them all off with the giggles again.

# SUNDAY, APRIL 14

## Charlotte

When Charlotte arrived in the kitchen, she was surprised that neither Meg nor Dani had started the coffee. She'd heard both of them earlier, but neither was in the house now. She looked outside and saw that Meg's car was gone. Maybe she'd gone for the paper, Charlotte thought hopefully. She couldn't believe Dani would have gone running, not if her head felt anything like her own.

Charlotte thought of the upcoming week. Her house was like a tomb without Will. Brett was never there, and when he was he had nothing to say. She could predict every comment that might emit from his mouth. Sometimes she found herself playing a little game of betting what Brett would say. She'd be downstairs in her exercise room and she'd hear him come home from work and she'd make little bets with herself. If he yelled, "You down there?" she'd do ten more sit ups, but if he just said, "Anybody home?" in his little sing-song way, she'd have to do twenty-five more. Every now and then, she'd hear his car and turn off the lights and lie on the couch pretending to be asleep, just so she didn't have to hear his predictable greeting.

Would she spend the rest of her life like this? Would they become that couple who sits across from each other in a restaurant saying nothing except, "Pass the salt"? Somewhere underneath all the flotsam of their life, was a love affair still buried?

And how on the earth did she get it back? Maybe Brett didn't love her like he used to. Maybe he was as tired of her as she was of him. All she knew was she couldn't go on like this. Something had to give. And this time it would have to be him.

She dreaded driving home today. She felt so good here with her friends. She was funny and interesting and alive. She couldn't stand the idea of pulling in her driveway and hearing Brett ask, "Did you have a nice time?" even as he continued to read his magazine and didn't listen for her answer. Then he'd suggest they get takeout so she didn't have to cook. After they ate, he'd say he was beat and had to be in the office early and would retire to their room to watch TV. She never thought her life would be so predictable.

## Meg

Meg sat in the sanctuary and breathed in the rich smell of candles. She loved the shower of color from the stained glass, the feel of the groove in the pew from the thousands of bodies who had sat here before her, people like her, looking for comfort, for answers. She listened to the soft music from the organ, the rustle of papers and coats as people entered and settled into the pews. The church was small, with few congregants this time of year. Even a Catholic church couldn't guilt people into attending in a beach town.

She hadn't planned on going to Mass. Her head was splitting and her stomach was churning. Before she was fully awake, she'd found herself driving to the Catholic church she'd driven by so many times in previous summers. She'd never been to Mass here, even when they came down as a family for vacation. Peter said *vacation* meant vacation from everything, and she hadn't fought him on it.

When the service started and the priest began reading the familiar words, Meg automatically kneeled, stood, or sat; familiar motions, even if the meaning was lost on her this morning.

Instead of following the service, her mind relived her weekend. She hadn't felt so alive in years. For once, she wasn't the mourning mother, the dutiful wife, the dedicated volunteer, the person who always did the right thing. She was just herself. It felt odd and wonderful, like returning to a place she'd long forgotten.

Meg tuned in and out as the priest droned on with his homily. He was giving a message she'd heard many times. You are not alone, God is here with you, blah, blah, blah. But something in his tone caught her attention. "Maybe you misunderstand what God is doing in your life. Maybe he has plans you can't imagine." The priest smiled widely at the congregation.

"Right," said Meg, doubtfully. She didn't realize she'd said it out loud until the couple in the row in front of her turned to gape at her.

Meg ducked her head. What was wrong with her? Maybe she was still drunk. She listened as the music finished and the priest gave a benediction. As the service ended, she remained in her pew. The sanctuary grew ever quieter, voices echoed down the stairwell towards coffee and gossip.

"Are you all right, my child?"

At first, Meg thought it was God speaking, but then she realized it was the voice of the elderly priest as he sat down behind her.

"Oh, yes, I'm fine. Just resting."

"This is a good place for that. Is this the first time you've been here?"

She turned to look at him and managed a weak smile.

"Actually, yes. I'm only here for the weekend."

"And did the service help you?"

Meg looked at his kind face. There were many lines, but his eyes shone a bright blue. His thinning hair was snow white. He looked at her expectantly.

"It did," she lied. "Thanks for your message."

"It wasn't my message. It was God's. But I believe each person hears the things God means for her to hear."

Meg was quiet as she tried to will the tears away. The priest reached over the pew to hand her his handkerchief.

"It's all right. This is also a good place for tears. Stay as long as you need," he said and headed down the stairs after his flock. Meg watched him go. She felt like he'd poked a tiny hole in the dam of her life. She needed to get out of there before the whole thing blew. The heavy air of the sanctuary was choking her. She stumbled out the door on the side of the church and found herself in a garden. She looked desperately for an exit. High brick walls seemed to block her every way. She stumbled over the carcasses of zinnias, Russian sage, and coreopsis. Where was the gate?

Finally, she spotted it, just past the trellis with the wisteria. Her own garden at home must be a jumble, she thought, pausing to pull free a plastic bag from the thorns of last year's roses. For the past two summers since Logan died, Peter had paid a neighbor kid to clean it up. He couldn't tell a weed from a perennial, so the space had grown wild. She intended to clean it up, but hadn't had the chance. Peter suggested they might want to tear it out and plant more lawn. She hadn't argued. She jammed the plastic bag in her pocket and tried the gate. It was unlocked.

When she arrived back at the cottage, she headed upstairs, calling to Charlotte in the kitchen, "I'm just going to get a quick shower, and then I'll cook breakfast."

"No need," Charlotte answered her. "I can't stomach anything anyway. I was thinking we could go out for brunch later, when Dani gets back."

"Sounds good." Meg disappeared up the stairs.

## Dani

Dani walked along the beach for hours, watching the sun come up. Occasionally, she ran and chased the noisy gulls vying for the offerings left by the receding tide. Sometimes she sat and watched their battles. She needed more time.

How would she ever explain it and who would believe her?

Was she being selfish? Childish? Spoiled? Her life felt so stagnant. It was like she was treading water, going through the motions of a happy life, but not actually being happy. Why couldn't she just be content? And would she ever find her way back to the happy woman she used to be? It wasn't so much she wanted to stay here, as she couldn't go back. It didn't make sense, but she felt something here—a clue to where she'd gone off the path her life was supposed to take. It was crazy, she knew. She didn't believe in fate or God, but something was telling her to stay, and she knew if she went back now she might spend the rest of her life just going through the motions.

She was forty. How had that happened? How was it, in all this time, she'd gotten nowhere? Done nothing? Her life was spinning away and she was missing it. What had happened to the future that included traveling the world, creating art, being in love, feeling alive? How had she wound up deciphering the scrawl of physicians too busy to write neatly and battling with a three-year-old over Pull-Ups?

But what would she say to her kids? To Joe? How could she do this?

She watched the water coming in and going out. They would keep going, she knew. They had to. Look at Meg, she'd kept moving despite the worst nightmare any parent could face. The world wouldn't stop spinning if Dani Harper decided to take a break. And maybe with a little time and perspective she could figure out why she was so unhappy. Maybe she could find what was missing. She stood up and began walking with determination.

When she reached the house, she found Meg and Charlotte in the kitchen nursing hangovers with coffee.

"You're just the person I need," said Meg. "What was the Chinese dynasty of two thousand years ago?"

"I'm not going back," Dani announced.

"To the Chinese dynasty?" laughed Meg. "Wait! The Han Dynasty? That fits."

"I'm serious. I'm not going back today. I can't go back."

"You can't be serious." Meg's face changed from laughter to shock instantly. "Why would you leave Joe? Who will take care of your kids?"

"They'll figure it out."

"You can't!" exclaimed Meg.

Charlotte got up and began looking through her purse.

"What are you doing?" asked Dani.

"I'm looking for the agent's number. We have to stay here. This house is meant for us."

"*Us*? You're staying too?" asked Meg incredulously.

"What do I need to go back for? Will won't be back until June. Brett probably hasn't even noticed I'm gone."

"You can't do this. You have lives! You have children! This is nuts."

"Charlotte, you don't have to do this," began Dani.

"I can't go back. I'm suffocating there."

"But I can't drag you into this."

"You're not dragging me. I'm miserable. I have no reason to go back. What I don't understand is why you don't want to go back."

Dani shook her head. She poured a cup of coffee and leaned against the counter. "I don't know for sure this is the right thing; I just know that I can't go back. I've got to make some kind of change. I don't like who I've become—some sorry sack middle-aged woman living in sweatpants who types for a living and spends her days chasing a three-year-old and being outwitted by a twelve-year-old. I'm boring. I'm unhappy. This isn't the life I want. There has to be more than cleaning my house and chauffeuring kids around and typing indecipherable scribble."

"What will you tell Joe?"

"I'm not sure yet."

"Let me call the real estate agent," said Charlotte, opening the door to the porch. Dani and Meg watched in silence as Charlotte paced the yard and talked into her cell phone. At first she looked upset, but then she smiled, and when she turned to come back in, she gave them a thumbs up.

"It's ours. The owners hadn't planned on renting it, but the agent was able to reach them immediately and they said we sounded like the perfect tenants. They were happy to have someone other than college kids on break. I think we're meant to have this place."

"What will it cost?" asked Dani, holding her breath. She'd only brought about a hundred dollars with her. And she couldn't expect Joe to pay for this. The whole weekend had been a stretch.

"Oh, don't worry, we'll sort that all out. It's reasonable," said Charlotte, not meeting her eye.

Dani said nothing, but she couldn't hide her disappointment. She hated taking charity from her friend.

"I'll spot you," Charlotte said. "I mean it. You can pay me back whenever or not at all. I want this to happen."

Meg stood up. She stared at them. "You're really going to do this?"

Dani grimaced and Charlotte nodded.

"I have to get out of here," she said and fled from the room.

"Well, I better go get this over with," said Dani as she went upstairs to find her cell phone.

"'Lo?" Jordan's voice answered sleepily.

"Did I wake you?" asked Dani. "It's 10:45!"

"We stayed up late watching movies. When are you coming back?"

"That's kind of why I called. Can I talk to your dad?"

"Daaaaad!" her daughter yelled, not bothering to cover the mouthpiece.

"Hello?" Joe's voice sounded cheery.

"Hang up the phone Jordan; I'll talk to you again after I talk to your father."

"Whatever." Click.

"So how is the weekend going?" asked Joe. "Sorry I missed you last night."

"The weekend's been great," Dani began. There was not going to be any easy way to tell him, so she plunged ahead, "I'm going to stay a little longer."

"What do you mean?" Joe's voice immediately lost its cheerfulness.

"I need to figure out a few things. I'm going to stay longer."

"Define longer."

"I don't know."

"Dani, what is going on? I was not aware you had *things* to figure out. What are you not telling me?"

"I'm not *not* telling you anything. I don't know what's wrong; I need some time alone to figure it out."

"This is just great. Is this a midlife crisis? I thought I was the one who got to have that! And what am I supposed to do? Who will take care of the kids?"

"Can't you take some time off? You have a ton of vacation and comp time due."

"This is crazy. You can't just *not* come back. We need you here."

"I need this. Please, please, just let me have this," Dani kept her voice even. She would not cry and she would not back down.

Joe was quiet. She knew he loved her, but she was asking a lot. He had every right to be angry. She said nothing, just waited for his decision, knowing it didn't matter. She was staying.

"You will come back, won't you?"

Dani could hear the pain in his voice and it broke her heart.

"This has nothing to do with you. This is me. I love you, I do. I just don't know what is going on in my life. I know I'm not explaining this well. I've never felt so strongly about something. I need to stay and sort things out."

"How can it have nothing to do with me? I'm your husband. I don't understand."

"Maybe I don't understand either. I just know I need something to change. I can't keep going like this. I feel like I'm disappearing. I'm becoming this gray person who is simply existing, not living. I know I can't make you understand, but you have to trust me on this. I love you, Joe. I do. But right now I need to be just me for a little while."

Joe was quiet on the other end for a few moments. Then she heard him take a deep breath.

"Do you need me to bring some things down? Do you need money?"

His acceptance brought the tears she'd been holding back.

"No, I'm okay for now. I've got a little money and I'll figure something out. I don't need any more clothes, I'll just wash what I have. I packed too much anyway."

"Dani," Joe said through his own audible tears. "Just do this and come back soon. Please."

"I'll try. Let me talk with Jordan; I want to explain this to her myself."

"Good luck, she's not likely to see past how this will inconvenience her."

"Let me try."

While Joe went to get Jordan, Dani steeled herself for her daughter's attitude. What could she possibly say to explain?

"Hey, Mom."

"Hi, sweetie. Are you ready for school tomorrow, got all the homework done?"

"I did it on Friday. Dad made me."

"I need to tell you something," Dani began.

"Uh-huh."

"I'm going to stay down here for a little while. I'm not sure how long. You can call me on my cell phone whenever you need to. Daddy's going to take some time off and take care of you."

There was quiet.

"Jordan?"

"Are you and Daddy getting a divorce?"

The question struck at Dani's heart.

"Of course not. I love your dad. I just need some time to take care of some stuff."

"What stuff?"

"Some things I need to do," Dani prayed her daughter would not press her to explain something she couldn't.

"Okay. Do I still get to go swimming on Thursday?"

Dani was relieved to hear Jordan switch back to the world that revolved around herself.

"Of course, but you might need to remind your dad."

"Is that it?"

"Yes, unless you want to talk about something else."

"Un-uh. Joey wants to talk to you. He's trying to take the phone from me . . . MOM! Make him stop!"

"Let me talk to him for a minute, and go get your dad."

"Here, have the phone!" Dani winced as Jordan yelled, but in a moment Joey's heavy breathing filled her ears.

"Hi, Joey."

"Hi." More heavy breathing.

"Are you being a good boy?"

"Yeah."

"I'm glad. Joey, Mommy's going to be away a little while longer, but Daddy will take care of you."

"Come home." Joey's command was simple.

"I can't right now, but I will soon," Dani promised.

"Come home," Joey said again.

Dani heard Joe telling him to say good-bye in the background.

"Bye."

"I love you, Joey."

"He's gone," Joe's voice said.

"I'm not sure he gets it," Dani sighed.

"That makes two of us."

❧

"How'd it go?" asked Charlotte when Dani sat down on the sofa beside her.

"I don't know. Better than expected, but I don't know what I expected."

"What does that mean?"

"It means he didn't understand and I didn't explain it well, but for now, he'll live with it."

"What did you tell Brett?"

"Nothing."

"You didn't call him?"

"I'm going to wait for him to call. I'm curious how long it will take him to notice I didn't come home."

❧

## Meg

Meg paced her room. She flung things into her suitcase, then couldn't bear it and took them out again, folding everything neatly before putting them in again. Why did she always have to be the good girl? Why did she always feel compelled to do what was right? How could Dani just walk away from her children? Meg couldn't possibly leave her kids. They would be lost without her. What if something happened? And Peter certainly couldn't take care of things by himself. The poor man couldn't even make his own lunch! No, she had to be there. They needed her.

She closed her suitcase and snapped it shut. Then she did a quick check of the bathroom to be sure she hadn't left anything. She looked around at the buttery yellow walls. She'd felt so safe here, having slept soundly for the first time since losing Logan. She sighed, lifted her suitcase, and headed for the stairs, nearly colliding with Dani coming down the steps from the third floor.

"Meg, you don't need to leave early."

"I've got to get back. Things will be crazy tomorrow if I don't get home and put the house back together."

"They'll survive."

"Maybe at your house they will, but my life is different."

"I'm sorry; I didn't mean anything by that, just that the weekend isn't over. We hadn't planned to leave until after lunch anyway. Stay and have lunch with us."

"I'm sorry; I've really got to go."

Charlotte met them at the bottom of the stairs.

"Hey, you can't leave yet. We have to go down to the boardwalk and have those greasy fat fries with vinegar!"

"And the ice cream cones made out of cookies," added Dani.

Meg pushed past them and called back over her shoulder, "Sorry, ladies, but I've got to get home. Too much to do, and I certainly don't need the extra calories!"

She knew she sounded shrill, but she was on the verge of tears or anger or maybe breaking down and staying with them. She shook her head and scooped up her purse from the couch, glancing around and then grabbing her sweater from the chair. She headed for the door. They followed her out.

"Please, stay just a little while longer," said Dani, taking her suitcase from her.

Meg reclaimed the suitcase, shoved it in the trunk and closed it with a slam. She looked at Charlotte and Dani. "I can't," she said as her voice cracked and the tears came. Dani put her arms around her. Charlotte circled them with her own. The three of them stood in the driveway holding each other as Meg cried harder. Finally, she pulled back and untangled herself.

"I wish I could be like you, but I can't. I have to go."

"You should," said Dani, wiping her own tears. "I didn't expect anyone to stay but me. This was supposed to be just a girls' weekend, nothing more. It's a crazy idea anyway. I'll probably wake up tomorrow and run for home."

"It's okay. It's not your fault. I'd like to stay for lunch. I would, but if I don't leave now, I won't be able to."

"I'm glad you came," said Dani. "I'm sorry it's ending this way."

"Me, too," said Meg as she climbed in her car.

Meg had been driving for an hour when she began seeing signs for Sadlersville. Without warning, her eyes welled up. The closer she got to home, the more she felt like a magnet from one of Michael's science projects. One of the ones that repels the others. It was as if the closer she got to her house, the stronger the force was that repelled her from it. She'd never understood how the magnets worked, even though Michael had explained it to her many times. It didn't make sense how something with an irresistible power to attract you could also repel you with equal force.

She pulled over at a park-and-ride lot. It was deserted on a Sunday. She turned off the engine and looked at her cell phone. Before she knew what she was doing, she was dialing her sister-in-law's number. Phoebe had always felt more like a sister to her than her own sister. They'd grown up together and when Meg started dating Peter, Phoebe predicted some day they would be sisters. She'd been the maid of honor at her wedding.

Meg could never have survived the months after Logan's death without Phoebe. She'd stepped in with her crazy energy and awful jokes, sorting casseroles, writing thank you notes, and catching Meg when she'd fainted while they were picking out the headstone. The kids adored Aunt Phoebe. Even though they were the same age, Phoebe seemed a decade younger than Meg.

Maybe it was just that she had yet to settle down. She went through boyfriends and houses like most people went through toothbrushes. As a real estate agent, she couldn't resist "the next great deal" and was continuously trading up. That seemed to be her tactic with men also. She was currently living in an amazing condo in the most sought-after area of town near the university. Meg was pretty sure Phoebe was between boyfriends, but couldn't be certain since they hadn't spoken in the last week. She'd been adamant that Meg should go when she'd heard about the girls' weekend.

If anyone would understand this crazy impulse, it would be Phoebe. She lived in a constant state of midlife crisis. Meg never knew what Phoebe would come up with next. She'd collected Longaberger baskets, and next she was following a heavy metal band across the country. She had held any number of bizarre jobs before she finally found her calling as a real estate agent. People liked her.

Phoebe answered on the first ring.

"Hey, sweet sister of mine!"

"Hey, Phoebe. Are you in the middle of something?"

"Nope, doing nothing. I'm at an open house for this little rancher that is never going to sell unless the owners agree to drop the price, or they spend some money to fix it up. I'm telling you Meg, it's a dump. Right now I'm sitting out on the porch because the house stinks so badly of cat urine. I don't know why I took this listing. So what's up?"

"Phoebe, I need your help."

"What can I do?"

"I need you to go stay at the house with Peter and the kids for a while."

"Wait? What? Meg, are you leaving him? What did he do?"

"He didn't do anything. He doesn't even know about this yet. I just need to take a break from my life," Meg was counting on Phoebe to be the one person in her family who would support her on this.

"Meggy, where are you? Can I come get you?"

Meg took a deep breath.

"I'm going to stay in Sweet Beach. I need to do some thinking."

"What's going on? You know you can count on me. I'll do whatever, but what is up with you?"

"I don't know. I really don't. I just can't go back to that house right now. Please, can you go there tonight? I'll call Peter and tell him. The kids will be thrilled to see you."

"You're covered. I don't have anything I can't get out of. Promise me you'll let me know what's going on soon, though."

"I will. You're the best."

"Good luck with Petey. I doubt he'll take it well."

"I doubt it, too."

The next phone call Meg made was to a local valet service. She'd found their card a week ago stuck under her windshield wiper outside the grocery store and stuck it in her glove box, just in case. The card said, *We run errands so you can run your life.* She dialed the number, wondering if her life had become simply a series of errands to run.

❧

It was quiet in the house at Sweet Beach when Meg pulled in the drive. She peered in a window. Charlotte was lying on a couch in the sunroom lost in a book. When Meg opened the door, Charlotte leapt off the couch ready to take on the intruder.

"Meg!"

Dani came out from the kitchen at the sound of Charlotte's voice.

"Meg? Did you forget something?"

"No, I'm here to stay, if there's still room."

"Of course there is!"

"What did you tell Peter?"

"Nothing really. He wasn't there, no one was, so I left a message."

"Wow, that's bold. I wish I could have done that with Joe. What about the kids?"

"Phoebe is going to stay with them for now. She doesn't cook, but she'll take care of the kids and they'll be happy to have her. I actually hired a valet service to deliver meals and pick up Peter's dry cleaning. So, really, nothing should change too drastically in Peter's world other than dealing with his little sister on a daily basis."

"You're amazing. You took care of that all in one afternoon? I really left Joe hanging, I guess."

Meg shrugged. She was used to taking care of everything; this didn't seem to be such a big task.

"I'm hungry and tired. I think I'll make a snack and head to my room and wait for Peter's call. I feel kind of bad I won't have talked to him before Phoebe shows up on the doorstep. But she can handle it. She's the queen of crisis."

❧

## Charlotte

When Charlotte's cell phone rang at 1:00 a.m., she assumed it would be Brett, but instead it was Will.

"Hey, Mom."

"Hey, yourself! It's so good to hear your voice!" Charlotte sat up and turned on her light, mentally doing the math to figure out what time it was in Spain.

"I talked to Dad but he didn't know where you were, which is kinda weird. Where are you?"

"I'm at the beach with Dani and Meg. We're having a sort of girls' weekend."

"Oh."

"How's Spain?"

"It's pretty good. I met a bunch of people this weekend at a party Teresa's family took me to."

"Nice people?"

"Cool people."

"How's your Spanish?"

"It's getting pretty good, but everybody wants me to talk to them in English mostly."

"That makes it easy."

"But it's not the point."

"True. How's school going?"

"All right. I like it. When I understand what they're talking about, the work is easy. Sometimes I don't understand though, but the teachers are really nice."

"I miss you, sweetie," said Charlotte. Suddenly, she felt scared. What the hell had she done? She couldn't let Will worry about her and Brett while he was over there.

"Yeah," said Will. "I miss you guys, too."

"Hey, just so you know, I'm going to stay down at the beach for a bit. Since you're not there, the house is pretty quiet. I'm going to see if I can drum up a few clients down here." Until it came out of her mouth, Charlotte hadn't thought of that. There had to be plenty of rich people and tacky houses down here in need of her help. It was the perfect excuse.

"Cool. Maybe you could get a beach house for us."

"Maybe," she said.

"That'd be awesome. Hey, I have to go. My bus is here."

Charlotte could hear voices in the background. Will was starting his day. His voice was like a balm. He sounded good. He was fine without them. It was hard to believe he was on the other side of the ocean just outside her window.

"Love you," she said, but she wasn't sure if Will heard her before his phone went silent.

She could hear Meg's phone ring on the other side of her wall. It had to have been the tenth call already. She sounded upset, definitely crying, but then she got angry. Charlotte was pretty sure she heard her call Peter an asshole. She arranged her throw pillows, found her earbuds, and turned up the music to drown out the drama. She couldn't imagine being married to a man like Peter. She supposed she should be grateful that she had Brett. But was she? Did love fade for every couple? The Hallmark specials made it sound like there were couples out there who stayed madly in love for decades. That didn't seem sustainable. Her love for Brett felt stale, like crackers left on the counter with the lid open. Bland, soft, in danger of rotting if someone didn't close the box.

Had she settled when it came to Brett? She'd been to so many weddings by that time. Her friends had been starting their lives and she'd been working every weekend. Her business had just begun to make real money. Maybe she'd been looking too hard for Mr. Right. Getting together with Brett was so easy. She'd thought that meant it was right, but maybe it was simply the timing. She'd been ripe. He'd been ready.

Charlotte had first met Brett in college at a local bar called Duffy's. It had been dime drafts night: from six to seven that night, draft beers were only ten cents. So by seven, the place had been full of drunks. For once, Charlotte hadn't been one of them. Her friends were completely toasted, but she'd still been working on her second beer. She'd needed to get back to the apartment later to work on a project.

It was her senior year, and she'd been carrying a heavy load plus putting together a plan to start her own business as soon as she graduated. She'd already found the money in the form of her Uncle Stan. He didn't have any children, and when she'd shared her business idea with him at Thanksgiving, he'd offered to partner with her. Her father had laughed and said he was wasting his money, but Charlotte had known otherwise.

She was going to be a success. She could feel it, and school was the only hurdle left in her way. Stan had insisted she had to graduate before he'd give her a penny. After changing her major to interior design in her junior year, it had been crazy trying to get through all the courses she needed to graduate on time. Her father had told her if she wasn't going to finish the business degree he'd agreed to pay for, she'd better at least finish something in four years. He wasn't paying for any more school. He'd worried that she was going to lose Stan's money and give Stan another reason to tease him. Charlotte's uncle was relentless in his harassment of her father. She'd always assumed it was all in fun, but once he offered to fund her dreams, her father had seemed to take everything the wrong way.

Suddenly, Charlotte had something to prove and she'd quit the partying and gotten serious about graduating and building her business. She'd already found a few potential customers, never mind that she'd slept with two of them.

That night at Duffy's, Charlotte had watched her roommates flirting with some guys from the medical school in town. Amanda had been completely lit and Charlotte had worried about the offers she might be making. She still had work to do and she hadn't wanted Amanda bringing home some show-off future physician to play doctor. She'd slid into a seat next to Amanda who'd thrown her arm around her and declared, "This is my friend Charlotte, she used to be a lot of fun, but now all she ever wants to do is work. Charlotte's like a

spider—always weaving her web!" It wasn't funny,
but they were all as drunk as Amanda and they'd
laughed like she was a comedian. It was a lost cause
for Charlotte, so she'd made for the door. Amanda
would obviously find her own way home. As she'd
waited for her jacket at the coat check, one of the
guys from the medical school approached her.

"Had enough?" he'd asked.

"That obvious?"

"Only to those of us who aren't completely
plastered." He'd smiled and introduced himself.
Her jacket came and he'd offered to walk her home.
He was easy to talk to, funny, sweet, and quite definitely cute. Great teeth. He was going to be a dentist. She never did get any work done that night. Or
the next. But by Sunday night, she'd been swearing
off sex and pulling an all-nighter to get her senior
project finished.

She saw Brett a few times after that, but had
broken it off just before graduation. She'd liked
him, but she had more important things on her
mind, like Stan's money and her father's doubt.
She'd tried to let Brett down gently, but he'd been
hurt and angry. When she returned his key and the
things he'd left at her place, he'd actually cried. The
tears had almost stopped her.

When they ran into each other five years later,
it had seemed like fate. She'd been hired to decorate his new office at the hot new dental practice
in town. Cosmetic dentistry was taking off. Bright
white teeth made the man, apparently.

The reunion sex had been amazing. They
couldn't get enough of each other. They'd been
young, rich, beautiful, and desperately in love. It
was like a movie. Until it wasn't. Those early years
had been good. They'd shared their bodies and
their hearts on a daily basis.

The decision to have a baby had sent their
relationship into overdrive. But then the resulting
pregnancy changed everything. From the beginning there had been health problems with the

unborn baby. It was like a war—every day a new plan of action, a new drug, a new problem. Nights spent in tears wondering if the baby would survive, if Charlotte would survive. The doctors, hospitals, monitors, tests, and fear had whittled away at their newly minted love. If they'd never had Will, would they have continued the way they'd been before the pregnancy? It wasn't possible; that kind of love was too intense—it would have burned them to the core. But she hadn't pictured this. She hadn't thought fifteen years later she'd be as unimportant to her husband as a potted plant.

# MONDAY, APRIL 15
--

## Dani

When Dani woke the next morning, the sun was not shining. The gray light made her room feel less like a secret tree house, and more like an attic. She reached for her phone and checked the time. At home, they would all be up and getting ready for their day.

She hoped Joe remembered Jordan had violin today. She swallowed her guilt and put on her running shoes. Once on the beach, she headed south toward the boardwalk. She sprinted past Jeremy's art gallery with the purple door, past Main Street and the Pelican.

She kept running until she came to a part of the boardwalk she hadn't been to before. There were no stores. The houses were old, some with patches of fresh siding bandaging the damage from recent storms. A few looked brand new, probably sitting on the ghosts of homes lost completely to a hurricane, or maybe new money building over old. Her legs felt like jelly. She balanced on a fence, stretching her tight, complaining muscles. Yesterday all she knew was she couldn't go home; today it wasn't so clear why she'd stayed.

What had she done and what had she gotten her friends into? She'd heard Meg crying last night and Charlotte acted as if it were her idea in the first place. This was her crisis, what were they doing here? She'd read somewhere that thirty-eight to forty-two were the hardest years for women emotionally.

The explanation had to do with a shift in hormones and the stress placed on women trapped between children, work, and aging parents. It made sense, but she couldn't help thinking maybe it was just plain boredom. Maybe we just got tired of our lives. Maybe we realized life was nearly half over and we began to wonder if this was all there is.

Depression seemed possible, but she didn't think her feelings of disconnection with her life had any roots in the physical. After all, she felt fine. Her body might be a little looser, lumpier than she wished it was, but nothing hurt. It was her mind that was unhappy; her heart that felt unsettled. Who was she to complain? Look at the people she heard about on the news. There were so many people barely living. People struggling in war-torn countries, mothers who couldn't feed their own children, women addicted to drugs, involved in prostitution, or battered by their husbands. No, she had nothing to complain about. And here she was running away from a life that seemed near perfect—at least on paper.

She began to run again, faster, then sprinting. When she reached the north end of the boardwalk, she launched herself into the sand and ran in and out of the waves, ruining her good running shoes but soaking her soul. She needed to wake up. She wanted to feel something, anything. Life needed to matter more.

When Dani arrived back at the cottage, she left her shoes in the yard, hoping the sun would dry them. She wrung out her wet socks and hung them over the bannister. She found Charlotte alone in the dining room with her coffee, bagel, and news-papers. Charlotte's red hair was frizzed from the humidity, but she'd tied it up neatly and was wear-ing another outfit Dani had never seen before. She looked like she lived here, or at the very least, that she had planned on staying indefinitely.

"Did Brett call?" Dani asked.

"He left a message while I was in the shower," said Charlotte without looking up from the paper.

"And?" prompted Dani. "What did he say when you called him back?"

Charlotte shrugged. "I didn't."

Dani plopped in an empty chair. "Why not?"

Charlotte shrugged again. "I don't feel like talking to him."

"Okay, but don't you at least need to let him know that you are safe and that plans have changed?"

"I will," she said and turned a page of her paper. "I'm going to go do some shopping. I can wait if you want to join me."

Dani shook her head and got up. Obviously, Charlotte wasn't going to talk about this. "Nah, I'm sure you can shop enough for the two of us."

Charlotte made a face.

"Any sign of Meg?"

"Nope, not a peep."

Charlotte's phone rang and she looked to see an unfamiliar number. Unable to resist, she answered.

"Hello?"

"Charlotte, this is Peter Fillamon. I'd like to know exactly what's going on!"

"Hi, Peter. Lovely day, isn't it?"

Dani raised her eyebrows at Charlotte and sat back down to listen. Peter spoke so loudly it was as if Charlotte had him on speaker phone.

"Look, Charlotte, I know this has something to do with you and your own problems, but you don't need to drag my wife into it. She's got this crazy idea she needs some *space*. This is not something Meg would do on her own. I'm sure you put her up to it. Do not drag my wife into your midlife crisis."

"Actually, it wasn't even my idea. And if you think Meg wouldn't do this on her own, you don't know your wife very well."

Dani looked at Charlotte with wide eyes.

Before Peter could answer, Charlotte continued, "I'm going to hang up now, I'm about to go into a tunnel." Charlotte clicked off the phone and laughed out loud.

"Charlotte, this isn't funny. I feel terrible I dragged her into this."

"Oh c'mon, you can't take all the credit. Meg's a big girl. Besides, what does Peter have to complain about? She took care of everything for him. All he has to do is hand over the credit card. He'll survive. Besides, I give Meg a week. She won't stay."

"I wouldn't be so sure. She's put on a brave front for too long. She's got a lot more to run from than either of us."

"Peter will survive. He's just angry because his easy life isn't so easy right now."

Dani poured a cup of coffee and paged through Charlotte's newspaper. The first thing she had to do was figure out how she was going to pay her share of the rent. Taking any money out of her checking account was out of the question. She located the classifieds; there were only a few listings, mostly for waitresses. Dani had had enough of waiting on people. She'd have to figure out something else.

"I'm off!" announced Charlotte from the kitchen where she'd gone to refill her coffee cup. She paused in the doorway. "Sure you don't want to come?"

"Have fun!" said Dani, biting into the bagel Charlotte had abandoned.

＊

## Meg

Meg rolled over in her bed and pulled the covers up higher. She peeked at her phone on the bedside table. She'd turned it off last night after listening to Peter for as long as she could stand it. Just like in court, he would have continued to argue until she saw it his way or was so confused and beaten down, she conceded. Meg had never been able to withstand his arguments. It was always much easier to see it his way. For maybe the first time in their relationship, she was holding her ground.

There was a time when she and Peter had seemed like equal partners in parenting, but ever since Logan's death, Peter had stepped back. Maybe that was because of her. She'd been putting all the energy she could muster, which didn't ever seem like enough, into the kids.

Logically, she knew she couldn't protect them from everything, but it didn't stop her from trying. She'd started driving them to school to avoid all that could go wrong on a bus. She'd made Sarah quit the ski team after one of her teammates had crashed into a tree and broken her collar bone. Timmy had asked to sign up for peewee football, but all Meg could picture were the headlines: *Student-Athlete in Wheelchair after Bad Tackle.*

She'd stepped down from committees and commitments so that she could be available for them. She'd even ducked out of carpools, preferring to be the one behind the wheel whenever her kids went anywhere. She spent her days at the school volunteering in their classrooms, or the office in Michael's case because parents were no longer allowed in the middle school classrooms. She told herself it had nothing to do with Logan's death. It had more to do with his life. She'd missed so many moments. She wouldn't miss any more of her kids' lives. Just in case.

So what was she doing here? Neither Phoebe nor Peter knew her kids like she did. How could she trust them to keep them safe?

She needed to call her kids today. She didn't know what Peter had told them. He might be angry and hurt, but she didn't think he'd take it out on them. She wished they could talk rationally and agree on what they should tell the kids, but since Peter had opted out of that possibility, she would make something up herself. She would call them later. Maybe by then she'd have some idea of what she was doing here. She got out of bed long enough to pull down all her shades and then climbed back in and fell immediately to sleep.

⚓

Later in the afternoon, Meg's hunger finally got the best of her. She fixed a peanut butter, honey, and banana sandwich and a big glass of milk and retreated to her room with the day's crossword puzzle and the one she hadn't finished from yesterday. She'd had to fish it out of the trash. Between bites, she wrestled with the Sunday crossword and what to tell her kids about her absence. She didn't make much headway with either. She threw the paper across the room and dialed home. Phoebe answered.

"Hello, Fillamon residence, this is the woman in charge."

Meg smiled. "Hey, Phoebe."

"How're you doing? Peter is going nuts. What the hell is going on? Are you sure you can't tell me? Did he cheat on you? I can't imagine *you* have time for an affair. I don't know how you keep everything straight with these kids. I almost let Timmy go to school in slippers today and Sarah was in tears over something called a reading log."

"I can't thank you enough, Phoebe."

"Just tell me it's not another man!"

Meg laughed. "It's nothing like that. I just need some space."

"That's the part Peter can't grasp. He thinks you're hiding something. He's called me from work three times today to speculate. First, he thought you were planning some big surprise, but I pointed out the holes in that theory, such as my presence at the last minute and your emotional state. Then he called to ask if I thought maybe you'd gotten mixed up in some credit card scheme or were in some kind of financial trouble. I reminded him that you are the most financially conservative person I know and asked him what exactly you could be spending it on. He called after lunch, sounding like he'd had a martini or two, and asked if I thought you could have taken a lover. That's exactly how he put it, 'Do you think Meg has taken a lover?' I don't know what you're up to, but you have truly made a basket case of my big brother. It's kind of nice to have switched roles for once."

"I need to talk to the kids. What has he told them?"

"That you decided to extend your trip by a day or two and you'll be home soon. They don't seem concerned."

Meg was not surprised by his marginalization of the moment.

"I'm going to call back in a half hour after the kids have gotten off the bus. Can you make sure they're all there so I can talk to each of them?"

"Sure. We're planning a marathon Monopoly session and then karaoke night. I didn't know you had your own machine!"

Meg almost told Phoebe to be sure their homework was done first, but decided to let it go. Peter was going to have to step up.

She said good-bye to Phoebe, got up, and made her bed. Then she found the paper on the floor and sat down to finish the puzzle. Sunday's puzzle was always the worst. She rarely finished it before Wednesday. She couldn't think anyway; her head hurt. She looked through the medicine cabinet for aspirin, but found none. Catching her reflection in the mirror, she paused. There were enormous bags under her eyes. How was that possible? She'd slept nearly eighteen hours.

She selected a few fancy bath salts from the crowded basket on the sink counter. When the oversize tub was full and steaming hot, she slid in, breathing in the scent of eucalyptus. Meg studied the rolls of fat that covered her stomach. She couldn't remember the last time she'd taken a bath, but it was definitely before her body boasted so much extra flesh. She poked at the puckered skin that was turning pink in the hot water. Before children, she'd never really needed to worry about her weight. She rolled over so she wouldn't have to look at her belly and said out loud, "What am I doing here?"

-●-

# Dani

Inspired by her visit to Jeremy's art gallery, Dani took her journal, a stubby pencil she'd found in the kitchen junk drawer, and a thermos of coffee and went up to the widow's walk. Watching the ocean was hypnotizing. Drawing it was frustrating. This was ridiculous. That art professor had been kind in steering her elsewhere. She may have been an art major, but she was no artist. She hadn't admitted it to anyone, not even Joe. That was the real reason she'd dropped out of college. Classes could only teach you so much. You had to have the raw talent and an eye that saw things other people didn't. She had been delusional to think she was an artist. She'd wanted to believe all those well-meaning people back in grade school. She wanted to be an artist. If desire was all it took, she had that. As her mother had always told her, "If wishes were horses, beggars would ride." After a few frustrating hours, she tore out the pages she'd drawn and went downstairs for lunch. She'd eat something and then walk to town.

When she set out, she had no destination, but as she got closer to town, she knew exactly where she was headed. When she reached Jeremy's art gallery, she hesitated. What if he was just being nice on Saturday? She didn't want him to think she was stalking him. She looked in the window and saw no one, she was about to go when Jeremy's curly head appeared. He smiled when he saw Dani and opened the door.

"Hey, I thought you were heading home yesterday?"

"I was, but plans changed. How're you doing?"

"It was a slow weekend, but I just got some great new works in today. It's Dani, right? Want to come in and see?"

Dani followed him inside, thrilled that he'd remembered her name. He showed her a set of modern paintings. The type that usually made Joe say, "I could do that!" The colors were startling and Dani couldn't help thinking Joe *could* have done that.

"I know. It's a little over the top, right?"

"Yeah, but I'm not a fan of modern art, so I don't have an appreciation."

"You'd be surprised. Some people like stuff like this. It makes you scratch your head."

"It makes you question the definition of art!" said Dani.

Jeremy laughed. "But!" he said, pointing at her, "It gets you thinking!"

He showed her the entire collection. She couldn't help catching his enthusiasm. He was a natural salesman. On a whim, she asked, "You take work on consignment, right?"

"I do. I keep about forty percent, but it's negotiable. Why? Have you got something for me?"

"I might. I'll let you know."

"That'd be great; I could use some new blood in here."

Dani smiled. "I've gotta run."

"Well, don't be a stranger!"

"I won't!" she called as she raced out of the gallery.

Walking back, her mind churned with ideas, occasionally interrupted by thoughts of Jeremy. He had such a positive energy. It was probably his youth, but it was contagious. When had she stopped creating art? Probably about the time she'd started creating children. Joe had never asked why she stopped. In fact, they never talked about art or went to art galleries anymore.

They were both busy and the kids were constantly underfoot. Most marriages reached this point, didn't they? Comfortable. Taken for granted, but not in a bad way. When your relationship was as solid as theirs, you could afford to ignore it, couldn't you? There wasn't that constant need for reassurance like in the beginning.

When she met Joe, she'd been enjoying college life. Maybe just a little too much. Her grades had slid up and down depending on who she was dating. In retrospect, she probably shouldn't have gone to college when she did. Her parents had told her since she could speak that she would go to college. She'd never questioned it, but she'd never thought about what she would actually do after college. She chose to major in art because everyone had said she was good at it and she loved to create things. She'd never given any serious thought to what she'd do once she finished her degree. But then, Joe swept in and she'd never had to.

She'd met Joe at the grocery store. Cliché for sure. He'd been stumped by the herb selection and asked for Dani's advice. He couldn't tell which herb was cilantro and which was parsley. He'd been wearing a tie and seemed so earnest.

"Do you always dress so nice to do your grocery shopping?" she'd teased.

"I was on my way home from work," he'd explained, blushing and loosening his tie.

"What do you do?"

"I'm an insurance salesman."

"Sounds exciting!" Dani had teased. She remembered the look on Joe's face. He hadn't been sure at first that she was teasing, but then he'd laughed. She might have fallen in love exactly at that point. Joe had the best laugh.

"What do you do?" he'd asked.

"I'm a college student," she'd said, handing him the cilantro. "What do you need cilantro for?"

"I wanted to make enchiladas. I'm kind of tired of takeout, but you can probably guess I'm no cook."

"I'm a great cook!" she'd said. And just like that, he'd invited her to his townhouse and set the wheels in motion. Dani loved being at his house. She loved cooking with him. She loved talking to him. And soon she loved him. So much for college, she'd gotten a job working as a receptionist for an office full of architects. Maybe not high glamour, and certainly not high art, but she'd been happy. She had no regrets. She still loved Joe. She just wished that were enough.

---

By the time Dani got back to the cottage, she was starving. She dug through the kitchen, assessing the options. She found pasta, chicken, tomatoes, and olives and went to work. Before long, the kitchen smelled of garlic and olive oil and comfort.

Meg came in still wearing her pajamas and sat in the window seat.

"Smells wonderful."

"It will be," said Dani as she searched the cupboards for a strainer.

Meg was quiet.

"Did you talk to your kids?"

"Yup. They weren't fazed. It's amazing how oblivious they can be to the people around them. I worried all day that there would be a big scene, but they were too anxious to get back to their computer screens to care about my crisis."

"Don't you remember? We were the same way, too. I don't remember much about my parents lives, other than when they got in the way of my plans."

"Too true. They'd much rather have Phoebe there to play with than me."

"That won't last long, you know it. Have you talked to Peter today?" Dani decided not to mention the phone call Charlotte had gotten.

"No, and I turned off my cell phone. For a man who has known me since I was twelve and who spends his days dealing with other people's drama, you'd think he could accept this. He should know I would never do this without a really good reason."

"Well, if the tables were turned, wouldn't you be freaking out?"

"No, I'd know he had another woman," Meg said.

"Really?"

Meg shrugged.

"I think if Joe left, I wouldn't be too worried. As long as I knew he was coming back. After all, he already travels for work. I'm comfortable running the show by myself."

"How's Joe handling it?"

"Kind of like Peter. He's confused, maybe a little angry, pretty worried. But, to his credit, he did try to be calm and accepting."

"And your kids?"

"Joey, of course, didn't understand, but Jordan was kind of like your kids and didn't think it was such a big deal. It will be good for them to have some solid time with Joe. He's been gone so much lately. He would have never cashed in all his comp time if I hadn't done this."

Meg watched Dani slicing tomatoes. "Were you planning to stay all along?"

Dani put down the knife she was using and turned to face Meg. She dried her hands on a towel and took a deep breath. "Honestly? No." She sat down next to Meg. "I can't explain why I stayed. All I know is that it's like I've been living on autopilot, like I'm waiting for something to change. But I don't know what needs to be changed. Some days my life seems pretty pointless." She held her hand up when Meg started to protest. "I'm not going to kill myself or anything. I just feel like time is slipping past, and I missed out on something. Like I misread the signals at some crucial moment and now I find myself in tears for no apparent reason. Maybe it's hormones, but it feels deeper than that. I feel like something is missing. That makes no sense I know. I mean, I've gotten what I thought I wanted. I love my husband, my kids. We have a nice house, a good life, good friends, everybody's healthy. So why isn't it enough? Why do I feel so empty? Why can't I just be happy?"

"I'm the wrong person to ask," said Meg.

"I need some air. Come outside with me." Dani turned off the stove and grabbed a bottle of wine and the opener.

Sitting in the descending darkness, Meg said, "I'm so glad we did this."

"Me, too. I only hope we don't have to pay too dearly."

"Let's not think about that now. Let's be these rebellious mamas on the loose."

Dani laughed, "That's us. Mamas on the loose!"

Meg laughed, too, but Dani could tell her heart wasn't in it. Dani lit one of the citronella candles on the railing, even though there were no bugs yet. It was too cool. The trees creaked in the wind and a horn sounded somewhere down the street. The candle sputtered and went out.

"Do you ever think about how if you made one decision differently, you'd be living an entirely different life?" asked Dani.

"Sure, but then you might still be asking that question."

Dani laughed. "So, you think I'd be unhappy right now no matter what decisions I'd made?"

"Maybe," said Meg.

"That's depressing."

"I think everybody's unhappy on some level. Some of us just fake it better than others."

"Okay, now that's even more depressing."

"Sorry."

Dani sipped her wine.

"How do you do it?"

"Do what?" asked Meg.

"How can you find happiness again after losing Logan?"

"What makes you think I have?"

"You seem so good."

"I've had a lifetime to perfect the art of appearing fine."

"I didn't know."

"You couldn't. Like you said, I seem good."

Dani took Meg's hand.

"Every day, when I get up, before I have a chance to even remember that Logan is gone, I get busy. I keep moving, I take care of the kids, I plan things, and whenever there's a lull, I pull out my crossword puzzles. I do anything, *anything,* to keep my mind off it."

"Maybe you shouldn't do that."

"Maybe. But what's the alternative?"

"Grieving."

"I've done that. I cried for months. And then everyone got tired of my crying. It's hard to live with someone who cries all the time. They'd already stopped. So I stopped, too. I got busy, instead."

"But maybe you needed more time than they needed."

"There will never be enough time. This hurt will never end."

"I'm not saying it would end, but it might change."

"If I stop missing Logan," said Meg through tears, "It'd be like he was never here."

Dani put her arms around Meg. "That could never happen."

Dani was crying too. "God, we're a mess," said Meg.

Dani went in the house for tissues. When she returned, Meg said, "Do you think everything happens for a reason?"

"Not so much."

"How does it work, then? Is it all just random?"

"Maybe. The big stuff is at least—floods, fires, accidents. I think the *reason* is found in how we react, what we do about the chaos. I think we have to listen to our hearts. It's when we stop listening to our hearts that the chaos wins."

"I like that idea," said Meg.

"Let's go with it then, for now," said Dani, smiling in the darkness.

## Charlotte

Meg and Dani were sitting down for dinner when Charlotte finally made it back to the house, arms loaded with so many bags it required two trips to the car.

"Just in time!" she sang out as she entered.

Charlotte decided not to tell Meg that Peter had left a message on her phone threatening to come down and find them if Charlotte didn't bring Meg back tomorrow. He would cool down. Besides, the guys only knew they were in Sweet Beach. They didn't know the address. Peter couldn't find Meg unless she wanted to be found.

Later, after everyone had gone to bed, Charlotte listened to her messages.

"Charlotte—where are you? I thought you were going to be home yesterday. Did I have the date wrong? Anyway, call me."

"Charlotte—I talked to Will and he said you're still in Sweet Beach. What's going on? Could you please call and fill me in?"

"Hey, now I'm starting to get worried. Should I be worried? Did I do something wrong? Are you upset about something? Please call me."

Charlotte stared at her phone. She should call Brett. She should. But what was there to say? Sorry, I've decided to take a vacation from you and our life. I'm sick of trying to get you to pay attention to me. I'm terrified that our marriage is over.

She looked at the time. 11:15 p.m. He'd be asleep by now with his phone on the charger downstairs. She dialed his number.

"Hey. Sorry I haven't returned your calls. I guess I don't know what to say. Maybe . . . I mean . . . I don't know what I mean." She knew she sounded ridiculous. She took a breath and plowed on. "I just need some time by myself. You and I aren't really working these days and maybe we both need a time-out. With Will gone, it's a good time. I'm going to see if I can find some business while I'm down here, but mostly, I just want to be left alone for a while. I hope you can understand that. I need it. Well, um, have a nice day. Bye."

*Have a nice day*? That was stupid. She flopped back on her bed and looked at the ceiling. There were bugs in the pretty stained glass overhead light. Lots of them.

This was crazy. She emptied the rest of the wine bottle she'd brought up with her into her glass and drank it in one long swallow. Sleep.

# TUESDAY, APRIL 16

## Dani

The next morning's run was much slower and Dani was walking by the time she reached the boardwalk. She sank down on a bench and watched the sun creep over the horizon. From this angle, it really did seem as though you could fall right off the edge of the earth if you went too far.

The week stretched out in front of her. She wished she had a therapist or a priest or someone to tell her what she should be doing. Someone with a better idea how to sort through her emotions and find what was true. Behind her, a light came on in a shop. It was a used book store called the Bookateria. Dani looked at her watch, what kind of book store was open at seven on a Tuesday in the off-season?

As she entered, she smelled strong coffee brewing. The warmth from the pinging radiators felt like a blanket around her goose-pimpled arms. A woman popped up from behind one of the stacks. She was dressed all in purple—flowing skirt, peasant blouse, multiple scarves, and even purple bifocals on a purple chain.

"Hello, welcome!" she smiled warmly at Dani.

"I was surprised you were open."

"I like to open early, gets me out of the house. I'm a morning person and I get a lot done in these hours; might as well be open for business at the same time. Have to say, though, I don't get many customers until after ten. Would you like some coffee?"

"That would be wonderful; it smells great."

"Might be a bit strong—I like it to jar my bones—so I won't be offended if you add a bit of cream. I'll go fetch some," she began to leave.

"Don't bother, I like it strong, too," Dani said.

"I'm Libby. Here you go," she said as she offered the steaming mug.

"Thanks, I'm Dani."

"Dani?"

"It's short for Danielle."

"And what brings you out so early, Dani?"

Libby seemed like the kind of person who might understand her crazy problem, but Dani smiled behind her mug and answered, "I'm just looking for something good to read." She took a sip of the steaming coffee and added, "Although, I'd be interested in any kind of self-development or career counseling books you might have."

"Can't say I have many of those, but I think there may be a copy of *What Color is Your Parachute* back there from 1985. Let me go look." She disappeared.

Dani looked through the titles. There were thousands. Mostly well-worn fiction—westerns, romances, and mysteries stacked two and three deep. Beach reading.

"The nonfiction is in the back. Are you doing a bit of soul searching? The beach is always good for that." Libby materialized at Dani's side, causing her to jump and spill some of the coffee on her hand. Libby offered her a handkerchief, purple, of course. Dani wiped herself off as she followed Libby to the back of the store.

"The ocean attracts lots of soul searchers, not sure why that is. Maybe because it's so huge and unending, it puts us back in our place."

Dani left the store two hours and three cups of coffee later with a grocery bag stuffed full of books. Libby had let her buy the books with an IOU. Where else in Dani's world would that have occurred? She was certain she had happened upon Libby's store for a reason. Maybe the answer would be in one of the books in her sack. First, she had to get them home. She called Charlotte.

Charlotte answered in a worried voice, "Are you okay? Where've you been? I thought you were going for a run."

"I need a ride."

"Are you hurt?"

"No, I found this great little used book store and bought more than I can carry."

"Glad you're okay, we were beginning to think you ran all the way home."

"Ha. Nope, still here. What are you up to? Could you come pick me up?"

"We were just sitting here plotting our laundromat run. I'll be right there."

"Thanks."

---

Dani hadn't spent a day in a laundromat since college. Charlotte popped in and out between scouting out potential business and getting her nails done. Meg spent most of her time bent over her crosswords, pausing a few times to ask for help from Dani and the other customers.

"Oh God, a math clue. Dani, who wrote, 'There is no royal road to geometry'?"

"I think that's history, not math."

"Euclid," said an elderly man who was dozing in a chair nearby.

"Wow," said Meg, "that fits!"

Dani spent the afternoon reading her books, eating M&M's from the vending machine, and watching daytime TV with strangers. She didn't find any great wisdom in her books, but she developed a greater appreciation for her own dryer and decided if she ever got on *The Price is Right*, she wouldn't be greedy. She'd just take the side-by-side refrigerator and the lifetime supply of dish soap and forget about the vacation in Bali.

Back at the cottage, Dani put her clean clothes in her dresser. They fit easily, not like at home where her drawers were overstuffed with clothes she never wore. She dialed home. Talking to Jordan helped ease her guilt. She sounded fine and talked endlessly about the new Delia's catalog and everything she wanted for her birthday, still several months away. Her story of the lunchroom drama actually enthralled Dani. It had been a while since she'd shared any tales of the lunchroom, and Dani listened attentively—for once she wasn't distracted by the million other tasks she needed to be doing.

Jordan talked to her less and less these days, but it seemed like whenever she finally opened up it was never a good time. Today she had all the time in the world. When Jordan finally came up for air, Dani asked to speak to Joe, but he'd taken Joey to the grocery store. Dani could just imagine that spectacle. Taking Joey to the grocery store was like taking a drunk frat boy to a bar full of coeds. He couldn't contain his excitement and he wanted it *all*. She told Jordan she loved her and promised to call again soon.

Dani sank down on the bed with the phone book and the local paper she'd purchased at the laundromat. She copied down the address she was looking for and then scanned the paper for yard sales. She circled several for Thursday.

## Meg

Meg hung up the phone. It had been good to talk to Phoebe and hear that things were fine with the kids. The service was supplying great meals and had taken Peter's shirts to the dry cleaner. Meg reminded Phoebe that the cleaning woman she'd hired to take care of the house in her absence would be there on Wednesday. She'd had a nice conversation with Michael, listening to him explain his plans for the spring science fair. Then Peter had gotten on the phone and begun interrogating her about her plans, so she'd said she loved him and hung up. She'd decided on a strategy for handling Peter. She would talk to him if he was civil and sane; she would hang up if he became angry or hurtful. He'd figure it out eventually. It was the same tactic she used with her kids to teach them manners, or their poodle to teach him to pee outside. If you wanted to change the behavior you had to give consistent positive response to the behavior you sought and negative to the one you didn't. Peter was a smart guy; he'd figure it out.

She went downstairs looking for company. Dani was already in bed, but Charlotte was sipping wine on the front porch.

"Hey," she said, sitting on the step beside Charlotte.

"I was just contemplating a cigarette, and then the cigarette police shows up," kidded Charlotte, putting the unlit cigarette in her hand back in the pack.

Meg smiled. "I won't stop you. If you want to kill yourself, go on and do it."

"How'd your call home go?"

Meg shook her head, unable to speak. She knew she'd cry.

"That well?" said Charlotte. "I keep my phone on mute, letting the messages pile up. It's easier to talk to him through voice mail."

They sat in silence for a long time. Then Meg spoke.

"I'm glad I'm here. I am. I just wish I knew what I'm supposed to do next."

Charlotte bumped shoulders with Meg. "You'll figure it out. Maybe first, you just need to breathe for a while."

"Maybe," said Meg.

"And then if you still don't know what to do, I'll put you to work for me."

"You found some work already?"

"Yup. Talked a horny guy with a tacky little shoe store into letting me do a modest redesign."

"I didn't know you did retail stores. I thought you did houses and offices."

"There's a first for everything," said Charlotte lifting her glass.

"Good for you," said Meg.

"You'll figure something out."

"I hope so. I need to come up with something to explain this to Peter."

"No, you don't."

"Oh, I think I do. If I don't he might send a private detective down here to get me. He keeps insisting he needs the address."

"Did you give it to him?"

Meg shook her head.

"Good. He's an adult, Meg. You both are. He can handle this."

"I don't know. He's been different since Logan."

"How?"

"I don't know. Distant, unengaged. He works crazy long hours and when he comes home he's always too exhausted to play with the kids like he used to. It's almost like he's afraid to be close to them."

"That's crazy."

"I don't know. I've been thinking about it. Maybe on some level he's afraid he might lose them, too, so he doesn't want to get so attached."

"He's their father!"

"I'm probably wrong. It just seems like I've pulled them closer and he's pushed them away."

"Wow," said Charlotte, pulling out her cigarette again and lighting it. "Don't you guys talk to a therapist?"

Meg shook her head. "Peter wants me to, but he says he doesn't need one. I did take the kids for a little while, but they didn't like it."

"Maybe it's time to revisit that option."

"Maybe," said Meg, standing up and yawning. "I'm going to leave you to your death stick. Have a good night."

"You, too," said Charlotte, taking a long drag.

# WEDNESDAY, APRIL 17
### Meg

The next morning, Meg woke up disoriented. In a panic, she jumped out of bed, certain the kids had missed the bus. It was Logan's first day of pre-school! When the butter yellow walls of her room came into focus, she remembered. She sank down on her bed and allowed the pain to wash over her. The thick, heavy, hot hurt filled her stomach and she ran for the bathroom, making it just in time.

She sat with her head resting on the side of the toilet wondering if this was her life now. There seemed to be no escape from her own guilt and sadness, it followed her, even here in this beautiful place.

She got up and brushed her teeth. She was not going to be swallowed by it today. She'd just get moving. That always helped. She made a list.

> *Clean*
> *Grocery shopping*
> *Get some exercise*

Dani was out running. Charlotte was gone, too—probably out shopping. After a quick breakfast, she began on her list.

She discovered a vacuum and other cleaning supplies in a closet on the landing of the second floor. She breathed a sigh of relief. Cleaning grounded her. Whenever she felt her life was out of control, she would get out the dust rag or sort out a closet. Almost always she felt better for it.

When she was first pregnant, Peter had begged her to hire a cleaning lady, but she wouldn't hear of it. Call it cleaning therapy, but with the addition of each child, her house got cleaner rather than messier. Since Logan's death, their home was clean enough for the queen—not a thing out of place, not a mote of dust to be found, and yet she cleaned daily for hours.

Wiping down the beautiful old furniture in the living room made her think of her mother. She would appreciate the simplicity and the taste with which this house had been so carefully decorated. For her mother, appearances were everything and she'd done her best to pass that value on to Meg. Meg knew how to put on a happy face, no matter what she felt beneath it. Hopefully, her mother wouldn't find out she'd abandoned her family. Growing up, she had craved her mother's approval. She still did. Whenever her mother visited, Meg outdid herself cleaning and cooking and presenting the perfect home. She was always exhausted when Francine left.

She didn't remember her mother ever explicitly saying she expected Meg to be perfect, but she didn't need to. When she was a little girl, Meg could never go out to join the other kids playing kick the can after supper until the dishes were done, her homework was finished, and her own room was spotless. Many nights Meg sat tortured on her bedroom floor sorting out her Barbies and stuffed animals, listening to the calls and the laughter of the neighborhood kids. Most nights she never made it out to play. She never argued with her mother, never put up a fight. She left that to her sister Annie.

Annie was four years older than Meg. When they were growing up, Annie resisted every piece of advice given, broke every rule made, and intentionally disregarded her mother's directions. Meg listened to Annie in her bedroom talking to boys on the telephone and saying things that fascinated, yet repulsed her. She remembered closing her window when the smoke drifted in from the roof where Annie would sit smoking clove cigarettes—sometimes alone, sometimes with friends  talking in hushed tones punctuated by bursts of harsh laughter.

Meg had never understood why Annie and her parents struggled so. When Annie finally graduated and left to travel Europe carrying only her backpack, the house itself seemed to breathe a sigh of relief. Most of her parents' emotional energy had already been spent trying to reform a resistant Annie and there was not much left for Meg. Meg had never made a conscious decision to be the perfect daughter, but looking back now, she realized that was exactly what she had been doing. And she had done it. Her life was neat, organized, perfectly run, complete with beautiful children, a successful husband, and a home in a trendy neighborhood.

Until Logan died. Some days she could remove herself from it and pretend that it had happened to someone else and it was terribly sad for them. But sometimes she woke up after long fitful nights with just snatches of sleep, sure she would find Logan in his little race car bed. For months she couldn't bring herself to put it away, and then she came home from Confirmation classes at the church with Lizzie one evening to find Peter had disassembled it and stored it in the basement. She'd been furious, locking herself in Logan's room and sliding to the floor, sniffing the carpet for the scent of him.

Peter had knocked on the door, apologizing, begging to be let in. She'd opened it and he'd pulled her into his arms. They'd lain on the floor and talked about Logan that night. It was the first time she'd seen Peter cry since the funeral. It was good to know he hadn't buried his grief with the casket. Meg realized then she'd been angry at him for not being sadder. Maybe she was angry now because he wasn't still sad, like she was. He'd managed his grief, just like he managed his work and his life.

Meg turned off the vacuum cleaner, midway through the living room. She went to sit on the porch, breathing in the clean, sweet air. She felt a tightness in her chest but for once her eyes were dry. What kind of life had she been living? She spent her days either trying not to think about Logan or looking desperately for him. If she let herself feel the pain that pulled at her every day like an anchor, she would drown with it. And if she stopped looking for Logan, would that mean she loved him less? Rationally, she knew that wouldn't be true, but letting go of wanting him back? She couldn't do that. But she couldn't live like this. It hurt too much.

Maybe being here would help her find a new way. Her world had become her children. Maybe that wasn't such a good idea, especially when one can be gone in an instant, taking your heart, even your soul, with him. She hadn't planned to build her life around children, letting them dictate her emotions, her days, her future. There was a time when she'd wanted something else. Wasn't there?

She shook her head to clear it. *Was* there a time when she'd wanted something else? She tried to remember what she'd dreamed of doing when she sat in her room listening to her parents argue in their bedroom, as her sister sat smugly in front of a television—homework untouched. Meg thought of calling Annie. They didn't talk much. Annie thought Meg's life was completely material and superficial. Annie had been sober now for several years, and was living in San Francisco working at a government job doing something that had never really made sense to Meg. She realized now that she treated Annie with the same indifference and disrespect she had accused Annie of heaping on her. She couldn't call her if she wanted to, the number was tucked away in her desk drawer at home, scrawled on the back of one of her mother's Christmas letters.

Besides, she and Annie were worlds apart. Even at the funeral, Annie hadn't known what to say to her. Meg hardly remembered her being there, but knew she had been. She sighed and went inside to finish cleaning.

## Dani

Dani tried to find the address she'd written down from the telephone directory. She'd been driving back and forth on the same stretch of road, in search of a sign for some time now. She should have called for directions. Joe was always telling her that. Call first and save yourself time. She banished thoughts of Joe and pulled into a shopping center. She scanned the storefronts, finally finding what she was looking for—The Artistic Touch. She parked and went inside.

Her pulse quickened at the sight of so many tubes and pots and cans of paint. There were more options than she'd ever seen before. She breathed in the familiar smell of oils and solvents, dust and possibilities. She selected a few brushes and studied the paints. Oil, she decided, and maybe some acrylics too. She wasn't sure what she would be painting—wood or glass or maybe both. She added a pan for mixing the paints, more brushes, and some cleaning supplies. She was amazed at the total when the cashier added it up. It had been a long time since Dani had purchased serious art supplies. Crayons and glue certainly didn't cost this much. With a wince, she pulled out her credit card.

She settled the packages on the passenger side floor and smiled to herself. She'd forgotten how happy fresh, new art supplies always made her. Maybe she should have worked in an art supply store. What she needed next was inspiration. She headed for Jeremy's gallery. She parked on the street and walked up the boardwalk, her enthusiasm evaporating when she saw the Closed sign hanging in the window. As she unlocked her car, she remembered her IOU at the Bookateria and headed back down the boardwalk.

Libby was happy to see Dani, and went to fill two coffee cups. When she returned, she asked, "So, this soul searching, any progress?"

Dani wrapped both hands around the warm cup, breathed in the rich scent, and smiled. "I don't know. Maybe, a little."

"What brought it about anyway, if you don't mind my asking? Was there some sort of crisis on the home front?" The question was personal, but Dani could tell Libby wasn't being nosy, she wanted to help. Besides, Libby had her own story; Dani was sure of that. She gave Libby the abbreviated version of the girls' weekend and her abrupt decision to stay, followed by her friends' decisions to join her.

"I don't even know why I'm down here. I mean, my friends both have real issues I never even realized they were dealing with. I guess we were busy with our own families. There wasn't time to talk or maybe we didn't ask each other the right questions. We say we're fine, even when we're not. But the thing is, there's nothing fundamentally wrong with my life. I feel guilty that I'm so unhappy and dissatisfied. It's seems petty and selfish. I've got everything; what right do I have to be unhappy?"

Libby took a sip of her coffee. Then she looked at Dani with her sparkling eyes and said, "Emotions are honest. They can't lie. You feel what you feel."

Just then the door opened and another elderly woman came in. She called, "Hey, Libby, is your pot hot? I've got stories to tell from the great land where the sun always shines!"

"That'll be Marian, returning from Florida and her winter in the sun. I wish I had an answer for you. But everybody digs their own row. You can't judge your feelings, but maybe you could set them aside for the time being and see what's underneath it all."

"Libby?" Marian's voice rang out.

"Don't be a stranger, Dani," said Libby and she squeezed her arm. Dani watched as she hugged her friend. She waved Dani away when she offered to pay her IOU.

"Not now, you can pay when you stop in next, that way you'll have an excuse to visit again." Dani thanked her and headed home.

As she walked back to the car, she nearly collided with Jeremy.

"Hey, Dani, were you coming to see me?"

"Actually, I was."

"I'm going to open up right now, you want some coffee?"

"I just had some at the Bookateria."

"Libby brews it strong, doesn't she?"

"Yeah. She's my kind of woman."

"So what can I do for you?" Jeremy asked as he unlocked the front door and flipped the sign to Open in the window.

"I was kind of looking for some inspiration," Dani said as she began to look around.

"Plenty of that here, at least on the walls."

"I'll just look around if you don't mind."

"Sure. I'll be in the back."

Dani wandered around the store. She stopped to muse on a beautiful watercolor of the marshes in early spring.

"So how come your stay was extended?" asked Jeremy, appearing with coffee cup in hand.

"Lots of reasons," said Dani. She couldn't tell Jeremy about her decision to stay. He was too young to understand. Besides, he'd been filling up too much of her daydreams. She was embarrassed thinking about it and hoped it didn't show.

"Hmm. Mysterious. I like that. So, why are you in need of inspiration?"

"I'm thinking I might do some painting, and it's been a while."

"Cool. What do you paint?"

"Glassware and chairs, sometimes coffee tables, picture frames," Dani said absentmindedly, caught in the flow of three paintings hung together. Gentle yellows gave way to harsh metal colors, which then morphed into screaming reds on the third painting. Each had echoes of the other in the shapes and waves, but they clashed in a huge way. The black frames and minimal white matting really set them off.

"This artist really surprises you," she observed.

"She does. Although, I've had that for a while. Not many people are partial to all the dissonant color and the price is pretty steep. So, glassware and chairs? Primitive stuff?"

"No," Dani laughed, "I paint *on* the glassware and chairs and other odds and ends. Silly stuff. Whimsical. Really just doodles."

"There's quite a market for stuff like that down here."

"Really?" Dani said. "I can't imagine people really buy that stuff."

"You'd be surprised. They love fun art like that for their fancy beach houses. It really sells. Serious art is a little harder to move."

They talked about the market for Dani's work, and she helped him set up a new display with the figurines he'd shown her over the weekend. Before they knew it, it was lunch time.

"You want to go grab some lunch? I usually close up for an hour around now."

"I'd love to, but I need to return my friend's car. She might have plans and I told her I only needed it for the morning."

"Well, come by if you need more inspiration," Jeremy said hopefully.

"I will," Dani promised.

When Dani arrived back at the cottage, Meg was washing windows in the sunroom. The whole house sparkled.

"Needed to expel some nervous energy?" Dani asked as she plopped down on one of the sofas.

"I figured the house could use it and I didn't have anything else to do. I'm going grocery shopping after lunch. I started a list in the kitchen, feel free to add anything."

"Okay," said Dani. "I'd help you clean but I don't think you left me any dust bunnies."

Dani went to the kitchen, studied the page-long list Meg had started. She added, "*Four gallons of Jell-O for the Jell-O wrestling Thursday.*"

As she was eating her lunch, Dani noticed the small shed in the corner of the back yard. Strange she hadn't noticed it before. She put her dishes in the sink and walked outside. The little shed had a moon and star carved above the door and ivy creeping up its sides. Inside there were garden implements and a potting bench. A window on the far side of the shed let in plenty of sunlight. Dani found a switch and turned on the light. It was "a clean, well-lighted place" as Hemingway would say. She was never a Hemingway fan, mostly stuck to the CliffsNotes, but that phrase had stuck with her. Clean, well-lighted places inspired her. This place would be perfect.

Now, all she needed was someone's old junk to paint. Hopefully, she'd find that tomorrow at the estate and yard sales she'd mapped out. Charlotte was coming along. It was her kind of adventure. She loved ferreting out treasures in unlikely places.

# Charlotte

Charlotte typed Martin O'Keefe's name into the search engine on the computer terminal at the public library. She didn't know why, but she couldn't bring herself to research him on her own laptop back at the cottage. She'd stopped by the Rum Runner, but he wasn't due to be there again for two weeks. She didn't have that kind of time. Any moment now, she'd lose her nerve. All she had to do was ask the bartender about him and she could have probably saved herself this trip, but she couldn't bring herself to say his name out loud.

As it turned out, there were lots of hits for Martin O'Keefe. Too many for her to reasonably check out, so she narrowed her search. She typed *Martin O'Keefe Irish folk singer.* This time there were fewer hits. After several sites full of shamrocks and set lists, she hit on his. She almost squealed when she saw his face on the screen. She poured over the site examining every word and following every link. He was forty-five and he really was a native of Ireland. He wrote most of his music, but did a few covers. He performed mostly in Oceanside and other beach towns in the area. She read about his family, with no mention of a current wife, only mention of a son in Ireland.

After borrowing headphones from the desk, she listened to every song available through the website. She went back to the calendar page to examine his show dates. He would be in Sweet Beach, of all places, this Sunday night at a Mexican place on Second Street. What was an Irish folk singer doing at a Mexican place? She hoped that didn't make him as desperate as it looked. She jotted down the time and place, smiling to herself as she folded up the note and put it in her purse.

She'd silenced her phone while in the library, but once outside again, she realized Brett had called.

"Hey, it's me. Look, I'd like to understand what's going on. It doesn't make sense to me. I hadn't realized anything was wrong. I knew you were a little annoyed I didn't take you to California with me, but this sounds like more than that. If you need some space . . ." There was a long pause, and Charlotte found herself holding her breath, but then Brett's message continued in a more business-like tone. "Fine, if you need some time, take it, but at some point I'd appreciate it if you could call and we could talk about this."

Charlotte deleted the message and dropped the phone in her purse. She didn't want to talk about it. She had nothing to say.

# THURSDAY, APRIL 18

## Dani

**D**ani hefted her box of new-found treasures out to the little shed in the back yard. She carefully unpacked each piece. After more than half the day spent traipsing all over Oceanside and the surrounding county, she was a bit disappointed to only have just a few things to show for it. Charlotte had been a shrewd negotiator. She'd gotten some great deals but forced Dani to walk away from several things she would have bought at any price. She looked at the prize—an iced tea pitcher and four glasses on a serving tray. She thought of what she might paint to make it a matched set. She unpacked the wooden window frames that could be painted and fitted with glass or mirrors. A small park bench and some glass serving bowls, including a beautiful punch bowl and ladle completed her lot.

She would start with one of the smaller bowls to get her creative juices flowing and test her deftness with the brush. It had been many years since Dani had painted anything but a wall.

When she was decorating Joe's townhouse, Dani and Joe had delighted in going to yard sales on the weekends, exploring the surrounding countryside. They would look for a small mom-and-pop-type restaurant to stop in for lunch and peruse the local real estate guides looking for their dream farm. Dani would carry home all kinds of broken and battered furniture and frames and dishes and decorations, and then she would take them to the basement where she spent her evenings transforming them into masterpieces. Joe had always said she should sell them and make their fortune, but she'd laughed at the idea. She did sell a few things at the Spring Market fundraiser for Jordan's preschool, but that was for charity. This would be different. There would be no art teacher judging her work and nobody bidding for it out of obligation. She wanted to create something . . . what, beautiful? No, inspiring. She didn't pretend to be an artist. She would see what each piece wanted and then she'd try to create its new life. She felt butterflies in her stomach, as if she were about to get away with something. She set a bowl on the rickety workbench and watched it. She tried to picture a vine of daisies swirling around it, but her phone rang and she saw her home number.

How was she ever going to sort out her own heart, if she let herself be dragged back into their world and their issues night after night? Just today she'd had two calls from Jordan. One was to tell her she got a B- on her spelling test and Daddy wouldn't let her watch television after school. She'd also called in the morning before school and left a message on Dani's phone while she was in the shower. She said she wanted to go over to Jillian's house that afternoon. How was it that Dani was still the authority when she wasn't even living in the house? Thank God Joey was too young to use a phone, or she could just imagine the incessant ringing. The phone was still buzzing. She answered and was at first relieved to hear Joe's voice instead of Jordan's, but then the conversation quickly regressed to the same conversation they'd been having for the past three days.

"I just don't understand. Can't you help me understand?" he asked.

"I can't explain it."

"Well, you need to try. You can't just walk away from our life."

"I'm not walking away. I'm taking a break. I need this, Joe. I thought you understood that."

"I understood that you wanted a few extra days, but this is more than that. At least give me a return date."

"I can't."

"Yes, you can. It's pretty simple."

"It's not. God, if it was simple, I wouldn't be here. I just need some room to breathe, to figure out why I'm so unhappy."

"That's the part I don't get! When did you become so unhappy?"

"I haven't been happy for a long time. I just get through the days, doing what needs to be done."

"I'm sorry we've been making you so miserable."

"It's not you guys. It's me. *I'm* not happy!"

Joe was silent. Dani cried softly.

"I want to understand, I do," he said. "But you're asking a lot of me. The kids aren't easy. I need to get back to work. I'm trying to figure out if I'm losing my wife. I know you've been tired of your job and the kids can make you nuts, and God knows I wish we had more money, but Dani, I love you and I want to fix this. You have to let me help."

"You can't," she said. "You can't. I wish you could, but I have to figure this out for myself."

"And you don't know how long that will take?"

"I don't. We've had this conversation every day for three days now. Would it be okay if we didn't keep doing it?"

"You don't want to talk to me now?"

"Not every day. I told you I need some space, and if I have to keep explaining myself and dictating menu plans, I can't be here. I need to be here, not there. That's the point."

Joe said nothing.

"Look, I do know I'm asking a lot of you. I promise I'll make it up to you."

"Right."

"Joe, I love you. Please just let me do this."

She heard him sigh.

"Okay."

"I'll call you after the weekend."

He didn't say anything.

"I love you."

Finally, she heard him whisper, "I love you, too."

## Meg

It was a gorgeous day. Meg decided to go for a walk on the beach. Wasn't she a lucky woman to be able to do that on a day like today? She slipped off her shoes, and in moments she was sweating from the effort of walking in the deep sand. She was out of shape. This she knew. Peter stopped at the gym every day on his way to work. He found the time to keep his body in the same shape it was in when he played football in college. He looked good, always had. Whenever Meg complained about the time he spent at the gym, he would say it was necessary for his success. He needed to look good for the jury. She knew his handsome face and trim body played a part in his success as a trial lawyer.

She wondered what he really thought of her body. She definitely didn't have the body she had in college. Five babies, no free time, and a nearly absent husband would do that to a person. She'd put on a little more weight with each pregnancy, and she'd gained even more since Logan's death. She was probably forty pounds heavier than she was on her wedding day. Granted, she'd been ridiculously thin on that day. She had starved herself for weeks to fit into the gown. In the pictures, her collar bones protruded in a frightening way and her shoulders looked bony and angular. Back then it was all about getting in the dress.

She wished she had the energy, even the desire to lose weight. Peter never mentioned her weight, but she knew how much he noticed appearances. It was usually the first thing he mentioned when describing a client or coworker. "God, that woman was a moose," or "No one could take their eyes off her—what an ass!"

Sand clung to her ankles, and somehow even her elbows, by the time she reached Sweet Beach. She sat on the steps to the boardwalk and wiped the sand from between her toes. She really wasn't a beach person. Sand irritated her. She hated the way the tiny crystals lodged themselves in the creases of the car seats and the cracks in the floor. She never felt truly clean when they vacationed at the beach and the feeling followed her home each summer. She put on her shoes and began walking on pavement, happy to have solid ground beneath her again.

She headed for the church she'd gone to on Sunday. Maybe the priest was hearing confession. When she reached the church, it turned out that confession was over, so she wandered the church garden. There were little paths and benches scattered about to encourage dawdling. Meg meandered through the pathways, noting the perennials poking their little green tips out of the ground. At home, what was left of her own garden would be a few weeks behind, but here the bulbs below the leaves were already waking up. She stopped to admire a carpet of snowbells underneath a weeping cherry tree just beginning to bud.

"It's quite a sight, isn't it?" said a voice behind her.

She turned to see the same priest she'd spoken to on Sunday.

"I admit a weakness for the snowdrops, every year I order more of them," he confessed.

"I love them, too. They always make me feel hopeful," Meg told him.

"That's what spring is about, isn't it? Hope."

Hope didn't begin to cover it. She immediately felt silly for coming to the church. How could she tell a stranger, priest or not, about her fractured world? If she told him about Logan, he would probably tell her Logan was in a better place. She was tired of that explanation. She hadn't been to her church at home since the new young priest at her parish told her she should be celebrating, not weeping, because her baby boy was with God.

"What brings you here today?"

"Oh, nothing really. I was going to go to confession, but I'm too late."

"Ahh," said the priest. "I'm available now, if that's what you need."

Meg felt the tears begin. The priest took her elbow and guided her to a nearby bench. He waited while she gathered her thoughts. She shouldn't be here. She should be home with her family. So why did the idea of going home cause her throat to constrict?

"I'm sorry," she said.

The priest pulled a tissue from the folds of his robe and handed it to her.

"I don't know why I'm here."

He nodded.

"I don't even really have anything to confess."

He smiled, waiting.

"I left my family and I can't go home," she blurted. Ever since she was little, she'd been unable to keep anything from priests. When her mother dragged her to confession, she'd be in the box so long, the priest would eventually say, "Let's pick this up right here, next week."

Her mother would admonish her not to "talk the father's ear off" but she couldn't help herself. It was something about that collar that just opened the floodgates for her every time. She'd plan on keeping it brief, but then she'd get started and feel that if she was keeping anything from him, God would know. So she'd blather on. Except about Peter. She'd never told her parish priest about sleeping with Peter before they were married, even though she knew at the time that she would marry Peter so it didn't seem like such a sin.

"It's not that I don't love my children. I do. I really do. And I'm pretty sure I still love my husband. I just can't breathe there."

Meg paused and took a deep breath. She wiped at her nose and eyes. "I lost my youngest child two years ago. He was three."

"I'm sorry," said the priest, nothing more.

"I miss him so much." Meg stared at the tissue, tearing it in her hands. "Everyone else has moved on. Why can't I?"

The priest handed her another tissue and she blew her nose.

"I've always done what was expected of me. I'm a good mom. A good wife." Meg laughed. "I'm sure it doesn't sound like that to you right now." She blew her nose again with the disintegrating tissue. "I'm sorry. I'm wasting your time." She stood. "I really better go." She rushed out of the garden before the priest could say a word. She ran down the sidewalk, frantic to get back to the safety of the cottage.

---

## Charlotte

Charlotte spent an hour at the library e-mailing Will and studying Martin's site before heading back to the cottage. As she passed a T-shirt shop with a cluttered window and bad lighting, she decided to stop in. Obviously, the owner was in need of her services.

A foreign-looking man studying a racing form raised his eyebrows and said, "You need T-shirt?"

"Maybe," she said. "But first I'd like to talk about the potential for improvement in your business."

"Huh?" He set down his form.

"Do you sell a lot of shirts?"

He shrugged his shoulders.

"I can change that," she said, and pulled the extra stool beside the counter over, climbing up and digging in her purse for her card.

After she'd explained her ideas for brighter lighting, more professional signage, cleaner layout, and popular music, the man asked, "How much this cost?"

"Not as much as you'd think. You can do most of this yourself. I'd just provide a plan including a new layout, lighting recommendations, contacts for reasonable sign companies, and suggestions for an appropriate playlist."

"This cost a lot?" he asked.

"I'm reasonable," she said. The key was getting a few stores on board, the rest would follow.

"You bring me plan and then I decide."

"Fair enough." She didn't usually work on spec and she guessed he might stiff her, but she needed some work. One shoe store in a strip mall wasn't going to keep her busy. "I'll be back tomorrow to take measurements and pictures."

"What that cost?"

"Nothing. It's part of the plan."

He smiled and looked at the card she had given him.

"Okay, Charlotte," he said (pronouncing her name "Char-lot"). "We see you tomorrow."

"Thanks, Mr. Abib, I'm looking forward to working with you."

He nodded and went back to his racing form.

When Charlotte arrived home, she found Dani wrapped in a soft pink afghan sitting on the couch and sipping a glass of wine in the fading sunlight.

"Hey, how was your day, Picasso?"

Dani shook her head. "I don't know what I'm doing."

"That makes two of us."

"I talked to Joe again. He's frustrated."

"Of course he is."

"And I don't know what to paint. I spent the whole afternoon out there, just staring at the stuff we bought. This whole thing is crazy. We shouldn't be here."

"Wow, this seems serious; hand me that wine bottle."

"How come you're so fine? No one else is," asked Dani reaching for the bottle and giving it to Charlotte.

"We're here aren't we? We already pissed off our husbands. So what's the point in being miserable? We need to capitalize on this time."

"But that makes it sound like we're here for fun."

"Aren't we?"

"No! My life isn't working anymore. I'm not happy. I didn't stay here so I could party with my girlfriends. I stayed here to figure things out."

"So it's really a midlife crisis!"

Dani smiled. "Well then it's a really boring, pathetic midlife crisis."

"Until now!"

"I was kidding. This isn't a midlife crisis."

"Of course that's what this is. I'm all for it. I say we embrace it. We should drink a lot and do something crazy."

"We already are drinking a lot."

"True," said Charlotte, taking a sip from the bottle.

"And staying here in Sweet Beach is kind of crazy."

"Not crazy enough!"

"What's not crazy enough?" asked Meg, walking in the door.

"Charlotte thinks that we're having a midlife crisis and we need to be doing something crazier than abandoning our families and drinking too much at the beach."

"I think this is pretty much my limit on crazy," said Meg, taking the bottle from Charlotte and going in search of wineglasses.

"I landed another job today," said Charlotte.

"What?" called Meg from the dining room. "You're kidding."

"Nope," she said and told them about the T-shirt shop and Mr. Abib.

135

"What do you know about redecorating retail stores? I thought you only did upscale offices and homes. I can't picture you in a T-shirt shop," laughed Dani.

"*And* a shoe shop," Charlotte reminded her. "It's all the same idea, though. I can do this. Besides, who spends more time in retail shops than me?"

"Uh, people who own them and work there," said Meg, handing Charlotte a glass and pouring one for herself.

"Well, being here makes me want to try something different. It makes me feel like someone different. I can do anything I want."

"Not *anything*," said Meg. "We'll have to go home someday."

"Why?" asked Charlotte, taking the bottle from Meg.

"You have a husband, for one!" sputtered Meg. "And a son, remember him?"

"They are both perfectly fine without me."

"You know that's not true," said Dani.

"I absolutely do know it's true. Maybe you guys are just here for a little extended vacation, but I might just stay." Charlotte drained the remainder of the wine into her glass. "Tell me, why are you here? You want to change your life, right? You're sick of it the way it is."

There was a stunned silence and then Dani said, "I think we need more of this," picking up the empty wine bottle and retreating to the kitchen for another.

"Well? C'mon Meg. This is our chance to change things. Don't you want more than a clean house full of perfect kids and a husband who makes more money than God? Things could be different. You could be different!"

"You know nothing about my life, Charlotte. Maybe I like it fine just the way it is," said Meg, her voice rising. "You're the one who has nothing to be running away from. One perfect, amazing, don't-we-all-wish-we-had kid. A husband who does most of the parenting. A fancy job, a fancy car, and you've never had to diet a day in your life. I'd trade you in a second!"

"Wait a minute," said Dani, returning with a new bottle. "What's going on here? It's not a competition! We all have our own shit to deal with. Being here isn't about judging, it's about just being."

"You're getting a little too new-agey for me, Dani," said Charlotte, holding her glass out for more.

Dani filled all of their glasses and sat back down.

"Look, I know I started this, but obviously we all have our own reasons for staying. I'm not going to pry into yours, but I'm here for you both if you need me."

No one said anything. Charlotte looked at Dani and Meg. How well did she really know her two best friends? How well did they know her?

"Now what do we do?" asked Meg.

Charlotte regretted challenging her friends' reasons for staying. They all needed to be here. That was the bottom line. She walked over to the stereo on the bookshelf, then turned back to them and smiled. "We dance!" she yelled and loud music erupted from the speakers. She laughed and dragged Dani to her feet. Soon they were all dancing. When the song ended, they collapsed on the floor.

"I don't think we're going to sort anything out tonight and I, for one, am exhausted," said Meg. "Good night, ladies." She disappeared up the stairs.

"I've got to find some food," said Charlotte, heading for the kitchen.

"I think I'm going to go work a little." Dani grabbed her jacket and went out to the garden shed.

---

## Dani

*No more judgment*, Dani said to herself as she picked up a paintbrush. She'd stared at the bowl all afternoon and hadn't been able to paint anything. Now she dipped her brush and began painting a vine of flowers around the clear glass bowl. She mixed together purples and blues for the flowers and buds and painted the leaves a bright lime green. She thought it looked happy, so she painted the word *happy* along the rim. After it was mostly dry, she turned the bowl over and signed her initials. It was when she was cleaning up the brushes that she realized she had signed the initials of her maiden name.

She smiled to herself, remembering the day she and Joe had gone to the DMV to fill out change of address forms for their licenses. They'd just returned from their honeymoon and moved into the house they were in now. Until that moment she'd planned to keep her maiden name, Godfrey. On a whim, she'd written Joe's last name on the form. After they were done, Joe had asked to see her new license. As he looked at it, a smile had crept over his face. Dani smiled now, picturing it. He'd pulled her to him on the sidewalk outside the DMV and kissed her while strangers filtered around them. Dani had never felt so connected to him. She was now, at least officially, Danielle Godfrey Harper. She'd never liked her middle name, Margaret. The only person who ever used it was her mother. And then it had never been a good thing. Advice always followed.

The early years with Joe were happy times. She remembered the first time she referred to Joe as "my husband." It was to the plumber who'd arrived to deal with a flooding basement. She'd loved the way it sounded. Saying "my husband" had made her feel like a grown up.

That seemed so long ago. Now she couldn't remember calling him anything. It was probably a normal thing for married people to rarely use each other's names. She'd said it more in the last few days on the phone than he had in the past few years. "We really take each other for granted," she said out loud to the empty shed before she shut off the light.

# FRIDAY, APRIL 19

## Meg

Meg pushed open the gate to the church gardens. She'd brought gardening gloves and a small trowel she'd purchased at the little hardware store in town. After her quick exit yesterday, she felt herself drawn back to the church. She hoped she would find the priest in the garden and she wasn't disappointed. He sat with his coffee and a newspaper at a little table under the arbor on the side of the building. Sun speckled the walkway and Meg could almost smell the lilacs that would be blooming in just a few short weeks. Father McMann looked up when he heard Meg come through the gate.

"Good morning, my dear. I see you've brought your work gloves, does that mean you're here to help?"

"I'd like to help, if you need it. I'm sorry about yesterday."

He waved away her apology. "I'm guessing you're a gardener yourself, so I probably don't have to tell you what needs to be done."

"No, you don't. I'll just get to work."

The priest turned back to his paper. He didn't seem surprised by her presence or her desire to work. As soon as she began, Meg felt herself relax. It felt good to get her hands in the dirt. Her mother had taught her that hard work was good for the soul. She pulled dead underbrush and fallen leaves out of the beds, making piles on the walkways to pick up later. She pulled off the stalks leftover from last year's perennials and added them to her piles. A few hardy weeds had survived the winter hidden under the blanket of leaves, and Meg yanked them out, too. She loved this part of gardening, the getting ready part. It was soothing to remove the dead, unneeded parts in preparation for new flowers to grow. Several hours passed before Meg stopped to rest. A moment later, the priest appeared with a glass of water. He sat beside her on the bench and offered her the glass. She took it gratefully.

"You've done good work."

"Thank you." Meg took a sip of the cool water. "Did you design this garden?"

"Not the original, but I add to it each year. It's my one indulgence." He looked around happily. "So what brought you back?"

"I'm not really sure. I've just always assumed if you're having a crisis, you should go to a church."

The priest chuckled.

"Actually, this morning when I got up, I felt drawn here," she confessed.

"God calling."

Meg shook her head. "That's not what I thought."

"You don't believe that God would call you specifically?"

"No, that's not it." She watched a robin rooting under the leaves at the base of a dogwood. "Lately, I find it hard to believe God has anything to do with my life." Meg stood up, not sure she wanted to talk about God. "I probably shouldn't take up any more of your time."

"I have nothing but time," said the priest, gesturing to the bench beside him.

"Well, if you can't tell a priest, who can you tell," sighed Meg as she sat back down.

He laughed. Meg unfolded her story for him. She told him about Peter and how they had been high school sweethearts, dating all through school, even being named prom queen and king, and then marrying after college. Her voice warmed as she told him about her children. How she'd given up teaching to stay home with them. When she told him about losing Logan and her inability to move forward since then, for once she didn't break down. It was as if she was reciting someone else's life. And thankfully, he didn't say that Logan was in a better place.

Then she told him about the girls' weekend, from Dani's first suggestion, to her attempt to return home and her avoidance of Peter's calls. When she was finished, she waited for him to tell her what to do.

"Guess you have a bit of figuring out to do," he said.

"Aren't you going to give me your priestly advice?" she pleaded.

"Sadly, I wasn't given the gift of perfect judgment and wisdom when I was given this collar. It's for you to sort out in your heart and with your God. I will tell you this: you needn't look to others for direction and understanding. Everything you need is inside you."

He got up and laid a hand on her head as she sat crying softly. Then he walked carefully over her piles of weeds on the walkway and went back into the church.

Meg sat on the bench in disbelief. Even the priest couldn't be bothered with her problems. She needed to get herself home before everyone thought she'd gone off the deep end.

She began clearing the debris away, filling a wheelbarrow and hauling it to the compost pile in the back of the garden near the dumpsters. When she was finished cleaning up, she walked home slowly on the beach. Peter probably thought she was nuts and would force her to go see that psychologist he kept mentioning. Was there anything really wrong with her besides sadness? People can live with sadness. They do it all the time. Maybe thinking she was supposed to stay here and have some big breakthrough was her own doing. She'd probably just wanted to be included in her friends' crises. She would eat some lunch and then head back to Sadlersville.

---

## Charlotte

Charlotte read the e-mail from Will. She sat at the terminal in the public library and tried to picture his life in Spain. He told her that in Spain everyone had wine with most meals, no one was in a hurry, and he got to come home every day at lunch for a few hours. He bragged that his soccer skills were improving, and that Teresa, his hostess, was teaching him some French in preparation for a trip they were going to take there in a few weeks. Charlotte tried to keep her motherly hysteria to a minimum as she wrote him back. How were his studies going? Had Spanish gotten easier? Was he playing on a soccer team or just kicking around? She did not ask him about the physical attributes of Teresa or whether he was also having wine with his meals.

When she was finished with her e-mails, she packed up and headed to the T-shirt shop.

There was a plump Mrs. Abib at the counter when she arrived.

"Good morning!" she called. "Is Mr. Abib available?"

"He not here. I can help," she said.

"Oh," Charlotte said. "I was speaking with him yesterday and told him I'd be in today to take a few measurements."

"Measure what?"

"I'm working on a proposal to help the business."

"Help, how?"

"Well, a more inviting layout would bring in more customers and better displays would increase sales."

Mrs. Abib furrowed her brow. "Not need," she said.

"Well, it won't cost anything for the proposal. If you don't like what you see and don't think it will help, you don't have to buy it."

"You do what you like, but we no need," she said.

"I'll just take a few measurements, then," said Charlotte. Mrs. Abib watched as she pulled out her tape measure and scowled at her when she produced a camera. Charlotte worked quickly, anxious to be out from under Mrs. Abib's suspicious eyes. She felt like she had during the first year of her business, when she'd had to prove herself on every job. But back then she was young and her charm had opened many doors. Mrs. Abib didn't seem like someone who could be charmed easily.

When she finished at the T-shirt shop, she stopped in the shoe store to take measurements. The owner, Brad, hovered over her as she worked. She knew it probably wasn't her designing skills or salesmanship that had sold him. She'd landed that job after buying two pairs of four-inch heels and allowing his anxious hands to fondle her feet as he fitted them. When he'd asked what she did for a living, she'd told him about her business. He'd practically begged her to help him with the store. He was at least ten years older than her, wore a wedding ring, and he stared at her chest as he spoke. She dealt with men like him all the time. It would be easy money and she was kind of excited at the idea of designing retail space. She hadn't done anything like it since college.

Brad was happy to see her. After she'd measured the store space and taken a few pictures, he insisted on showing her his office, a tiny windowless room in the back of the storage area.

"Maybe you'd have some ideas for this space, too," he said, holding the door for her and guiding her in with his hand on the small of her back.

"What were you thinking?"

"I don't know. Something to make it more inviting?"

Charlotte snapped a few pictures and Brad held the end of the tape as she took measurements.

"Are you attached to this desk?" she asked. The desk consumed most of the room and was barren except for a lamp and a laptop.

"I'm not attached to anything," Brad said with a leer.

Charlotte declined his invitations for lunch and headed back to the cottage to start working on designs.

# SATURDAY, APRIL 20

❧

## Meg

**M**eg heard Charlotte and Dani leave the house before six that morning. She glanced out the window and noticed the ominous gray sky. A perfect morning for sleeping, but not for shopping at yard sales.

Her resolve to go home yesterday had washed out with the tide. At nine thirty, she dragged herself out of bed, poured some coffee, and called home, knowing Peter would be golfing. The weather inland was forecast to be beautiful. Even if his wife was still AWOL, he wouldn't miss his tee time.

She enjoyed hearing the kids tell her about their week. Phoebe had to show some houses, so she'd left Michael in charge. Apparently, Peter had dropped Timmy at someone's house Meg had never heard of. Sarah informed her it was a playdate with the son of a coworker. Meg was slightly impressed he'd done it on his own initiative, although he lost points for the fact it was just so he wouldn't miss his golf game.

She listened to the news of softball tryouts and camp registrations. She assured them Peter could fill out the forms. Lizzie rattled on about the presidential fitness test in gym class. She'd been able to hang on the rope the longest.

Michael didn't have time to talk; he was deep into a research project. He said to tell her hello and asked when she was coming home. Meg told them she wasn't sure, but she was working on it. Before

145

they had time to press her any more, she said a quick good-bye and hung up.

The whole day stretched ahead of her. It looked like the skies could open up any moment. Maybe she would go to the movies. What a treat that would be, to lose herself in someone else's story and forget her own for a while.

Meg made toast and opened the paper to the movie section. She'd never been to the movies alone. It might be nice to sit anonymously in the dark for a few hours. There was a family film and a drama playing at the local theater. Maybe she'd stay to see both.

The rain was really coming down as Meg drove to town. She parked near the theater, but stayed in her car. She was early. She watched the theater-goers running through the parking lot trying to stay dry. Timmy had explained to her that you stay dryer by walking in the rain, not running. He'd learned that on *MythBusters*. She smiled at the thought.

What had that priest meant yesterday? Were the answers really inside her already? Were there clues she could study like in the crosswords? Maybe it was like a rebus answer. Maybe there was more than one letter needed to solve it. How was that possible? She didn't even know the questions.

Her days were consumed by cleaning, shopping, doctor's appointments, volunteering at school, shuttling kids to practice, rehearsal, or lessons. Peter couldn't be counted on anymore to help with any of it. She should have demanded that he help, but she didn't want his help anyway. She put everything she had left into caring for her kids. Maybe it was some kind of sick mother-martyr thing, but she didn't want to trust them with anyone else, not even Peter. His absence gave her the excuse to fill every waking minute with her children's needs and avoid her own. Was that why she couldn't do anything except get through each day, as if it were a battle in some unknown war?

Would she be feeling this lost if Logan were still here? She'd be busy with preschool, probably still be serving on their board. She had never questioned her choices, her commitments, until Logan died. Suddenly, it had all seemed pointless. Marking time until they all disappeared—not that she thought her children would die, but they would leave. They would have their own lives. And she would be more than alone. The work she did was important, though, wasn't it? Someone had to make the meals, do the shopping, take care of the kids, donate the cookies for the PTA, drive the carpool, do the spring cleaning, and decorate for the holidays. Those activities were once important to her, and now, now they just felt like killing time.

The movie would start in a few minutes. Meg made her way into the theater, she bought the biggest bucket of popcorn they sold and asked for extra butter. As she settled in her seat, she realized that for once she didn't have to share her popcorn.

➢

## Dani

When the rain really started coming down, Dani decided they had to head back. They still had several planned stops, but there wasn't much point since most people were closing up shop. Charlotte tried to convince her otherwise, but she was anxious to get back to the shed and continue the work she'd started on the pitcher and glasses. Besides, she thought they had a pretty good haul. She'd found several old picture frames, a big box of glass Christmas ornaments, a small coffee table, and a lamp. The back of the Saab couldn't hold anymore, even if they'd found something else.

Stopping in a diner for lunch, Dani was happy for the chance to get out of the rain. The steady downpour was fraying her nerves. They talked about their found treasures and Dani's plans to paint them. Charlotte rattled on endlessly about her plans for the shoe store and T-shirt shop. Dani was mystified by why Charlotte was taking on these jobs but bit her tongue. We're all working this out in our own ways, she thought.

Their food arrived. After they'd eaten only a few bites, Charlotte's cell phone rang. She looked at it and frowned. "Peter again. The man is nothing if not persistent." Charlotte switched off the ringer and sighed heavily.

"What kind of relationship do you have with Joe?" she asked.

Dani thought for a moment, considering the question as she worked on her sandwich.

"I think it's pretty good. Not *From Here to Eternity* kind of intensity, but real."

"Does it feel like you're equally committed?" asked Charlotte.

"In what way?"

"Like, you know how when you're first dating, maybe even first married, you try. You make romantic gestures, say nice things, tell each other I love you on a daily basis. Do you and Joe still do that for each other?"

Dani gave it a moment's thought.

"I don't know. Joe used to work at it more than he does now, but that's because he's busy with work. It's not always roses and romance, if that's what you mean. We have our moments, though." Dani smiled, thinking of a recent afternoon when Joey was at a friend's house and Jordan was at school and Joe had surprised her in the middle of the afternoon. That had been pretty good. And long overdue.

"Why do you ask?"

"I just wondered if all guys give up and stop trying at some point in their marriage. Maybe they figure you aren't going anywhere so they don't have to work so hard."

Dani laughed. "That's pretty cynical, don't you think?"

Charlotte shrugged.

"What about Brett? I know you don't think he's trying, but maybe he's busy, too. Maybe you need to drop a few hints."

"I have, believe me. To him, I'm Will's mother and the lady who washes his undershirts, nothing more."

"Oh c'mon, I can't believe that."

"I think it began the moment my pregnancy was confirmed and it has simply been gathering speed ever since."

"We all changed when we became parents. Joe doesn't look the same to me now as before. Everything about our relationship is colored by the fact that we created these little human beings who are dependent on us. We all wish our relationships were different. I wish Joe and I could laugh more and have real sex more than once a month, but most days we're lucky if we can be civil and kind by the end of the day."

"It's more than that for Brett and me." Charlotte looked out the window at the rain. "He never looks at me anymore—really looks at me. I could shave my head and I don't think he'd notice. For Christmas he told me to go buy what I'd like because he didn't know what to get me. He never holds my hand or asks me anything deeper than what's for dinner. He never considers a vacation that doesn't include Will. In fact, we never really talk about anything except Will. It's like the lines that connected us now have to travel through Will to reach each other."

"Maybe with Will gone, this time could be good for you and Brett. Maybe you should go back and see if you can figure out your relationship without Will in the house."

Charlotte looked at her. "We had a whole month to do that before I came down here. It didn't happen; if anything, we're even more disconnected."

"Did you try?"

"I suppose I could have met him at the door wearing nothing but an apron, but he rarely even came home before nine. I tried to suggest dinner out or a movie, but he said this was a good time for him to focus on his work. It was almost like he didn't want to come home if Will wasn't going to be there."

"You have to talk to him about this before Will comes back."

"Actually, I don't. He obviously doesn't see anything wrong with our relationship. I can't make him address a problem he doesn't think exists."

"Then maybe you have to make him see it."

"I think that's what I'm doing down here. Not that it seems to be working, since his last message said he'd wait for me to call him after I finish 'my little crisis.'"

"Maybe he's just giving you space. Isn't that what you wanted?"

"Or maybe he just doesn't care."

# SUNDAY, APRIL 21

## Dani

Sunday morning arrived without regret for the rain the day before. The world sparkled with spring. Dani breathed in the cleansed air as she ran along the wet wood of the boardwalk. She looked in Jeremy's gallery as she passed and thought she saw a light on in the back. She stopped to knock on the door. Jeremy smiled and hurried to let her in.

"Surprised to see you here so early."

"I was running by and wanted to be sure you'd be here later; I've got some work to show you. I want to see what you think of it. It was slow getting started again, but I think I found my groove!"

He smiled. "I can't wait to see it. You look good Dani—you're glowing."

"Sweating like a pig is more like it. I didn't dress for the weather."

"Well, you look good for whatever reason. I don't mind a sweaty woman."

Dani giggled girlishly and told Jeremy she'd be back later. *Was he flirting with her?*

Whatever it was, she liked it. Smiling to herself, she sprinted along the beach back to the cottage. She showered and dressed more carefully than she normally did.

She knocked on Meg's door to ask if she could borrow her car. Meg sat up in bed, bleary eyed, and pointed to the keys on her dresser then dived back under her covers.

Dani pulled up in the alley behind the gallery and honked the horn. Jeremy came right out and helped her unload the park bench. He loved it, and was really impressed by the pitcher and glasses with the matching tray. He assured Dani they would sell and then invited her out for a cappuccino to celebrate.

As they walked together talking happily, Dani looked up and her heart froze. Peter Fillamon was walking toward them, stopping to look in restaurant windows. Dani grabbed Jeremy's hand and dragged him back to the gallery.

"What's going on? Did you see a ghost?" Jeremy stood next to her in the gallery doorway, still holding her hand.

"No, much worse. I've got to go. I'll call you later to see if you have any questions about pricing. I trust your judgment, though."

Dani looked down, suddenly aware they were still holding hands. She dropped Jeremy's like a hot potato.

"Are you sure you have to go? If you don't want to be seen with me, I could go bring something back."

"It's not you; it's Meg. I just saw her husband on the boardwalk and I'm sure he's down here to find her."

"Wow, this is like a movie. Let's follow him! It'll be fun."

Dani looked at Jeremy; he was serious.

"I don't think you get it."

"Sure, I do," he said, smiling.

"Sorry, gotta go!" She hurried out the back door.

Dani crept up the alley in Meg's car, expecting Peter to appear at any moment. She pulled out onto the street and headed back to the cottage. Once she was out of town and on the beach road she floored it. Flying into the driveway, she sprayed gravel as she screeched to a halt. She raced out to get the tarp she knew was in the shed. She was frantically trying to cover Meg's car when Charlotte appeared on the porch.

"What'd you do? Rob a bank?" she called.

"Help me cover Meg's car, I just saw Peter!"

Charlotte walked down the steps and stood watching Dani.

"Dani, he'll never find us. He doesn't know where we are."

"I saw him on the boardwalk."

"He's hoping to run into one of us. We'll just stay here."

"Is Meg up?"

Charlotte shook her head. It was almost one. "I think she had a late night and whatever she ate didn't agree with her. She was retching this morning."

"Should we wake her?"

"I don't think we should tell her he's here. Let him do his little detective thing and go home."

"We have to tell her. I can't keep something like this from her. This is her life."

"She can't get out of bed. She said something about too much popcorn and candy when I asked her what was wrong. I'm not sure she can handle the idea of Peter now, mentally or physically." Charlotte sat down on the steps and continued to watch Dani attempt to cover Meg's car unsuccessfully.

Dani settled for covering the back end so the license plate didn't show. She sat down beside Charlotte.

"This is nuts. Don't you feel like we're living in some soap opera, suddenly?"

"More like a sorority house."

Dani laughed.

Dani and Charlotte waited on the porch, keeping vigil for Peter. There was no chance he would find the house, but the sun was shining and neither of them wanted to tell Meg. Charlotte lounged in the hammock, but Dani remained on the steps.

"So, what did Jeremy think of your work?"

"He loved it. Said it would definitely sell."

"Maybe you'll become a rich woman and you can buy this place for us."

"Not sure his gallery generates that kind of money, but I promise I'll spend my first million on this place."

"It'll cost more than that."

"Amazing, isn't it? That so many people can afford a place like this? I mean there are thousands just in this little town and there are probably tens of thousands of towns like this. That's a lot of people with a lot of money. Where does all the money come from?"

"I don't know, but when you figure it out, let me in on it."

"Maybe I should take your car and go scout around for him," suggested Dani.

"That would be stupid. Peter would recognize my car."

"No, he wouldn't," said Dani.

"Of course he would," said Charlotte without lifting her head from where she was napping in the hammock.

"How do you know?"

"All men notice cars. They probably notice that before they even take stock of your boobs."

"Peter has never noticed my car or my boobs."

"Peter definitely knows your car."

"Does that mean he's noticed my boobs, too?" asked Dani.

"Stop worrying about what Peter thinks about your boobs. It's not important. What's important now is whether or not we have a good supply of wine in the house just in case we're trapped here."

Dani laughed.

The door opened and Meg appeared. "Did I just hear you talking about Peter and boobs?"

Dani and Charlotte erupted. When they'd pulled themselves together, Dani patted the seat next to her and Meg sat down.

"Peter's here," she said.

"What?" Meg jumped up as if he were right there on the porch.

"Not here at this house, but here in Sweet Beach. I saw him on the boardwalk walking around this morning. I guess he's looking for you."

"Did you talk to him?"

"No, he didn't see me."

"I guess I kind of expected this. He was getting angrier by the day and I haven't answered his calls for the last two days. I've just been calling the kids and Phoebe when I know he'll be gone. I don't know why he has to take this so personally. What should I do?"

"Do you want to talk to him?"

"Not really, but if I don't he'll just keep trying to find me. Everything is so black-and-white to him. He doesn't understand things aren't so clear to the rest of us. You would think as a lawyer, especially with the number of divorce cases he handles, he'd realize this world is pretty gray."

She sat down next to Dani. "What should I say to him?"

"I don't know what to say to my own husband, I certainly wouldn't know what you should say to yours."

"He just can't stand not being in control of things. I think maybe that's it. He likes to think he's in charge."

"Maybe he needs to learn he's not in charge of you," said Charlotte.

"I'll go talk to him. Ask him for a little more time."

Meg went to find her phone. Charlotte and Dani waited on the porch.

"How's it going with your shoe shop?"

"And my T-shirt shop," Charlotte corrected. "Okay. I don't think the shoe guy is serious about anything except getting in my pants and I don't think the Abibs will actually ever pay me a cent."

"Then why are you doing it?"

"It's a challenge. I'm bored with my other work."

"What are you doing about your other work while you're down here?"

155

"Mostly making excuses, but I did set up a couple calls next week to talk through proposals."

The door opened and Meg reappeared. "I called him," she announced.

"What'd he say?"

"That he wants me to come home. That he came down here to get me and he still loves me." She sat down on the steps and put her head in her hands. "God, what makes him think all my problems can be solved by him declaring his love for me?"

"All men think that," said Charlotte.

"Really? I thought it was just Peter."

"So what did you tell him?"

"I agreed to meet him, but I told him I'm not ready to go back yet. He wants me to meet him for a drink."

"Where?"

"Some Mexican place on Second Street. He wanted to meet me there in an hour, but I told him I'd be there at five."

Charlotte looked at her watch.

"I know he thinks if he can get me tipsy, I'll agree to go back."

"Can he?" asked Charlotte.

"No! I'm just going to have dinner with him. I need to convince him this isn't about him. Even though, the more I think about it, part of it probably is. I'm just going to talk to him, that's all."

"What's the name of the place?" asked Charlotte.

"El Sombrero."

"If you're going to meet him, I'm going with you," announced Charlotte.

"Me, too," added Dani.

"You don't need to come with me. It's not like Peter's going to kidnap me."

"We're just going as moral support," said Charlotte. "We'll even drive separately so he doesn't see us."

"We'll sit at the bar and not even look at you," added Dani.

"We'll be like your posse," said Charlotte.

"It's not necessary, but I appreciate it."

# Meg

When they entered the restaurant, Peter was sitting in a booth watching the door. He looked surprised when Charlotte and Dani walked in behind Meg. He stood up.

"So much for him not seeing you," muttered Meg as Peter approached.

"Well, I didn't expect all of you," he said. "I'm not armed or anything." He smiled, but his annoyance was evident.

"Hi, Peter," said Dani.

"Dani."

"Peter," said Charlotte. Meg didn't like the way Charlotte spoke so icily to Peter. She wished she hadn't told Dani or Charlotte so much, but it was good to have friends on her side, especially when it came to Peter. She'd always given him the upper hand.

"Charlotte. I think Brett is hoping you will call him."

Charlotte grabbed Dani by the arm and turned to Meg, "We'll be at the bar, if you need us."

When they left, Meg didn't move. She wasn't sure what was expected at this point. Should she embrace him like a long lost lover just to reassure his fragile ego, or should she sit coolly without touching him to make him nervous? Before she made up her mind, Peter put his arms around her. Meg felt herself reach up for him, out of habit. If he noticed her lack of enthusiasm, he didn't mention it. He helped her to her seat and hung her coat on the hook behind her.

"It's good to see you," he said.

Meg noticed the empties on the table and realized Peter had probably been drinking for most of the afternoon. She wasn't sure why that made her nervous, but it did. He was fortified; she suddenly felt vulnerable.

"I need to tell you before you even begin that I'm not leaving Sweet Beach today. I won't stay here forever, but I need some more time. It wasn't necessary for you to come down here."

"I felt it was since you weren't taking my calls."

"I'm sorry about that, but you weren't listening to me."

"What if there had been an emergency with the kids?"

"I talk to the kids every day."

"Meg, you can't do this. I get it, you're still hurting. Let's get you some help, but you can't just desert us without warning."

"If I'd given you warning, would you have let me come?"

"Of course I would. But maybe if you'd told me you were so unhappy, it wouldn't be necessary for you to leave to solve your issues."

A waitress appeared and Meg ordered a beer.

"We've been together for over twenty years. You know me better than anyone else. Do you think I'd stay down here if I didn't desperately need to? Can you really sit there and tell me honestly you didn't know anything was wrong? Oh, wait! You're never home—so how would you know? And even when you are, we never talk. You never ask how I'm feeling. It's like you're just waiting for me to forget him!"

"That's not true. I just don't know what to say. If you're not running the kids around, you're busy with the house or cooking or doing your damn crossword puzzles. When I try to touch you, you cringe."

"That's because you think if we just have sex, everything will be fine again!"

The waitress appeared with Meg's beer.

"Apparently, I can't do anything right." Peter took a long swing of his beer.

"You never asked me why I don't go back to teaching. Wasn't that supposed to be the plan once Logan was . . . once Logan didn't need me?"

"I just thought after everything, you'd want to be home for the kids."

"I do, but . . ." Meg bit her lip. She wasn't going to cry. She was tired of crying. She tore at her napkin and shook her head.

Peter reached across the table and took the napkin from her. "You know I love you."

She was trembling now. Silent tears fell to the table. "Peter, that's not enough. If you love me, you'd know I can't just move on, like our world is fine without Logan, like I can just stop crying and be over it. It doesn't work that way."

"How does it work, then? Everybody's sad, Meg. You don't hold the market on that. I'm sad, too. I miss him. But we have to resume our lives. We can't mourn forever."

"I don't know how to do that."

Peter took a drink of his beer and Meg pulled a fresh napkin from the stack on the table and wiped her face.

"Maybe we should have another baby," said Peter.

Meg shook her head, fury rising. "It doesn't work like that. I don't know you anymore. And you obviously don't know me. Why bring another child into this? You hardly see the ones you already have!"

She took a long drink, seething quietly. Peter ordered an enchilada for himself. When the waitress turned to Meg, she waved her off. For once, Meg found eating wasn't going to help.

Peter made small talk about the kids. Meg pretended to be interested and even tried to laugh as he told her about trying to help the girls with their hair, or how difficult it was get Timmy to dress himself in anything but his pajamas. He didn't ask what she'd been doing at the beach.

As she sat listening, she wondered—had their relationship always been about him? She remembered how lucky she felt when he had asked her out. All of her girlfriends had been jealous. Her own mother had been so proud. Everyone told her how lucky she was. It was like a broken record of her life until Logan died. She'd never stopped to consider that maybe Peter had been the lucky one.

Ever since she could remember, she only wanted to be Mrs. Peter Fillamon. She'd doodled it on her notebooks and written it on the back of a bus seat. Everyone knew she would marry Peter. She'd never wavered from that plan. And she'd always been the kind of girl who did what she was supposed to do.

Had she ever wanted something else?

Live music began. Meg recognized the Irish singer from a week ago. That seemed like a lifetime ago. She listened to the sound of Peter's voice droning on about his latest case, and felt herself aging. It was as if her skin were sagging by the minute, her hair thinning and the curls losing their bounce, the shiny blond being replaced by pale white. She felt herself disappearing, melting in a puddle of condensation from the beer Peter had just placed in front of her. She had to get out of there. She knew now better than she'd known a week ago, why she needed to be here.

She stood up and said, "It's been good to see you. It's helped more than you could know. Thank you for coming. I've really got to be going."

He looked at her in shock. He was halfway through a story about a colleague and his golf vacation.

"Meg, sit down. Finish your beer."

"No, I've got things to do. Please give the kids a hug for me," she turned to leave and he bolted from the booth. He hurried around a table and cut her off.

"What do you mean, 'you've got things to do'? Yes, you do. You have things to do for your children, for our home, for our lives. You can't just leave. Come back and sit down and finish your beer. We'll talk about this and figure out what needs to be done. Then you can get your things together and follow me back."

"I'm not going back tonight."

"Tomorrow then, I'll come stay with you. Or better yet, we'll get a hotel room."

His suggestive smile caused fresh anger to rise up in Meg. Her voice grew shrill. "No, you're not listening to me. You haven't been listening to me. I'm starting to realize maybe you've never listened to me. *I've* never listened to me! I'm not coming back tonight or tomorrow. I'm not sure when I'm coming back."

Peter took hold of her arm, trying to steer her back to the booth.

"Meg, you're making a scene," he hissed. "This is ridiculous. I don't know what kind of garbage your friends have been filling your head with, but it's time for this little fantasy to end. You need to come home now." Peter's voice was just above a whisper. Meg had never heard such intensity in his voice except when he would lean in and speak to a jury in the midst of a closing argument. Before she could respond, Dani appeared.

"Hey, Meg, I've got to get back. You ready?" she asked brightly.

Dani handed Meg her coat from the hook where she'd forgotten it and turned to Peter.

"Really good seeing you, Peter. Have a safe trip back."

Peter dropped Meg's arm. He looked at her and suddenly he laughed. "Fine, you go off with your girlfriends, but don't think you can keep playing this little game forever. And don't think I'm going to continue to finance this trip much longer. You'd better be home by the end of the week. I'll see you then." He turned and sat back down in the booth, picking up Meg's untouched beer and drinking without looking up.

When they got outside, Dani led Meg to her car and opened the passenger side door for her. "I'll drive," she said.

"Thank you. I needed to get out of there."

"That's what it looked like."

161

"Where's Charlotte?"

"She wanted to stay and have dinner. She said she'd keep an eye on Peter. I think she really just wanted to see that Irish guy again."

They drove back in silence. Meg was grateful Dani didn't say anything about what had just happened. Meg wasn't quite sure herself. As she sat looking at the passing landscape, she wondered who Peter was. She wondered if he was still the same person she'd fallen in love with. People change. Had he changed?

When they got back to the cottage, Meg made herself an omelet while Dani sat in the window seat keeping her company. When she sat down at the dining room table with her plate, Dani followed her.

"You know, when this whole thing started, I thought I was the one who didn't have a real reason to stay here. It's been almost two years. I should be over that by now, right?" Meg took a bite of her eggs.

"I wouldn't be over it," said Dani. Meg stopped chewing and looked at her.

"Thank you," said Meg quietly. Then she continued, "I understand what Charlotte's doing here. Obviously, she and Brett have issues. I mean, she hasn't even talked to him all week. And I figure you must have a really good reason since this was your idea. And look at you—you're rediscovering the artist in you. But I didn't understand what made me stay. Everybody says keep moving and the grief will recede, but it doesn't. Peter doesn't get that. It's not his fault, he is who he is, and probably I still love him anyway. But I have to figure this out for myself. If the grief never goes away, then maybe I have to figure out how to live with it, better yet, how to use it to live." She began eating her omelet.

Dani got up to leave, but paused, "Meg, I think you're the bravest person I know." She squeezed Meg's shoulder.

# Charlotte

Charlotte sipped her beer from the far side of the bar, out of sight of Peter, who looked shell-shocked. She imagined his little world was skewing pretty badly right now. She honestly didn't think Meg had it in her to stand up to his bluster. Charlotte knew his type. She worked for them all the time. Stuffed full of self-importance, with an ego that was actually wafer thin. Scratch beneath the surface and you'd find an actor playing a part. He'd survive. Once he sobered up, he'd go home, lick his wounds, and boss around a few paralegals. All would be well with his soul. He'd pretend it was his idea to give Meg the time down here.

Martin O'Keefe started his second set. How Peter had managed to pick this bar of all the places to meet Meg was almost comical. Or maybe it was fate. Charlotte knew so much more about Martin O'Keefe since the last time she saw him. She'd seen him shirtless, holding his newborn son and singing him a lullaby. Playing catch with that same child and teaching him to strum a guitar. His website was full of quick videos documenting a loving father. She wondered about his ex-wife. There were no pictures of her on the website, not even a mention of her name.

When the set was over, Charlotte ordered another beer. She watched Peter leaving. He was talking on his cell phone. She hoped he was calling a cab. He didn't look too steady on his feet. She studied the flyer about Martin she'd picked up from the stack on the bar. It listed his upcoming dates. She mentally noted the ones nearby. A man sat down on the stool next to her.

"Handsome devil, isn't he?"

She heard the accent, before she registered the question. She turned, her face immediately going red. He grinned at her.

"One of the Irish dancers from last week, right? Aren't you going to favor this Mexican crowd with your fancy footwork?"

She laughed. "That was my friend Meg; I'd have to have a lot more alcohol in me before you'd catch me out there on that floor."

"Then bring the lady a drink!" he called to the bartender.

She raised her newly filled glass. "I'm fine."

"That you certainly are." Martin smiled at her.

"I'm enjoying your music. You're very talented. Do you play other instruments as well?"

"I play all kinds of things," he teased.

Charlotte could not believe the man she had been lusting over for more than a week was sitting on this barstool, coming on to her like she was a freshman at a fraternity party.

"I imagine you do," she said with a knowing smile. Charlotte hadn't acted so brazenly since she *was* a drunk coed and it felt great.

"I've got to go back up, but you sit right there. Don't move. Hey, Chris, anything the lady wants, it's on my tab!" he called to the bartender. He leaned so close she could smell his aftershave and asked, "I know you know my name, but what might yours be?"

"Charlotte," she said, fluttering her eyelids shamelessly.

He smiled. "Lovely." He held her eyes a few seconds longer than necessary, but long enough to send heat searing through her. Finally, he turned, jumped up on the little platform stage, and picked up his guitar. He turned to his partner on the keyboards and said something before they launched into a fast, jig-like number. They played several more upbeat tunes that actually got some of the patrons sitting close to the stage to start clapping along. Charlotte watched him. Now and again, he would smile at her. She hadn't felt a thrill like this since high school. She looked down at her wedding ring. If it wasn't so tight, she would have slipped it off right then.

When he finished his last set, Martin thanked everyone, set his guitar down, and returned to the bar. He asked her if she lived around here and she said she did—with two roommates. He asked her what she did for a living and she told him she was doing some design work for the shoe shop out on the coastal highway and a few other places.

"Design work?" he asked.

"I'm an interior decorator," she explained.

"That must mean you have good taste."

"I do," said Charlotte, with a wink.

They flirted and Martin teased her endlessly, glancing at her ring, but never mentioning it. Charlotte was sure he'd ask her back to his place, and when he didn't she wasn't sure if she was disappointed or relieved. The lights came on in the bar and his bandmate yelled for him to help break down the equipment.

"I've got an early call, but I'll see you soon," he said. She nodded. Then he kissed her chastely on the cheek. He laughed a little as he pulled away. Then he was gone.

Charlotte's entire body tingled. What the hell was she doing? All evening she could hardly contain her excitement at where she thought their flirtations were leading. She knew she would have been powerless to stop it. In a weird way she was grateful it hadn't gone anywhere.

This wasn't the last she would see of him. She folded up the flyer with his schedule and tucked it in her jeans. She tried to pay her tab, but was told it was taken care of. Driving home, her head spun. When Brett's face appeared in her thoughts, she tried to brush it aside. She didn't want to think about him tonight. She wanted to think about the possibilities of Martin O'Keefe and not about the price she could pay for it.

When she got to the cottage, it was dark and quiet. Instead of going inside, she sat on the porch railing and lit a cigarette. She didn't want to go to sleep. She would wake to reality and right now she wanted to stay in the dream that had been her evening.

Behind her she heard the front door open. Meg appeared in the doorway.

"Charlotte?"

"Yep."

"Want some company?"

"Sure."

Meg sat next to Charlotte on the railing and turned down the cigarette she offered.

"Did you talk to that Irish guy?"

"I did more than that," Charlotte was glad it was dark, so Meg couldn't see her blush.

"Really? Oh my God. You're kidding, right?"

"Nothing really happened. We just talked. He kissed me good-bye."

"Are you sure you want to be doing this?"

"I'm absolutely sure I *want* to be doing this. Now, if you're asking *should* I be doing this? I don't know." Charlotte took a deep drag of her cigarette. She waved it in the air, "For all I know, Brett's doing similar things with his hygienists."

"He wouldn't."

"No, probably not," Charlotte had to agree. Secretly, she wished he was, then Meg's words wouldn't make her feel so guilty.

"So how were things with Peter?"

"He was pretty mad. Did he stay much longer after we left?"

"No, he just finished his beer and called someone and took off."

"I'm sure he either called a cab or is staying in town. He'd never take a chance on a DUI. Something like that could ruin him."

"Not to mention, kill someone."

"That, too."

"So, what did he want?"

"He wanted me to come home, of course. And earlier today I was ready to. In fact, several times this week I've thought I should go back. But once he told me I *had* to come back, it changed everything. I realized he has told me what to do for twenty years."

"It worked up until now, didn't it?"

"Yes, it did. And I can't say I was unhappy all these years. Maybe I needed someone directing my life. But everything's changed. He thinks he can tell me how I should feel. And that . . . that's not possible.

"How'd that sit with Peter?"

"He seemed more annoyed that I wasn't doing what he wanted than that something might really be the matter. It was like I was a disobedient child and he was here to collect me. He never even asked what I've been doing all week. Or even why I was here in the first place."

"Guess you have a lot to figure out."

"I guess so."

Charlotte leaned into Meg, resting her head on her shoulder. They heard cats scuffling a few houses over. Meg took Charlotte's cigarette and stubbed it out.

"Charlotte?"

"Uh-huh?"

"What are you doing tomorrow?"

"I don't know, why?"

"Do you want to go bungee jumping?"

"What?" Charlotte laughed.

"Really. I saw a sign for it in town. I want to do something I would never have done a week ago."

"I don't think my stomach would be up for it, but I'd go watch you do it. I was planning on picking out carpet and tile samples for the shoe store."

"Wow, that sounds like fun," said Meg, very deadpan.

"Depends on your definition of fun. It could be. Want to come along?"

"I don't know."

"A week ago, you wouldn't have been choosing carpet for a sleaze ball shoe store owner," said Charlotte.

"That's true," said Meg as she got up. "Maybe I'll start with that."

Charlotte smiled.

"Good night."

"Good night, Meg."

Charlotte lit another cigarette. Maybe she was becoming a smoker. She did need to call Brett eventually, but not tonight; tonight she didn't want there to be any Brett.

# MONDAY, APRIL 22

## Dani

After her run, but before she cloistered herself out in the potting shed, Dani tried to call Joe. She figured she could catch him just after Jordan got on the bus, when Joey would be clamoring to watch *Thomas*. No one answered. Dani looked at her watch. Maybe he'd driven them to the bus and gone to run errands. After last night's scene with Peter, she was feeling like she needed to check in with Joe. He hadn't called her since their painful talk last Wednesday and Jordan hadn't called much either. She left a message for Joe to call her and took her phone to the shed. When her phone rang a half hour later, she answered assuming it would be Joe, not even looking to see the incoming number. It was Jeremy. She didn't remember giving him her cell number, but she must have.

"Hi, Dani, I've got great news!"

"Really?"

"I sold your bowls, plus the pitcher and glasses set."

"Wow, I can't believe it."

"How about meeting me for lunch and I'll write you your first commission check?"

"That would be great. I'll come down around one, would that work?"

"Perfect, I'll see you then," he said happily.

She smiled to herself. Maybe she really was an artist. Somebody had actually paid money for her work, even if it was just doodling. She couldn't wait to tell Joe.

At noon, Dani went in to take a quick shower. Stepping out of the shower, she caught her reflection in the mirror. She didn't look so bad. It had only been a week of running daily, but her legs looked firmer and her stomach a bit less droopy. She searched for something clean to wear. She'd have to go to the laundromat this afternoon or buy more clothes. She did her makeup carefully, even though it meant she would be late, scolding herself for worrying so much about what Jeremy thought of her appearance.

She was still embarrassed about holding onto his hand yesterday. It was only because she'd been freaked out by the appearance of Peter. Hopefully, Jeremy hadn't picked up on her silly crush. She wanted this art deal to work and her unwanted admiration might ruin that. Hopefully, he hadn't read anything into it.

When they got together that afternoon, he didn't mention it, only asking if her own husband would be coming to look for her soon. She shook her head and laughed. She knew Joe would wait for her. He wasn't the type to make the big scene. In some ways, she wished he would come banging down doors in Sweet Beach to find her.

Dani and Jeremy sat on the porch at the Pelican. Jeremy told her about the couple who bought the glassware and the older ladies who purchased the bowls for gifts. He said he'd had inquiries about the bench and several people had said they would be back. After they ate, he presented her with her check.

"I should probably frame it instead of cashing it, but I really need the money."

Jeremy smiled. "You have a real talent. You know what people like. I think you should consider a career in this. Maybe you could set up a website. I can help you. You're welcome to use my computer; it's completely underutilized as it is."

Dani blushed with pleasure. It was exciting to imagine.

"Jeremy, eventually, I'll have to get back to my life."

"Why? You could make a living here doing something you love."

Dani looked at him. His eyes were a dark green, nearly black. He smiled at her as she studied him. For a moment, she almost reached out to touch his soft curls.

"I'll think about it."

---

Back at the gallery, Jeremy asked, "Why don't you come in? I could show you some programs on the computer for building websites."

"Tempting as you are, I've got to go do laundry, or I'll be spending tomorrow in my underwear!" Dani laughed.

"A sight to see, I'm sure," said Jeremy as he raised his eyebrows and smiled.

"It might frighten you as much as it does me," she joked.

Jeremy didn't laugh. "I'm so glad you stumbled into my gallery. Your work is a great fit and I enjoy your company."

"Well, I can't thank you enough for how much you've helped me."

"Will I see you again soon?" he asked.

"I'll try to have some more pieces for you on Wednesday."

"Well, think about what I said. There are great possibilities here."

Dani was certain Jeremy wasn't picturing the same possibilities she was and she turned before Jeremy could see the desire in her eyes. Walking back, she scolded herself. She was married, for Christ's sake. And he was young enough to be her son. Well, maybe not that young, but still too young for her. She could never abandon her family and start a new life here, but it was kind of fun to imagine. Maybe she could have been an artist like she dreamed. She envisioned herself living in the cottage, painting until the wee hours of the night, and then spending her mornings at Jeremy's gallery working on the computer. Laughing with him about the people who came in. Eating leisurely lunches at the Pelican.

When she reached the cottage, she gathered her laundry and a book from the stack she'd purchased at the Bookateria. She needed to get back down to see Libby soon. So far most of the advice in the books she'd read felt like platitudes. "Follow your dreams, model yourself after someone you admire, imagine the life you want and then make it happen, blah, blah, blah." As if it were that simple.

There was no one in the house to give her a lift, so she set off on foot. She wondered why Joe hadn't called. He must have gotten her message. Certainly, he hadn't been out of the house all day. What would they be doing? Besides, Joey should be napping by now. She fished her phone out of her pocket and peered at it over her laundry bag. No calls. On a whim, she dialed Joe's work number. He answered immediately.

"Dani?"

"Hi. What'd you do with Joey, tie him to a file cabinet?"

"No, he's at the Montgomerys."

"What's he doing there?" The Montgomerys were their nearest neighbor. They shared an elementary school bus stop. Dani had probably spent hundreds of hours with Cheryl Montgomery at that bus stop when you added it all up, but she didn't really know the woman. They talked about the weather and school activities, and Cheryl spent a great deal of time telling Dani about her church. In fact, she invited her practically every week. It was awkward.

Cheryl's kids were always dressed neatly and stood quietly waiting for the bus. Joey, on the other hand, ran around looking for anything alive to mess with—bugs, butterflies, salamanders, his sister. Jordan never hesitated to call him a name or shove him away if he got too close. Lately, Jordan stood with her earbuds in, ignoring the rest of them. Cheryl Montgomery and her neat little brood never failed to make Dani feel inadequate. There were five Montgomery children—three rode the bus with Jordan, one was only three, and Cheryl was home schooling the oldest, Joshua, because "the public school just doesn't meet his needs."

"Cheryl offered to watch Joey for me so I could get some work done. I know you're a little freaked out by the woman, but she seems completely sane to me. Her kids are well-mannered and she's been very helpful this past week. So this morning, when she saw you were still not back, she offered to take Joey for me."

"Joey doesn't know her."

"Sure he does, he was happy to go there. He loves to play with Miranda. Look, Dani, I'm trying to be patient with this little crisis of yours, but I have a life, too. I needed to get back to work. I can't just be out indefinitely. What am I supposed to say, 'Sorry, Brian, I'll be back to work when my wife figures out what she wants to be when she grows up'?"

"What *did* you tell Brian?" Brian was Joe's boss; he had assumed almost a father figure role in Joe's life ever since Joe's own father died several years ago.

"I told him you had a family emergency."

"That's kind of what this is."

"It sure is from this end."

"I'm sorry, Joe. Peter was here yesterday and he was a mess. He tried to force Meg to leave. I couldn't believe the level of his anger. It made me appreciate how great you've been about this."

She heard him sigh. "I'm doing my best. But I'm not going to be patient forever."

"Are you paying Cheryl?"

"She said we could work that out later."

"What did you tell her about me?"

"That you needed to deal with some personal issues."

"Wow. Did she go for that?"

"I guess. She didn't ask any more questions."

"I can just imagine what's going through her mind. I'm probably condemned to the fires of hell if I wasn't already."

"I get the feeling you already are."

"Hmm. Is she watching Jordan, too?"

"Just for an hour until I can get them at five. She said she'd give her a snack and get her started on homework."

"Probably sneak in a little bible lesson while she's at it."

"I don't think you're in any position to question the child care situation."

"I won't."

"So, can I ask what you're doing with your time?"

"You could, but I probably couldn't explain it right now. I'm actually walking to the laundromat as we speak. I'm good though. This has been really good for me." Dani didn't know why she didn't tell him about the painting. She'd tell him later. Hearing that Cheryl Montgomery was taking care of her family had taken the wind out of her sails.

"How's everyone else?" Joe asked.

"Meg's a mess and Charlotte is living in some bizarre alternate reality."

"Really? What's Charlotte up to?"

"Well, she's redesigning a shoe store owned by some guy who has the hots for her and trying to sell her ideas to a T-shirt stand owned by a skeptical older couple on the boardwalk. Oh, and she's become the lone groupie for an Irish folk singer."

Joe laughed. It was good to hear him laugh. It made Dani feel safe.

"I love you, you know that, right?" he said quietly.

"I do know that."

After Dani hung up, she tried not to think of her kids sitting in Cheryl Montgomery's kitchen eating homemade oatmeal cookies and reciting bible verses amidst the painted wooden Amish people and the lace doilies.

The steady noise of the laundromat was soothing and her eyelids kept closing as she tried to focus on the book she'd bought at Libby's store—*Forty New Attitudes for a New Life.*

# TUESDAY, APRIL 23

## Meg

On Tuesday, Meg decided to go shopping. Looking at carpet samples the day before had bored her beyond belief, so she declined Charlotte's invitation to the paint store. She needed a makeover of her own.

She drove to the mall in Oceanside and waited for the doors to open. In her excitement, she hadn't factored that stores near the beach don't open at 8:00 a.m. like they did at home. It gave her time to catch up on the crosswords from the last few days' papers. Each morning, she'd carefully cut them out and clipped them to the growing stack in her purse. At home, she finished the puzzle the day it was published. If she didn't, her day felt off-kilter and the undone puzzle nagged at her conscience. Sometimes, if she hadn't finished the day's puzzle, she'd find herself unable to fall asleep and finish the puzzle by flashlight while Peter slept beside her. Here she didn't feel that pressure. Still, it was good to have them done. Finally at 9:30, some of the bigger department stores opened.

Meg went first to the makeup counter and told the stylist she wanted a new look. She tried not to stare at the woman's hair, which was dyed a shade of red bordering on fuchsia or her fake eyelashes coated with purple mascara. When the stylist finished, Meg looked in the mirror. She hadn't had so much makeup on her face since her junior prom.

She liked the way the eye shadow made her eyes seem bigger and how the blush created the illusion of defined cheek bones. She purchased all the products, plus makeup remover and a perfume she tried while waiting for her order to be packaged.

Next, she walked to the first hair salon she found inside the mall. Again, she threw caution to the wind and went with the first person available. It was an older woman with hair plastered up into a strict bun with the ends coaxed to small spikes across the back of her head. She also had colored mascara, blue this time, and skintight leopard print pants with a hot pink top. Meg told her she wanted a new look. She pulled the headband from her curly blond hair. Meg had worn her hair in her trademark hairband for years. She never had time to style it the way she had before kids. Back then she'd spent hours on it. Sometimes Peter would pull the hairband off and run his fingers through her hair, tangling them in it as he kissed her. He would always ask her why she never wore it down anymore, and she would laugh and say there was no time.

Meg closed her eyes as the woman worked. She didn't open them until the woman shut off the hair dryer, spritzed a little hair spray, and said, "Ta-da!" Meg didn't recognize the woman in the mirror. The stylist had thinned and layered her hair until it framed her face and fell just below her ears. It looked lovely and simple. Meg blinked back tears and thanked her.

She felt like a new woman as she drove away from the mall. She was hungry for lunch, so she pulled in the drive-thru lane of a burger place. Studying the menu she knew by heart, it dawned on her that she didn't even like fast food but had turned in out of habit. She maneuvered her car out of the lane, soliciting a few angry looks from the drivers who were forced to back up to accommodate her. She stopped at the farmers' market and bought every piece of fruit that appealed to her, plus a huge bran muffin from an old woman with one leg. She took her picnic to the beach. After she ate she built a sand castle and then combed the beach for shells, collecting a pile to take home to her girls. She spent the rest of her afternoon wandering in and out of the shops in downtown Sweet Beach. She couldn't remember the last time she'd spent a day with herself. Had she ever?

Driving back to the cottage, Meg realized she hadn't cried all day. She'd thought momentarily about Logan at the hair salon while the stylist worked, but it had been a happy memory of his first haircut. She'd taken him to an old-fashioned barber shop and the old men there had made a big fuss, even pretending to shave him. He'd loved it. She had pictures of it somewhere. She couldn't remember if she'd ever had them printed.

When she got home, Dani was already at work in the kitchen. She squealed at the beautiful produce from the farmers' market, but shooed Meg from the kitchen so she could focus on the fancy risotto she was concocting.

Meg went to her room to shower and write a letter to Peter. He worked with the written word every day. Maybe if she wasn't there in person to arouse his anger, he'd be able to hear her. Wrapped in her towel, Meg sat on the bed with the scented paper she'd purchased from a little boutique at the boardwalk.

> *Dear Peter,*
>
> *I'm writing in the hopes this will help you know what is going on in my heart.*
>
> *I'm still hurting. I miss Logan every day. <u>Every day</u>. I thought if I just worked very hard at doing the things I was supposed to be doing—caring for our kids and our house—I would begin to feel better.*

*Everyone said Logan was in a better place, but I've never been able to believe that. Maybe that's selfish or maybe that shows how little faith I really have. I do know that he is still very much in my heart. At first, when I decided to stay here I thought maybe it was because being here would help me let go of him. But it won't. And I don't want it to.*

*This might sound crazy, but I think losing Logan may help me find myself. I've been so busy being your wife and the kids' mother that I'm not sure who I am. I've felt stuck in my own pain, unable to move forward. But for the first time in a long while, I feel awake, alive.*

*When you came down here on Sunday, I realized something else. You did miss me. But you didn't miss Meg, you missed the woman who makes your life run so smoothly. You miss the person who takes care of your house and your children and your meals. I hear you, right now, denying this. But Peter, you never even asked me why I left, or what I've been doing down here. You never asked how I felt.*

*I think I've been missing for years, and no one noticed, not even me.*

*As difficult as I know this time is for you, I hope you're discovering your own ability to take care of yourself and your children. Maybe you'll figure out that you don't*

*need me as much as you think
you do! I think our lives have been
intertwined for so long that our
own edges are blurry. I need to figure out where you end and I begin.*

*Most of all, I need to let Logan's life
change mine. I need for Logan's life
to have mattered.*

*Meg*

Meg sealed the letter, addressed it, put it in her purse to mail in the morning, and went downstairs. She sat in the kitchen window seat watching Dani work.

"I can't get used to how different you look."

"In a good way or a bad way?" asked Meg.

"Definitely a good way. You've had your hair the same way since the day I met you. It's just not what I expect of you."

"I'm thinking of trying lots of things no one would expect of me."

Charlotte arrived with her arms full of paint chips, fabric swatches, and tile samples.

"Don't you think you're going a little overboard on these jobs?" asked Dani.

"Absolutely," agreed Charlotte, "and it's so much fun."

"Somehow, I don't think the Abibs are going to go for a new floor," said Meg, noticing the flooring samples, "But you could probably get Brad to install marble if you showed a little more cleavage."

---

After dinner, Meg cleaned up the dishes. Dani sat in the window seat with a book as she sipped her tea.

"Dani?"

"Uh-huh," said Dani, not looking up or putting down the book.

"I'd like to run with you tomorrow."

Dani didn't say anything.

"Dani?"

"Huh?" said Dani still glued to her book.

Meg stopped what she was doing and sat down next to Dani. Dani looked up.

"Sorry. What?"

"I'd like to go running with you tomorrow."

"Really? Is this part of the new and improved Meg?"

"I've never done it before. I'd like to try. I still have most of the baby weight I've gained and I think it's time to lose it. Besides, exercise might help clear my head."

"It will do that."

"So can I come with you? You don't have to stay with me, just get me started."

"I'll run with you. I don't run very fast anyway, don't worry. I run around 6:30, if you're not up, I'll knock on your door."

"I'll be up."

"Good, it'll be nice to have company."

Meg went back to her dishes and Dani to her book. A few minutes later, Meg interrupted Dani again.

"Remember when we talked about God and whether he's involved in your life?" asked Meg.

Dani looked up from her book. "Wow, now that's pretty much out of left field."

"No, I'm serious. Do you think God's got a plan?"

"I thought we covered this."

"I've just been thinking about it more."

"Right now, I don't seem to have a plan of my own, I hardly believe God could spare the time to worry about my pathetically self-involved life," said Dani, sighing.

"Really? You don't think he cares?"

"I don't know, Meg. Now's not a good time to ask. Right now my life feels a bit off course. It would be nice to trust God is involved in this, but I've never believed that was how He worked."

"Huh," Meg considered this for a moment. "So how do you think God works?"

Dani dog-eared her place in the book and hugged it to her chest. "I guess I've always believed God is here in the good stuff, in the people who are kind—the ones that don't act like assholes. I guess I believe he might be here, but not that he's necessarily directing or controlling or even influencing my life. I think he assumes he gave me a brain and a heart and imagination and I will eventually figure this out."

Meg wrinkled her brow as she reflected on Dani's theory. "I think that interpretation of God hugely overestimates humanity," she concluded.

Meg finished the dishes and dried her hands on a towel as she looked at Dani who had gone back to her book. As far as she knew, Dani never went to church. How was it that Dani's faith seemed much more solid than her own?

"I'll see you in the morning, bright and early," she said as she left the kitchen. Dani didn't look up from her book.

# WEDNESDAY, APRIL 24

## Meg

The next morning, Meg and Dani walked the two blocks to the beach for their run.

"It's about a mile to the boardwalk. You can do that much."

"I don't know," said Meg.

"Anyone who's walking around on a daily basis can run a mile, trust me."

They ran slowly on the firm sand near the water, and to Meg's amazement, she made it. When they reached the boardwalk, Dani said, "I'm going to run down to the end of the boardwalk, it's another mile. Why don't you walk, and then when I catch up to you on my way back, you can run again."

"Sounds good," Meg said. She watched Dani running down the boardwalk. Dani never worked very hard at being beautiful, but she was. Meg envied her. She was always joking about her weight or her hair, but Meg would be happy with either. She had those Ivory Girl natural good looks. Her hair was a mixture of soft brown with blond streaks highlighting it. It was long and straight and thick.

Meg was tired of looking like a housewife. She never had to work at being fit when she was younger. Her body had been something she simply took for granted. She remembered how Peter had trembled when he touched her bare skin for the first time. They'd been in the basement of her parents' house. It was a rec room equipped with pool table, TV, and couch. If only that couch could talk, Meg thought. She remembered when her parents had gotten rid of it. She'd been home from school on break and saw the familiar green plaid frame lying abandoned on its side at the curb. The stained cushions were piled next to it already wet from the rain the night before. Her father had broken off the legs to get it up the stairs from the basement.

She and Peter had started dating when Meg was in ninth grade and Peter was a junior. Meg had worshipped him from afar ever since she was in sixth grade and met him at a party at Phoebe's house. Phoebe and Peter had attended Jefferson, the other elementary school in town. Meg had attended Engleside. When they reached sixth grade, kids from both schools were mixed together at the middle school. Meg remembered how the kids from Jefferson seemed so much cooler and older than the kids she'd spent the previous six years with. In retrospect, it was probably just that Meg had known the kids from Engleside when they couldn't tie their shoes and cried because they forgot their lunch. Meg had been drawn to the kids from Jefferson and became fast friends with Phoebe. The fact her brother was in eighth grade and gorgeous made it all the better.

Meg and Peter had said only a few words to each other in the years before she reached high school. Meg had been rendered mute by infatuation and immaturity every time she was near Peter, which was fairly often since she and Phoebe became inseparable. Meg finally admitted to Phoebe how she felt about her brother the summer before they started high school. Phoebe was sworn to secrecy, but once Peter and Meg started dating she confessed to Meg she had told Peter that past September.

Much had happened between Peter and Meg on that couch in her parents' basement, but Meg managed to hold him off for months because she'd wanted the moment to be perfect. She laughed at herself as she thought about it. The *perfect moment* turned out to be an afternoon when they were left home alone because her parents had to attend a funeral. Meg had been nervous and jumpy and Peter tried to be gentle and slow, not an easy feat for a horny sixteen-year-old. Meg assumed she was his first and had been shocked to learn years later that she wasn't. Apparently, he'd had his share of eager, drunk girls that flocked to the after-game parties the football players attended. Even as a freshman, Peter had attracted the girls. The parties had been held in a deserted field or a home when parents were out, so the opportunities were ample.

Meg and Peter stayed together all through high school, breaking up briefly in college, only to get back together when Peter appeared at her dorm one night to propose. She missed the passion they used to share. Before Logan died, they'd made love fairly often, but it had become kind of routine— more obligation or relief than passion.

Meg wondered about Peter now. He'd been so absent from their lives, she'd gotten used to running the house without him. No wonder he was struggling. He'd been so angry on Sunday night. She'd never seen him like that, but then again she'd never given him a reason to be angry. Had she always been so compliant? She loved Peter. She always would; she wasn't as certain he loved her in the same way. When he was in law school and they didn't have much, their love had felt like a lifeboat. She meant the world to him. But now, she seemed to be only a necessary part of his life as much as the car or the garbage men, something he noticed more when it didn't work.

Meg was startled out of her thoughts by the bench Dani had painted in the window of a gallery. She looked down the boardwalk for Dani and didn't see her coming, so she tried the door. It was early, and she was surprised when the door opened. A bell rang somewhere in the back as she entered. A handsome young man in jeans and a ragged sweater appeared.

"May I help you?" he asked.

"Are you open?"

"Not technically, but I'd be happy to let you look around if you'd like."

"I was just admiring this bench," said Meg innocently.

He looked surprised and pleased.

"It is fun, isn't it?"

"Yes, but I have to confess, I know the artist," Meg told him with a giggle.

Jeremy's eyes widened.

"Don't tell me. You must be Meg." He smiled warmly at her.

"And you must be Jeremy. Dani's spoken highly of you. In fact, we were just running together, but I needed a breather. I'd better get back out and keep an eye out for her."

"She's an amazing woman," said Jeremy.

Meg registered the intensity in Jeremy's voice and noted he said *woman* and not *artist*. She looked at him again, more carefully. He looked young, but not fresh out of college, probably still well under thirty. He had a natural, hippy guy kind of look, but there was something mysterious about him. Plus those curls and those gorgeous eyes, Meg could see why Dani was spending so much time with him.

"I think so, too," agreed Meg. "But I don't want to miss her, so I better run. I hope we'll get to talk again soon. Dani should invite you out to the house."

"I'd like that."

"I'll suggest it. Nice to meet you, Jeremy. Gotta run—literally!" Meg laughed at her own little joke as she left.

Outside, she looked down the boardwalk and spotted Dani. She waved to her and started running in place like she was getting revved up to race. When Dani reached her, Meg saw her search Jeremy's window.

"I just talked to him," Meg told her.

"Who?"

186

"Jeremy. Who else? I see why you're so captivated by him. He's a doll. Wouldn't we all just love to take him home?" Meg teased.

"He's a little young, don't you think?"

"Young can be good. They have more stamina."

"Meg! I'm a happily married woman. Besides, what would a man like Jeremy possibly want with an old fart like me?"

"I could imagine a young guy like Jeremy would want a lot with an older, experienced woman like you."

"You're insane," Dani told her and sprinted ahead, but not before Meg saw the blush creep up her cheeks.

After running with Dani, Meg didn't know what to do with the rest of her day. Charlotte was locked in her room having phone meetings with her clients from home and Dani was in the shed painting. She finished the daily crossword in record time, impressing even herself, and decided to visit the church garden again. Maybe there was more work to do or maybe Father McMann would offer her better advice than "figure it out yourself." She was still confused by his refusal to tell her what to do. That's what priests were supposed to do, wasn't it?

She found her gardening gloves and set off on foot. Her new commitment to fitness included not driving her car anywhere she could walk.

As she walked, she thought about the conversation with Dani the night before. She was sure there must have been another plan for her before she closed off all her options and settled down with Peter. What if she hadn't followed him to college? What if she'd gone to school somewhere else? Would they have still married? Every option she considered meant she wouldn't have produced her children, so maybe she was on the path she was meant to follow.

Meg was relieved to find Father McMann working in the garden. He was pulling tall dead grass from behind the bright yellow forsythia bushes next to the building and humming to himself.

"Father McMann?"

He turned at her voice and smiled. He didn't look surprised to see her.

"Meg, my dear friend, have you come back to join in this labor of love?"

"I have," Meg smiled as she held up her gloves.

"Lovely! If you could just bring me one of the big buckets by the gate for these weeds it would be a great help."

Meg hurried to find the buckets. After she helped him finish the weeding, Father McMann brought out a tray of seedlings. They were hollyhocks, one of Meg's favorites. As they worked together to prepare a bed near the trellis on the side of the garden, he asked if she had made any decisions about what she would do now. Meg shook her head.

"I just wish I knew what it is I'm supposed to be doing with my life," Meg said.

"Have you asked God about it?"

"I've had a bit of trouble praying lately, so the idea that he might have a plan for me, specifically, seems kind of vain. And the idea that Logan dying could be part of that plan makes me angry."

"That's understandable, but I'm quite certain God does have a plan for your life. Sometimes it's not entirely clear He's at work here, but later it becomes evident, a little like this garden."

Meg picked dead leaves from a bank of snow bells. She wanted to believe the priest. She watched as Father McMann cleaned up the empty plant containers and markers.

"Do you think after a while God gets tired of waiting on us?" asked Meg.

"God is more faithful than we are," he replied.

"That's probably a good thing."

Meg got up, dusted off her jeans, and handed him her trowel.

"I've got some mulch being delivered early Friday morning. Would you be available to give me a hand with it?" he asked.

"Sure."

"That would be wonderful. I'll see you then!"

"Isn't there more we could do today?"

"There is much work to be done today, but none of it involves a garden trowel, I'm afraid. I'll see you Friday, then?"

Meg nodded. She watched the old priest disappear into the church building. She had nowhere to go and nothing to do. She was completely unfamiliar with this feeling. Even when she was a little girl, her mother had kept her busy with piano lessons, dance class, play dates. Time was not something to be wasted. Meg looked around her at the garden; it was almost humming with the promise of spring. Flowers were snaking their way up through the dirt from the bulbs below. Bushes were greening up and perennials were appearing in what had looked to be barren ground. Such hope. She was normally inspired by the appearance of spring, but now she felt adrift.

How many times had she wished for more hours in the day or even just one hour to herself? And here it was, but she didn't know what to do with it.

She dialed her house. Phoebe answered and they talked for a while about the details of the life that used to be all she knew. Phoebe told her Peter seemed more resigned today. She assured Meg she was enjoying the kids. She was getting the chance to really know them. Meg watched an elderly couple walking along the beach hand in hand. She felt strangely unsettled. What if all she'd ever known wasn't enough? The afternoon stretched out in front of her. She could do anything she wanted. If only she knew what that was.

# THURSDAY, APRIL 25

## Charlotte

Charlotte spent Thursday morning, at Brad's request, getting to know Shoes 4 Everyone. He told her he thought she'd get a better idea of how to improve the place if she spent some time in the store. Although, judging by the intensity of his aftershave, what she really got was a better idea of how desperately he wanted her.

"I'm going to draw up a few ideas," she said, retreating to a chair near the front window, trying to stay in the safe zone of the public view. She opened her laptop and tried to piece together a few options so she could get out of the over-perfumed air. Brad hovered nearby, rearranging shoe displays.

"I'm still in the creating phase. I promise I'll show you something when it's ready."

She worked for almost an hour before Brad's hovering began to drive her nuts.

"I'm just going to go grab a cup of inspiration," she said when he approached again.

"I've got plenty of ideas I could run past you. Why don't we go back to my office and see what we can come up with?"

"I was thinking more like a cup of caffeinated inspiration," she said, smiling and grabbing her purse. Normally, in a situation like this she'd ask if he wanted anything also, but she was considering making a run for it and slipped her laptop into her bag, too.

Lucky for her, a mom with three school-age kids came in right at that moment.

"Looks like you've got business to attend to," she said. "I'll be in touch."

She hurried out, closing the door behind her and muttering, "Thank God." She turned to make for her car and ran into Martin O'Keefe, who was headed into the store.

"And what would you be thanking God for on this glorious morning?" he asked, smiling.

"Martin! What are you doing here?" she asked, taking in his wet hair, freshly shaven cheeks, tight jeans, and Guinness T-shirt.

"Actually, I was looking for you. The shoe place was my only clue—a bit like Cinderella, don't ya think?"

Charlotte laughed.

"Would you care for a cup of coffee?" he asked.

"That's exactly what I need," she said.

"I know just the place," he said and led her to a coffee shop only two doors down in the strip mall.

Her cell phone rang. She looked at the number. Brett. "Give me a minute," she said, holding up her finger. He shrugged and entered the coffee shop without her.

She couldn't ignore Brett's call again. He'd already called twice that morning. Obviously, he had something to say.

"I'm glad you finally answered," Brett sounded relieved.

"Is something the matter?"

"Well, other than the fact that my wife took off a week ago and doesn't seem to be intent on coming home, sure, everything's great."

"Very funny," said Charlotte, tapping her foot. "What do you want?"

"I'm sorry, I didn't mean to be flippant. I was calling because I have an unexpectedly light day tomorrow and I thought I could leave early and come down to see you. Maybe we could have din-ner? Talk a bit about all this?"

"I don't think so."

"Oh," said Brett. There was an awkward silence. She wasn't going to explain herself.

"Well, I just thought we needed to start sorting this out," said Brett.

"Sorting what out?" she asked.

"Whatever this is," said Brett.

"I don't know what this is," said Charlotte, sighing in annoyance.

"Believe me, I don't either, but I think talking in person might give us a start."

"No. That won't work. I'm not ready to talk. I told you I'd call you when I was."

"Yes, well, when do you think that might be?"

"I don't know."

"Charlotte, this whole thing isn't making sense. You're worrying me. I didn't realize we had such a big problem."

"You not realizing that we have a problem is the problem!" Charlotte hissed. Then she ended the call, silencing her phone just as Martin came out the door of the coffee shop and walked towards her. God, he had such a swagger. She wondered if he even knew it, if he practiced it at home. Brett used to have a little swagger himself. He was confident that people liked him. Charlotte had been attracted to his way of looking for the good in people and situations. He could always find something redeeming to say about anyone. He was ready to excuse anything.

Charlotte imagined he was already preparing to forgive her for this whole scene. He'd sounded irritated, for once, but Brett never really got angry. When they were first together that had been a major attraction for her. He was fun, it was impossible to ruffle his feathers. He didn't let people get to him. After growing up with a single father who yelled all the time, it was refreshing to be with someone who never raised his voice. But over time, his calmness had become an irritant. There seemed to be nothing she could do to provoke his anger. Lately, it was almost a game. Sometimes she couldn't help herself. She baited him, wanting a fight, anything to reveal there was still passion hidden in there somewhere.

She knew some of their friends shook their heads when they heard what Brett put up with from her. She was ready for Brett to call her on the carpet for something, anything. After a while, if someone never gets upset with your behavior, you begin to think maybe it's not that they're tolerant and patient, but that they just don't care. At least if a person was angry with you, you knew you mattered.

Martin handed her a tall cup. "One sugar, as I imagine you to be a woman who's only slightly sweet."

"You're good," she said and smiled.

"They all tell me that." His confidence was almost comical, but Charlotte suspected it wasn't unfounded. He led her to one of the tables set up on the sidewalk for customers. He'd also bought doughnuts and they shared them, playfully fighting over the jelly-filled one.

Charlotte told him about her "roommates," conveniently leaving out the part about all of them being married. He told her about the CD he was working on and about his recent trip back to Ireland to visit his son. He lit up when he talked about his son, and never mentioned his ex-wife.

He made up a song for her, causing her to blush and giggle like a school girl, and when he wiped powder off her face she almost swooned at his touch. She was ready to follow the man home, but Brad poked his head out of the shoe store and called, "Charlotte? I've got something I need you to take a look at!"

"Be there in a moment," she called. "The man is driving me crazy. He has trouble keeping his hands to himself. And he's married!"

"I could have a word with him," Martin offered.

Charlotte laughed at his chivalry. "No, it's a job. I can handle it. I've had much worse, believe me."

"Sorry you have to go. Perhaps I could take you to lunch somewhere a little more private?"

Charlotte felt her whole body heat up at the thought of being alone anywhere with him.

"Uh, I've actually got to stop in at my other job, but I could meet you somewhere near the board-walk. How about one at the fountain, and we can stop at one of the fry stands?"

"My kind of woman," said Martin, brushing her arm as he gathered up the trash on their table. She shivered at his touch.

Over fries, Charlotte asked him about Ireland. He assured her it was as green as the stories claimed, but there weren't any Leprechauns that he knew of. She wanted to hear about his childhood and he regaled her with stories that were probably exaggerated, but very entertaining. He was charming and funny. Charlotte loved listening to his accent. Even when he was talking, he seemed to be singing.

·"But what about you, lass? I've talked on and on and heard nothing of you."

Charlotte didn't want to tell him about her boring life as an interior designer. She didn't want to tell him about her husband the dentist, or their beautiful house which was always featured in the Tour of Homes each summer. Instead, she told him about her son who was away in Spain on an exchange program. She told him of her fears that he would be corrupted by a European teenager, of her worries he would want to go there to live some-day. She avoided any mention of Brett, and Martin didn't ask.

"You look much too young to have a thirteen-year-old son," said Martin, as he pushed his plate away and rested his chin on his hand, gazing at her. Charlotte blushed from the compliment and his hungry eyes.

"Flattery will get you everywhere," she laughed.

"Oh, but I mean it. You're a beautiful woman," he said. "How about I make you dinner tonight at my place?"

When was the last time Brett had called her beautiful?

"I'd love to," she said, glancing at her phone, which was lit up with texts from both Brett and Will. "But tonight is my night to cook. We kind of take turns and Thursday is my night." Meg would love to hear they had a schedule.

"I'm not sure I can take no for an answer," said Martin with mock-pain in his voice, "You wound me." But he smiled and got up to take the trash from her. "I'm playing at the Pelican tomorrow night. Maybe we could get a late supper afterward?"

"I'll try to be there," said Charlotte.

"You'll try?" he asked.

What was she doing? All she'd been thinking about for days was getting Martin alone and now here he was offering it and she was waffling.

"No, I'll be there," she said. He leaned down and placed one slow, soft, chaste kiss on her lips. Then he looked at her from only inches away. He didn't need to say a word, she knew what that look meant. If she was wax, she would have melted right there.

"I'll be there," she said again.

"I'm glad. Guess I better let you get to your work now."

Charlotte smiled, wishing she was leaving with him. Instead, she walked to the Abib's T-shirt shop. Why hadn't she gone with him? She didn't need this job and odds were that she'd never see a cent from it. But she hardly knew Martin. Where was this crazy desire coming from? She couldn't remember if she'd ever been this hungry for Brett. She must have been, but back then she'd been young and hungry for everything.

Now, she was a completely different person. She'd grown up and so had Brett, but had they grown in the same direction? It certainly didn't feel like it. Brett was more stable now, more constant. He wasn't nearly as exciting as he had once been. His passions had cooled. He rarely wanted to argue politics or world economics with her. There'd been a time when they would have debated far into the night and through several bottles of wine, before the intensity of their talks and the suspense of the sex to come became too much for them and they wound up in bed. Sometimes they didn't make it to the bed. But those days seemed so long ago. Now she could as much imagine having sex with Brett on the kitchen table as walking on the moon. Besides, Brett was always worried they'd wake Will up or, heaven forbid, he'd see them. It drove Charlotte nuts that he refused to lock the door; he insisted Will would knock and he didn't want to give him the message that he wasn't welcome in their room. It was impossible to have a decent orgasm with the door unlocked.

-●-

## Meg

Meg sat on a bench in the park, struggling with her crossword. She'd needed to get out of the house, but wasn't up for more running. The muscles in her legs felt tight as drums. So, she'd found a little park near town and had gone for a lazy walk before settling on this bench. Thursday puzzles didn't normally take her this long. The theme for this one had something to do with death. Maybe that's what was causing her to stumble. What rapper co-founded Death Row Records? D_D_E? Hmmm.

She was distracted by the squeals of the children arriving at the playground. There were five of them. Two looked preschool age and immediately claimed the swings, kicking their legs higher and higher. Two were toddlers, swaying about on new legs, tripping over fallen twigs and their own feet. They mostly stuck to the sandbox where periodic battles ensued over the rights to the dump truck. The other child was barely crawling. He had been placed on a large blanket but kept creeping to the edge to sample the grass. His mother would scoop him up, fish out the grass and mud from his mouth, and set him back in the center of the blanket and he would begin the cycle again.

Meg couldn't take her eyes off the children. Even as adults, it seemed people hadn't progressed beyond the sandbox. She saw it all the time. Some sailed by, oblivious to those around them and under them, not noticing the ones they kicked over mid-swing. Still others toiled day in and day out, fighting for their share of everything. And then there were those who seemed to be constantly struggling, only to find themselves starting over again and again, just like the infant inching across the blanket.

A woman about her age, maybe a little younger, moved across the grass, pulled by two overweight bulldogs on a double leash. When she reached the bench, she plopped down, jerking the dogs to a halt. One immediately began gagging and the other accosted Meg with his snuffly nose.

"Brutus, leave the poor woman alone," said his keeper as she dragged him over to her side of the bench. Meg reached in her bag for a napkin to wipe the drool dripping from her pants. She smiled politely at the woman and watched her attempt to get both dogs to sit. She managed to get one dog to sit down by leaning all her weight (which was considerable) on the dog's hind end. The other one was having none of it and simply stood staring off in the distance, straining against the leash.

"Suit yourself," the woman said as she sat back down with a heavy sigh and began rummaging through her backpack. She pulled out a badly bruised banana and began peeling it. She noticed Meg watching her and held the banana out to her, "Hungry? I've got another in my pack."

Meg shook her head.

"My name's Earlene. I don't think I've seen you around before and I know everyone. Are you new or just visiting?"

"Sort of both," Meg answered.

"Huh, well, do you have any dogs?"

"No."

"See, I'm a dog-walker by trade. I love the animals. I even have a few cats I look in on during the day, and one I actually walk on a leash. Animals shouldn't be left alone all day, you know?"

"I didn't know."

"You need a dog. I volunteer at the shelter in Oceanside. They've got lots of dogs that need homes. Or maybe you're more of a cat person, you kind of look like one."

Meg hesitated, and then ventured, "What does a cat person look like?"

"Well, they're generally skinny," the woman squinted at her. "Or they were once. They do things like read and listen to public radio, and they fill out those surveys that come in the mail with all the little tiny boxes to check off. Oh, and they watch people a lot. They study life, as opposed to dog people who tend to just experience it without knowing for sure what they're in for. You just seem to have a cat aura about you. Me, I'm a dog person, always have been. Not that I don't like cats, I do. Just prefer the honesty of a dog."

Meg didn't say anything. Earlene finished the banana and dropped the peel into her bag. Meg winced.

"I was a Pekinese in my last life," Earlene said matter-of-factly.

"How do you know?" asked Meg, regretting the words the moment she said them.

"I was. See, I believe we are all reincarnated, and we just keep coming back. We keep evolving. There are only so many souls, you see. So we take turns being the people. I'm certain I was a Pekingese in my last life. I was carried around in one of those dog carriers, and always wore matching bows and collars."

Meg continued to stare, not quite sure if there was a punch line to follow, and not daring to ask.

"This time around, I'm a person. But I identify with the little dogs so much. Feel like a kindred spirit. Whenever I get to walk a little dog, I always suggest to the owner she shouldn't put bows in the dog's hair, that it makes the dog a bit self-conscious. I can see it in their eyes because I'm the same way— hate frilly stuff, too. Now, dogs like Brutus and Caesar here, they're bound to come back as uptight little white guys who wear suits every day and carry a briefcase."

Meg looked at Brutus and Caesar and burst out laughing. She covered her mouth to try to contain herself. Earlene looked shocked at first, but then joined in the laughter. Meg was relieved that Earlene had only been kidding, but then Earlene stopped laughing and squinted at her. "I'm betting you were one of those fluffy cats with the long hair who had her own bed with a canopy. Your owners put pink ribbons in your hair and a rhinestone collar on you." Earlene squinted at her, picturing her previous life as a cat.

"You know, Earlene, this has been very enlightening, but I've got to run. Enjoy your day," Meg said and she picked up her bag and her work gloves and headed for the church.

"Oh, I will darlin'. Always do. You take care and think about that shelter down in Oceanside, lots of nice cats there," Earlene called.

# FRIDAY, APRIL 26

## Dani

Friday morning, Dani knocked softly at Meg's door.

"Meg, you running this morning?"

There was no answer, so Dani cracked the door open softly. Meg's bed was made and the room was neat as a pin, but empty. Maybe she had plans. Dani had worked until late in the potting shed and eaten dinner by herself after the others had already gone to bed. She wondered where Meg could be this early.

Dani ran fast on the sand. Her legs had grown accustomed to the deep footing. She could feel their newfound strength and stability. Her body was growing stronger, her muscles tighter, while her soul felt like it had been let loose. Her life at home seemed more distant than ever. The beach felt real. It seemed crazy that she could disconnect herself from her life that easily. When she was at home, the idea of leaving seemed impossible. But apparently it wasn't. Their world kept spinning and hers was opening up.

Dani reached the boardwalk in record time. She passed the Bookateria. The lights were already on. Libby was most likely perched on her stool with her cup of coffee. There were no lights on in Jeremy's gallery; she smiled to herself as she pictured his handsome face. She passed a homeless woman sitting on a bench talking to herself. Dani yelled, "Good morning!" and waved. The woman scowled.

On her way back, Dani stopped outside the Bookateria and leaned on a bench. She pulled her ankle up behind her like a stork to stretch out her quadriceps. The ocean was a gorgeous blue today, a reflection of the clear sky. There would be quite a few day trippers on a day like this. Jeremy would be busy. She hoped he would have time to look at the work she'd finished this week.

The bell rang as she entered the Bookateria. Libby called hello from where she sat cross-legged on the floor, reading a book. "Just had to check this one out. It's called, *Learning to Fall: the Blessings of an Imperfect Life.* Father McMann brought it in. He's a huge reader. But what else can you do in an empty church all day? How've you been Dani?"

"Pretty good, actually." Dani poured herself some coffee.

"You're still here, so I guess you haven't sorted out your life yet."

Dani smiled and sat down beside her. Libby handed her the book, and she scanned the back cover.

"Has anyone?" she asked.

"No one that I know of. So how goes the art business?"

Dani set down the book. "It's great. Jeremy's sold a bunch of my things and he really thinks there's a market here for me."

Libby looked surprised. "Amazing he's sold anything at all, the crowds have been low so far this spring. Summer will be here before we know it, though, and then things will start hopping." Libby smiled at her and clinked coffee cups. "You look different since I saw you last. The salt air must be good for you."

"You know, I feel better, like I can breathe again. I feel like I'm doing something meaningful."

"You don't feel you do anything meaningful at home?"

Dani shook her head. "Not really. I transcribe medical records. Other than that, I take care of my kids. Some days it feels like I'm just marking my place. I never accomplish anything. I do the things that have to be done, but I never make any progress. The same tasks, or ones just like them, have to be done again the next day. I pick up and vacuum, do the dishes, wipe the counters, but by dinner it looks as if I've done nothing but sit on my butt all day, it all needs to be done again."

"Ahh, the work of a mother. A thankless job, I'm afraid." She patted Dani's knee. "Someday there won't be messes to clean up, that's when life will truly be hard."

Libby hauled herself up off the floor and shuffled to the front counter to get a new pile of books. Dani flipped through the book in her hand. Libby was right. Joey had only been toilet trained for a few months and already Dani had forgotten the drudgery of changing his diapers every day. The work didn't go away; it just changed.

"C'mon, can't miss the morning," said Libby, offering Dani her hand and pulling her to her feet with unexpected strength for someone her age. She filled Dani's cup and led her outside to a bench facing the ocean.

They watched the waves break in easy silence. Libby took a sip of her coffee, and hummed a tune Dani couldn't place. Dani sighed.

"That sounds like a serious sigh."

Dani smiled.

"What's on your mind?" asked Libby, taking a sip of her coffee and turning to look at Dani.

"I know I should be happy. I've got a good life, so I don't understand this restlessness. My head keeps telling me to just be happy, but I'm not."

"What makes you happy?"

"I don't know. That's the problem."

"Sure you do. Don't think too hard. What makes you happy?"

Dani closed her eyes and lifted her face to the sunshine. "Quiet. The smell of garlic cooking. The woods in the summertime. Creating something—a picture, a poem, a list, a meal even. My husband, when he surprises me, or when he really listens to me and doesn't just pretend to. Making my children laugh. A neat, orderly house." She laughed to herself. "I guess the neat, orderly house isn't going to happen for fifteen years or so."

"If you're lucky. They don't always go away and they don't always take their messes with them. Besides, maybe by then you'll have grown fond of the mess." Libby's eyes twinkled with affection, most likely for her own mess makers. Dani realized she didn't know anything about Libby's world.

"Do you live alone, Libby?"

"I do. I rather like it. I was afraid of it at first. I've been surrounded by children or husbands for nearly sixty years. I like the quiet and the ability to go to bed without brushing my teeth and not offending anyone but myself."

Dani laughed. "How many children do you have?"

"I had two, but they're both gone now. I lost my son in Vietnam and my daughter to cancer. I do have a stepson from my second husband who visits from time to time. He misses his father dearly. Me, not so much, but then he had a lifetime with him and I only put up with him for twenty years."

"What happened to your first husband?"

"Don't really know. He might still be alive. He left one night to help a friend with car trouble and then called later to say he wasn't coming back. I'd guess that friend was female. I think he couldn't handle the pressure of supporting a wife and two children. He never really grew up himself, so it was for the best."

"Were you angry?"

"I didn't have time to be. I had two babies to take care of, and Herb came along eventually."

Jeremy's door was propped open, so Dani decided to stop in. He was busy with a customer, but waved to her. Dani waited at his workbench in the back, mindlessly eating the M&M's he kept in a clear glass bowl.

She heard the customer leave and Jeremy appeared. "Coffee?"

"I just had two cups with Libby."

"Wow, a two-cup conversation. Must have been serious."

Dani laughed. "Kind of," she said.

"Can I ask?"

"We were talking about what makes people happy. It made me wonder if anyone is truly happy."

"I'm pretty happy. I like what I do. I like my shop. I like the artists I encounter, like yourself, for instance. I like living by the ocean."

"Do you like being alone?"

"I'm not always alone." He blushed. "Most summers I hook up with someone who's just here for the season."

"You like it that way?"

"It's worked for me, so far."

"But are you happy?"

"I think I am. I take it from your line of questioning that you are not?"

"I don't know. I'm working on it."

"Can I help?"

"You already have."

"How's that?"

"By selling my creations and encouraging me to do more."

He smiled. "How about if I buy lunch for my most successful artist? I've just got a few things to take care of here. You could help and then we could grab an early lunch."

"I'd like that."

Dani spent the rest of the morning helping Jeremy pack up some things to ship to another gallery.

She helped him frame a new print and tried to tidy up the workroom. Her stomach was just beginning to ache when Jeremy pronounced it time for lunch. The coffee and M&M's were beginning to make her feel jittery.

They walked to the Pelican, and over lunch Dani told Jeremy about her kids and Joe. He was a good listener and kept her talking with a steady stream of questions. It might have been her imagination, but Jeremy seemed to change the subject whenever she talked about Joe. She found herself sharing stories of her younger self—the self who wanted to be an artist. It seemed surreal to be sitting in her favorite restaurant at the beach talking about her family, her life, and her dreams with a man who'd been a complete stranger only two weeks ago.

When she turned the conversation to him, Jeremy was not as free with the details of his life, telling her briefly of his childhood and talking mostly about his art education at several prestigious art institutes. He measured his words, doling out only what made him sound good. His vanity reminded her of how young he was and she wondered what she was doing here or, more to the point, what he was doing here with a woman clearly too old for him who was obviously emotional, possibly even unbalanced.

It wasn't until the restaurant started clearing out completely that Dani realized Jeremy had stayed way past a typical lunch hour.

"Oh my goodness, you've got to get back to the gallery."

He laughed. "That's the beauty of being the owner; I don't have to be anywhere."

"But we should get back."

"So we should," he agreed not sounding very convinced.

As they walked back on the boardwalk, Jeremy said, "I've really enjoyed this afternoon."

Dani's cheeks colored. She knew he was only being polite, but it sounded more like something you'd say after a nice date in the hopes of getting another. "I'm going to estate sales on Sunday. Hopefully, I'll find some new pieces to paint," she babbled nervously.

"Are you taking Charlotte with you again?"

Dani shook her head. "She's had a lot of work lately. It's the strangest thing, her commitment to these odd little shops. It's not her style at all."

"Maybe I could come along for company."

"Could you do that?" Dani asked, hopefully.

He laughed again, "Probably. Let me work on it. It could be a business trip. Who knows, maybe I'll find something for myself."

---

## Meg

It was still early when Meg reached the church garden. She should have been running with Dani, but she hadn't been able to sleep much the night before. She'd lain awake thinking about the message her mother had left on her phone. She'd demanded an explanation for Meg's "little adventure," as she called it. Was there any explanation? It was all so out of character for Meg. Her mother kept asking in her message if Meg had thought about what people might say. What would they say? That she'd had a nervous breakdown? Maybe she had. Maybe that wasn't a bad thing.

The garden was an oasis in the chaos surrounding it. The beach season was approaching, and Meg could hear the buzz of saws at the house next door and the shouts of workmen as they tossed down damaged shingles from the home across the street.

Near the gate sat a mammoth pile of mulch, its fragrant rot filling the air. Father McMann was nowhere to be seen. Meg sank down on a bench and closed her eyes. She meant to pray but, as always, no matter how good her intentions or how fervent her desire, her everyday thoughts took over and before she knew it she was calculating how much she owed Timmy's school for snack money, instead of communicating with God. Today, her thoughts drifted to Peter. She wondered if he'd gotten her letter. Despite the noise, she couldn't keep her eyes open, and eventually her head dropped and she slept sitting upright on the bench. A sudden noise woke her and she opened her eyes.

Father McMann was leaning on his shovel surveying the huge mound of mulch. He was dressed in coveralls, his white collar poking out beneath his chin. Next to him were two wheelbarrows and another shovel. He smiled when his eyes met hers.

"Glad you're rested. I don't know what I was thinking ordering this much mulch. It seemed like a good idea at the time, save time on weeding later."

"That it will, Father. Let's get to work," said Meg, rising and lifting a shovel.

By noon they had only made a small dent in the pile. It was clearly a job that would take several days. Meg was covered in mulch. She pulled off her hairband and wiped her brow.

"Enough for today, I think," said Father McMann, sitting down on the bench and motioning her to join him.

"To look at that pile, you'd think we hadn't even started," sighed Meg.

"Sometimes that's the way with work. You can't always see the fruits of your labor. I'm sure it's much the same with raising children," he turned to her and smiled.

"Pretty much," agreed Meg.

"And how are your children doing without their mother?"

"Surprisingly well. I guess I never appreciated how self-sufficient they can be."

"People do surprise us, don't they?"

"They do."

Meg pictured her children making their own lunches and sorting their laundry as Phoebe said they were doing.

"You know, Father, I think maybe I'm the one who needs them to need me so much. As long as they're completely dependent on me, I have a purpose. I've been thinking lately about what I will do when they don't need me."

"I can't imagine there is ever a time a person doesn't need his mother."

"I mean when they don't need me so much. I don't know what I will do with myself."

"I would wager, when the time comes, you'll be busier than ever and wonder how you ever had time to take care of children. Now, I've got my own children to attend to." He smiled and squeezed her arm before shuffling into the church.

Meg shook her head. She was tired of trying to figure it all out. She was tired of managing everyone's life, including her own. The memory of Logan was like an ocean she was holding back, measuring out just a cup at a time. The effort exhausted her. Being here in the quiet with no real responsibilities and nothing to distract her mind except crossword puzzles and too much wine, Logan was everywhere.

She stared at the pile of mulch. Logan would want to climb up to the top of it. He had always been the child who got into every mess he could find. She glanced around, then set down her shovel and began climbing. The pile crumbled beneath her as she struggled to make it to the top. She sat down, raised her arms in victory and felt the heat from the fermenting mulch seeping through her pants. Maybe she needed to stop stifling her feelings with lists and puzzles and busyness. Maybe she needed to let herself feel, even if it meant feeling the pain. She didn't need to always do the right thing. She didn't need to have it together. Maybe what she needed for a while was to be a mess. A big, fat, mulchy, smelly, overheated mess.

Two elderly ladies walked through the garden unaware of Meg perched atop the mulch. Meg stifled her giggles as she listened to them argue about where somebody's ashes had been placed. The garden looked different with the knowledge there were dead people about. Strange to think she had been raking and planting in someone's grand-mother. The giggles she'd been holding in exploded out in a snort.

The two women startled and then stared up at her. Meg waved. Shaking their heads, they contin-ued up the path and out the side entrance.

Meg climbed back down off the pile and headed for town. She was covered head to toe in mulch. She walked down to the water and used it to wipe off her arms and face. She took off her shoes and waded in. It was icy cold. When the waves hit her, she jumped in vain to avoid them. Laughing out loud, she plunged in head first, only regretting it when she came up for air, gasping from the cold. She ran out of the water. Grabbing her shoes, she looked around, shaking from the cold. Where had Charlotte said that T-shirt shop was? Maybe she could borrow her car.

Sixty degrees was warm if you were sitting on a bench in the sun, but it was bracing when you were soaking wet with ocean water. At least the mulch was gone. Meg's teeth were chattering as she climbed the steps to the boardwalk. She spot-ted Sweet Beach Tees right where Charlotte said it would be, across from the fountain on Main Street. Charlotte's Saab was parked out front.

When Meg entered the shop, Charlotte leapt to her feet. She'd been measuring a display rack and there were chalk marks on the floor around her.

"What happened?"

"I need your car!" Meg begged through chatter-ing teeth.

Charlotte fumbled in her purse and produced the keys. "Wait! Let me get you a towel so you don't ruin my seats!" She grabbed a large Hannah Mon-tana towel and shoved it at Meg.

"That towel no free!" exclaimed a foreign woman.

"I'll pay for it," said Meg.

"No worries; I got it," said Charlotte, leading her out the door despite Mrs. Abib's protests.

Once they were outside, she asked again, "What happened?"

"I went for a swim," said Meg, wrapping the towel around herself as Charlotte opened the car door.

"Have you completely lost your mind?"

"Yes."

Charlotte shook her head and burst out laughing.

"It just seemed like the right thing to do at the time." Meg looked at her defiantly.

Charlotte laughed harder and, after a moment, Meg laughed too. "Don't worry about the car. I can walk back when I'm finished."

"Thanks! Call if you want a ride," said Meg, slamming the door and roaring off.

-•-

## Dani

Meg, Dani, and Charlotte arrived at the Pelican just as Martin was getting set up on a small stage on the deck. The evening was warm and management was probably hoping the sound of live music might pull in customers lingering on the boardwalk. They found a table near the railing separating the restaurant from the boardwalk. It was a gorgeous night. Dani was glad she'd given in to Charlotte's insistence that they eat here.

"So, Dani, has Jeremy sold more of your things at his gallery?" asked Meg.

"Unbelievably, yes. I suppose I should be buying all the drinks tonight."

"I'm all for that," said Charlotte as she waved down a waiter to order.

"You must feel so great about your work selling," said Meg after they'd ordered a pitcher of beer.

"It's a weird feeling. Almost too good to believe, you know? But Jeremy thinks I've found a market."

Dani noticed Charlotte watching the singer as he finished his set. As he put down his guitar and turned to acknowledge the scant applause from the partially filled deck, Charlotte climbed up on the railing behind her and raised her beer to him. He smiled at her and Dani thought she saw him wink.

"Charlotte, what have you not been telling us?" demanded Dani.

Charlotte sat back down and shrugged. "I had lunch with Martin yesterday."

"What?" shrieked Meg and Dani.

"Just lunch. I ran into him and he bought me lunch." Charlotte's guilty smile gave her away.

"Are you nuts? What's going on with this guy?" asked Dani.

"Relax, it was only lunch . . . and coffee that morning," she laughed.

"You *are* nuts! I realize you and Brett are going through some stuff, but this is crazy. He's a real person." Dani pointed at Martin. "What are you getting yourself into?"

"Nothing I can't handle. I don't need the scolding, Dani. I'm not asking you to keep any secrets here."

Dani looked at Meg to back her up, but she only shrugged. Dani glared at her and Meg started to say something, but then took a drink of her beer instead.

"What?" asked Charlotte, looking at Meg.

"I didn't say anything," said Meg.

"That's just it. I didn't bring you guys here so you could judge me. I thought this would be a fun night out for us."

"So we're not here to see the Irish guy?" asked Dani.

"I like his music," said Charlotte, shrugging.

"And?" prompted Dani.

"We're friends. That's it."

Dani rolled her eyes. The forced casualness of Charlotte's tone gave away much more than the looks she kept shooting at Martin.

211

"So why are we here?" asked Dani. "To keep you from becoming more than that tonight?"

"No," said Charlotte, tearing her eyes off Martin and fumbling for a cigarette. "I just felt silly coming here by myself."

They ordered dinner. Martin finished his set, and Dani could see Charlotte clearly hoped he'd come by their table. She scanned the restaurant and didn't touch her food when it came. When he started his new set, Meg suggested they should head home.

"Not yet, it's too early!" exclaimed a clearly tipsy Charlotte who had only nibbled on a salad, but consumed three beers.

"I don't know what you're up to here, but I'm not interested in being a party to it. You're on your own," announced Dani, getting up.

Charlotte looked at Meg, who only shrugged and drank the last sip of her beer.

"Fine. Go, here are my keys, I'll find my own way home." Charlotte fished in her purse for her keys and held them out to Dani.

"Charlotte, this is clearly not a good idea," said Dani.

"For whom?"

"Come home with us. If you want to have an affair, at least make the decision when you're sober."

Charlotte watched Martin. She looked at her friends and grimaced. She put the keys back in her purse.

"Just let me stay to the end of this set. I want to talk to him."

Meg and Dani looked at each other and sat back down. When the set was over, Charlotte went to the bar and asked the bartender if she could speak with Martin. He shook his head, but delivered the message. Martin appeared moments later and pulled an empty chair to their table, turning it around and sitting on it backwards like a high school kid. He waved down a waitress, who handed him a beer.

"So what's with the chaperones?" he asked.

Meg waved and Dani held out her hand, which he ignored.

"Are you sticking around?" he asked.

"I can't."

"Why not?"

Charlotte looked pleadingly at Dani and then said, "It's complicated."

He didn't say anything.

"Are you playing anywhere tomorrow?"

"I'll be back down at the Rum Runner. You should come."

Dani got up. "We've got to go," she said, standing with hands on hips, watching them.

Martin smiled at Dani and then stared at Charlotte as he took a long swig of his beer. He leaned down, his mouth next to Charlotte's ear and whispered something. Dani could see Charlotte visibly shiver. Then Martin kissed her on the cheek and left. Charlotte sat for a minute, seemingly in a trance.

"Okay, satisfied?" asked Dani, taking her arm and pulling her up.

Charlotte said nothing but had a goofy, drunken smile plastered all over her face.

Dani sighed and held out her hand for Charlotte's keys. They walked in silence to her car.

# SATURDAY, APRIL 27

## Dani

On Saturday morning, Dani skipped her run. She was tired and there was too much to do. She loaded the pieces she'd finished in Charlotte's car. The plan was to drive Charlotte to the T-shirt shop and then take her things to Jeremy's. As she passed Meg's room, she noticed she was already gone.

"No Meg again. What do you think she's up to?" she asked as she entered the kitchen.

Charlotte looked up from her bowl of cereal, "Maybe she's got a man on the side." She smiled innocently at Dani.

"That's not even funny. You seriously need to think about this."

Charlotte waved her spoon at Dani. "I'm going to think about this as little as possible."

"Weird about Meg," said Dani as she peeled an orange for breakfast.

Charlotte shrugged and went back to her cereal.

Dani thought she knew Meg pretty well, but this time together was proving her wrong. They'd met when their girls were in preschool together. All those hours, standing outside the classroom waiting for class to end, they'd shared everything from their angst over toilet training to the debate with their husbands about vasectomies. Meg wasn't the affair type, but she was wrestling with something. Maybe it was Peter, but more likely it was Logan.

She was spending long hours at the church and she'd been so quiet the night before.

Dani watched as Charlotte typed rapidly on her computer. Just like Meg, Charlotte was a different person here. Dani had always looked up to Charlotte. She was successful, confident, happy. She said anything, did what she wanted, and she was the most capable person Dani knew. But here, she seemed vulnerable, searching, hungry, looking for trouble. Like Meg, whatever Charlotte was struggling with went way back before the decision to stay in Sweet Beach. How is it they could all be so close, and Dani not know her friends were so unhappy? Maybe the same could be asked of her. They told each other so much, but maybe some hurts went too deep to share.

Dani felt partly responsible for whatever it was Charlotte was headed for. Would Charlotte be acting like this if they were still at home? Dani thought of her own little flirtations with Jeremy, but that was different. Charlotte was serious. Dani wasn't. And Martin seemed awfully interested in Charlotte. She couldn't believe Charlotte would go through with it, but she felt powerless to stop her. Maybe questioning her every move wasn't the answer. Maybe being her friend was. But what did that mean?

"I'm sorry I'm hounding you about Martin."

"Apology accepted."

"What's he like?"

Charlotte stopped typing and a smile crept across her face. She blushed, something Dani rarely saw her do.

"He's amazing. I don't know him that well yet, but he makes me feel like a kid in junior high with my first crush. I know it's ridiculous, God, I'm forty-two years old, I didn't think I'd feel like this ever again."

Dani tried to smile, but couldn't. "What about your family?"

"It's like Brett and Will are from another lifetime. Maybe that's because Will is in Spain, and well, Brett's Brett. With Martin, I don't have a history. I don't have any baggage. It's just fun." She laughed. "And he is so incredibly sexy."

Dani gave her a questioning look.

"Oh, I know he doesn't necessarily look like a pin-up poster guy, but once he starts talking or singing, I totally melt. I do. He's amazing."

"Are you really going to see him today?"

"I am."

"And then what?"

"I don't know." She shrugged. "I'm going to see where it leads. All I know is I like being with the guy. I like not having to talk about serious stuff or kids or finances or home repair. I'm just going to go with this."

"You do realize if you throw away what you have for this guy, you'll just be talking about kids and finances and home repair and divorce settlements with him in a few years."

"It's not like that, Dani. It's not serious."

"But it changes everything."

Charlotte went back to her typing.

Dani's phone rang. It was Joe. She walked out on the deck to answer.

"Hi," said Joe.

"Hi. Is something wrong?" asked Dani. She hadn't expected his call.

"No, just wanted to touch base about Jordan's birthday party. She's giving me a hard time."

"Her birthday isn't until the end of June."

"I do remember when she was born. Give me some credit. She wants to start planning the party and every day she has more ideas. Every time I say no, she says you would let her do it. Every suggestion I have, she shoots down. She wants a sleepover at the mall at this point."

Dani laughed. It was funny to hear Joe stressing over a birthday party, something that wouldn't even have appeared on his radar until Dani asked him to pick up the balloons on the day of the party.

"Tell her I'll call her tonight and we can talk about it."

"Thanks."

"No problem."

"So, how're you doing?" he asked softly. The gentleness in his voice broke Dani's heart.

"I'm okay." She didn't want to say more, feeling unexpected tears rising.

"I'm glad, but I miss you."

"I know," said Dani.

"Guess you have things to do."

"Kind of."

"Well, I love you, please keep that in mind." Joe's voice wavered for a moment.

"I will."

"Okay, bye."

"Joe?"

"Yeah?"

"I love you, too."

---

Dani dropped Charlotte off at the T-shirt shop without another word about Martin, promising to have her car back in time for her to drive down to the Rum Runner that afternoon. She parked in the back alley and knocked on the door. When Jeremy opened the door and saw Dani, he grabbed her by the hand and dragged her inside.

"Jeremy, what's going on?" Dani laughed as she allowed herself to be pulled along. He led her to the front window of the gallery where her bench had been displayed. It was gone. Dani stared for a moment before she realized what he was telling her.

"You've sold it?" she shrieked.

"Not for as much as we had originally asked, but the man who bought it really had his heart set on it." Jeremy smiled at her. Dani hugged him and turned to look for her other things; they were gone, too.

"You have a fan," Jeremy said as he continued to smile at her. "I hope you have more for me."

"I do. Come see. Whatever you don't want, I'll take down to Oceanside to the other gallery you mentioned. I need you to write down the address or maybe tell me how to get there. I was going to run down there next. I've got to get Charlotte's car back to her by four; she's got a hot date."

"Really? I thought you were all married."

"Some more than others, I guess. Come on; come see what I've done." Dani raced back to the car and began pulling out several frames, a huge mirror, and the ornaments.

"I don't have anything left to paint," she told Jeremy as they brought the things inside. "But I think the sales tomorrow will be good so, hopefully, I'll find some more stuff. I've got to get more paint, too."

"I really would like to go with you tomorrow if you need me. Unless Charlotte's plans have changed," said Jeremy.

"Somehow I think she'll be busy with other projects."

"Then I'll keep you company," he offered.

Dani stopped wiping the glass on the mirror and turned to look at Jeremy.

"Really? Don't you need to be here?"

"Must I remind you again about the benefits of being the owner of an establishment such as this?"

"It'd be good to have you along. You can help me figure out what things are worth. Charlotte's great at haggling, but I'm a total pushover, I just pay what it says and never know if I'm being taken."

"What time do we leave?"

"That's the tough part; most of the sales are way out in the county, so I need to head out of Sweet Beach by 5:30 at the latest."

"I can do that."

"Jeremy, this is great," Dani gushed.

He smiled and turned to examine the ornaments he was unpacking. Dani continued wiping things off and Jeremy went to get his log book. He wrote quietly while Dani worked.

"Okay, I'll take them," Jeremy concluded as he closed his book and began carrying the mirror up to the front window.

"Which ones?" asked Dani.

"All of them. You're my hottest seller right now."

"You really want everything? You don't have to do this; I can take some stuff down to Oceanside, really."

He set the mirror on an easel and turned to Dani.

"Dani, I'm a business man, you know. I want exclusive rights to you. Right now you are one hot commodity, and I'd like to keep you here."

## Charlotte

When Dani showed up with the keys, Charlotte was just on the verge of getting Mr. Abib to sign the contract she'd drawn up. Never mind that she hadn't billed them for any of the hours she'd already spent.

"You give it some thought. I'll be right back," she said, meeting Dani at the door to get the keys.

"Going well?" asked Dani.

"Better than expected, but only because Mrs. Abib isn't here. You look happy. Things go well with your art?"

"Jeremy loved everything I made. He took all of it for his gallery. That's why I'm finished with your car already. I don't have to drive around to any other galleries. And he's going to go with me to the estate sales tomorrow, so you're off the hook."

"I would go if you need me," Charlotte offered.

"I know, but Jeremy really wants to come."

"You be careful, I think that young pup might be interested in more than your artwork."

"You're ridiculous. Not all men are after sex."

"No, just the ones that are breathing," said Charlotte.

"Still going down to Oceanside?"

Charlotte nodded and tried to contain her smile. She knew Dani didn't think she should go, but it wasn't up to her.

"I'll be fine. Don't you worry about me. I can take care of myself."

"I know you can," said Dani. "I just don't think this is such a good idea."

"Thanks for your input. I gotta get back in there," said Charlotte, trying to contain her anger. She was tired of this holier-than-thou thing that Dani had going. What was she doing with Jeremy anyway? Seemed like the pot calling the kettle black, but she bit her tongue and ducked back in the store.

She spent another forty minutes repeating everything she'd already said, and just when Mr. Abib was about to sign the contract, Mrs. Abib appeared.

"We think about this," she assured Charlotte, waving her away.

Charlotte drove to the shoe store already dreading Brad's horrible breath and handsy help. Maybe this retail design work wasn't for her. She spent over two hours going over the contract with Brad, making changes only to change them back. She knew he was only trying to keep her there. She tried not to be distracted by the anticipation of seeing Martin.

"I'll make all these changes and then get this contract back to you on Monday."

"The store isn't open tomorrow, but I could meet you somewhere else," suggested Brad.

"Sorry, I make it a policy not to work on Sundays."

"Oh, you're religious?"

"Not in the slightest. I just like my Sundays to myself," said Charlotte closing her laptop and standing up.

Brad wiped his hands on his pants before offering his sweaty palm. Charlotte shook it, but when she tried to let go, he held on. "How about I buy my designer some dinner? We could talk some more about your ideas."

Charlotte wrenched her hand free. "Sorry, but I've got a date."

Brad's face fell. "Oh, I thought you were married."

"I am," she sang out as the door swung shut behind her.

Driving to Oceanside, her mind kept flipping to Brett. It must have been talking to Dani that brought on the guilt. Maybe it really was time for her and Brett to . . . what? Separate? Divorce? She couldn't keep going like they had been. If only one person sees a problem, it's very difficult to bring about change in a relationship.

She had tried to get his attention, but nothing she did ever seemed to get the slightest rise out of him. She'd spent thousands on designer clothes, haircuts, manicures, facials, even bikini waxes. Neither the expense nor the change in her appearance had any effect. She'd redecorated their bedroom in purple; a color Brett had always told her was too garrulous for his taste. He never mentioned it, not even the fourteen throw pillows crowding the bed or the purple gauze canopy she'd secured above it.

As she got closer to Oceanside, her confidence began to wane. Was she crazy to be starting this affair? She wasn't naïve. She knew where this was headed. There was nothing innocent in the flirtations of Martin O'Keefe. It had been a lot of years since she was in the dating scene. There were so many new infectious diseases these days. She had only just begun to pay attention to those possibilities so she could properly worry about Will and the amorous European teenagers. She had talked to him just yesterday and he had assured her he was not romantically involved with anyone. They went out in groups, and he was enjoying being the novel American and all the teasing that went with it.

She spent a little time fixing her makeup as she sat in the parking lot gathering her nerve. Putting her things back in her purse, she found condom packets on the bottom. Flavored. She laughed. She couldn't decide who would have put them there. Most likely Dani, but Meg had been surprising her lately.

She entered the restaurant and sat down at the bar. Martin was setting up with his keyboardist and soundman, Jerry. Intent on his work, he didn't notice her come in. She ordered ice tea and watched him. Martin's sandy hair was tousled, as if he'd taken a nap this afternoon and hadn't had a chance to comb it. His sky blue T-shirt was tight on his biceps and across his chest. When he turned to the microphone to do a sound check, he spotted Charlotte. He winked. Charlotte blushed. He sang a few notes and Jerry gave him the thumbs up from the back of the room. Then he launched into a silly ballad about a carnival dancer, using Charlotte's name in place of Marian, the character in the song. Charlotte laughed and began to relax.

After conferring with Jerry a bit more, Martin joined her at the bar. He indicated something to the restaurant manager and then took Charlotte by the hand. They went upstairs to the roof deck, which wasn't yet open for the season. A table was set with table cloth and dishes. Tired chrysanthemums filled a vase. Martin pulled out his lighter and quickly lit several candles which flickered out in the wind. He smiled and shrugged, then held a chair out for Charlotte.

"Are all Irish men this charming?"

"Why do you think they have so many children?"

"I thought that had more to do with being Catholic."

"Oh no, it's all the charm," Martin assured her.

Under the table, Martin rested a hand on her thigh. Charlotte thought she might just explode if he even wiggled a finger. She tried to calm herself. She tried to picture carpet samples. Martin watched her with a look of amusement. Then he removed his hand and opened a bottle of wine.

"To finally having you alone," he said, lifting his glass in a toast. Charlotte raised hers, trying to keep her hands from trembling.

She drank her wine in gulps. She asked him about Jerry and the places they played in Oceanside, anything to keep the conversation from turning to why they were sitting here and what might come later.

Martin reached across the table and took her hand, "I've told you my story and too much about my work, but I haven't heard much about you. I'm sure you do other things beside rearrange furniture."

"There's really not much to tell." Charlotte didn't want to think about her real life, let alone tell him about it.

"You've told me about Will. What happened with his father?" He glanced at the ring she was still wearing.

Charlotte hesitated.

"Oh, a story similar to your own. A failed relationship, but a great kid; life goes on."

Now they both looked at her ring.

"I've never taken it off. Habit I guess. And it's kind of stuck, plus it keeps away men like you."

"And why would you want to keep a man like me away?"

"I've been asking myself that very same question."

Charlotte managed to maneuver the talk back to Martin's life and adventures. They ate the food that the manager brought unceremoniously and dropped on the table, packaged for takeout. Martin slowed down on his wine consumption, but continued to refill Charlotte's glass liberally.

When it was time for Martin to start his show, he led Charlotte back in and left her at the bar, kissing her sweetly on the forehead before going to join Jerry, who was already warming up.

As Charlotte sat alone at the bar, she consumed more alcohol, her nerves on edge. As the alcohol began to erode her inhibitions, she had to contain her urges to touch Martin in completely inappropriate ways for a public place or a married woman. Between sets, he stood next to her, sipping water, teasing her and laughing. While he was playing, he watched her and every now and then he would wink, which always made her smile. He was irresistible. Charlotte looked around the restaurant and noticed more than a few women eyeing Martin. She savored the knowledge that Martin was hers tonight.

As she concentrated on remaining atop her stool and willing the room to stop spinning, Charlotte's phone rang. It was an international number. That could only be Will. She rushed outside, trying to sober up instantaneously.

"Will?"

"Hi, Mom."

"Are you all right?"

"I'm more than all right."

"What time is it there; it must be the middle of the night." Charlotte sucked in the cool night air, trying to clear her head.

"Actually, it's almost six in the morning. I wanted to catch you before you went to bed. I need to tell you something." His voice was serious.

Charlotte braced herself. She watched two drunk kids wobbling out of the restaurant for a cigarette.

"What is it, Will?"

"I know you've been freaking out about the girls here and all that, so I wanted to tell you myself."

"What?"

"Mom, I'm in love."

Charlotte sank down on the sidewalk in relief. He's only in love, not sick or hurt or arrested.

"Will, you're only thirteen; you can't be in love."

"I knew you'd say something like that. But you're wrong; I am. And anyway, I'm almost fourteen."

Will would have a birthday while he was in Spain. The first time Charlotte would not be there for it.

"Is it Teresa?"

Teresa was Will's host and would be coming to Charlotte's house this fall.

"No, not Teresa. God, she's like my sister. No, her name is Natalia. She's beautiful, Mom."

"Where did you meet her?"

"At school. She's fifteen and she's really smart."

"I thought you told me you always go out with groups."

"I do. That's how I've gotten to know her."

"Does she feel the same way about you?"

"I don't know."

Charlotte digested this information with another wave of relief.

"You mean you haven't actually gone out with this person?"

"Not just the two of us. But, Mom, I meant it, I think she's the one."

Charlotte smiled and imagined Will's sweet face. She remembered the power of those first feelings of love. She was happy for him, but secretly hoped Natalia wouldn't feel the same for him.

"So, what are you going to do about this?"

"I don't know. What do you think?"

"Well, maybe you should try talking to her."

"I thought maybe I could ask her out, just the two of us. Maybe for lunch or something."

"I think that's a good idea. Do you have money to buy her lunch?"

"Yeah, Dad's been sending me some. What's up with him? He doesn't seem so happy lately."

"He's been working hard."

"Well, I'd better go. I've got to get ready for school."

"Don't you have a few hours?" Charlotte didn't want to let his voice go.

"Yeah, but I need to do some of the homework I never finished yesterday."

"Love has a way of distracting people, Will, so try to stay focused on why you're there."

"Don't worry, Mom, I get it."

"And, Will," Charlotte hesitated. There was so much she wanted to tell him. Love is dangerous and painful, she wanted to say, but instead she settled for, "Be careful, be smart."

"I know, don't worry."

"I'll try. I love you, Will."

"Love you, too."

Charlotte tried to reconcile the conversation she just had with her current situation. She was drunk at a bar waiting for a man she barely knew to finish singing so they could go have sex. She had to get out of here. She called Dani.

A half hour later, Dani and Meg walked through the doors of the bar. Martin was in the middle of a song, but watched their progress with a worried look. He tried to catch Charlotte's eye, but she wouldn't look at him.

"Thank God you're here. I'm way too drunk to drive home. I don't know what I'm doing." Charlotte was swaying on her feet and Meg reached out to steady her.

"It's okay, let's just go," said Dani.

"No, I've got to at least say good-bye to Martin. We had plans."

"You can talk to him tomorrow. Let's go," said Meg, taking Charlotte's arm.

Martin finished his song, set down his guitar, and left a confused Jerry noodling on his keyboard for an interlude.

"Well, how lovely to see you again," Martin said, smiling at the women as he made his way between them to Charlotte. Before he could reach her, Dani held out her hand to block him.

"We've got this."

"Ah, Dani, good to see you again."

"I'd wish I could say likewise."

Charlotte couldn't look at Martin. She kept her eyes focused on Dani, who was leaning closer to Martin and speaking in a stage whisper that Charlotte could clearly hear.

"I need to tell you something," said Dani, not letting go of his hand. He nodded and cast a worried glance at Charlotte.

"Charlotte's had way too much to drink. She's embarrassed to tell you this herself. And the thing is, when she's had as much as she's had, she tends to start throwing up uncontrollably. She doesn't want you to see her like this. So, we're going to take her home now."

"Whoa there, lassie, I've got that under control," Martin said and reached for Charlotte, who stared at the floor trying to keep the room from spinning. She felt the tears coming. Why was she such a colossal screw up? What would she do without Dani?

"That's just it, she doesn't want to make a fool of herself in front of you. So, we'll take care of her. I'll be sure to have her call you tomorrow," Dani assured him. Jerry approached Martin.

"Are we on a break, mate?" he asked.

"No, I'll be right there," Martin said tensely. He pulled Charlotte closer and lifted her face to look at him. She closed her eyes rather than let him see her tears.

"Are you okay?"

"No, but I'm sure I will be," she said, nodding and gripping his arm.

"I was really looking forward to having more time with you tonight."

"I'm sorry," she looked at him now with tear-stained, bloodshot eyes. His hand cradled her cheek. She leaned into it and closed her eyes.

He sighed. "Okay, you take care of yourself, I'll be in touch."

Charlotte let Dani lead her out of the restaurant and deposit her in the backseat of the Saab. Meg went to get her own car. On the drive back, Charlotte cried softly. She didn't understand herself. She wanted Martin in a way she hadn't wanted a man in years. But each time she had an opportunity to act on that desire, she found herself terrified. Martin probably thought she was a terrible tease. She hated herself for acting so juvenile. Dani watched her in the rearview mirror but didn't say a word.

# SUNDAY, APRIL 28

## Charlotte

Sunday morning, Charlotte heard a soft knock on her door and groaned. She wasn't ready to face Meg or Dani or her own stupidity.

Meg cracked the door open. "How're you feeling?"

Charlotte emerged from under the tumble of blankets. "I've felt better."

"I've got some orange juice and Tylenol."

"You are a saint," said Charlotte, sitting up in bed. Meg brought her the drink and pills and then sat down on the side of the bed.

"So . . . ?" she looked at Charlotte expectantly.

"I don't know what I'm doing." She swallowed the pills and took a long drink of the orange juice, then flung herself back on her bed again. "I thought I knew what I wanted. God, Meg, last night Martin made me feel like a princess, not some middle-aged woman with wrinkles and dyed hair. I couldn't believe this gorgeous man was trying to impress *me*, actually wanted *me*. I don't think Brett was ever that interested in me, even when he was interested in me. But then Will called and told me he was in love and I guess I just freaked out. Plus, I had way too much to drink. I'm an idiot. Martin must think I'm such a tease." Charlotte pulled the blankets up to hide her face.

"Oh, c'mon, you're not an idiot."

Charlotte pulled the blanket down and made a face.

"Okay, maybe a little bit of an idiot."

"What am I going to do?"

"You're going to get up and take a shower and then do whatever it is you do on your computer or go down to one of these stores you're redesigning. You know, get on with your life such as it is at the moment."

Meg hugged Charlotte.

"C'mon, you'll figure it out. You did the right thing last night, eventually."

After Meg left, Charlotte got out of bed. She turned on the shower, pulled off the pajamas she didn't remember putting on the night before, and studied herself in the bathroom mirror. She looked good for her age. She looked damn good. And she wanted someone besides Brett to attest to that. She didn't have many years left before sex with the lights on would be out of the question.

Martin made her feel desired. She might never get this chance again. The last two weeks felt like a dream. She wasn't ready for reality yet. Eventually, reality would be right here in the form of Will and Brett and work and her future. Oh, screw reality. She wanted Martin.

---

Charlotte spent the morning on her computer going through her e-mail. Her phone rang three times—twice it was Brad and once it was Brett. Two men she definitely didn't want to deal with. After lunch, she dragged herself down to the shoe store. She was in no mood for Brad, but she needed him to sign the contract so that she could give the sign guys the go-ahead. On the way there, she left a voice message for Martin, apologizing and saying she wanted to make it up to him, but she had to deal with the shoe store contract. Maybe she could meet up with him later? She knew he didn't have a gig that evening. When he didn't call back, she assumed he wasn't interested in seeing her anymore. Who could blame him after all their false starts?

Brad was busy taking orders for dye jobs on prom shoes, so Charlotte wrote a long e-mail to Will about the dangers of love and using contraceptives and then never sent it, knowing that the teenage mind, even her exceptional son's teenage mind, would have no interest in her wisdom. Besides, she didn't want to be the one to sink Will's boat. The Spanish crush could do that for him—hopefully.

When Brad had a few minutes, he scanned the contract for what seemed like the millionth time. She knew he was only stalling. She'd be pissed if this was all only a ploy to get her in the store and didn't even pan out as a job.

"So, it's all there. I made the changes you asked for, but we need to move this along if you want the new signage in time for the summer season."

"It looks good," said Brad, still not signing. "Will you be overseeing all the work?"

"Only when they need me. I'm not familiar with most of the contractors, so I'll definitely be involved, but they'll depend on you to get in the store during off hours to work, especially the floor guys."

"But you'll be here each day, making sure it's done right?"

"I'll be here when I need to be here. You can call me if you see any issues."

He didn't say anything, just tapped the pen on the paper and began reading again. Charlotte couldn't help herself. Maybe it was because she was so hungover. A heavy, annoyed sigh escaped her lips.

Brad looked up at her. "I know I'm dragging this out, but it's a big deal for me."

"I'm sorry, I know it is. I don't mean to rush you." She smiled sweetly.

Finally, he signed his name and handed the contract to Charlotte to sign. "And here's a copy for you," she said, handing him an identical copy with her neat signature at the bottom.

"So, that's it?"

"Yup."

"Could I take you to dinner to celebrate?" he asked.

Charlotte shook her head. "I'm sorry, Brad. I've got other work to deal with, and," she stood up and offered her hand, "I try to keep things professional with all my clients." They shook hands, but Charlotte didn't miss the look of disappointment in Brad's eyes. Maybe he'd finally give up. She just hoped his checks wouldn't bounce.

She walked out of the store, relieved to have finally closed the deal and dreading her next stop at the T-shirt shop, but when she walked around the side of the building to where she'd parked her car in the shade, she stopped in her tracks. There, leaning against her car, holding an enormous bouquet of roses, stood Martin. She thought her heart might beat completely out of her chest. She walked to him calmly, stood in front of him for a moment smiling like the Cheshire Cat, then raised herself on her tiptoes and kissed his lips. He kissed her back, gently at first, then with increasing intensity, pulling her against him. Any questions lingering in her mind as to where all this was leading vanished like smoke. Finally, he broke it off.

"I don't have a gig. So tonight I'm yours. That is if you don't have plans and none of the gang is going to come drag you away." He raised his eyebrows questioningly and looked around the empty alley.

"Oh, I have plans," she said. "And they all involve you wearing a lot less than you are now." She reached for him again, but he held up his hand and pointed to her car. She sighed.

Following him in her car, Charlotte tuned her radio to a rock station and turned it up loud to drown out all her doubts. She could still taste him on her lips. He lived in an old apartment building that looked like it might have been a motel in a previous lifetime. As they walked in, Martin apologized for the mess. Charlotte vaguely registered the clothes strewn about and the beer cans and books as she looked in vain for his bedroom. The apartment was small, with a tiny galley kitchen, a living room with just enough room for his couch and television, and a bathroom so small the toilet was practically in the shower stall. Just off of the living room was a balcony. Martin began moving things off the couch as he pulled it out to make up a sofa bed.

Needing to fortify her nerves, she looked in the fridge and found a selection of beers. She chose one that looked strong and dark and drank it steadily. When Martin finished making up the bed, he took the beer from her and finished it in one swig. Then he took her by the hand.

He laid her down gently and slowly removed her clothes. When she made a move to help him, he shooed her hand away. She tried not to think about the stretch marks from pregnancy, the looseness of her once-taut thighs, her breasts that seemed to have shrunk with age. As he exposed more and more of her, his eyes softened. He ran his fingers over her skin with such reverence and longing that she finally relaxed. His hands were warm, the tips of his fingers calloused from years on the guitar. When she was completely naked, he leaned back on his knees and pulled off his T-shirt, causing her to gasp. He was beautiful. Every muscle defined and deep. A perfect line of hair disappeared into his jeans. She ran her hands over his nipples and felt him shiver.

When he got up to remove his jeans, Brett's face flashed across her mind, but the Brett she saw wasn't the Brett she'd left at home just weeks before; it was the Brett she'd made love to in her dorm room so many years ago.

Charlotte tried to focus on Martin's body outlined by the fading sunlight. She concentrated on the sensation of his fingers against her skin. He explored her body with his warm breath—his lips barely grazing her, a smile playing on his lips. She breathed deeply, pushing away Brett's face and reaching for Martin.

As he lay down beside her and pulled her to him, she was trying with all her willpower to stop the orgasm welling up in her body from only his touch; she wanted this to last. He began caressing her body with a more definite goal in mind, lingering in the places that caused her to catch her breath. When he brought her to orgasm, she opened her eyes and saw him watching her with a satisfied smile. A moment later, he rummaged in the drawer of the coffee table. He produced a condom, much to Charlotte's relief. He reached for her and, with one motion, lifted her on top of him. She wrapped herself around him, burrowing her face in his chest, breathing in his scent. She moved with him and all too soon felt his body stiffen and shudder. He let out a low moan and whispered, "That was lovely."

Rolling onto his side, he pulled Charlotte against him. She nestled against his shoulder, completely satisfied, not wanting to think past this moment.

When Charlotte awoke, Martin was still holding her and snoring softly. She looked for a clock; the fading light told her it was nearly eight. She wriggled out from under Martin's arm, got up, and found her sweater. Then, spying Martin's boxers, she put those on, too. They barely held onto her hips, in the same fashion as the teenagers she always complained about.

She went into the bathroom and tried to repair the damage to her hair, then giving up she took all the clips out and set them on the side of the sink. She looked in the medicine chest for toothpaste and found cigarettes stashed there. She grabbed them and another beer from the fridge and went out on the balcony. She closed the door quietly, pausing to look at Martin's face so different in repose. *He's real*, she thought. *He's right there.*

She lit a cigarette and leaned over the railing to take in the view. She'd been too distracted to pay attention to her surroundings when they arrived earlier. Now, she understood why the place was so tiny. The balcony overlooked the beach. Martin paid for the view, not the square footage.

Charlotte sipped her beer. She had broken her marriage vows. When she married Brett she'd been certain those vows were forever. She and Brett would be different from all the failed marriages that plagued her family. It surprised her that she felt no regret. She'd enjoyed sex with Martin. He was an experienced and confident lover. Charlotte hadn't slept with anyone but Brett for nearly twenty years. Most of her experiences, other than Brett, had been fumbling college boys. And most of those escapades had been under the heavy influence of alcohol. This was different. This was quality sex.

Before Charlotte could process what this meant for her marriage, the door behind her opened and Martin appeared wrapped in a blanket.

"Someone stole my undershorts," he said, smiling sheepishly at her. "And my cigarettes, I see."

Charlotte moved over to make room next to her on the balcony and said, "Guilty on both counts, but I'll make it up to you later."

"I'll look forward to that," Martin said as he shook another cigarette from the pack and lit it. Charlotte shared her beer with him and they watched children chase ghost crabs scuttling across the sand in the fading light.

Martin ordered Chinese food and they ate on the balcony, talking about their first sexual experiences. Charlotte was wide-eyed as Martin told her of his at the tender age of twelve. It was easy to laugh about their early experiences, but she edited out any mention of Brett, and Martin didn't ask. When the evening's chill chased them indoors, Martin lit candles, creating a romantic glow in the tiny apartment, and Charlotte made good on her promise to pay Martin back, exploring the expanse of his body until exhaustion forced them to sleep.

## Dani

Dani pulled up behind the gallery at 5:25 Sunday morning in Meg's car. She turned off the engine and again wondered about the scene last night at the Rum Runner. Charlotte had come so close to crossing the line. It was almost like she was daring herself to cross it and kept being pulled back by chance, or maybe something bigger. She worried for her friend and for Brett, but she worried the most for Will. He was a great kid. If Charlotte threw away her marriage, it was one thing. Brett was a big boy and he shouldered some of the blame, but Will would be devastated. Dani was startled from her own thoughts when Jeremy knocked on her window holding steaming travel mugs of coffee and a bag of donuts.

"You think of everything!" exclaimed Dani as he got in and handed her a cup.

"Just happy to be along for the ride," he said.

She handed him the list of places and the map.

"I trust you know your way around better than I, so you navigate."

Dani and Jeremy spent the day gathering treasures. Dani found plenty of new things to paint and Jeremy even found a few pieces to sell directly in the gallery. They stopped for lunch at a roadside pit beef stand. They sat, side by side, on the hood of Meg's car.

"This has been great," said Dani. "I'm glad you came along."

"Me, too."

"I feel terrible for taking your whole day."

"It was worth it. I love that set of beach prints I found. They were a steal. I'll easily sell them for five times that price."

"You have a good eye. Have you always wanted to work with art?"

"I wanted to be an artist, like you," said Jeremy, wrapping up the remainder of his sandwich, and sliding off the car.

"I'm not an artist," protested Dani.

"Why do you always deny that you're an artist?" he asked.

"I'm not an *artist*, not in comparison to someone like the person who painted those beach scenes. I just doodle and draw and I've got really neat handwriting."

"The things you create are beautiful. You take something like that those old frames we found and you breathe new life into them with your imagination and paintbrush. I'd call that art."

"I'd call it craft."

"Okay, you can call it craft, but I'm selling it as art in my gallery, so I still call it art and I call you an artist." Jeremy reached for her hand and helped her off the hood. "We'd better get back at it. There's still room in the car."

"Barely," said Dani, laughing.

On the drive back, Jeremy restarted their earlier conversation.

"Dani, I don't understand why you're so adamant that you aren't an artist. I work with artists every day and their styles and abilities vary, but every one of them is an artist."

Dani was quiet, staring out the windshield, waiting her turn to enter the highway.

"I mean, technically, *I'm* an artist," he continued. "Because I draw pictures for my niece when she visits." Dani smiled. "There's no set definition of an artist."

Dani wished he'd let it go. She'd spent the last few weeks shoving aside the memory of her professor's pronouncement.

"It's just something I heard from one of my professors in college."

"What?"

"That artists make a statement, they change the way people see things."

"You certainly change the way people see things with your art!"

"No, he was talking about something different. You know how sometimes you can look at a piece of art and you're transported? It's like you are actually in the picture or you think the sculpture might move at any moment?"

"Yeah."

"That! I don't do that!"

"So? That's not the only definition of art."

"It is for me."

"I think that's pretty limiting, and whoever taught you that at school did the world and you a disservice."

"Maybe," said Dani as she flicked on the radio.

They made it back to Sweet Beach just as it was getting dark. Dani helped Jeremy unload the things he'd purchased.

"Want to grab dinner?" he asked.

"I'm really tired. I think I'll just head home and scrounge something up there."

Jeremy put down the painting he was holding and turned to Dani.

"I had such a great time. I really enjoy being with you."

"It was fun. Thanks so much for your help."

"It was all my pleasure, really. Any chance you'll be free to grab lunch tomorrow?"

"I'm really anxious to put in some time on this new stuff, but if I come up for air, I'll stop by, okay?"

"Good. You sure I can't come back with you and help you unload your stuff?"

"No, I'll be fine; I've taken enough of your time already. Do you want me to drop you home?"

"Actually, I've got some stuff to take care of here, but thanks. And thanks for the day, Dani. I really did enjoy it."

"Thank you. I'll see you soon."

❧

When Dani got back to the cottage, she found Meg unpacking a takeout dinner she'd picked up at the grocery store—rotisserie chicken, salad, and an enormous chocolate cream pie.

"Where's Charlotte?"

"Who knows? She should have been home hours ago. She's probably chasing after that Irish singer."

"Do you really think she's going to sleep with him?"

"I'm not going to answer that. I think maybe we should practice 'Don't Ask, Don't Tell' from now on when it comes to Charlotte."

Dani tried Charlotte's cell phone, but there was no answer. "Looks like it's just us," she said.

"I'm starving, so that's fine with me. I could eat this entire chocolate pie myself," said Meg when they sat down to eat.

"Hard work will do that to you. Did you work in the church garden again today?"

"Yeah. That mulch pile is endless. It was just me and a couple church members after services, but they were pretty elderly and couldn't move much. We quit around two because there was some kind of reception happening in the garden at three."

"What'd you do after that?"

"I played golf."

"Really?"

"Well, miniature golf. I played two games by myself, and then one with the assistant manager because he was bored and there wasn't anyone else there."

"Really?"

"Yeah, it was fun. I kind of understand Peter's obsession with it a little better now. You're really competing with yourself."

"But I bet the course where Peter plays doesn't have moving windmills and snapping alligator jaws."

Meg made a face. Dani pushed aside her chicken and opened the chocolate pie.

"Have you heard from Peter?"

"He left a message on my phone yesterday and said he wasn't going to keep bothering me. He hoped I would sort myself out soon and come home. Oh, and that Phoebe was a terrible cook and the kids missed me. I wrote him a letter earlier in the week. I guess he got it."

"You wrote him a letter? Why didn't you just call him?"

"Sometimes when we argue, he gets all lawyerly and I get intimidated and confused and never say what I really mean. A letter gave me a chance to say what I wanted to say."

"Smart," said Dani through a mouthful of pie.

"Are you going to eat that entire pie?" asked Meg, looking at the huge cavern Dani had created in the pie.

"Maybe. Want some?"

Meg picked up her fork. "Now I have to run with you tomorrow."

"Good, I've missed you all week."

# MONDAY, APRIL 29

## Charlotte

When Charlotte awoke, the sun was shining and Martin was gone. Looking at the ceiling mottled with water stains, she wondered if she had just cast similar stains on her life. But what she was feeling wasn't regret, it was anticipation. Now things would change. Now she'd really done it.

She folded the bed up and cleared their trash and dishes from the night before. She was just about to leave when Martin arrived with bagels and coffee.

"Sleep okay?" he asked.

Charlotte smiled. "I did."

"Hate to eat and run, but I've got to get to a meeting out in Burnley."

"No problem."

"You have to work?"

"Yeah, but most of it is on the phone."

"Not with your lovesick shoe salesman?"

"No, but I've got to get back to the cottage." *And I've got some explaining to do, I'm sure.*

After they ate, Martin walked her to her car. Neither seemed to know what to say. Martin hugged her and kissed the top of her head. He held her door for her and closed it behind her. As she started the car, she looked at him and he winked. Then he sauntered to his truck and was gone.

Charlotte arrived back at the cottage just in time to join Dani and Meg for a run. Neither made any comment about her night away as they took off up the beach to the north, away from the boardwalk for a change. The beach was deserted. They ran until Charlotte begged them to stop.

"I am so out of shape. How did that happen so fast?" said Charlotte, gasping for air and collapsing in the sand.

"Maybe it's all your smoking," suggested Meg, sitting next to her.

"Or the fact that you haven't put on your running shoes since we got here," said Dani.

Charlotte didn't acknowledge their comments.

Dani picked up a piece of drift wood and began writing in the sand with it. She wrote *Dani + Joe* in four-foot letters and then watched as the waves washed it away. She frowned and then sank down in the sand next to Meg.

"I really like running," said Meg. "I didn't think I would, but it's not so bad."

"I couldn't live without it," said Dani. "It's the only time I have to myself anymore. It's the only place my family won't follow me."

"But your friends will," said Charlotte, who was lying down now, shielding her eyes from the sun with her arm. "I used to like it, but now it gives me too much time to think."

"And heaven forbid you should do that," Dani said.

Charlotte didn't reply. They watched another runner pass by wearing purple spandex. Dani raised her eyebrows at Meg and giggled.

"How come you guys didn't tell me I was getting so fat?" asked Meg.

"You aren't," mumbled Charlotte.

"You look fine," said Dani.

"No, I don't. I've gotten fat and frumpy and no one had the nerve to tell me."

"What do you expect?" asked Charlotte. "We're your friends; we don't care how you look. But I promise you that if you topped three hundred, I would have said something."

"Thanks a lot."

"What are you worried about, Meg?"

"Nothing. This time here is just making me reconsider everything."

"Such as?" mumbled Charlotte.

"I don't know. I'm trying to unearth me; figure out what's left of me, so I can decide where I go from here. I think I've got to do something besides just take care of my kids and house and husband. That used to be enough." She paused, staring out to sea. Then shook her head. "But losing Logan made me realize I'm going to lose everybody eventually. Maybe even me, if I'm not careful." She pulled her knees to her chest and rested her chin on them. "I'm going to change. And not just by getting manicures and new haircuts. I want to be healthier and more grateful for what I have. I want to teach my kids that, too."

"Noble words, my friend," said Dani.

"It's not like you're an unhealthy, ungrateful slob to begin with. You've just been too busy taking care of everyone else," said Charlotte.

"I know, but I think I buried *me* under all the *us*."

"I think we all do that to a certain extent when we get married and have kids. We can no longer be just a *me*. Everything has to be thought of in terms of *us*," said Dani.

"But why? Why can't I still be me?"

"You can. I'm only saying that your kids take a little part of you, I mean, God, they are a part of you, right?" said Dani.

"You mean each time we have a kid, we lose part of ourselves?" asked Meg.

"Maybe. It's just a theory."

"Well, I guess most of you is long gone then, Meg," laughed Charlotte.

Meg threw a handful of sand at Charlotte.

"Hey!" she yelled, sitting up.

"Okay, Charlotte, fess up," said Meg, "What is going on with Mr. Irish?"

Charlotte smiled guiltily and lay back down. She didn't say anything, but she knew she didn't need to.

"Charlotte! Oh my God, you slept with him!" Meg accused.

"And if I did?"

"You're married!" Meg and Dani said together.

"Oh, c'mon, you mean neither of you has ever given infidelity a thought? I'm just enjoying myself for the first time in a long time. Martin's great, but it's not like I'm going to leave Brett for him, at least not yet, anyway."

"I can't believe you're saying this," said Meg.

"Look, I don't want to be lectured. I'm a big girl."

"That's true," admitted Dani. For a few minutes they sat quietly with their own thoughts. Then Dani said, "Charlotte, I'll shut up about Martin on one condition."

"What?"

"You tell me how he is in bed!"

Charlotte laughed, sitting up. Then she leapt to her feet and started running. She yelled back over her shoulder, "I will, but you'll have to catch me to find out!"

Dani and Meg scrambled to their feet to run after her. Charlotte was far ahead, sprinting hard. They chased her the whole mile back. When they reached the steps leading up to their street, Charlotte was already stretching.

"Guess I don't have to tell you anything," she teased.

"He was good, huh?" asked Dani.

"You just want to live vicariously through me. Why don't you go track down your hot, young art dealer and have your own fling?"

"He's a bit young for me, don't you think?"

"No, I think young men like him, with a sensitive side, like older women with experience. I'm sure you could teach him a thing or two."

Dani rolled her eyes as she headed up the steps past Charlotte.

"Speaking of my young, hot art dealer, I'd better get to work and make him some more art."

"I think you should make him something else!" called Charlotte from the steps and she and Meg laughed.

Meg and Charlotte sat on the bottom of the beach steps watching an old man wave his metal detector across the sand. Occasionally, he stopped to dig up lost coins and bottle caps. Intent on his task, he didn't notice the women on the steps.

"So how's Peter taking all this?"

"I guess he's decided to wait it out."

"Huh. I bet he's doing a bit of soul searching himself."

"That's not really his style."

"Well, neither is taking care of his kids and it sounds like he's doing okay with that."

"True. Phoebe says he is really stepping up. She's got some new man on the line, so I know she's itching to get out of there."

Charlotte laughed. "I love Phoebe."

"Me, too," said Meg.

There was a lull in the conversation. Charlotte still couldn't believe that Meg had really stood up to Peter. She'd underestimated her.

"Are you glad you stayed?" she asked Meg.

Meg fiddled with the laces on her shoes and didn't answer.

"You don't have to answer that," said Charlotte.

"I am glad I stayed. It's weird to be here and have all this time, all this quiet."

"I can only imagine how strange it must feel for you. You're the busiest person I know."

Meg picked up a handful of sand and let it run through her fingers. "Even before we lost Logan, I was busy, but after the funeral, I made myself busy. It was easier that way. I couldn't bear the quiet. I shut Peter out, too. It made me angry that he could just move on. He could laugh and be happy."

"I didn't know how much you were still hurting, Meg. You seemed to be doing so well. You were back to doing all the things you do."

"I'm good at pretending. I've had a lifetime of practice. Since being here, I've begun to wonder if that's all my life's been. When we went dancing on that first weekend and I really cut loose, that was the first time in a long time that I've felt real. I'm always being someone's mom or someone's wife, the PTA president, the chair of this committee or that, the parent chaperone; I always have a role to play. I haven't been Meg in a long time."

"Wow," said Charlotte, looking at Meg, searching for tears and seeing only resolve. Meg really was changing right before their very eyes.

"And I'm scared to death my husband is only in love with this person I've been pretending to be."

"Peter's known you a long time. Christ, you guys have been together practically since you got out of diapers."

"No, just since high school."

"Still, he must know you better than anyone else."

"Sometimes I think he's just one more person I'm trying to please."

They sat for a while, watching the waves. Soon people started arriving at the beach and they had to move off of the steps.

"You want to walk to town?" asked Meg. "I could show you the garden at St. Bart's."

"Sure."

Charlotte was glad for the diversion. She could think of nothing else but seeing Martin again. After Meg showed Charlotte the garden, they stopped in the church to say hello to Father McMann.

"I'm glad you stopped by," he said. "I wanted to give you this." He handed Meg a light-blue piece of paper.

*Widows' Group*

*"Coping with the Everyday" will be our topic this week.*

*Join us Tuesday at 9:00 a.m.*

"I don't understand," said Meg.

"I know you're not a widow," said Father McMann, placing a hand on her shoulder. "But I think grief is grief and you might find these ladies helpful."

"I'll think about it," said Meg, folding the flyer and putting it in her pocket.

Meg and Charlotte had lunch at the sub shop on the boardwalk. Meg listened as Charlotte told her about Martin's disastrous marriage and his remarkable son. Charlotte found that, like a junior high kid in the midst of her first puppy love, she couldn't stop thinking or talking about Martin. Focusing on Martin kept her from thinking about Brett.

They ordered ice cream cones and then walked the boardwalk.

"Do we have to ever go back?" Charlotte asked.

"I think Dani is expecting us for dinner."

"I mean to Sadlersville, to our lives."

"I suppose that all depends," said Meg.

"On what?"

"On whether there is anything to go back to."

# TUESDAY, APRIL 30

### Meg

Tomorrow would be May 1. The anniversary of Logan's death. *Father McMann couldn't have known that, could he?* Meg walked to the beach early, before anyone else was up. She sat in the sand and watched the sun creep over the horizon. Last year, on the anniversary of Logan's death, she hadn't gotten out of bed until Phoebe showed up at two. She'd forced Meg to dress and then they'd taken flowers to Logan's grave. Phoebe brought champagne and had proceeded to toast Logan, talking to him like he was right there listening. Meg had thought she would pass out from the pain, but she'd gotten through it. Later, Peter had taken the kids out to dinner and she'd gone to bed early, complaining of a headache, only to spend the evening sobbing into her pillow. This year she could tell the pain was still there, waiting for her invitation.

Dolphins appeared in the waves close to shore right in front of her, leaping and spraying, as if their show was just for Meg. She thought of Logan and his collection of plastic dolphins. They were eight different colors. It was how she'd taught him his colors. He loved to play with them in the bath and in the sandbox, even dragging them with him to preschool for show-and-tell. They'd gone to the aquarium with her in-laws when they visited that spring before Logan died. Her father-in-law had stayed with Logan at the dolphin exhibit the whole morning. He didn't want to see anything else. Maybe the dolphins were a sign. Maybe Logan was telling her that he was happy wherever he was, or maybe he was letting her know that he was still here with her. Or maybe they were just dolphins.

At 9:15, Meg entered the church. She followed the scent of coffee to a meeting room near Father McMann's office. She was late and the group had started, so she took a seat in the back. Several of the older women smiled warmly at her. She sat down next to a woman wearing a baseball cap over her gray hair who nodded at her. A handsome woman with a pretty green scarf had just finished speaking. Everyone clapped quietly, and then a voice from the front said, "I don't know how you do it, Isabel."

The woman in the green scarf laughed and said, "You know what? Nothing scares me anymore. I figure the worst that could possibly happen, has happened. What do I have to be afraid of now? I survived this; I can survive anything."

Meg's neighbor leaned over and whispered, "Isabel's husband died in her arms. She'd only been married two years!" When she saw Meg's surprised look, she added, "They met at the senior center. Neither had ever been married—can you imagine? All those years alone, and then poof!" She gestured with her hand like a magician.

"I know what you mean, Isabel," said another woman who was clearly wearing a wig. "I've felt the same way since I lost Genevieve. Somehow her death has made me fearless. I'm getting ready to launch my own business!" There were words of congratulations and some scattered applause.

Meg's neighbor, whispered, "Susan and Genevieve were partners for twelve years. They never got to marry because Genevieve got sick before the law passed."

Meg listened as a woman about her mother's age talked about making dinner for one.

"Sometimes I forget and I make enough for both of us. The other day I made a whole pot roast.

Can you imagine? I don't know what I was thinking. Most of it went in the trash. My George could really put the food away." She smiled sadly and shook her head. "Most days, though, I hardly cook. I think, what's the point?"

"You're the point, Betty," said the group leader, a tiny woman with a clipboard and a fierce look. "You still need to eat and it's important that you eat well."

Another woman, with hair so thin you could see the age spots on her head, spoke up. "I just go out to eat. It's easier."

"But I wouldn't want to sit by myself in a restaurant. It would feel awkward," said Betty.

"I take a book."

"Maybe I could do that."

"The thing is, ladies," said the leader, "It's not the mourning that is so hard, it's the living."

"I've started taking myself out on dates," said a quiet, thin woman who fiddled with the pearl buttons on her sweater. "I go places I always wanted to go. Sometimes I go places that Simon has gone with me and I imagine what he'd say now."

"But doesn't that make you sad?"

She smiled. "No. I think it would make him happy to know I'm doing things for myself. Simon was a man full of life and energy and happiness. I'm certain he'd want me to be happy, not sitting around feeling sorry for myself and eating TV meals."

"I'm not sure I'm ready to go out," said a heavy-set woman with sad eyes. Meg could feel her pain from across the room.

"But, Josie, that's just it," said Isabel. "You can't just sit around waiting for the pain to go away. You have to go out and dispel it!"

After the meeting, the woman with the pearl buttons approached Meg. "Welcome! I'm glad you joined us today. Was it was helpful?"

"Yes, I think so," said Meg shyly.

"How long since you lost yours?" she asked.

"It'll be two years tomorrow."

"Oh, that's still fresh. Do you want my advice?"

"Yes!" said Meg eagerly.

"Instead of trying to forget, you need to focus on ways to remember."

All these stories. Meg knew they would tumble around her heart for days. So much pain. But so much courage.

Later in the afternoon, Meg sat on the front porch swing. She needed to make a decision about going back. It was time. It was almost as if the dolphins that morning and the women at the grief group were messages telling her it was time to get back to living. Besides, she couldn't put it off much longer. Peter was bound to throw Phoebe out any day. Either that or Phoebe would abandon them for the current Mr. Maybe. Phoebe said Peter was doing the bulk of the work. She couldn't imagine him doing dishes. He hadn't touched a dish since they were first married. She also could not imagine him doing laundry or driving car pool or coaching Timmy's Little League team, but Phoebe said those things were happening, too. So maybe he was trying. Maybe her absence had pulled him back.

The front door opened, breaking into Meg's thoughts. Charlotte sat down next to her on the swing and gave it a push.

"Hey," she said.

Meg wiped her eyes.

Charlotte looked at her. "Stuck on a hard one?" she asked, nodding towards the puzzle in Meg's lap.

Meg laughed.

"Paranormal power, for short?"

"Oh, c'mon, that's an easy one. You can't be stuck on that!"

"I'm not," said Meg.

"You okay?"

"More than okay. I think I'm ready to go back."

"Really?"

"Yeah. I just hope I can make things different."

"You can."

"I have a few ideas, but I'm not sure whether I'll have time for them once I'm back and dealing with the kids and the house and our schedules."

"What ideas?"

"I was thinking of starting a group for grieving parents and maybe a garden in memory of Logan."

"Wow! Those are great ideas!"

"Yeah, but it'll take time and that's the one thing I don't have."

"You'll make the time."

"How?"

"Hire a babysitter. Eat a few more takeout meals. Pay somebody to clean your house. How do you think I ran my business when Will was young? I haven't cleaned my house since Will was born. I told Brett I didn't have time for it. We hired a cleaning woman, and she's been there every Saturday ever since."

"I can't do that. I'm home all day. You have a business, but I'm just a stay-at-home mom. I can't really justify a cleaning person. That seems selfish or lazy."

"Excuse me? Your husband makes a shit-load of money, and while you may be *home* all day, you're running around taking care of his children, his house, his life. Which is the only reason he can play golf all day on Saturdays and go to the gym every day. Did you ever think maybe this extended vacation might be the best thing for him? I have no doubt he has a much greater appreciation for all you do.

And as for being selfish, you are. But everyone's selfish. It's necessary for the survival of the species. Some, like Peter, are just better at it than others."

"I don't know."

"Why is it when women become mothers, they are expected to instantly stop being selfish?" Charlotte got up and began pacing the porch. Meg tried not to giggle at her intensity. She was like a preacher on a rant. "I mean we're all born selfish, yet we spend our lives trying to teach ourselves to stop being selfish. It starts as soon as we can sit up. Everyone's always saying 'share, take turns, you can't have all of it, leave some for the others,' when really every instinct in our body is saying 'mine, mine, mine.' I think it's completely unfair to expect mothers to give up every selfish whim the moment they procreate. Look at the fathers; no one expects it of them. Most dads play golf instead of taking the kids to the park, and watch their television shows instead of reading *The Cat in the Hat* for the fifty-sixth time. And they never feel bad about it. We need to take a page from their book."

"I thought that was just Peter," said Meg.

Charlotte sat back down. "Okay, well maybe it is, but the bottom line is you don't have to always be the perfect cookie-baking mom. You have to do some things for yourself. I think this group is a great idea. I think you should go home and tell Peter things need to change and then I think you just make it happen."

"That sounds so simple."

"It is. Unlike my situation."

"Which is?"

Charlotte didn't answer.

"C'mon, Char, why can't you talk to me about this?"

"Because you will make me feel bad, and I'm not ready to feel bad about this yet."

"Look, this Irish guy is your business. I just want to know you've thought it through and you know what you're doing."

"No, I haven't thought it through. All I know is he makes me feel sexy and young and interesting and fun. None of which I have felt with Brett for a long time."

"Everyone goes through droughts in a marriage; it's no reason to throw it away."

"I'm not talking about a drought. Brett treats me like a roommate he can occasionally have sex with. He's been doing it for so long I don't think he even sees me anymore. I don't need some big extravagant gesture, just a few little ones."

Meg cut her eyes at Charlotte. She knew her too well.

"Okay, so I like to be romanced. But I'd settle for a phone call in the middle of the day to say he loves me or a look across the dinner table or even holding my hand in the checkout line at the Home Depot. Or how about that he show up for the god-damn dinner I made the night before I leave for a weekend away with my girlfriends? Your husband has been freaking out and calling here and asking you to come home, and even doing the goddamn dishes, but not mine. He leaves messages like, 'When you're ready to talk, let's talk. Hope you're having a good time with your girlfriends.' He doesn't even get it that I've left him. He doesn't even think there's a serious problem! Really, I imagine for him it's much simpler this way. I'm not there forcing him to have a conversation over dinner, or nagging him to go see a movie."

"Brett loves you, Charlotte."

"How would you know?"

"If Brett showed up and brought you roses and confessed his undying love for you, would you go back to him?"

"Never in a million years would Brett ever do that."

"But if he did?"

"I don't know, Meg. I really don't."

As if on cue, Charlotte's phone rang. It was Brett. "Speak of the devil," she said.

"I'm going to take a nap," said Meg.

"ESP," said Charlotte.

"What?" asked Meg.

"Paranormal power, for short."

Meg smiled. "I knew that."

With a sigh, Charlotte answered her phone.

"Brett."

"How are you?" he asked.

"I'm good. And you?"

"I'm feeling pretty lousy."

Charlotte didn't say anything.

"I miss Will and I miss you. The house is so quiet."

She knew it. It wasn't that he missed her personally; he was just lonely and bored.

"Have you talked to Will?" she asked.

"Briefly. He was headed out over the weekend to France for a little vacation. He didn't sound so excited about it."

"Maybe he's worried about his French," Charlotte suggested, knowing it was more likely he didn't want to leave his Spanish sweetheart. She'd gotten an e-mail from Will during the week. He was hoping to take his crush out for lunch the following weekend, after he got back from France. He was working up his nerve to ask her out.

"Charlotte, what exactly are you doing down there? I'm beginning to be concerned."

"You should be."

"And why is that? You've left me completely in the dark here."

"Oh please, how can you say that?"

"I don't know what you want from me!" Brett sounded exasperated. Charlotte tried to check her anger. She hated that she had to spell it out for him. She took a deep breath.

"Do you remember when we used to do things like go to gallery openings and theater fundraisers?"

"That was a long time ago. I never really enjoyed them then; I can only imagine they are even more stifling now."

"What do you mean? We had fun! We went out! We partied, we laughed, we lived. Now, we go nowhere, except occasionally to the Home Depot if you need my advice on tile for the basement or siding for the shed."

"That's what married people do."

"No! That's what some married people do! That's not what I want."

"I don't understand. You want us to go out more?"

"You don't get it."

"What don't I get? Help me here."

"If I have to spell this out for you, there's really no point."

Charlotte was silent.

"I'm sorry to be so dense, but I think I do need you to spell it out."

Charlotte sighed. She couldn't speak, tears were choking her words.

"Charlotte, I want to understand."

She remained silent, a deep abiding sadness overwhelming her.

"Are you going to say anything?"

Charlotte shook her head, ending the call. She set down the phone and went upstairs to shower.

# WEDNESDAY, MAY 1

## Meg

The nine o'clock chimes had just sounded when Meg entered the garden. Father McMann was working on one of the benches in the back corner. He was using sandpaper to rough off splinters. She pictured Peter's basement full of power tools, including a cordless sander that would do this job. He used to love any excuse to use his tools around the house, now they sat abandoned. He was always too busy, and when anything needed to be fixed, he told Meg to call the local handyman.

"Need some help?"

He looked up from his work and smiled.

"Meg! You've already helped enough with the mulch."

"I was just looking for something to do."

"That's not surprising. You like to stay busy, don't you?"

"Guilty," said Meg.

"Well, there are some dead branches on the cherry trees near the gate and the wisteria is already starting to take over a bit. You could take some shears to them."

"I'd be happy to." Meg went to the storage shed to find the clippers.

She'd finished the cherry trees and was working on the wisteria when Father McMann joined her. "Did you make it to the widows' group yesterday?"

"I did. You were right—grief is grief. It was very helpful. In fact, it inspired me."

"How so?"

"I'm going to start my own group when I get home."

"That's wonderful! I take it that means you've decided to go home."

"I have."

"And have you sorted things out in your heart, then?"

"Maybe not everything, but enough."

Meg worked for another hour after Father McMann left to get cleaned up for noonday mass. After she finished in the garden, she went to the boardwalk and bought a sandwich for herself. She sat near the water, watching a family with young children building sandcastles.

Her cellphone rang. It was Peter. She'd known he would call.

"Hey," she said.

"How're you holding up?" he asked.

"I think I'm doing pretty good. How about you?"

"As well as can be expected," said Peter.

"Will it ever feel like any other day?" she asked.

"I don't think so, but it shouldn't."

Sadness colored Peter's voice and Meg wished he were here. What were they doing apart on today of all days?

"I still miss him, you know?" he said.

"I know."

Meg watched a little boy about Logan's age run shrieking to his mother when the tide caught his sneakers. She smiled.

"Things need to be different," she said.

"They can be."

"I want to be different."

"You already are," he said. "And I think maybe I am, too. I told the partners I was cutting back. I need more time at home."

Meg caught her breath. "Has something happened?"

"I just finally realized how much I could lose."

"We can figure this out, right?" she asked.

There was a pause on the line, and when Peter spoke, Meg could hear he was crying.

"I know we can. I lost my baby boy; I can't lose you, too."

Meg shook her head, but couldn't speak through her own tears.

"You'll come home, won't you?"

Finally, she said, "I will."

## Charlotte

Charlotte watched the clock. It was almost lunchtime. She hadn't heard from Martin in three days. She was angry—at him for not calling, and herself for caring that he hadn't called. It didn't help that she'd spent the morning sorting out bills for the clients she was avoiding back in Sadlersville. Numbers drove her nuts. Her cell phone rang with an unfamiliar local number.

"Hello?"

"Hey, my little Irish lass," Martin cooed.

"I'm not Irish, at least I don't think I am."

"Where'd you get the red hair then?"

"The Irish don't own the rights to red hair; I think Scottish people have red hair, too."

"'Tis true. How are you?"

"I'm fine. How was your meeting in Burnley?"

"Long, boring, but necessary."

"You sound tired."

"I could use a little personal sympathy."

"I wish I could give it, but I'm working right now, and tonight we kind of have a special dinner planned." It was the second anniversary of Logan's death, and while Meg hadn't said anything specific about it, they all knew what the date meant. Dani had offered to cook dinner for the three of them.

"Girls only?"

"Definitely."

"You have to eat lunch, don't you?"

"No time," she said. "I have to go down to Sweet Beach Tees; the Abibs said they've finally made a decision. And then I have to go to that damn shoe store. Brad's got some issue with the carpet."

"I'd really like to see you. Can't you squeeze me in? I thought you worked for yourself."

Charlotte's earlier irritation with Martin had evaporated. Hearing his voice made her desperate to see him. "Could you meet me at Sweet Beach Tees?"

"Sure. Thirty minutes?"

"Miss me?" she asked, happy that he was eager for her, too.

"You could say that."

"Give me an hour."

"Deal. There's an alley behind the shop. I'll pick you up there and we can grab lunch."

Charlotte changed into the new power suit she'd bought for her meeting last week with the contractors bidding on the shoe shop. The suit was bright yellow with a shorter skirt than her regular work suits, but then this was the beach and things were less formal.

When she walked into the T-shirt shop, she could see from Mr. Abib's fallen face and the way Mrs. Abib looked disapprovingly at her short skirt, that she hadn't gotten the job.

"Ms. Char-lot, you look so lovely today," said Mr. Abib, still not meeting her eye.

She didn't miss the scolding scowl Mrs. Abib cast his way. "Thanks. I brought the final contract with the couple changes you mentioned the last time we talked."

"Not necessary," said Mrs. Abib.

"Oh, well, we could just go with the original then."

"No contract. Nothing need changing. We are happy with what we have."

"You don't even want to consider the simple rearrangement of the floor plan? That's not very expensive and I could cut the labor costs if you wanted to do it yourselves."

"Moving things around not necessary."

"Well, then maybe just a new coat of paint or a brighter sign?"

"Newer is not always better," said Mrs. Abib, crossing her arms and shaking her head.

"I'm sorry we wasted your time," said Mr. Abib.

"No, no, don't apologize. I was the one who came in with the proposal. I'm sorry I couldn't help you."

"Yes, we are happy with what we have. Need nothing more," said Mrs. Abib again, nodding.

"You're lucky, then," said Charlotte, picking up the contract that lay on the counter.

"You come back with family and we give you discount," said Mr. Abib, a sad smile on his face.

Charlotte thanked them and backed out of the store. What was she thinking? This was not the kind of work for her. And really, they were right, the T-shirt shop was a Sweet Beach staple. No one cared if it had a new sign. She sighed and found the walkway that led to the back alley behind the boardwalk shops.

Martin spotted her and waved, "Hungry for lunch?" he asked.

"Or something," said Charlotte, feeling her pulse already quickening. Food wasn't what she needed.

"Oh?" said Martin, smiling impishly and looking around at the deserted alley. They watched as a woman wearing a hairnet and plastic gloves opened the back door of a restaurant and tossed a box in the dumpster.

Martin was wearing a baseball cap backwards to hide his bedhead. His blue sweatshirt set off his gorgeous eyes and Charlotte could hardly stop staring at his tight jeans. She reached for him and he responded immediately, leaning her against the side of his truck, kissing her face, her neck, and pulling her as close as he could. She let out a moan as his hands reached under her shirt.

"Get in the truck," she struggled to say through her own panting.

Martin opened the door and they practically fell across the bench seat. Martin hiked up her skirt as she worked at the button on his jeans. His eagerness made it difficult. He stopped momentarily to put on a condom that had materialized from somewhere inside the truck. Charlotte tried not to think about how practiced Martin seemed to be in this situation. It only took a few seconds before Martin called out and Charlotte opened her eyes to watch his face register ecstasy. She and Brett rarely made love with the light on. She watched his face as he reached orgasm. It was a raw image; as if she could see the inside of his happiness. For just those few moments, he was vulnerable and exposed, and then he was gathering himself again and it was gone. They straightened their clothes and slumped back against the seat.

"Woman, you are amazing," sighed Martin, closing his eyes in the sunshine and resting his hand on her thigh.

Charlotte grinned at him.

"I am."

"Lunch?"

Charlotte shook her head. She was hungry, but there wasn't time. Brad had texted that he needed her there before one. She looked down at her wrinkled suit and tried to smooth out the creases in the skirt.

"Gotta get to the shoe store."

"You have to eat. We can grab something quick. I'll drive you to the shoe store and you can eat on the way."

When they reached the shoe store, Brad was waiting out front. He looked agitated.

"Want me to wait around?" asked Martin. "You'll need a ride back to your car."

"This may take a while," said Charlotte drinking the last of her soda.

"I've got a couple errands to run. I'll be back." He leaned over and kissed her slowly, lingering. "You're too good to me," he said.

Charlotte hopped down out of the truck and Brad strode towards her.

"Is that your husband?" he asked.

"What's going on?" asked Charlotte, not wanting to explain Martin to Brad.

"The carpet people were here and the carpet they brought was awful."

"It wasn't the one you picked?"

"It was the one *you* picked," he said. "But it looked terrible. They said if they don't install today it will be three weeks before they can get back here. They want me to come down there and pick out something else, but I have no coverage for the store. I can't just shut down."

"Why not?" she asked, looking around at the nearly deserted parking lot.

"That's just not good business. Can you go down there and pick something better out."

"I thought what I'd picked was fine."

"It wasn't."

"So it seems. How about if I watch the store and you go down there and pick out a new carpet?"

"It's all the way down in Oceanside. That could take at least an hour and a half!"

"I think I can handle this. Just show me how to work the register."

After Brad explained the register to her, he insisted on showing her how to measure feet, demonstrating on her feet. Charlotte was certain he had a foot fetish, as he couldn't keep his hands off her feet, cradling them in his palms as he explained the metal measuring tool. Finally, he left. Charlotte prowled the aisles, trying on different shoes. One customer came in, an over-dyed blond woman who'd obviously had work done. When she found out Brad wasn't there, she left immediately.

Charlotte wondered if he handled all women's feet the way he'd handled hers.

Martin strolled into the shop about an hour after Brad left.

"Where's the owner?" he asked.

"In Oceanside."

"So, you're in charge?"

"Yup. I even know how to measure feet."

"Want to measure mine?"

Charlotte raised her eyebrows at him. "Your what?"

They laughed and then Martin produced the bag of chocolate chip cookies he'd bought at the bakery Charlotte loved. It was next door to Jeremy's art gallery and Charlotte told him about Dani's art selling so well there. It was a small town and Martin knew who Jeremy was, although he didn't know him personally. He was curious about the details of his relationship with Dani. Charlotte speculated for him.

"He is adorable, I'll say that. But Dani denies any ulterior motives outside of friendship and art dealing."

"Unless he's gay, he's got other things on his mind, too. And if he's gay he still has it on his mind, just not with Dani."

"Not every man is as horny as you."

"Yes, they are."

"How would you know?"

"You forget that I make my living in bars."

"Dani swears he thinks of her as a sister or mother figure."

"No man in his right mind would think of Dani that way."

"Hey, have you got the hots for my friend?"

"No, I've got you; I'm just saying she's pretty nicely put together."

"So you've noticed."

"I notice every woman."

"Just so you notice me," teased Charlotte as she got up and walked as seductively as she could to throw away their trash. The phone in the back office rang and Charlotte went to answer it. Martin followed her.

"Brad called and said he picked out the carpet and they're loading it now. He's on his way back and the installers will work tonight."

"So we've got a little time," Martin asked, eyeing the large empty desk.

"I can't do anything in here! What if Brad comes in?"

"He just left Oceanside. He won't be here for thirty minutes."

"What if a customer comes in?"

Martin walked to the front window and flipped the sign to CLOSED. Charlotte laughed. He took her hand and led her to the back office.

When Brad returned, Charlotte was standing behind the counter studying a spreadsheet on her laptop.

"Any problems?" asked Brad.

"It went fine. I actually enjoyed it," smiled Charlotte.

"It is a fun place to work," agreed Brad.

"I'm glad you were able to sort out the carpet. I can't wait to see what you picked out. I'll stop by tomorrow," said Charlotte, gathering her things.

"You sure you don't want to hang around. I could let you measure the next person who comes in."

Charlotte smiled. "As tempting as that is, I've really got to go. I have another appointment." Martin was waiting in his truck when she came out. She slid onto the bench seat and sat as close as she could, just like the teenagers did.

"Wish I was a younger man," said Martin, when she put her hand on his thigh.

$\triangleleft$

## Dani

Dani worked all morning, finishing up a brush and comb set and starting work on a coffee table. She carefully sketched out a pattern of waves on the table top. She would use bright shades of blues and turquoise and periwinkle. She looked at the clock and decided to wait until tomorrow to paint. She needed to get to the grocery store and farmers' market to get things for dinner. She knew it would be a tough day for Meg and she'd promised to make a special dinner for them. Even Charlotte was forgoing chasing down her Irish guy to be there for it.

After the farmers' market and the grocery story, she stopped and bought several bottles of wine and, on a whim, a bottle of champagne, too. She had a few minutes to spare, so she ducked into Libby's bookstore.

"Hey Libby," she called as she entered.

"I'm back here!" Libby's voice came from the backroom. Dani had never been in the workroom before. She followed the sound of Libby's frustration—books dropping to the floor, papers being pushed aside, and heavy sighs. Libby sat at a small table staring at a computer screen, surrounded by piles of books and a plethora of filing cabinets.

"Maybe you can help. I'm trying to move into the computer age, here. My nephew thought I needed to. He bought me this contraption and put some kind of program on it that's supposed to make my job easier. So far it's just made me feel old."

Dani smiled at her.

"I haven't got a whole lot of time to help now, but I could come back in the morning and give it a shot."

"Would you?"

"Sure."

"So, you and your girls figure anything out yet?"

She shook her head. "I'm beginning to think maybe we'll never have all the answers. We might have to go with what we've got."

"It's not that I don't like having you here. In fact, if you were a permanent fixture, I'd offer you a job, just for the company. But a mother should be with her children. They grow up so fast."

Dani pulled a book from the stack on the table and examined the cover, swallowing the guilt Libby had dredged up. "It's hard to explain. Charlotte thinks I'm depressed."

"Are you?"

"I don't know. I feel a lot better now. When I was at home, things seemed fuzzier—like I was seeing the world through a veil or something. I was tired and frustrated. Every day was like the one before and it all seemed so pointless."

"Sounds a bit like depression to me, although you don't strike me as the type."

"Exactly. There's nothing fundamentally wrong with me or my life. I don't know where these emotions are coming from. When I think of going back I feel trapped and sad, which makes me feel guilty and petty. I have a great life. What right do I have to be sad?"

Libby said, "Dani, I've told you this before, emotions are honest. They can't lie. You feel what you feel. If your feelings are overwhelming you, find someone to help you with that. Someone with an office, not a store full of books no one wants. I will tell you this, though, I find that just when you figure one thing out, a new problem rears its head. Best to just trust your gut and lead with your heart."

Dani looked at Libby and smiled. "You are possibly the wisest person I know."

"Don't tell me that, might go to my head and I'll start believing all the things that come out of my mouth. I've just lived a life, Dani; you will too. You make enough mistakes, eventually you learn from them."

Dani hugged her. "Thank you, Libby."

"You're welcome. I'll see you in the morning then?"

"Count on it!" said Dani as she raced out the door.

Dani spent the afternoon in the kitchen. It had been a long time since she'd fixed such a nice meal or been able to focus solely on cooking without children and life interrupting. She found herself humming as she made bread, kneading the sticky dough until it became elastic. She shaped it into three rough loaves and set them with their sides touching in a large cake pan. She covered the loaves with a damp towel and left them to rise in the sun coming through the window.

Next, she began making a key lime pie for dessert. Zesting the lime, she remembered how Jordan used to love to chew on lemon and lime peels as a baby. Joe was horrified the first time Dani had met him for lunch at a restaurant with the baby. Jordan started fussing and Dani handed her a lemon peel from her tea. Joe leapt out of his seat to retrieve the peel, much to Dani's shock. When she confessed that she'd been feeding her peels for months, he was amazed.

"How do you know it's safe for her?"

"She got one by accident the first time. It made her happy and it didn't hurt her, so I figured it was okay."

"Dani, you can't do that!"

"What?"

"Parent her by trial and error."

"Do you know any other way?"

Parenting had always been a joint effort for them. They got pregnant with Jordan on their first try. Dani enjoyed the pregnancy. Joe had been fabulous. He'd read the books right alongside her. He would fall asleep with his hand on her belly. They'd always been close, but when Dani was pregnant they couldn't get enough of each other and the miracle they had created together. Dani would be in the middle of something as mundane as sorting socks, and would look up to see Joe staring at her in awe. It had been a rich time for them. Dani didn't think they'd ever appreciated each other so much. But then the baby arrived and they were too tired and overwhelmed even to be civil at times. There'd never been that closeness again. Not even when she was pregnant with Joey.

She put the pie in to bake and sat down in the window seat. She dialed Joe.

"I'm so glad you called!" Joe said. Dani could hear background noises.

"Where are you?" she asked.

"Dress shop with Jordan. I'll explain in a minute. Is everything okay? Why'd you call?"

"I was just thinking of you," she said.

"You were?"

"I was."

"In a good way?"

"I was remembering when we were first pregnant with Jordan."

"That was a special time."

"It was. What's up?"

"Actually, your firstborn is in need of advice. We're at the mall shopping for a dress for the spring dance."

"Spring dance? How come no one told me?"

"She hadn't planned on going, but then some kid named Patrick asked her," Joe explained.

"She's going on a date? She can't do that, she's twelve!"

"Just about thirteen, actually."

"Since when are there dances in middle school?"

"It's at the rec center, and it's really a spring social. The dancing is supervised. There will be board games, too."

"Who is this Patrick kid?"

"I've never laid eyes on him."

"And you said she could go with him?"

"She'll be supervised the whole time. Lizzie is going. I wasn't going to be the one to wipe that smile off her face."

"Wow. Have I been gone that long?"

Joe was quiet.

"Here she is."

"Mom, I really, really, really want to buy the blue one, but Lizzie told me I have to wear black and the black one is itchy and hot. But there's nothing else and Daddy says we have to leave soon to get Joey, and I can't decide!"

Dani smiled. She could handle this crisis.

"Jordan, first of all, you should wear what you want, and not what someone says you should wear. Second of all, always go for comfort over trend, rule of thumb, sweetie."

"But what if everyone else is wearing black?"

"It will seem more like a funeral than a spring dance. Besides, if everyone else is wearing black, it will just set off your blue and make you look special."

"I'm not sure I want to look special."

"Not much you can do about that, darling, you are special."

"You're just saying that because you're my mom and you feel guilty for not being here."

Dani caught her breath. When did her little girl grow up so much?

"No, I'm saying it because it's true."

"Whatever."

"So buy the blue. When is this dance?"

"This Friday and it's a social, not a dance."

"Will there be dancing?"

"I guess."

"Take pictures, okay? And thank your dad for going dress shopping with you. A lot of men wouldn't."

"Okay. When are you coming home?"

"I'm not sure."

"Can we come down there?"

Dani hadn't thought of that.

"There's not really room here."

"That's okay, we can bring the tent."

"I'll let you know."

"All right. Bye, Mom."

"I love you."

Dani heard Jordan calling for her father, who was probably slouching in one of the chairs outside the dressing rooms, trying to look invisible.

"Did you solve the crisis?"

"I think so. She's grown up so much."

"Not sure how that happened. Maybe we shouldn't have fed her so much."

"How are things?"

"Okay. Jordan's kind of tired of the after-school at the Montgomery's house. But Joey's doing pretty well. He likes being there. Cheryl bakes a lot of cookies."

"How are you?"

"I kind of vacillate between worried something's really wrong with you or me or us, and angry I have to do so much. You will be back soon, won't you?"

Dani didn't answer. She was saved by Jordan's whining demand over the top of the dressing room door that Joe go find a different size.

"I'd better help her. I'll talk to you soon."

"Okay. I love you, Joe."

"I love you, too."

Dani hung up, but didn't move from her perch. She didn't know why she wasn't ready to go home. She was feeling so much better, she really was. Being here was like living in an alternate reality— one where she was happy.

"You feel what you feel," Dani said out loud to herself as she rose to finish making dinner. As she washed and chopped the herbs she would use with the scallops she'd bought, she wondered how much control she really had over her feelings. Was it possible to decide to feel happy? There was a sign in the office at Jordan's school that said, "You may not be able to change your situation, but you can change your attitude towards it." But could she? Maybe all Dani needed was to decide she was going to be happy and act like it. But was it real if she had to work at it? She felt happy when she was painting, and last Sunday with Jeremy at the tag sales, she'd had such a happy day. She felt alive and authentic. When she sat in the dark on the deck with Meg or Charlotte and talked into the night through several bottles of wine, she felt like she was putting pieces of the puzzle together.

Dani's thoughts were interrupted by the bustle of the others arriving. Charlotte appeared first with more wine, fresh flowers, and a giddiness that meant she'd seen Martin. Dani found a pitcher for the flowers and set them on the table. They were spectacular—huge lilies and bright tulips, plus freesia, and several types of flowers Dani had never seen before. Their brightness and fragrance transformed the room instantly. Charlotte always went for the extravagant; she was not one to do things in a small way. She told Dani she needed a quick shower, then disappeared with wineglass, bottle, and opener in hand. Dani returned to her cooking.

Then Meg arrived. She stopped in the kitchen to breathe in the aroma of the fresh bread. "I don't know if there is a better smell in this world," she said.

Dani watched Meg standing over the loaves fresh from the oven waving her hands and literally gulping their scent. She looked different. She'd definitely lost a few pounds since they'd gotten here, but she seemed to be holding herself differently. Meg was beautiful in that homecoming queen kind of way. Blue eyes, blond curls and, even with a few extra pounds, a body men noticed, but ever since Logan's death, she'd seemed to shrink—walking with her shoulders hunched and her head down, like she was ducking from an onslaught. Here was the light, playful friend she remembered.

Dani caught her in a hug. "How are you doing?" she asked.

Meg smiled. "I'm good. I really am. In fact, I'm so good, I'm thinking of going home soon."

"Really?"

Meg nodded. "How about you. Any plans to go back?"

"I don't know. I think I'm waiting for some kind of answer to a question I've never asked."

"That sounds pretty deep."

Dani looked around the warm kitchen in the fading sunlight, rich with the yeasty smell of bread.

She still thought there were answers here, but she didn't know if she'd recognize them if she saw them.

"I think maybe I've been looking for the fix-all, instant solution and life just might not be like that."

"You think?" Meg smiled and winked.

Dani laughed and went back to her preparations.

◆

## Charlotte

Charlotte opened the bottle of wine and poured herself a glass. She wanted to revel in her day before she joined Meg and Dani. She found a jazz station on her clock radio. She eyed her cigarettes. She desperately wanted one, but wouldn't dare light up inside.

Instead, she turned on the shower and waited for the water to turn as hot as she could stand it. Being here felt like living a new life. She wished it could stay like this. God, she was having too much fun, why did it have to end? She stood under the hot spray and let it wash over her. Once Meg and Dani went back, Brett would start expecting her. And how could she go back to him? She felt like she was tasting life again for the first time. She was daring and exciting. Gone was the dull routine of her predictable life.

What had happened to them? When did everything change? It probably happened gradually, like the wrinkles on her forehead and the gray in Brett's hair. Had it been inevitable? And like her wrinkles, was it irreversible?

Charlotte shook her head, banishing thoughts of Brett. Sex with Martin today had been amazing—illicit, thrilling, maybe even crazy. It was something she would have done when she was young, before life with Brett tamed her. Had sex ever been like that with Brett? Maybe at one time, but now the house, their jobs, the family obligations, the teacher conferences, carpools, and soccer practices just sucked the thrill right out of a relationship. Charlotte wished she could bottle what she felt this afternoon. An all-consuming desire that overrode her senses and certainly her sensibility. Charlotte Branson would never have sex on the seat of a pickup in an alley in broad daylight. Or would she? She smiled to herself.

Meg and Dani were in the kitchen when Charlotte came downstairs. She tried not to look too guilty as she entered.

"Now that we're all here," said Dani. "I'll open the champagne."

"None for me," said Meg.

"I'll drink hers," said Charlotte.

"I'm just not in the mood for alcohol," she said when Dani questioned her.

"That's okay, you can have ginger ale," said Dani, searching in the fridge for the bottle.

"Let's take it out on the deck," suggested Charlotte, fingering her cigarettes.

Dani popped the cork, watching it fly off the deck into the dark night. She filled their glasses.

"I want to make a toast," said Meg, her eyes welling up. They raised their glasses. Meg's voice trembled as she said, "To Logan, my beautiful boy. Thank you for teaching your mother how to live." Tears ran down Meg's face, but she was smiling.

Charlotte and Dani wrapped their arms around Meg. "Thank you," she whispered. They were all crying now.

"Look at us," said Charlotte. "We're a mess!"

"Absolutely," said Dani.

"But in a good way," said Meg, laughing and wiping her eyes.

Dani raised her glass, "To you, the best friends I've ever known. You make me laugh. You make me happy. You make me better."

"Oh, Dani, you're making me cry again," said Charlotte, waving her hand in front of her face, but she lifted her glass. "To reinventing ourselves!"

After dinner, they lounged in the living room, stuffed and content. No one was ready for the pie yet, so Dani put on some coffee. Charlotte told them about Brad and his foot fetish and the woman who came looking for him. She didn't mention her rendezvous with Martin in the store office. She imitated Mrs. Abib's expression when Charlotte arrived with her short yellow skirt and her contract. It was easy to make fun of her efforts at finding business in Sweet Beach, and Meg and Dani laughed at Charlotte's stories.

"People are funny. Of course, you don't really know them, especially the Abibs," said Meg. "They might be really nice people when you're not trying to sell them a crazy new floor plan."

"It wasn't crazy," said Charlotte, smiling. "It's just me that's crazy."

"No, you just give off a crazy first impression. I remember when Dani introduced me to you. You were so loud and so *right*. And you had these crazy ideas about how Peter's office needed more metal! I was kind of scared." Meg giggled.

"I *was* right!" insisted Charlotte. "I thought you were such a cheerleader with your perfect hair and your perfect clothes, and then when I went to Joey's first birthday party and you were there with all your kids dressed in matching outfits, it was a bit much."

"Oh Gosh, I remember now. We had just been to Sears to have pictures taken and I had dressed them all alike. Michael had a cute little bowtie and vest and the girls wore dresses with pinafores! I must have been pregnant with Timmy."

"No, not yet, because I remember when you told me you were pregnant."

"Oh yes, you looked right at me and said, 'What? Are you one of those Catholics who doesn't believe in birth control?'"

They all laughed. And then Meg started crying again. Dani looked at Charlotte, who shrugged.

"Meg?" asked Dani.

Meg waved them away and sat up. She started to speak, but the tears came again. Charlotte and Dani sat down on the sofa on either side of her.

"What is it?" asked Charlotte. "It's not as if you can't tell us anything."

"I just can't believe I did this," said Meg, putting her face in her hands.

"You couldn't have done anything worse than me," said Charlotte, placing a hand on her back.

"True," said Dani and Charlotte made a face.

Meg looked from Dani to Charlotte and back to Dani. "You aren't going to believe this."

"Don't underestimate us," said Dani.

"Holy shit!" said Charlotte.

"What?" asked Dani.

"She's pregnant!" shrieked Charlotte. She'd heard Meg in the bathroom getting sick on too many mornings for it to have been just the wine, like she'd claimed.

"What?" asked Dani again.

Meg just nodded through her tears.

"Meg," said Dani. "Aren't you happy about this? Another baby is great."

"Not right now," said Meg. "I just took a test this afternoon. I don't know how it happened."

"I could take a good guess," said Charlotte. Dani smacked her.

"It's just that I was finally feeling like I've got a purpose and Peter's changed. The timing is terrible."

"No, it's not," said Dani at the same time Charlotte said, "How has Peter changed?"

"I do want this baby, but not now, not when it seems like I'm finally figuring out how to accept Logan's death."

"Have you told Peter?" asked Dani.

Meg shook her head. "He's been trying so hard. Phoebe said he's doing everything at home, so much they hardly need her. And he told his partners he was going to cut back his hours."

"Wow," said Charlotte. "Good for Peter."

"How can I tell him there's another baby?"

# THURSDAY, MAY 2

## Meg

After spending over an hour on the phone with Phoebe, Meg drove to Sweet Beach. She spent the morning in the library researching grief and grief support groups. Turns out there were lots of national grief groups who sponsored local chapters. She couldn't find one for Sadlersville. Did the group she started have to be so formal? She would rather pull together something more organic with the people nearby. She couldn't be the only person in Sadlersville who was mourning someone. But how would she find them?

The task seemed too daunting, so instead she went in search of the gardening books and spent another hour paging through garden designs. Maybe the country club would let her have a small space for a memorial garden, after all that's where Logan died. He was gone before he reached the hospital, despite the paramedics' best efforts. Meg sometimes wondered if Peter played golf so much because Logan's spirit was still there. She had only been back for the holiday party this past New Year's, but now she longed to go there again.

Lists were piling up in Meg's head, so she stopped in a stationery shop nearby and bought a notebook. She made list after list of possibilities until her mind was empty. Satisfied, she went in search of lunch.

While munching on fries, she called Phoebe again. She was in her office surfing the Internet.

"What is your problem? Your kids are fine. You'd be amazed at how self-sufficient they've become. And Peter, he's a new man. He's even cooking dinner tonight."

"You're kidding!"

"No, he's tired of my vegetarian fare and Lizzy's frozen food. I think he's doing a stir-fry. He gave me a list and asked if I would have time to pick up a few things for him this afternoon. Here it is—*snow peas, shrimp, rice, teriyaki sauce, lemon, garlic.* Sounds good, huh?"

"I'm amazed. I should go away more often."

"Probably not the best idea for your marriage. Peter's working himself up again. He even bought some kind of self-help book."

"Peter?"

"Yeah, it was called something like, Keeping the Love You've Got."

"Wow. I'm impressed. I didn't think Peter needed anybody's advice."

"You've definitely sat him on his butt, Meg. He looks a bit lost these days."

"You told me how everyone else was doing this morning, but you didn't mention Michael. How is he?"

"He's pretty good. He asked about you for the first time yesterday."

"He hasn't been asking about me?"

"I think he was trying to be patient. But yesterday at breakfast he asked Peter if you were getting a divorce."

"Oh my God. What did Peter say?"

"He said no. Said that wasn't even on the table."

Meg smiled at the idea of Peter using his lawyer-speak on the kids. Meg finished her conversation with Phoebe, and promised to call the kids after school and talk with Michael.

She wanted to tell Phoebe about the baby, but she knew she could never keep a secret. Not one this big. Meg ran her hand over her stomach. *Oh baby, do you know what you're getting yourself into?*

# FRIDAY, MAY 3

## Charlotte

**M**eg and Dani sang "Happy Birthday" as they burst into Charlotte's bedroom with hot cinnamon rolls covered with glowing candles.

"Oh my God, you're going to burn the house down," she protested. Charlotte hadn't mentioned her birthday to anyone. She was trying to forget about it herself.

"Blow them out!" squealed Meg as she held the flaming plate towards Charlotte.

Charlotte looked sternly at Meg and then sighed. She took a deep breath and blew until every candle was out. Smoke swirled upwards for a moment and then all the candles reignited one by one. Meg's laugh was maniacal, and Charlotte couldn't help but laugh, too.

"HA! Everlasting birthday candles! Did you make your wish?"

Setting the plate down on the nightstand, Meg and Dani both launched themselves onto Charlotte's bed.

"Oh my God, what are you, like, five?" laughed Charlotte as Meg and Dani climbed under the covers with her.

"Well? What did you wish for?" asked Dani.

"Nothing I'll ever tell you!"

Charlotte sat between her two friends, giggling with happiness. Maybe it was just sticky buns and girl company, but she hadn't had a better birthday wakeup call since Will was three and had serenaded her in a ballet tutu waving his sippy cup full of orange juice.

"So what are you doing on your special day?" asked Dani.

"Working, I guess." She had to go down and check out Brad's new carpet and be sure the new displays had arrived.

"So no plans with Martin?"

"He doesn't know it's my birthday."

"Guess you're stuck with us, then."

"How's that?"

"Meg's going to teach us to play miniature golf."

Charlotte narrowed her eyes. "I hate miniature golf."

"Good, you already know how to play!" said Dani. "Get dressed!"

---

Despite Charlotte's reluctance, she actually did enjoy her morning of miniature golf and birthday lunch at the Pelican. It was much better than dealing with Brad and his carpet.

When they arrived back at the cottage, there was an enormous bouquet of flowers on the front porch.

"I think somebody got birthday flowers," sang Meg.

"Who would send me flowers?"

Charlotte pulled the card from the vase full of birds-of-paradise, calla lilies, and other exotic blooms. "These are amazing!"

"Whoever sent them knows you well," observed Meg as she poked through the bouquet.

"They're from Brett," said Charlotte. "How does he know where I am?"

"He called me and said he'd ordered flowers for you from a florist in Sweet Beach, but didn't know where to send them," said Dani.

"Why didn't you tell me?"

"He wanted to surprise you."

They all stared at the flowers.

"They are pretty incredible," admitted Charlotte.

"The man has good taste," said Dani. "Always has."

"Well, I'm going to get a shower and take a long nap. That was awesome, but I'm exhausted," said Meg as she went inside.

Dani sat down on the porch railing and watched Charlotte.

"I'm a jerk, huh?" said Charlotte.

"No, nobody's a jerk on their birthday. But tomorrow you'll probably be a jerk. I still love you, though."

Charlotte sighed and stared at the card. She ran her hands over the blooms and breathed in their scent. In a quiet voice she said, "What am I doing?"

"I thought you knew what you were doing. I've never known you not to."

Charlotte put her head in her hands, the card dropping to the floor.

"What's the card say?" asked Dani.

Charlotte picked it up and handed it to Dani.

*Happy Birthday to the love of my life. I'm miserable without you. Come home to me.*

Charlotte rubbed her eyes. "I've got to deal with my work e-mail and return a few calls," she said, picking up the vase of flowers.

"Are you going to call him?"

"I can't."

"You should; you owe him that," said Dani.

## Meg

Meg knew it was time to leave, but she wasn't ready to say good-bye. Secretly, she hoped Charlotte and Dani would leave, too. Maybe she was jealous of the idea of them at the cottage without her. She heard her phone ringing in the kitchen where she'd left it charging on the counter. She ran to get it.

"Hey, Phoebe."

"Hey, yourself. What's the Spring Hullabaloo?"

"Oh God, I forgot. That's a fundraiser the PTA does. I'm on one of the committees to organize it."

"Apparently. Some lady who sounds like she's got something stuck up her nose keeps calling. She's getting pretty irritated at this point. I'm running out of excuses for you. What should I tell her?"

"What have you told her so far?"

"That you are out of town due to an illness in the family."

"Can't you tell her the illness got worse or somebody died?"

"You really want me to?"

"I guess not. I'll call her."

"How's it going down there?"

"Oh, Phoebe, I feel so much better. I'm gonna come home soon, I am. I don't know what's keeping me here. Maybe I'm afraid I'll come home and just go back to being the same over-busy robot mom."

"No, you won't."

"How do you know?"

"The first step to change is awareness. Now you're aware of your behavior, so you have a chance at changing it."

"Where'd you get that?"

"The self-help book Peter is reading."

"He's really reading it?"

"I don't know, but he left it on the back of the toilet in the downstairs bathroom, so I read it when the opportunity arises."

"You're too much. I love you, Phoebe."

"I know. I love you too, but come home soon. I've had just about enough of my brother."

"Are the kids making you nuts?"

"The kids are great, a little exhausting, but great. But Peter is getting on my last nerve."

"I'll be home soon, I promise."

# Charlotte

Charlotte sat in her room staring at the flowers. Why hadn't Martin called? She needed to see him. Brett's flowers were beautiful and expensive and so not him. She watched them sitting on her bureau innocently screaming out a warning that this whole affair with Martin might possibly be an enormous, life-destroying mistake. She picked up the flowers and took them out in the hallway, setting them on the little phone table on the landing.

Maybe she should tell Martin that she was married. But why? Did she want more than what she'd gotten with him? Maybe. Was that why it bothered her so much that he hadn't called? She'd chosen Martin. She'd made it happen. She would be the one to make it unhappen. Or not. Brett couldn't just send flowers and write a beautiful note and think she'd come running home. It wasn't that easy.

Martin was playing at a bar in Oceanside tonight. She should just call him. Why couldn't she? He was supposed to want her, not the other way around. She was tired of making people want her.

She sat on the floor trying to remember some of the yoga poses she used to know. She needed to relax. She was getting way too uptight over this whole Martin thing. It was supposed to be about having fun. Screwing her husband by screwing someone else. Great plan. She just hadn't thought through what came next.

When the phone rang, it was Brett. She hit 'ignore' and wished it were that easy. She'd begged off when Meg offered to buy her a birthday dinner, saying she was going to have an early night, but now she prowled her room, anxious. She didn't understand why Martin hadn't called. She knew where he was playing tonight, but if he didn't call, she wasn't going to go there.

How had this guy she barely knew gotten her tied up in such knots already? She could tell that he was well-practiced at seduction, but still she thought she was special to him. Martin was more like the men she'd dated prior to marrying Brett. He was good-looking and popular and exciting. Brett was good-looking, but he certainly wasn't popular, and exciting would have been a stretch. He was solid. She remembered telling her cousin Dara that. Dara had asked, "Like a tree?" Solid was what you wanted in a husband, not popular and exciting.

---

## Dani

Dani loaded up Meg's car and took her latest pieces to the gallery. Jeremy was on the phone with someone. She heard him talking low and serious. When he finished, Dani thought he looked exhausted.

"How about I buy you dinner tonight, since I'm making so much money?" she asked.

He brightened. "That would be great, let me just close up." He went back out front and changed the sign, locked the door, and turned off the lights. As they left together, Jeremy placed his hand on Dani's back to guide her to his car.

"I'll drive. Let's go somewhere other than the Pelican for a change," suggested Jeremy.

"Fine with me."

They drove towards Oceanside, stopping at a small Thai restaurant just outside of the city limits. It was even smaller inside than it looked from the outside. There were just six tables. The waiter was very polite, but spoke marginal English until Jeremy ordered for both of them in fluent Thai and then he was all smiles. Dani stared at Jeremy.

"You have other talents I knew nothing about!"

"I have lots of talents you know nothing about," he said.

They talked about Jeremy's studies and his travels in the Far East. Dani was amazed at how much he had seen and done at such a young age. She told him about her meager travels to Italy and to the Caribbean. When they finished eating, Jeremy ordered more wine and Dani tried to protest.

"I'll pay for it; it was my idea," he assured her.

"No, that's not it. I'm just feeling a little tipsy as it is."

"I'll take good care of you," he promised.

They drank the second bottle of wine and talked more about art and Jeremy's opinion that art appreciation in general was deteriorating. Dani told him stories of Jordan's forays into art and the art teacher at their school who seemed to be more of a craft teacher. Everything Jordan brought home looked exactly like what everyone else brought home. There was no allowance for personal expression. Jordan loved to paint, but was extremely critical of her own work, regularly tearing up her finished products before anyone could see them. Dani hung the precious few surviving pieces on the walls of her office. They inspired Dani, but Jordan began sneaking in to take them down, so now Dani kept them in an under-the-bed box beneath the couch.

"That's just it; it's hard to find anything original these days. At least original without being offensive or ridiculous," Jeremy lamented. "Your stuff is original and energetic and fun; that's why it sells."

"I'm not sure my work's going to have an impact on the world."

"You underestimate your abilities."

She smiled. "You're kind, but I realize my limitations."

"I don't think you have any. You are one of the most competent, talented, intelligent women I've ever met."

"Now you've had too much wine!"

"No, I'm serious, wine or not. You're an impressive woman." He stared at her forcefully. Then he took a deep breath and said, "I'd like this to be more than a business relationship."

Dani was thrown off-balance, unsure how to respond. In her hazy state, she thought she might be misinterpreting his intentions. She didn't say anything, just stared at her glass, which Jeremy instantly refilled with the last of the bottle.

"A toast," he began, lifting his glass, "To a bright, new talented artist, and a long collaboration."

She touched her glass to his and took a small sip. The room was beginning to spin. Maybe it was the hot Thai food and the wine, but suddenly being with Jeremy felt awkward and illicit. She waved to the waiter who brought the check. Dani reached for it and Jeremy caught her hand.

"Jeremy, I said I'd pay."

"I'd really like to pay and you'll have to wrestle me for it if you don't let me."

Dani tried to pull her hand away, but he held it tight.

"Dani, I meant what I said. I want a relationship with you outside of business."

Shock registered in Dani's mind, but everything seemed to move in slow motion. Jeremy let go of her hand and handed his credit card to the waiter. He finished his wine, smiling at Dani, and said they should go dancing tomorrow night. Had something changed? Why would she go dancing with Jeremy?

Still, in a state of confusion and knowing she wasn't sober, Dani allowed him to lead her out of the restaurant and seat her in his car. He drove slowly and carefully, the music on the stereo was some Wynton Marsalis-sounding jazz turned low. Dani stared out at the darkness. The road between Oceanside and Sweet Beach was mostly government land. It paralleled the water. There were no street lamps, only deserted dunes. She searched for the stars, but the clouds were so thick only an occasional glimmer could be seen.

When they reached the gallery, Jeremy got out of the car and hurried around to open the door for Dani. She wobbled as she got out of the car.

"I really don't think I should drive home like this. I think I'll walk on the beach and come back for Meg's car tomorrow."

"I'll walk you, but maybe first we could go inside and have a nightcap."

"I think I just need to get home to bed."

"You could stay here. I have a bedroom upstairs; I used to live here before I got my place."

She looked at Jeremy and considered the long walk back.

"Maybe that's a good idea. But I better call Meg and Charlotte just to let them know where I am."

"Dani, it's 10:30. They have your cell phone number."

"Yeah, that's true. I guess they'd call if they were worried. Meg's probably asleep and Charlotte's probably with Martin, anyway."

"She's still with him?"

"You sound surprised. It hasn't been very long."

"It's just that he doesn't tend to stay with one woman; he kind of likes to sample, never buy."

"Charlotte's pretty into him and he seems to like her, too."

"That's good," said Jeremy, heading to the little fridge he kept in the back work area and producing a bottle of wine.

Dani held up her hand. "No more for me. I've definitely reached my limit."

"You can keep me company then, no one likes to drink alone."

She smiled at him weakly and sat down on one of the work tables. He poured himself a glass and sat next to her. He took a long sip and stared at her. Dani blushed and looked away.

"You don't take me seriously do you?" he asked.

"What do you mean?"

"When I say you're an amazing woman and I want to be with you, what are you thinking?"

Dani was confused again. Why was Jeremy coming on to her? Just the idea of it seemed completely out of touch with reality. It must be the alcohol. He couldn't be interested in her. It made no sense. But when she looked back on their time together with this new information, it suddenly did make sense. All the little looks, the inadvertent touches, the more-than-friendly welcomes and the overly eager willingness to accompany her to lunch, yard sales, and now dinner. Whoa. Now it wasn't just the room that was spinning.

"I'm happily married. Did I give you some idea I was available?"

"I don't think you're very happily married. Look where you are."

"Right now?"

"Well, you've run away from your husband, haven't you?"

"I ran away from my life, not my husband specifically."

"I'd wager he was a big part of your life."

"Yes, but . . ." Dani was unable to finish because Jeremy set down his wineglass, took her face in his hands, and kissed her. Without thinking, Dani instinctively kissed him back, before the wine cleared from her head and she opened her eyes and pulled away.

"Jeremy, I can't do this. I've been drinking. This isn't what I'm looking for."

"I think it is. Aren't you looking for a new life? This could be it."

"I have to go," said Dani. She began searching for the sweater she had shed when they first walked in. She stumbled around in the dimly lit room as Jeremy watched her.

"You don't need to be scared. I can be discreet. You can stay here until you settle things at home and then we can be together. We can go wherever you want. I have money."

She found her sweater and turned to Jeremy.

"I think I've given you the wrong idea, completely. I need to go." She made for the door, but Jeremy jumped up and beat her to it.

"Dani, what's wrong? I thought you wanted this. That kiss just now said you did."

"That kiss was wrong. I've had too much to drink and I'm confused. I've got to go, please, just let me leave."

"Let me take you home, then."

"No, I really need to walk. The air will help."

"Then I'll walk you."

Dani looked up at him.

"I want to walk by myself. I need to think."

"All right, as long as you promise to think about what I said."

"I don't know how I couldn't," said Dani.

He smiled. He leaned down to kiss her and she turned her head. His lips grazed her cheek. She opened the door and glanced back at him.

"Thanks for dinner."

"I'll be here when you come for the car tomorrow. Maybe we can get breakfast."

"Maybe." She waved and hurried up the alley. She needed to get away from him as fast as she could. When she got to the beach, she took off her shoes and walked fast. There were lights on the ocean, barely visible in the foggy night. Ships passing miles away. The moon danced in and out of cloud cover, making the beach nearly pitch dark. Dani stumbled over driftwood and former sand castles. She gulped big breaths of air, trying to sober up. What had just happened?

How could Jeremy have been so misled? What had she said? She'd been flattered by his company and, admittedly, she'd found him attractive. She'd enjoyed flirting with him and even fantasizing about him a bit, but it had seemed safe at the time. She never imagined he would be attracted to her. He was so young! How could he possibly be interested in a future with her? She laughed out loud. She didn't want to hurt his feelings. He'd been a huge help to her. Without him, she might not have redis-covered her creative side. She owed him a lot, plus he was effectively her boss at the present moment since all her work was in his gallery. She couldn't very well slink away in the dark of night. She would have to face him again. And tiptoe around his frag-ile male ego.

A pounding was beginning behind her tem-ples. She started to run.

When she reached the cottage, Meg and Char-lotte were in the living room playing Scrabble.

"Hey," she said and collapsed on a chair, winded.

"She's killing me," said Meg. "But I'm plying her with alcohol so I should soon have the advantage!"

"Where've you been?" asked Charlotte.

"You're not going to believe this," said Dani.

"Are you okay? You look like you've seen a ghost. Here, have my wine, I'm not drinking it any-way," said Charlotte, holding her glass out to Dani.

"I've had more than enough to drink," said Dani.

Meg got up from where she was pinned behind the coffee table and sat on the arm of Dani's chair. "What happened to you? You do stink like wine," she said.

"You aren't going to believe this," repeated Dani. "I'm not sure I do."

"Well, try us."

Dani unfolded the evening for them, hardly believing it herself.

"Oh my God, Dani! Did you sleep with him?" Charlotte sat up.

"No! God, no."

"But you kissed him?" asked Meg, waving Char-lotte away.

"When I realized what was happening, I stopped it. What am I doing? I feel like such an idiot. This is crazy, right? Staying here was insane. Why did you let me do this to all of us? What was so horrible about our lives that we had to run away?"

The question hung in the air and no one dared touch it. Dani began crying and Meg wrapped her arms around her. Charlotte stared at the ceiling.

"So how did it end?" asked Charlotte, matter-of-factly.

Dani pulled away from Meg and wiped her eyes with her sleeve.

"I told him I had to go, I needed air. He wanted to walk with me, but I told him I had to think. He thought I would seriously consider leaving Joe to start a new life with him. Oh my God. What did I do? I keep going back over all the time I spent with him, and when I look at it in this light, maybe I did lead him on a bit. I just never thought he was thinking of me in that way. I mean, when he flirted with me, I thought he was just humoring an old lady for fun."

"Dani, you are not an old lady in anyone's book. Even Martin said so."

"That's not saying much. I hate to bring this up at this point, but Jeremy said something tonight about Martin's habit of hopping from girl to girl."

"Can we leave Martin out of this? I thought we were dealing with your crisis."

"Is it me, or do we sound like we're in high school?" asked Meg.

"Meg, I'm sorry I left your car there."

"No biggie," said Meg. "We'll get it in the morning."

"Thanks," said Dani.

"I think this birthday is officially one for the books," said Charlotte. "Good night ladies."

"Happy birthday," said Dani.

"I'm going up, too," said Meg. "You sure you're all right?"

Dani nodded. "I'm just going to read down here for a while. Try to calm my mind down."

"Okay, good night."

Meg's phone was ringing somewhere. Dani could hear it and didn't understand why she wasn't answering. Opening her eyes, Dani realized she was still on the sofa where she'd fallen asleep with a book. Meg's phone was charging on the counter in the kitchen. Dani dragged herself up to answer it, but it stopped ringing just as she reached it. She looked at the time, 2:17 a.m. She turned and launched herself back onto the sofa, pulling the afghan up to her chin again. She was almost asleep when the phone began ringing again. Sleep was pulling at her so strongly; she turned over and pulled the pillow over her head. The phone stopped, only to begin ringing again almost immediately. Dani groaned and got up. She stumbled to the phone.

"Hello?"

"Who's this?" Dani registered Peter's frantic voice. "Peter?"

"Dani?"

"Do you know what time it is?"

"I've got to talk to Meg. It's an emergency."

"Hold on. I'll find her," Peter's words startled Dani into action. She set the phone down and took off for the stairs. When she reached the stairs, she realized she should have brought the phone with her. She ran back to get the phone, banging her shin on the coffee table. Cursing, she grabbed the phone and limped up the stairs. She knocked on Meg's door as she opened it.

"Meg! Wake up! It's Peter!"

"What?" Meg crawled out from her covers, looking confused. "Where?"

"On the phone. Here." Dani handed her the phone and sat down on the bed.

"Peter?"

Dani could hear Peter shouting over the sound of a child screaming.

"Meg, I need you here. Lizzie's broken her arm, I think."

"Hold on. How could she have broken her arm, isn't she in bed?" asked Meg.

"She was. She slept in Sarah's top bunk. They were telling each other ghost stories and got so spooked they wanted to sleep in the same room."

"Did she fall out?"

"Yeah. And her arm is bent funny. Phoebe's not here, she had a hot date and I guess it worked out for her. I'm going to leave Timmy and Sarah with Michael, but Meg, I need you. I'm not good at this and she won't stop crying."

"I'll be there. Are you going to University?"

"Is that the closest?"

"Yes. Try not to move the arm. Give her some Tylenol before you go. I'll be there as soon as I can."

"When?"

"I don't know, two hours or so?"

"Okay, hurry, but be careful."

Meg hung up the phone and jumped out of bed.

"You're leaving?" asked Dani.

"Peter is completely paralyzed by stuff like this. I need to be with her. Help me find my stuff."

"Just get dressed and grab a few things. I'll bring the rest later."

Meg stopped and looked at Dani.

"Am I going back?" Her face suddenly registered fear.

"It looks like it," said Dani as she frantically threw things on the bed to pack.

Charlotte appeared in the doorway.

"What's going on?" she asked.

"Meg has to get back. Lizzie broke her arm."

Meg came out of the bathroom with a toothbrush hanging from her mouth and her arms filled with her toiletries. "My car!"

"Shit. It's at Jeremy's!" said Dani.

"You can't go by yourself anyway. I'll drive you," said Charlotte.

Meg and Dani both looked at Charlotte.

"C'mon, I'm fine. I'll make coffee." She went downstairs.

"I don't want it to end like this," mumbled Meg through her toothpaste-filled mouth.

Dani shut her suitcase. "I'll bring the rest of your stuff back with your car."

"I hate to leave this way," said Meg.

"It's a pretty sucky ending," said Dani, "But you have to go. You've been ready for days."

Dani followed Meg down the stairs, colliding with her at the bottom when she stopped suddenly.

"What if nothing's different?"

"Meg, we're all different, even Peter. You said so yourself. Besides, we can't figure out the secret to life in a few stolen weeks at the beach. But you've changed. You know you have. Everything's different."

"You're ready," said Charlotte, appearing behind them. "Now get your butt in the car. I'm gonna grab some food."

Dani and Meg went outside and loaded Meg's suitcase into Charlotte's Saab. Meg turned to Dani. "Thank you," she said, hugging her. "For everything, for this crazy idea and for always being there for me. I don't know what I'd do without you."

"Same," said Dani, her eyes misting.

Charlotte came outside, bounding down the steps with a bag of grapes, a crumpled bag of Oreos, and a stale bagel.

"Here," she said, thrusting the food at Meg. "It's all I could find." She pulled out a Diet Coke from her coat pocket and handed that to her also.

"Now get out of here," said Dani, opening the car door.

# SATURDAY, MAY 4

## Dani

Dani slept fitfully. Her mind ping-ponged between Meg and Charlotte racing home in the middle of the night and Jeremy's words earlier. By seven, she still hadn't heard anything from anyone, so she decided to go get Meg's car and deal with Jeremy. When she reached the gallery, she knocked on the back door. It opened almost immediately.

"You up for breakfast?" asked Jeremy brightly.

"Actually, I'm not hungry."

"You want to come in? I haven't opened up yet."

"Maybe we could go for a walk?" asked Dani.

"Sure, just let me turn off some lights." Jeremy came back with his hand held behind his back. Dani had a momentary panic, but laughed nervously when he pulled out a rose.

"For you," he said and kissed her on the cheek.

They walked to the beach. Jeremy chattered about a shipment he was expecting today and the predicted good weather that should bring the crowds in. Dani fiddled with the rose and pretended to listen while she rehearsed what she would say.

"So, did you have time to think?" he asked.

"I did."

"And?"

Dani's stomach churned as she looked at his sweet face, full of hope. She swallowed and then stopped, turning to him.

"The thing is, Jeremy, I may be in a vulnerable place right now. I'm confused about my life and trying to sort things out. But I'm not confused about my feelings for my husband. I love him deeply and I made vows to him."

Jeremy looked out at the ocean as if not hearing Dani. She continued.

"We have children who need their parents, both their parents, full time. I'm not sure what made me decide to stay here." Dani paused, touching Jeremy's arm. She knew it was hard for him to hear this. "I can't thank you enough for all the help you've given me in rediscovering my art. It's made me feel so alive. Being here has felt like being in a different life. But it's not. It's still my life and my life involves a marriage to the love of my life and two beautiful children who love me and count on me. So, I'm sorry if I led you to believe I had run from that. I ran from me, not them. And it's time to go back."

Jeremy glanced at Dani and then looked back out at the sea again.

"Jeremy, you're an amazing man. I will admit when I met you I was almost intimidated by you. I had a junior high-size crush on you, I did."

He turned to look at her and a smile slid out the side of his mouth.

"But I never thought you would look at me in that way. Flirting with you seemed harmless; I knew it would never lead anywhere. And I swear I had no idea you thought it would. I really never thought you'd be interested in someone like me."

"Dani, I . . ." he began, choking back emotion.

"No, Jeremy, I'm certain you can have your pick of women. They must swarm you in the summer. I'm unbelievably flattered by your feelings. I wish I could return them. I do. But I can't."

"I wish you'd reconsider," he said flatly, not looking at her.

Dani started walking again, but back in the direction they had come. She didn't know what to do. It seemed like he hadn't heard her. What was it about men, were they deaf to anything they didn't want to hear? Jeremy took her arm and stopped her.

"I know you say you love your husband. But I think you're just trying to convince yourself. I could make you happy."

"You're not listening to me," said Dani, her voice rising with her frustration. "I can't have a relationship with you."

"You can't or you shouldn't? There's a big difference."

"No, there's not. I can't and I shouldn't and I don't want to." There, she'd said it as plain as day. "I have to get back." She began walking again, but faster and with determination. She wanted to run. How could someone change so completely overnight? This was not the Jeremy she knew. Or maybe this was Jeremy and she'd imagined he was someone else. Now, instead of passionate and endearing, he seemed unstable and desperate. She glanced back over her shoulder and saw he was still standing there, watching her leave. She shuddered and ran up the steps to the boardwalk.

---

## Meg

The break was bad and required surgery. Meg found Peter in the surgical waiting room. He looked disheveled, unshaven, terrified, and more handsome than she could remember him ever looking. She paused in the doorway.

"Hey," she said softly.

Their eyes met, but he said nothing. He stood and reached for her and she fell into his arms. He stroked her hair and waited for her tears to abate.

"She's going to be fine," he said. "The doc says it's an easy fix. There was no way around the surgery, though."

Meg nodded.

"And us?" she asked.

"Maybe not such an easy fix, but I'm ready to try." He took her hands and led her to the chairs. Now it was his turn to cry.

"Things have to be different."

He nodded. "They already are."

"No, I mean I need you to be a part of our family. I need us to talk about Logan. We have to remember him. We can't pretend. He has to stay a part of our lives."

"I know," said Peter. "I've been trying to be the strong one. I knew you were hurting, and I didn't know what to do. I thought if I just acted like our family was fine, it would be. But that wasn't working and you seemed so unreachable. I just couldn't be there. It was too hard to pretend to be fine. Does that make any sense at all?"

"It does. I was doing the same thing, even though I was in the house. I kept my mind off the pain by keeping busy —doing too much and by doing those stupid puzzles."

"I got you a new book of puzzles," he said.

"I don't think I need it." She smiled. He squeezed her hand.

"How are we going to do this?" he asked.

"I don't know, but I'm done trying to do it by myself."

He nodded. "You don't have to."

"I was thinking of starting a grief support group," she said, watching his face, looking for his doubt.

"What's that?" he asked.

"A safe place for people to talk about how much they still hurt and how they're handling it. I've been doing some research."

"I think that's a great idea."

"You do?"

He smiled. "I do."

"And I want to build a memorial garden. I want to have it at the club."

"They'd like that. The manager has asked me several times if they could plant a tree in Logan's

297

memory, but I never gave him an answer. I didn't want to bring it up with you."

Meg leaned her head on his shoulder. "We can't do that anymore."

"What?"

"We can't keep things from each other—good or bad."

"You're right."

"So, I have to tell you something else." Meg's tears started again. She sat back up and searched his worried face. Would this news make him happy? Or would it scare him like it scared her?

"I'm pregnant."

"What?"

Meg just looked at him. She knew he'd heard.

"But, when . . . how?"

"In your study. I did the math. It had to have happened then."

Peter looked at their hands entwined. When he looked up, his smile was the smile Meg had fallen in love with. Only then did she realize she hadn't seen it since Logan died. He pulled her into his arms and kissed her with a passion she also hadn't felt since then.

"Do you know how much I love you?" he whispered.

Meg nodded. "As much as I love you."

❧

## Dani

When she reached the boardwalk, Dani dropped Jeremy's rose in the first trash can she came to. She dialed Meg's number and she answered on the first ring.

"Hey," she said. Dani could hear a new happiness in her voice. "The surgery went well. Lizzie's doing great."

"Is Charlotte still with you?"

"I haven't seen her since she dropped me off, and she isn't answering her cell phone."

"And how are you?"

"I'm good," said Meg. "It feels right. I'm glad I'm here. I told Peter my plans while we were waiting during surgery. He thinks the country club would be thrilled to let me build a garden and he had some great ideas about networking to learn more about support groups. I'm exhausted, but I feel good. Maybe it isn't the way I wanted to leave, but I'm glad I'm here."

"And is Peter happy with your news?"

"He can't take his eyes off me!" Meg whispered.

Dani laughed. "I'm glad."

"Take care of Charlotte, she seemed a little too wired on our drive."

"I haven't seen her yet, but I'll do my best."

After she hung up with Meg, Dani tried Charlotte's cell phone and left a message. Had she decided to go home, too? Dani didn't want to go back to the empty cottage. There was no point in painting, she wasn't in the mood, and besides, she couldn't keep doing business with Jeremy. She'd go see Libby.

When Dani reached the Bookateria, Libby was busy with customers, so she fixed herself a cup of coffee and waited as Libby rang up a sale. When she'd finished, she turned to Dani.

"Well, every week I wonder if you will still be here. When I didn't see you with the sun this morning, I thought maybe you'd finally gone home."

"I'll be going home soon. I just have to take care of a few things first."

Libby raised her eyebrows. She told Libby about Meg, and then gave her an edited version of the events with Jeremy. Jeremy was Libby's friend also, and Dani didn't want to paint him in too harsh of a light.

"I feel terrible. I didn't want to hurt him. I had no idea."

"He's a big boy, I'm sure he can handle it. Although, I doubt that he's had too much rejection in his life."

"So how are things going with your computer inventory?" asked Dani. It had only taken one morning for Dani to help Libby master the relatively simple program.

"I think I've got the hang of it. I still use the cheat sheets you gave me, though. I hope in the end it will all be worth it."

"This is the hardest part, getting the stuff you currently have into the system, but it won't require nearly as much time once you only have to enter new inventory and the books you sell."

"Actually, I kind of enjoy it. Makes me feel 'hip,' as you say. I hate feeling like an old fart who was left behind by the computer age."

"Libby, you could never be an old fart," Dani put her arm around her. "You have been such a dear friend to me. I can't believe I only met you a few weeks ago."

"I think it's been nearly a month, my dear. You really need to be getting back to those children of yours. Your husband may be a patient man, but you are approaching something beyond patience."

"I know I am. I just have to settle things with Jeremy. And I don't know if Charlotte is ready to leave yet."

"You can't make her go back, you know. She'll only resent you if you drag her back out of guilt."

Dani knew she was right. She didn't understand Charlotte's obsession with the man. Dani didn't trust him as far as she could throw him. But maybe Charlotte's marriage was past the point of no return. Who was she to say? If she forced Charlotte to go home now, her obsession with Martin would most likely only continue. Memory had a way of warping reality. No, Charlotte would have to make the decision for herself.

"You're absolutely right, Libby. I've got to keep my opinions to myself."

"I didn't say that, but there's no point in offering an opinion that can't be heard and wasn't asked for."

"True. I seem to forget that sometimes."

"We all do, and we waste too much breath, I think."

Dani stuck around for lunch and helped Libby reshelf the books that had piled up waiting to be entered in the new inventory system. It was nearly four when Dani finally said good-bye, promising to visit in the summer and bring her family.

## Charlotte

After she left the hospital, Charlotte felt compelled to drive past her house. It was early, Brett would probably still be asleep. If Will was home, they'd be off on some adventure—fishing or hiking or kayaking, something that didn't include her. It was going to be a gorgeous day, but she didn't lower the top of the Saab.

She pulled onto her street and spotted Brett's car in the driveway. It was dripping wet, Brett must have just finished washing it. Wait—it was Saturday, wasn't it? Brett always washed his car on Mondays. Three years ago, he'd started closing the office on Mondays, presumably so they could have time together. Funny, she'd forgotten that was the real reason.

She remembered the teary night the first time she'd confronted him about their relationship. She'd lost her temper, yelling that they never spent any time together and that their marriage was empty. He'd calmly told her he disagreed and then came up with the plan for Mondays. They thought spending a day together would reignite their relationship, but it hadn't worked out that way. It had taken three months to wean the patients and staff to a four-day week and by then Charlotte had given up. Brett used Mondays to wash the car, work out, and catch up on his dental journals. She was always busiest on Mondays. Seemed clients had their best ideas over the weekend and Charlotte's phone would ring off the hook with changes and new business.

She parked up the hill behind another car that belonged to new neighbors who had moved in this winter. She found her scarf in her glove compartment, tied it around her head, and got out of the car. Crouching behind the neighbor's car, she felt a little foolish and was about to leave when she saw Brett come out of the house carrying towels. When she saw that he was using the good guest towels, she had to force herself to stay put and not run down there to yank the towels from his hands before he ruined them drying the car. Taking a deep breath, she steeled herself and stayed put. Brett looked pretty much the same. He needed a haircut and he looked a little thinner to her. He was drying the car very methodically, a panel at a time.

Just as he was finishing, a car pulled in the driveway and a young woman got out. Charlotte felt her pulse start racing. Was Brett having an affair? She couldn't imagine it. The woman looked to be in her twenties. She wore jeans and a pink sweatshirt. She waved to Brett and went into the house. Charlotte's face felt hot. She sat down and leaned against the car. Could Brett be having an affair with a younger woman? Damn him. She didn't think he was capable of something like this.

She snatched the scarf off her head and marched back to her car, squealing the wheels as she pulled out. She didn't even care if he saw her. She sped back to Sweet Beach. She'd go deal with Brad and his stupid carpet and then she was going to get good and drunk. She'd had enough of all the men in her life.

***

## Dani

"You're here!" said Dani when she got back to the cottage later that afternoon and found Charlotte there. She was sitting in the kitchen window seat painting her nails and sipping a gin and tonic.

"Here I am!"

"How did it go?"

Charlotte shrugged. "Went fine. By the time I parked and found Meg, she and Peter were making out in the surgical waiting area. I figured she was fine and took off. How'd it go with Jeremy?"

"Not well," said Dani, tossing her purse on the counter and opening the fridge in search of juice.

"What do you mean?"

"I told him in no uncertain terms I wasn't interested in having a relationship with him, but he was like Joey when I tell him we're out of chocolate milk. He just keeps asking for the chocolate milk no matter how many times I tell him we don't have any. It was like he couldn't hear me. I finally had to walk away."

Dani sat down on the window seat next to Charlotte.

"That's bold," said Dani, nodding at Charlotte's bright red nails and taking a swig of juice. "You don't think he's the kind of guy who could become a stalker or anything do you?"

"You've seen too many movies," said Charlotte. "His ego's just bruised, he'll bounce back. Give him a few days."

"You think?" asked Dani, relieved.

"I do. He's a man, he'll move on," she said bitterly.

"What happened to you today? You were AWOL."

"I was in Sweet Beach. Drove back after I left the hospital. I promised Brad I'd come check on the carpet install."

"Oh, that's right. How'd the shoe store look with the new carpet?"

Charlotte shrugged. "I don't know."

"I thought today was the big unveiling."

"It would have been, if I hadn't been fired."

"What? That slime ball fired you after all the work you've done?"

"He found out I had sex in his office."

"What?"

Charlotte smiled and took a sip of her gin and tonic. "Me and Martin."

"You didn't! How'd he find out?"

"Video surveillance tape. Who looks at those? And it wasn't the fact that I had sex with Martin in his office, it was the fact that I turned him down when he asked if he could have sex with me in his office!" Charlotte shrieked.

"And that's funny?" said Dani.

"Kind of, don't you think?"

"Not really."

"Oh, c'mon. It is kind of funny. It has to be, because if it isn't then I am truly losing my mind."

"Losing? I'm thinking it's long gone."

Charlotte shot her a look.

"Sorry," said Dani.

"I know you think I'm nuts, but Martin makes me happy. It's not just the sex, either, which is unbelievable." Charlotte raised her eyebrows, then continued, "It's the way he's so content all the time. Like where he is is exactly where he wants to be. And he makes me feel beautiful."

"You are beautiful. You don't need some singing Irish playboy to make you beautiful," said Dani.

Charlotte stuck out her tongue at Dani. "You know what I mean," she said.

"Not really. Sure, everybody feels all gaga when they're first seeing someone, especially if sex is involved and the sex is good, but it goes away."

"Why does it have to?"

"Because you aren't living in a romance novel. Life is messy and complicated and eventually the gaga fades."

"I've read about couples who've sustained a romantic love for decades."

"That's not realistic, and just because someone wrote about it doesn't mean it really happens that way. I think romance comes and goes. It kind of cycles throughout your relationship," said Dani.

"Maybe yours, but other than the desperate birthday flowers, I can't remember the last time Brett did the slightest romantic thing."

"Well, when did you?"

"I've tried, and he's always appreciative, but he never reciprocates. Eventually, I just stopped trying. I mean, what's the point?"

"Do you really think if you dumped Brett and moved in with Mr. Irish hot pants, things would be any different in, say, five years?"

"I'm not moving in with him. Can't you just stop riding me about this?"

"I could, if I didn't love Brett and Will so much," said Dani, getting up to rinse her juice glass.

The air was thick with unspoken thoughts.

"I'm on your side, Charlotte," she said quietly as she walked by her. The screen door slammed as Dani went out to the potting shed.

Charlotte sighed.

# SUNDAY, MAY 5

## Dani

The bell jingled when Dani entered the Bookateria.

"Back so soon?"

"Do you know why Jeremy isn't open?"

"He isn't? That's strange; he didn't say anything to me and he would have told me if he wasn't going to be open today. The season's started."

"I know. I hope he's okay. He's not answering his phone."

"I'm sure he's fine."

"I kind of wanted to settle up with him."

"You could always go to his place," said Libby. "He just lives down on Pelican Way."

"Do you know the house number?"

"I don't know the number, but it's the little green house with the wood shutters. He's got an amazing garden out front with lots of those little carved up bushes."

"Bonsai?"

"Yes! You can't miss it."

"Thanks, Libby."

Dani started to leave, but Libby called after her, "Dani?"

"Yes?"

"Don't be a stranger."

"Don't worry. I'll e-mail you. Take care, Libby. And thank you for everything."

Libby waved her off as she poured herself another cup of coffee.

❧

Dani walked down the boardwalk to Pelican Way. It was only four blocks. As she walked past the Pelican, she thought of the lunches she'd had there with Jeremy. She couldn't believe she had been so naïve.

Jeremy's house was just as Libby described it. Dani stopped to admire the garden before knocking on the door. There was no answer to her knock, although she was sure she'd heard music when she first approached the house. She peered in a window.

She was shocked to recognize a table and chair set she'd painted in what looked like Jeremy's dining room. And on top of the table were most of the frames she'd painted. Dani walked to another window. She saw boxes on the floor next to a piano. She thought she could see the edge of one of her trays sticking out of the side of the box. And there was the coffee table and the bench. Her head was spinning. What did this mean?

Dani walked back to the front door and began pounding.

"Jeremy! I know you're in there! Please, open the door!"

When there was no answer, she walked around to the back door. She was sure she saw movement inside. She pounded again.

"I'm not leaving until you open the door!"

Finally, the door opened a crack and Jeremy's dark eyes appeared. He didn't say anything.

"Can I come in?"

"I'm not feeling so great."

"I just want to talk."

He hesitated, then opened the door. Dani walked in. She glanced at Jeremy and then took a brief tour of the first floor, noting all of her work piled throughout the house. She stopped in front of Jeremy, who wouldn't look at her.

"Why?"

Jeremy shrugged and sat down at his kitchen table.

"You could have just told me the stuff was crap."

"It's not crap."

"Then why did you have to buy it all?"

"It would have sold, eventually. But I wanted to inspire you and keep you coming back to see me."

Dani softened and took a seat opposite Jeremy at the table.

"You want coffee?" he asked.

"No, I just came to say good-bye. I'm sorry it's like this."

"Are you going home?"

Dani nodded. "It's where I belong."

Jeremy didn't say anything, just stared at a stain on the table cloth.

"What will you do with my stuff?"

He looked up.

"Some of it, I'll put back in the gallery."

"And the rest?"

"I don't know yet. I used to love having it here with me. It was like having part of you here. But now I just feel so stupid when I look at it."

"You shouldn't feel stupid."

"Oh yeah? How should I feel?"

Dani looked at him sadly. "I don't know. But you're not stupid to feel something for someone else. Feelings are honest, not right or wrong, just what they are. Libby taught me that."

Jeremy continued to stare at the stain, not looking at Dani.

"I haven't given up, Dani. My feelings haven't changed. I wish yours would."

Dani stood up.

"Well, my feelings aren't going to change."

Jeremy snorted.

"I'm going to go. You do what you want with the pieces that are still left."

"Maybe I'll have a bonfire," said Jeremy half-heartedly.

"You do that."

He looked up at Dani.

"I wouldn't."

"Jeremy, I can't thank you enough for encouraging me to paint again. I realize now, although I'm sure I've known this all along, it's not great art. But it's my art and if no one ever buys a piece, that's okay. I'm doing it for me, not for them. Thanks for helping me to see that."

Jeremy stood up. Dani held out her hand. He looked at her through bloodshot eyes, she knew he wanted much more than a handshake. Slowly, he took her hand and squeezed it.

"Dani?"

"Yes?"

"You are an artist. You should never have let anyone convince you otherwise."

Dani nodded, biting her lip and holding in her tears. She reached for the door.

"Have a nice life," he said.

"I will; you do the same," she told him and quickly walked out. She closed the door behind her before he could say another word, but Jeremy opened the door and called to her.

"Dani! Wait!"

She turned.

"Here, I want you to have this." He held out a tiny soapstone statue. It was one from the collection she'd seen the first time she entered the store. It was a painter working at her easel with a palette in hand. You could even see the separate blotches of paint on the palette and the tiny brush making contact with the paper on the easel. The painter had a dreamy look in her eyes, as if studying something no one else could see.

Dani took the statue from Jeremy.

"Thank you. It's beautiful."

"I hope all your memories of me won't be bad ones."

Dani shook her head. "They won't be."

He smiled at Dani and she could tell he was fighting tears. This time she did reach over and hug him. Then she held up the statue.

"Thank you for this, I will treasure it."

She turned and hurried off before he could say anything else.

---

When she got back to the cottage, Dani threw her energy into cleaning up the potting shed. It was time to go. She'd stayed too long. Charlotte would have to survive without her.

She picked up the box of clean brushes and unused paint she'd packed the night before and stared at it. Take it home? Throw it out? There would be no time or place for painting at home. She set it outside. Maybe Jordan would want it.

She cleaned the shed from top to bottom, her old Girl Scout leader's voice in her head, "Leave it cleaner than you found it." Well, it was that. When she'd finished in the shed, she set to work in the house. She packed up the rest of Meg's things and then her own. Exhausted, she collapsed in the hammock late in the afternoon and fell fast asleep.

---

## Charlotte

When Charlotte got out of bed, the house was quiet. It was nearly lunchtime and her head pounded from all the gin and tonic the night before. She made coffee and found some Tylenol. She could see Dani out in the potting shed. She was cleaning out, dumping bags of stuff on the lawn. Guess that meant she was headed home, too.

She couldn't face Dani. She couldn't tell her that Brett was having an affair, she would surely take his side.

Instead, she drove to Oceanside. She had no idea where Martin was and she hadn't talked to him since the day they'd had sex in Brad's office. She pulled over and lowered the top of the Saab, letting the wind whip her hair into a tangled mess. Maybe she should just take off; drive until she found a more interesting life. Why had she never left Sadlersville? Surely, she was meant for more.

Will. He was the only thing that anchored her to this life. He would be home in about three weeks. Things weren't working out so well with him and Natalia. Natalia had given him the "you're too nice and I don't want to lose you as a friend" speech, which was apparently the same in any language. Charlotte was secretly glad, but knew Will was suffering. Only the beginning for him, she was certain. He was such a sensitive soul. Just like his father.

His father. Who was Brett anymore? She thought she knew him. Was this woman the first or had there been many? Was that why he was rarely interested in sex? Did he buy flowers for the woman with the pink sweatshirt and the pony tail?

She pulled into a gas station and bought another coffee.

"You okay, honey?" asked the attendant. It was then that Charlotte realized she was crying.

"I'm fine," said Charlotte, irritated. Why was she crying over Brett? He certainly wasn't shedding any tears for her. She fished in her wallet and threw a ten on the counter and then went in search of the restroom.

She starred at her reflection in the smoked glass for a long time. Twice, other women had to ask her to move so they could reach the soap dispenser. She couldn't take her eyes off herself. Finally, she broke away. She used a paper towel to wipe away her smeared makeup. She needed to find Martin. She checked his website. He was playing at the Rum Runner. She knew he and Jerry would be there early to set up before the dinner crowd. That's what she needed. Martin.

Charlotte entered the bar and spotted Jerry and Martin setting up. She slipped into a booth in the back of the restaurant and watched them laughing and joking as they worked. A waitress stopped to talk to them and Charlotte couldn't help but notice the way her hand lingered on Martin's shoulder as he was bent over fiddling with one of their amps. When she turned to walk away, Martin watched her. Charlotte knew that hungry look. Charlotte could hear Dani in her head. *Playboy.*

The waitress approached and she ordered a Long Island Iced Tea. She watched Martin joke with Jerry. They played through a new number she hadn't heard before. Martin, periodically, put down his guitar and hopped down off the stage to walk back to the center of the restaurant to check the sound. Charlotte shifted to the back of her booth and ducked her head, not wanting to be recognized yet.

She tried to drink slowly, knowing how potent her drink was. The sweetness was an illusion. She and Brett used to make Long Island Iced Teas. Charlotte discovered the drink on one of their rare nights out and Brett had called several bars to get the recipe. They'd experimented with the recipe, never managing to get it to taste like it did the first time, but almost always managing to get completely drunk. It had led to all kinds of sexual experimentation. Charlotte flushed at the thought. But those days were so long ago. She wondered if Brett ever remembered them.

Lost in her memories, she managed to finish her entire drink. The waitress appeared and asked if she would like another. She asked for ice water instead. She watched Martin working on his playlist, making notes and conferring with Jerry who was noodling on his keyboard, nodding when necessary. Martin's brow was furrowed in concentration. She knew his body, certainly, but she didn't know who he really was. Was he just a playboy who only thought of Charlotte as a future good memory? Was he just a nice guy who liked to indulge his desires without regrets? Maybe he wasn't actually divorced. This was never going to be anything but a fling, right?

She watched Martin put his guitar in the case and hop down off the stage. He grabbed a barstool and joked with the bartender who brought him a rum and coke with two limes, his regular drink. She couldn't resist him so near to her. She made her way to the bar.

Charlotte slipped her hands around Martin's chest, leaning against his back and putting her chin on his shoulder.

"Guess who."

"Dorothy? No, wait, Gertrude? No, no, that's not it, Charlene? That's close, I know!" Martin laughed, spinning his chair around, he pulled her up into his lap, straddling his waist.

"Now, this gives me some ideas," said Charlotte.

"Does it now?" asked Martin as he kissed her.

"How soon are you needed?" she asked.

"By whom?"

"Anyone else but me."

"I've got some time." Martin turned to the bartender. "Tell Hank I had to run home to get something. I'll be back by 5:30."

The bartender gave him a knowing smile.

It was only a few blocks to his place and they made it there quickly. Ushering Charlotte upstairs, Martin stopped at the door.

"Wait here," he said, holding up his hand.

He went in. Charlotte turned and surveyed the parking lot. She watched an overweight tattooed man sitting on the hood of a car. He lit a cigarette and shook his fist at the woman on the balcony above him who screeched about a window he needed to fix. The man looked at Charlotte and smiled, revealing a few missing teeth. This infuriated the woman, who threw an empty beer can at him and gestured to Charlotte. When Charlotte looked away, embarrassed, the woman's cackling laugh echoed across the almost empty lot. She felt like an actress in a B movie. This wasn't her. The Charlotte who had been carrying on this affair with Martin was not the Charlotte she had been up until this point in her life. She wondered which Charlotte was more real. She shuddered to herself just as Martin opened the door.

He led her into the living room already consumed by the bed he had pulled out and thrown a blanket over. The lights were off and the curtains drawn, casting the apartment in darkness. There was a candle on the kitchen counter giving off the smell of something sweet—apple pie? It was a bizarre smell for the apartment. It belonged in a shop selling Precious Moments figurines and wooden cutouts for your lawn. Charlotte tried to picture Martin buying the candle, smelling each scent and choosing this particular smell to mask the stench of cigarettes, dirty laundry, and stale food that lingered in his apartment. Charlotte shook her head and pulled herself back to the moment. She watched Martin pull his T-shirt off. Her head was beginning to spin, she wasn't sure if it was from the Long Island Iced Tea or her conscience trying to catch up with her.

Again she shook her head, trying to bring herself back to the moment. She set her jaw and walked to Martin. She traced his face gently with her fingers, feeling the stubble that had already formed. He closed his eyes. He kissed her fingers and ran his tongue over them. Then he smiled and scooped her up and set her gently on the bed.

She remembered trying to get Brett to carry her over the threshold when they had gone back to their apartment to change after the wedding. Brett had picked her up with great gusto but then practically dropped her as he struggled with the door, which had been locked. She batted away the memory.

Martin didn't say a word, just undressed her and then himself. She couldn't remember the last time Brett had even glanced at her naked body. She wondered if it held even the slightest thrill for him anymore.

"What is it?" asked Martin when she stiffened at his touch.

"I need a minute," she said, sitting up and pulling on her shirt and panties. She opened the door to the balcony and stepped out. The beach was packed with the weekend crowd trying to get summer started.

Martin appeared, beer in hand and cigarette dangling between his lips. In the bright sunlight, he looked old and worn. He'd spent too many hours in the sun, drank too many beers, and definitely smoked too many cigarettes. His skin showed it. In all the times Charlotte had caressed his skin, she'd never noticed that before. He stepped behind her, his arms resting on the railing on either side of her, trapping her in his embrace.

"You got something on your mind?"

Charlotte didn't answer. She shouldn't be here. She should have never been here. She felt sick to her stomach. She had led this man to believe so much about her that wasn't true. She had led herself to believe it.

"What will you do when the season begins?"

"Hopefully, I'll have some better paying gigs and a lot more work. There won't be many more Sunday afternoons to lounge about in bed." He pulled her hair aside and kissed the back of her neck.

Charlotte struggled to keep from flinching at his touch.

"Let's go inside. I've been thinking about you all morning. I even put on clean sheets."

Martin turned to go, but Charlotte didn't move. He sat down in the rusty folding chair with an impatient thud.

"So what's up, Charlotte? Is it time for the talk?"

"What talk?"

"The one where you tell me you need to know where this is going."

Charlotte turned and looked Martin in the eye. "This isn't going anywhere. I'm married."

He laughed. "What? Did you think I didn't know that? C'mon, you've been wearing your damn ring, for Christ's sake. You think I didn't notice all the stuff you weren't telling me?"

"If you knew I was married, why have you been seeing me?"

Martin laughed again.

"Half the women I sleep with are married. I think I've come to prefer them. They generally don't have any illusions of me settling down with them. And the sex is much better with married women— they have years of frustration to work out."

Charlotte looked at him, horrified. Never in her life had she ever felt so completely used. Charlotte Marie Branson was not the kind of woman to let men take advantage of her. She wanted to be angry, but her embarrassment won out. He had never taken her seriously. She needed to leave.

"I think I'll go."

"Oh c'mon, one more time before you go, I promise to make it something you'll remember."

Charlotte felt repulsed at the thought.

"No, you save that for the next married woman you bed." She turned and opened the sliding glass door.

Martin got up. "Hey, don't be mad. You didn't think this was going anywhere either. You were never going to leave your guy. You know it. Can't you just let this be a good memory? A little beach fling? Let's end on a good note."

"I don't know what I've been doing here. Thank you, though, I think you've taught me a few things." He was standing in front of her now.

"You sure I can't teach you one more thing?" he asked and took a swig of his beer.

She smiled at him. "Good-bye, Martin."

She ducked back inside the apartment and found the rest of her clothes. He followed her and watched her dress in silence, but just as she reached the front door, he called to her.

"Charlotte!"

"Yes?" She paused in the open doorway, but didn't turn to look at him.

"I've said all along that you're a remarkable woman. I hope you find what you're looking for, but if you don't, be sure to look me up when you're down here at the beach."

"I'll keep that in mind," she said, and closed the door behind her.

When Charlotte arrived home, Dani was asleep in the hammock. She crept by her and went in the house to find food. She was starving. There wasn't much to choose from, so she put cream cheese and jelly on crackers. It was too nice of a night to stay inside. Balancing the plate in one hand and a wineglass in the other, she pushed the front door open with her backside. Dani's shout startled her and the plate of crackers went flying.

"Shit! You scared me!"

"You scared me!"

Dani jumped up from the hammock. "I'm so sorry!" She began picking up the crackers, which were mostly stuck jelly side down on the porch floor. Charlotte waved her away.

"It wasn't the most nutritious dinner, anyway."

Dani laughed.

"Here, hold this, I'm going to get the rest of the bottle." She handed Dani her glass and returned with the box of crackers and the bottle of wine. She poured a glass for Dani and tapped it with her own. "And then there were two," she said, raising her eyebrows in a question. "Unless you're headed home, too."

"In the morning," said Dani, sipping her wine.

"Well, then I guess that just leaves little ole me."

"You could go, too, you know."

"Not sure there's anything to go home to." Charlotte looked away, tired of her tears, tired of hiding them.

"What's really going on, Charlotte?" asked Dani, setting down her wine and putting her arm around Charlotte.

"I don't know what I've done." Charlotte's voice cracked. She shook her head. "I feel like I've just gotten home from a trip that went way wrong." She laughed half-heartedly and drank her wine.

"I was so into him."

Dani waited.

"And then I realized he's just some sad, middle-aged man who plays music in bars at the beach in the off-season. He exists in the now. He's not part of anyone's tomorrow. I can't believe I wasted all this time down here chasing him, when I could have been hanging with you and Meg. I've been a rotten friend." She leaned against Dani's shoulder. "What am I gonna do? I've fucked up everything."

"Maybe, maybe not."

"Why have you stayed so long?" asked Charlotte.

"What? You want to be alone?"

"That's not what I meant and you know it."

"I told you I'm leaving tomorrow."

"But why have you stayed so long? I've been so busy screwing Martin, I haven't been a very good friend to you. Did you figure things out?"

"Not really. But I think I did realize one thing. I have always had incredibly high expectations, probably from reading so many novels with happy endings. I had everything I thought I wanted in this life and couldn't understand why I wasn't the happiest person on the planet. But that's not what it's about. Getting everything you ever wanted doesn't make you happy."

"Couldn't hurt."

"But it doesn't automatically make you happy."

"So what does?"

"It's the daily stuff. You know? Different things make people happy, but I don't think it's something you arrive at. Happiness isn't static. I think you have to create your happiness on a daily basis."

Charlotte looked down at her drink.

"I'm not sure I have the energy to create any happiness in my life right now."

Dani took Charlotte's hand and squeezed it.

"Will you tell Brett?"

"He's having an affair."

"Wait? What? How do you know this?"

"I saw her."

"Who?"

"Yesterday morning when I went by the house. I saw a woman go in the house like she'd been living there."

"That doesn't mean anything!"

"He'd just finished washing his car and she showed up. She's young, too, much younger than we are."

"She could be anyone. Have you asked Brett?"

"Right. What am I supposed to do? Call him and say, 'Hey, I was spying on you yesterday morning and saw you with your hot young thing'?"

"Well, not exactly like that, but something like that."

"No."

"You've got to talk to him! This isn't high school, this is your marriage! This is your life!"

"Maybe it's for the best. I had an affair, he's had an affair. Now we're even."

"But your affair is over."

Charlotte shrugged.

"Isn't it?"

"Yes, but that doesn't change the fact that it happened. I can't take that back."

"What do you think would happen if you told him?"

Charlotte considered this. If there was ever any man who could honestly forgive her and not hold it against her forever, it would be Brett. He was a man with an expansive heart, but even he might not have room for this one. He didn't tolerate pain well and his usual tactic was to avoid it all together. That's probably why he was so sympathetic to his dental patients and tended to over-use the local anesthetic.

"I don't know. I don't think I could tell him, anyway."

Dani studied her for a moment. "Could you really live with that?"

"If I told him, he would forgive me and that might be more painful than living with the knowledge that I've kept this from him."

---

Late that night, Charlotte tried not to listen as Dani called Joe to tell him she was coming home. Her happy laughter echoed out the open window above to Charlotte on the porch below. In an effort to numb her mind, she'd gotten decidedly drunk. She'd never painted herself into such a corner. There didn't seem to be an escape route available.

Her phone rang. It was Brett. She reached for the ignore button, but on second thought answered. At this point, she had nothing to lose.

"Hello?"

"Charlotte? Is that you?"

"Hey there, Brett!"

"You sound like you've been drinking."

"I have."

"I've been trying to reach you for days. How was your birthday? Did you get the flowers?"

"I did. They were spectacular. Did your girl-friend help you pick them out?"

"My what?"

"Your girlfriend."

"What girlfriend?"

"The one with the pink sweatshirt and the ponytail."

"I have no idea what you're talking about. How much have you had to drink?"

"Jesus Christ, Brett, you're a terrible liar."

"I'm not lying. Maybe we should have this conversation when you're sober."

"Oh, right. That gives you time to get your story straight."

"What story? You're making no sense!"

"It's okay. I just want you to know that two can play at this game. You might have found a sweet young thing, but I found a hot Irish singer."

"A what? You are making no sense!"

"And I slept with him! And it was pretty damn good, just so you know," pronounced Charlotte triumphantly.

The phone was silent.

"Brett? Did you hear me?"

"I heard you, Charlotte."

"So?"

"What am I supposed to say?"

"I don't know, maybe you can tell me about your date Saturday morning."

"What? Saturday morning I was here. I washed the car."

"I know."

"How do you know?"

"I saw you and I saw her go into our house."

"No one was here! Wait, yes, there was some-one here. That was the new house cleaner. Sandra quit so she could take care of her grandbabies. She found us this other woman, Vie. She started last week. She doesn't speak much English, but she does a good job."

Charlotte dropped her wineglass and it shat-tered on the steps below.

"Christ."

"Did you think I was having an affair with her? Why were you here Saturday? Were you coming home?"

"I drove Meg home and I came by the house and I saw her. I saw you. I thought, shit, I thought . . ." Charlotte was choking on her own tears.

"Maybe we should have this conversation in person," suggested Brett. His tone had become business-like. It frightened Charlotte. "Maybe you should come home."

# MONDAY, MAY 6

## Dani

Dani went for a quick run before she loaded Meg's car. She ran further than she normally did, but when she finally turned around to run back, she was barely winded and her legs still felt strong. If nothing else, she'd gotten in shape during these weeks away from home. She sprinted for the cottage, anxious to be home with her family.

Back at the cottage, Charlotte was camped out at the dining room table, which was littered with paper.

"Back to work?" asked Dani, using a chair for balance as she stretched.

"Such as it is," said Charlotte. "I forgot to ask if you'd settled things with Jeremy."

"He had all my stuff."

"What stuff?"

"Everything I've painted."

"I thought he'd sold it."

"Apparently, there was only one buyer. I went to his house to find him when he didn't show up at the gallery and all my things were there."

"Oh God, how creepy. What did he say?"

"That he wanted to keep me coming back."

"That's sick. You know that, right?"

"We all have our desperate moments."

Charlotte winced. "That's a bit more than desperate. You don't seem too upset."

"I was. But then I realized it doesn't really matter." She shrugged. "So, I'm not an artist."

"But you are!" protested Charlotte.

Dani held up her hand. "I'm not the artist I wanted to be, the one I dreamed of being. But I think despite everything, being here, creating my art again, it made me realize it's not about the finished work, it never was; it was about the creating. Just like my life. I guess that's the lesson I needed to learn."

Charlotte didn't say anything. Her phone buzzed with a text and she read it, then made a note. "So you're headed home today?" she asked.

"I am. I'm going to take Meg's stuff. What about you?"

Charlotte set down her pen and looked up at Dani.

"Eventually, but maybe not today. I have to figure out what I'm going to say to Brett."

"How about the truth?"

"I don't know if either of us can handle that."

"But what's the other option? Giving up?"

"I'll figure something out."

Dani sat down at the table and looked at Charlotte. "Do you love him?"

"I didn't think I still did, but now I don't know. It really hurt to see that other woman at my house, and even when I was with Martin, I kept thinking of Brett. Is that love or habit? It might not matter because, even if I do love him, it's probably too late."

"You don't know that."

"I've got a pretty good idea."

"But instead of assuming it, maybe you should go find out."

"I want to fix this, but it might not be fixable."

"Maybe you need to put a little of that Charlotte-energy into this," said Dani. "I've never known you to walk away from a challenge."

"I think this is a little more complicated."

"It is."

Dani got up and poured a cup of coffee. She refilled Charlotte's cup and squeezed her shoulder.

"I'm gonna load up."

Charlotte smiled at her and put down her pen. "You know how you always say that a real artist can see things other people can't?"

Dani nodded.

"I think you're a real artist. You've always been able to see things in me that I don't see in myself."

Dani was quiet for a moment and then asked, "Was it a mistake? Us staying here?"

Charlotte took a sip of her coffee, then smiled at her friend.

"There are no mistakes, only lessons to be learned," she said.

---

## Charlotte

Charlotte helped Dani pack up Meg's things. They loaded them in the car.

"Guess this is it," said Charlotte.

"You'll call me?" asked Dani.

"I will."

"You sure you have to stay here?"

"For now," said Charlotte.

Just then, a car pulled in the driveway. Brett. Charlotte's heart began to race.

"Did you know he was coming?" asked Dani.

Charlotte shook her head. "What do I do?"

"I guess you'll figure that out. I'm going to get out of your way."

"Don't leave!" hissed Charlotte as Brett got out of the car. He looked sad, impossibly sad, but there was something else in his expression. His jaw was set. Was it anger or determination?

"Hey, Brett!" called Dani, cheerfully.

"Hi, Dani," said Brett, accepting her embrace.

"Good to see you. Sorry, I gotta run. Joe's expecting me."

Brett stared at Charlotte, who said nothing.

"Well, I'm sure you two have lots to catch up on!" she called. Then she slammed the door to Meg's car and pulled out quickly before Charlotte could stop her.

Brett hadn't moved from where he stood beside his car.

"So," began Charlotte. "Do you want to see the place?"

"Sure," said Brett, following her in. She gave him the tour, both of them were impossibly polite. When they'd finished, she poured him a glass of tea and they sat on the deck.

"Charlotte, I don't know where to start," said Brett.

"Then don't," said Charlotte. "Let me speak."

Brett took a sip of his tea and waited.

"I don't know what happened to us. We used to be so good together. Remember?"

Brett nodded.

"And then things started to change. Maybe around the time Will was born. We stopped being a couple. We were only a family."

"That's what we wanted!" protested Brett. "I loved our family."

Charlotte noted his past tense. "I do, too; but I miss *us*."

"What is that supposed to mean? Until this past month, there was still an us."

"No! There wasn't! Don't you see that? We never do things without Will; we never do things just you and me. We used to have fun! We used to go out to exciting places; we took vacations; we used to be in love! We used to *make* love!"

Brett set his face. Charlotte knew he wanted to protest, but couldn't. She was right.

"And it's always you and Will. Sometimes I feel like I'm the third wheel."

"You aren't the third wheel. That's ridiculous— you're his mother!"

"But the two of you have something special. I feel like an outsider. You have jokes and hobbies and you spend all your free time with him."

"He's my son."

"I know! And you're a great father! Probably the best father I know. It's hard to compete with."

"It's not a competition."

"It's not, but I've never been very good at this mother thing and you are so natural, so good with Will—with all kids, but especially Will. It's like you prefer his company to mine."

Brett didn't say anything. They both watched a squirrel make his way across the grass, pause to look at them, and then scamper up a tree.

"It's not easy being married to you," said Brett quietly.

"What's that supposed to mean?"

"It means you expect things. You expect big things all the time—romance, excitement, fun. And you're so capable and confident. You can do anything, Charlotte! You don't even realize what a big person you are. It's hard to keep up with. I guess after a while I realized I'd found something I could do really well. I was good at being a dad, even if I wasn't so great as an exciting husband. Going to gallery openings and fundraisers and staging romantic gestures exhausts me as much as it energizes you. It was easier to leave that to you and put my energy into being a really good dad."

"Why does it have to be one or the other?" asked Charlotte. "Why can't you be a really good dad and still love me?"

Brett had tears in his eyes when he looked at her. "You need more than I have."

"No, I don't!" protested Charlotte. "Why do you think that?"

"Because it's true," he said, letting the tears flow down his cheeks. "I think I've always known I couldn't be enough for you. This past month only proves it."

"No, Brett! That's not true. You are enough!" cried Charlotte, getting up from her chair and kneeling beside his.

He ran his hand gently around Charlotte's face, wiping her tears. "I wish it were different. But it's not and we both know it."

Charlotte shook her head back and forth, denying it with all her being.

"Now what?" she asked.

"I don't know," said Brett, pulling Charlotte to her feet and holding her tight. "I don't know."

---

**Dani**

Dani pulled into her drive and turned off Meg's car. It was only two. She'd made good time. Jordan wouldn't be home yet. Joey should be napping. She'd called Joe that morning to say she was on her way. He'd sounded happy, but would he be happy? Or would there be some lingering resentment?

Her house looked different. Not just because spring had truly sprung and tulips and lilacs were blooming. She was nervous about seeing Joe after all this time. Maybe the house looked different because she was different. Would Joe notice?

She couldn't wait to see her kids. Trying on a different life had made it clear that she belonged in this one. She took a deep breath and opened the car door. At the same moment, her front door burst open and Joey came flying down the steps.

She scooped him into her arms and nuzzled his neck as he shouted, "I MISSED YOU MOMMY! WHY DID YOU STAY AWAY SO LONG?"

She shook her head and breathed him in. "I'm sorry, baby, but I'm here now and I'm not going anywhere."

He scrambled out of her arms and asked, "Promise?"

She smiled and nodded, wiping the tears from his eyes. "Promise."

"C'mon," said Joey, taking her hand and pulling her around to the side of the house.

"Where are we going?" she asked, laughing.

"To see your new house!"

Before Dani could respond, they reached the backyard and there was Joe standing in front of an adorable shed. It was the kind you bought at Home Depot and plunked down already built. It had green siding and window boxes full of pansies.

"What is this?"

"It's for you!" said Joey.

"So you can have a place to paint," said Joe, pulling her into his arms.

"I don't understand," said Dani.

"When you talked about your painting you sounded so alive. I don't want you to have to run away from us to be happy. I want you here. With us."

"That's just where I want to be," whispered Dani holding him tighter.

# Acknowledgments

I started this book nearly twelve years ago as therapy. I wanted to run away from my overloaded, underfunded life. I didn't, though, because of friends and family who took my dream seriously.

Grateful thanks to Judy Shannon, Mary Beth Stapleton, and Nick Achterberg, who read the first version of this book so long ago, they probably don't remember reading it!

If I was running away for my own extended girls' weekend, I would have done it with Linda Soper and Elizabeth Kunde whose lifelong friendships surely color my world.

Bringing this book into the light wouldn't have been possible without the faithful editorial assistance and endless encouragement of Lisa Weigard, Gina Moltz, Margot Tillitson, and Pat Hazlebeck. Huge debt of gratitude to my beta-reading-copy-editing-proof-reading wonder-friend, Candace Shaffer.

Lou Aronica's editorial guidance helped me to cut (and cut) and carve out the real story. He gently taught me how to tell a story properly, and stopped me before I re-wrote iT for the hundredth time.

I've been blessed with more girlfriends and girls' weekends than I probably deserved. Each of them and all those heartfelt, wine-fueled conversations inspired and informed this book. Mine is a grateful heart.

## About the Author

Cara Achterberg is the author the novels *I'm Not Her* and *Practicing Normal*, and the memoirs, *Another Good Dog: One Family and Fifty Foster Dogs* and *One Hundred Dogs & Counting: One Woman, Ten Thousand Miles, and a Journey into the Heart of Shelters and Rescues*. She lives on a hillside farm in Pennsylvania but pines for the mountains of Virginia. For more information visit CaraWrites.com.